SHADOW
COUNTER

SHADOW
COUNTER

Tom Kakonis

A DUTTON BOOK

DUTTON
Published by the Penguin Group
Penguin Books USA Inc., 375 Hudson Street,
New York, New York 10014, U.S.A.
Penguin Books Ltd, 27 Wrights Lane,
London W8 5TZ, England
Penguin Books Australia Ltd, Ringwood,
Victoria, Australia
Penguin Books Canada Ltd, 10 Alcorn Avenue,
Toronto, Ontario, Canada M4V 3B2
Penguin Books (N.Z.) Ltd, 182–190 Wairau Road,
Auckland 10, New Zealand

Penguin Books Ltd, Registered Offices:
Harmondsworth, Middlesex, England

First published by Dutton, an imprint of New American Library,
a division of Penguin Books USA Inc.
Distributed in Canada by McClelland & Stewart Inc.

First Printing, July, 1993
10 9 8 7 6 5 4 3 2 1

 REGISTERED TRADEMARK—MARCA REGISTRADA

LIBRARY OF CONGRESS CATALOGING-IN-PUBLICATION DATA
Kakonis, Tom E.
  Shadow counter / Tom Kakonis.
    p.   cm.
  ISBN 0-525-93633-5
  I. Title.
PS3561.A4154S48   1993
813'.54—dc20   92-37595
                                                               CIP

Printed in the United States of America
Set in Caledonia

PUBLISHER'S NOTE
This is a work of fiction. Names, characters, places, and incidents either are the products of
the author's imagination or are used fictitiously, and any resemblance to actual persons, living
or dead, events, or locales is entirely coincidental.

For Helen, Marge, Bonnie—and a lifetime of memories.
Also for Allan Sonnenschein, a steady voice out of the wicked city.

A driver 30 years ago could maintain a sense of orientation in space. At the simple crossroad a little sign with an arrow confirmed what was obvious. One knew where one was. When the crossroads becomes a cloverleaf, one must turn right to turn left. . . . But the driver has no time to ponder paradoxical subtleties within a dangerous, sinuous maze. He or she relies on signs for guidance—enormous signs in vast spaces at high speeds.

from Robert Venturi et al., *Learning from Las Vegas*

PART
ONE

1

S ay what you like, gild it however you will, blackjack has to be, finally, a dreary way to eke out a living. All the infinite variety and intoxicating tingle of bagging groceries, say, or flipping burgers or clerking in a bank. Almost enough to make an honest job look tolerable. Well, almost. Even at the pretzel-bet level there's the occasional heady rush: the bullet dodged, the count confirmed on the unveiling of the cards, the risk rewarded. Got to give it that. To be fair. But otherwise, as vocation, livelihood—face it—it's pretty grim.

Not much as entertainment either, if the company at this table was any measure. Anchoring down first base with a lubberly rump overspilling his chair was the male half of a golden years couple, grit-suckers, judging by their blackstrap-molasses drawls. "Ah be go to *shee*-it!" bawled this canny player after splitting fives and gaping, chute-jawed, as the dealer efficiently busted both hands and scooped in his chips. Ten big soldiers vanished. It was tragic. But his wife, a waxy-cheeked bluehead, animated as a zombie, caught a natural and contemplated her plunder and her luckless mate, each in turn, with a glassy smile. So the palliative laws of compensation were still more or less in place.

Next to these two merrymakers sat another couple, much younger, wholesome hay shakers by the looks of them and by the giveaway twang that located them somewhere around the middle of Nebraska. Transparently greenies (the girl kept saying "Hit me," while the dealer, a tiny oriental woman of saintly patience, Little Miss Roundeyes, gently reminded her of the hand signal protocol), they wore the blank, slightly dazed expression of born victims. Now their pink country faces contracted in the enormous effort of decision as they weighed stiffs, fifteen and thirteen respectively, against Miss Roundeyes's exposed three. They hesitated, exchanged timid glances, called for hits. Into thy hands, O Lord. Both went blotto. Sometimes He giveth, more often He taketh away.

And next to the cornhuskers, last and least, was an uncommonly ugly fellow—lank grease-gunned hair, ferret eyes, collapsed cheeks, mail slot mouth, undershot chin—whose night-of-the-living-dead pallor, as much as his colorless mechanical play, stamped him unmistakably a local, a casino rat. Also the way he lit a cigarette and sneered out jets of bitter smoke through clenched yellow teeth. Shrewd master of basic strategy, he wiggled an affirmative finger, got a four laid on his twelve, expelled a whistling sigh around another jet stream, and made a reflex swipe of the hand. Master or not, Roundeyes was grinding him down, and he sat hunkered over his dwindling pillars of chips like a starved hound guarding a bone.

Fun in Vegas. The American way to play. It was a melancholy scene, when you thought about it. Better not, there lies madness. And anyway, since you're as much a figure in this joyless *tableau vivant* as the rest of them, a little more Christian forbearance, Mr. Waverly, if you please.

"Sir?"

Madame Butterfly, polite but urgent (time is money, sir, here at the Barbary Coast), hauling him back from these gloomy reveries.

Waverly looked at his cards, brought up the tally on the screen behind his eyes, slid out another four reds, and doubled his soft eight/eighteen. If he had the count right, the shoe, a little over half down, ought to be spot-card heavy. So there was a better than good chance of moving up a notch or, at worst, staying even. And the forty score wouldn't hurt any either, which was of course no way to be thinking but when you're scrambling after cab fare, next week's TV dinners, next month's rent—okay, call it what it is: a couple of coins to rub together, chump change—when you're doing that, then that's the way you think.

She dealt him an ace. Nineteen. Gratifying to see there were still some constants left in this world, even if only of the mathematical variety. Nevertheless, it was all academic once she turned up her hole card, revealing one of those plenteous spots he had reckoned on and then effortlessly dropped an eight on her thirteen, and he and the sharpie went down together. The thing about blackjack is, artful count notwithstanding, sometimes you just can't catch a break.

"Whoo-ee!" exclaimed the rhino rump, pride of the Deep South. " 'Cept for the mizzus here, this little lady done delivered a downhome butt-whuppin'."

The dealer acknowledged the praise or complaint or limp sally of wit or whatever it was with a neutral smile, the mizzus with the same vacant one she'd displayed all evening. The Nebraskas grinned weakly. Adonis scowled, said nothing.

Neither did Waverly. He occupied third base, removed from his fellow players and the burden of any gratuitous chitchat by a single, mercifully empty chair. But not for long. Soon a squat, square fireplug of a man came weaving through the crowd of railbirds, settled into the seat, and in a voice somewhat nasal, somewhat slurred, commenced a nonstop bantering monologue delivered at anyone who would listen or respond, Waverly not excluded. Scratch mercy.

Waverly did his best to tune him out, narrow in on the cards. Without much success. In principle, he was opposed to table-jumping and all the other tattered superstitions that spring up around this or any game. Better by far to rely on the fidelity of the numbers. All the same, his count was badly thrown off by the ceaseless chatter, the flood of words. Live and partner with a B. Epstein and you soon enough get your fill of words. More than plenty.

So he played through a few more shoes and when he could absolutely tolerate it no longer (for by then the fireplug had magically transformed this heretofore funereal table into a jolly social club, himself as chairman and everyone else, even the surly rat, joining in, trading *Where you froms*, *How's the lucks*, prattling, cackling), he got to his feet and gathered up his chips. He wasn't about to count them now, but from their heft and color he figured to be up maybe a couple bills, no more than that. Nothing sensational, though not a bad take for four numbing hours of five and ten play. Of course, the shift wasn't over yet either, but he was due for a break.

"Hey, you leaving?" boomed the chairman. Keen observer.

"That's right."

"C'mon, you're the only one doing any good here. You can't quit now."

"That's the best time," said Waverly, strolling away.

He went over to the long marble-topped bar opposite the tables, sank onto a stool, ordered a ginger ale. He let his taut shoulders sag, emptied his head of tallies, numbers. The relentless rackety symphony of the slots, punctuated now and again by ecstatic squeals, expiring groans, assailed his ears. He watched the cocktail waitresses prance about, powdered jugs spilling out of abbreviated, bordello-red outfits. Watched the parade of eager marks and wised-up hustlers come and go, faces scored with anxiety, tension, doubt, various shades of malaise. He watched them. And recognizing he was no different, certainly no better, probably worse, equally snared in the frantic swirl of self-delusion—recognizing all that, he was for a splinter of a moment overtaken by an immense weariness that had nothing to do with fatigue, and a loneliness vast and basic. Backlash of the poison myth of Starting Over. Talk about madness.

In the four months they'd been here he'd graduated from the two-dollar tables (operating off under a thin dime, that's where the starting over starts) to the fives. Worked his way out of the sawdust joints downtown and onto the fabled Strip, but slowly, cautiously, sidestepping the tinsel palaces (where the pit bosses picked up the scent of a counter quicker than a cat sniffing out a fallen crippled sparrow) in favor of cut-rates like this one. Digging out of the Florida hole. And a long, steep climb it was, too: one step up, two back down. Often as not, the backsliding could be traced to Bennie's sports bets, for he was sadly out of practice, out of touch. Though no less optimistic. "Soon's we build ourselves a little nut," he'd declared on their arrival, "get ahead, oh, say ten, fifteen long, we'll get you back in the serious action, doin' what you do best. Start livin' like white folks again." No arguing with that kind of buoyant faith, even though four months later they'd amassed, between them, the princely sum of 7K. Or somewhere in that neighborhood; Bennie kept the books. Not your most inspiriting rally, whatever the total.

Two stools over, a woman in an electric-green dress sipped daintily at a drink. The dress, for all its neon shimmer, did little to enhance a figure stout through the middle and wide across the beam. The face, puffy, used, downside of forty, was so glossy with paint it appeared almost shellacked. She gave him an appraising glance, assembled a labored smile, and chirped a sprightly "Hi."

Waverly gave her back a noncommittal nod. Also in those four lusterless months he had yet to be hit on by a hooker. Till now. Testimony, no doubt, to the somber bleakness engraved on his face. Or to her desperation.

"Having any luck tonight?"

He made the so-so gesture with a flat hand in the air.

"Where you from?"

The uniform Vegas queries, this one demanding of a voiced response. "Nebraska," he said.

"Really. Nebraska. I've got a girlfriend lives in Omaha."

"There's a coincidence."

"Oh? You from Omaha too?"

"No. Grand Island." Far as he knew, that was in Nebraska.

The non sequitur puzzled or interested her not at all. "So how do you like Vegas?"

Routine operating moves, never mind the nature of the hustle. Which had to be coming up soon. One thing they weren't long on out here was invention. "Most spectacular city," he allowed.

"Isn't it though. So much to see. Do."

Nothing to say to that. She took a time-out. Another decorous sip. Now it comes.

"You, uh, looking for company tonight?" she asked, putting some coquettish lilt in it.

"I don't think so."

"I wouldn't be too quick to say no," she counseled. "See those two little darlins over there?" She elevated a scarlet-taloned finger, directing his gaze to a pair of girls busily feeding coins into a slot across the room.

Waverly affirmed he saw them.

"They're with me. Cute, aren't they."

The girls were young, scarcely old enough to be in here, by his estimate. One of them had hard, mean, pretty, butch features; the other a heart-shaped baby-doll face, skin white as the face of the moon, and hair an extravagant cotton candy confection of approximately the same hue but for some streaks of pink. Both had remote incurious eyes, ice-locked. Both chomped wads of gum. They were outfitted in identical ankle-length leopard-print Spandex pants and sleeveless V-back tops that exhibited an abundance of silky young flesh. Sheenas, direct from the jungle. "Very fetching," he agreed.

"They come with the package. No pun intended, you understand."

"Oh, I think I understand."

"What we do is, first we oil ourselves up. I'm talking all over. Everywhere. You follow what I'm saying?"

"I seem to be getting the picture."

"Then we put on a show for you. It's really something to see. Guaranteed to please."

Traveling in packs of three now. New dimensions in sybaritic delights, whole new galaxies of unexplored sensations. Maybe he was wrong; maybe they weren't so destitute of invention after all. He said innocently, "Comes with a guarantee, does it? No pun there either, by the way."

"Like nothing in your wildest, naughtiest dreams," she said, evidently impervious to irony. "And after that you get to join the party. Think about it."

"All three of you, this show?"

"Correct. We work as a team."

A certain lickerish breathiness, quite unfeigned, quickened her voice. Her eyes glittered. It was cheering to see there were some people still happy in their work. "With you as den mother?" Waverly said.

The forged smile slackened just a bit. "What's that supposed to mean?"

"Nothing. Strike it, means nothing. Appreciate the offer but I'm going to pass tonight. Thanks anyway."

The shellacked face turned suddenly to stone. She swiveled about on her stool, showed him her back. He thought he heard her muttering something about goddam time-wasting bumblefucks, something like that. Out here time, lest we forget, is money, *money*! Waverly looked away, finished his ginger ale, and when a moment later he looked again she was gone. He glanced over at the slots and the jungle queens were gone, too, the three of them vanished so suddenly he had to wonder if they'd been nothing more than a fanciful hallucination.

Either way, real or imagined, it was of scant importance. Time (to which he was no less accountable) to go back to work. He scanned the tables, searching for a vacant third base. None in sight. He waited. Eventually one opened, and he hurried over and secured it. Settled in, laid out his chips, and made some innocuous mid-shoe bets, donations, most of them. At the shuffle he leaned back, lit a cigarette, cleared his head.

This table showed considerably more promise than the last. Couple of dink kids at the other end, empty seat, middle-aged lady who periodically snorted from a Vicks inhaler and applied Blistex to seriously cracked lips, two more empty seats, himself. Dealer was a scrawny young man with blotchy skin, bad teeth, and a greased ponytail dangling between his bony shoulder blades. Studiedly supercool, but without the dextrous moves or the rocket speed to carry it off. Dinks and the lady played decent games, no major gaffes, and none of them had anything to say. So this was about as good as it got.

The cards came out. Waverly locked onto the count, adjusting his strategy to the rise and fall of the numbers churning in his head. Sometimes those numbers dictated strange choices: doubling an ace-nine against an eight, standing on a stiff thirteen against a seven, or on a fourteen staring down a mighty ten. Once they even obliged him to hit a seventeen (happily for his cover, he forfeited that one). The curious, erratic play lifted some eyebrows around the table and elicited an occasional superior smirk from the dealer. That part was okay. Marked you as a hunch player, chump. It was the pendulum wagering gave you away, got you an accelerated passage out the door. Which was the last thing he needed. "Get made in one joint"—in Bennie's elegant injunction—"and you're made all across town. Comes to counters, they're tighter'n a nun's twat. And lemme tellya, boy, they got your elephant memories, this vicinity." Sound advice. Accordingly, he stayed clear of the wide conspicuous swings. When the count got fifteen or better to the good, he'd go trips but never any more than that; five and under dropped him back to the base unit, a humble ten bones. That kind of pocket change, nobody was going to notice, or care. All he wanted to do was walk out of here three, four yards ahead. Anymore, even that qualified as handsome booty.

Slowly, steadily, the clusters of chips multiplied under his fingers, and inside of an hour he was getting close. Very agreeable prospect. But somewhat less agreeable was the uneasy sense of a presence hovering directly behind him, watching him, scrutinizing his play. He kept his eyes fastened on the cards, tried to stay centered. Railbirds were notoriously restless, addicted to cruising; ignore them and eventually they'll fade away. Not this one. This one was static, rooted to the floor. After a few more hands Waverly considered turning and drilling him—her—whoever—with a frosty glare, but then he thought better of it. Centered, centered.

No need anyway. At the next shuffle the presence, in the ample shape of the gasbag from the other table, materialized in the adjacent chair. He squinted at Waverly as though seeing for the first time a mythical creature he had heard about somewhere but never actually encountered, like a cyclops or a winged Nike. His eyes were slushy, his brick-red face punished by drink. A violent spray of terra cotta freckles spangled his chipmunk cheeks and nose and high patrician brow, above which rose an unruly whoosh of hair, its fire-engine shade softened hardly at all by flecks of gray at the temples. Some dim cognition insinuated itself into that squinty gaze, and he leaned in close, establishing a confidential zone, and murmured *sotto voce,* "You're a counter."

Now Waverly produced the glare. For all the good it did. The gasbag stared right back, a wily spark kindling his bleary eyes. Waverly looked around, inspecting the nearby tables. Scarcely an empty seat anywhere, and certainly no more third bases. Not good. The dealer offered the cut card to one of the dinks, and the play resumed. Waverly picked up the count, which swung wildly the first several hands and then settled into the low positive figures, good enough for a few nice scores. But it didn't escape him that the gasbag (who, having lapsed into an uncharacteristic silence, could no longer be described as such) was slavishly apeing his betting patterns. Playing off a big quarter base unit, he was raking in the loot. By the end of the shoe the dealer was casting wary sidelong glances at both of them. No, this was not good at all.

The way Waverly saw it, his options were reduced to two. He could get out of there, go down the street, start in again somewhere else. Or he could pack it in for the night. Either one he could of course do, but neither was to his liking and neither in his plan. It was annoying to be victimized by a prying, meddlesome juicer looking to ride your coattails, reckless of all caution, throwing everything into jeopardy. More than annoying, it was galling. Maybe there was another way.

For the next couple of shoes he held his bets flat. Freckles (by now that's how Waverly identified him) did the same. They seesawed, won some but lost more than they won. The dealer began to loosen up. Then a moment arrived when the count soared well above twenty. Waverly waited till the dealer was occupied with the other end of the table, and then he turned to Freckles and whispered in his ear, "Now's the time to zing it in."

"Now?"

"Right now."

"How much?"

Under the table Waverly displayed five fingers.

On the next deal Freckles stacked five green chips in his bet box. Waverly stayed with the sawbuck.

"What about you?" Freckles said doubtfully.

"All I can risk. Trust me, this deck is spot rich."

About that he was right, though it came through the back door, hard way. Freckles caught a fifteen, Waverly a twelve. Dealer showed a powerful ten. Freckles looked stricken. Waverly nudged him, made a slight negative gesture, and at their turns they both stood. Dealer flipped over his hole card, revealing a four. He dropped the foreordained face on it, and in an instant Freckles was a hundred and twenty-five General Georges to the good. His lips parted in a sunburst grin.

"What did I say?" Waverly said, but softly and out of the corner of his mouth.

Same story next hand. And the next, and the ones after that. Except that Waverly, still betting an even ten, deliberately threw some of them, while his exuberant confederate, innocent of the dealer's deepening frown, continued to hammer it in. When finally he'd had enough, the dealer shot an over-the-shoulder glance at a pit boss, who came sidling up to the table. A significant look passed between them. No words were exchanged. The boss planted himself by first base and studied the play and the players with unblinking cushioned eyes full of a sullen malice. A swarthy Med, he had a bald spot round and symmetrical as a radar screen sculpted into the crown of his head, like some oversized third ear alert to signals outside the auricular range of other mortals. And those signals were telling him something was gravely wrong. Waverly figured it wouldn't be long now.

The shoe was almost run out. Once more around the block. Freckles got dealt a pair of paints, Waverly a soft seventeen. Dealer's up card was a puny four. Just beneath the rim of the table, out of the boss's line of sight, Waverly made a scissoring motion with two fingers, and Freckles dutifully pushed in another five green chips and declared, "Split 'em."

The dealer hesitated just a beat. Around a curling lip he said, "You sure you wanna do that?"

"I'm sure," said the stalwart Freckles.

No reason not to be sure. He pulled an ace on the first, another face on the second. Couple of spoiler hands, two and a half bills in one deft touch, coming right up. The dinks and the Blistex lady, spear-carriers in this unfolding drama, supplied some appreciative gasps. The dealer shook his head, confounded, all the rehearsed cool long since evaporated. In the judgmental eyes of the pit boss a black storm gathered. Waverly declined a hit even though the count said double. When that storm broke, he was looking for shelter. The dealer rolled over a hole five, laid a ten on it, and cancelled everyone but the flushed and beaming Freckles. Then he turned to the boss and said, "Shuffle," a trace of a question in it. "Shuffle 'em," the boss echoed, squeezing behind first base and coming around the outer perimeter of the table. Waverly followed his progress narrowly. Crunch time.

The boss stepped up to Freckles, tapped him on the shoulder, and growled, "Sir, gotta talk to you."

Freckles, busily arranging his towers of chips, didn't bother to look up. "I'm playing."

"That part you got wrong. Your playin', it's over."

Now he looked up, genuine bewilderment stamped on his face. "What do you mean, over?"

"Over," the boss repeated. "Like in done. Diced. Cut off. Finito. That plain enough? C'mon, let's cash 'em in."

"I don't get it. What the hell have I done?"

"Counters ain't welcome here."

"Counter!" Freckles spluttered. He stabbed an accusing finger at Waverly. "*He's* the one running a count."

Waverly shrugged, made an innocent face. He swept a hand over his modest pile of chips, but offered nothing in his own defense. Flash point like this, less is always more. The dealer smiled thinly and kept right on shuffling. The three other players at the table got down behind their eyes. Who needs trouble?

"It's you I'm askin' to leave," said the boss, nostrils flaring dangerously. A rumbly menace edged his sandpaper voice. "Been goin' about it real polite. So far. Do I gotta call in security?"

Freckles looked back and forth between him and Waverly, taking their respective measures. His hands trembled pathetically. Indignation ruddled his pouchy cheeks. His mouth moved in desperate, wordless twists. Center stage in this tragicomic playlet, he looked rather like a man who's just swallowed a worm. Finally, and with stiff inebriate dignity, he pronounced, "This is not *fair.*" Fair or not, he came to his feet anyway, collected his chips, and marched off to the cashier's cage, the boss in escort, clutching at his elbow. Poor Freckles.

Bets down, the game rolled on. Waverly suppressed a smile.

Back to business. No one at the table had anything to say, but all of them, dealer in particular, examined his play critically, still a little dubious. Guilt by association. And in a moment the boss reappeared, shadowed his corner. Waverly let go of the count. Business, as business, was effectively done in for the night.

2

In a ninth-floor room of the north tower of the Dunes Hotel diagonally across the street, another sort of business, somewhat more bizarre, was being conducted at that same hour. Five men occupied the room. Four of them sat tensely on the twin double beds, two to a bed; the fifth was folded into a chair backed up to a wall and positioned so as to face them. The man in the chair was speaking. His voice was feathery, whispery, yet softly resonant too, with a peculiar bludgeoning energy in it. His words seemed to emanate not so much from the mouth, a narrow seam bracketed by harsh gorges carved into the gaunt cheeks, as from some remote chamber located deep behind the zealous, hard-cut eyes. His topic: homeopathic healing.

"The human body is nothing more than an expression of consciousness, an epiphenomenon, you might say. The slightest flicker of thought, intention, is a quantum of consciousness. Even as I speak to you this very moment, I create fluctuations in the cosmic field that binds us all, healer and sufferer alike. The fundamental premise of homeopathic medicine, you see, is that consciousness is primary, matter secondary. Or, put another way, the body itself is merely a ripple in that dynamic field we call the universe."

He paused sufficiently to allow this nugget of wisdom to dissolve and settle like an ineffable mist over the room. A smile faintly beatific played across his slit of a mouth. The men on the beds regarded him with baffled expressions, waiting out a moment charged with expectancy. Though the oldest among them could have been no more than thirty, they were all of them stiletto-thin, with ravaged fissured faces and eyes like tombs. Their skins had the color and texture of withered lemons. Their breathing came in hard, dry, obstructed rasps.

The silence lengthened. Beyond the glass slider opening onto a deck, the steady industrial hum of urgent traffic whisking down Flamingo Road rose and floated on the night air. At last one of the bed-sitters, in a voice mincing, skeptical, though with the vibrato of fear mounting through it, ventured, "All this is very instructive, I'm sure. But how exactly do these lofty sentiments translate into a treatment, Dr. Brewster?"

"Mister," the man in the chair corrected him, firmly but not unkindly. "I take no pride in that title conferred on me by the deceitful practitioners of traditional—" He hesitated, ransacking his own noncosmic consciousness for the properly odious epithet, settling finally on "dogma. I'll not dignify their sorcery with the word medicine."

"All right. Fine. Call it whatever you like. But the question remains the same, *Mr.* Brewster."

"Please, Howie," his bed companion pleaded. "Don't be bitchy."

"Shut up, Barry."

For all his testiness, Howie looked to be on the perilous edge of a crumpling swoon, as if all the life juices were oozing out of him at an alarming rate. The chastened Barry, an elfin wisp of a man, fanned him listlessly with a hotel entertainment guide and did as he was told. A dog-collar necklace girdled his stringy throat. Dull resignation glazed his sunken eyes. The little eruption excited a nervous giggle from the twosome on the other bed. Howie silenced it with a wicked glare.

"As does the answer to your question," said the imperturbable man in the chair. "Treatment is more than simply the relief of pain. Much more. As who should know better than the four of you. No, true healing is a delicate balancing of the physical, emotional, and spiritual sides of a man's nature. Through such perfect balance will he access his inner self, and from there proceed to function once again in health and peace and harmony. On the walls of the temples of the ancients were inscribed these words: 'The doctor dresses the wound, but the Universal Spirit heals the patient.' "

Serene, gentle-spoken, relaxed to a point of near-drowsiness, there was nevertheless about him a certain mesmerizing power. Call it a bearing, an intoxicating aura, as though all his impenetrable words orbited a central source of light distant as heaven's farthest star; as though he alone were privy to alien mysterious voices subject to no earthly laws.

Howie, however, was not impressed. "I'm afraid you'll have to be more explicit than that, sir. We didn't travel two thousand miles to listen to some half-baked mysticism. We were told you have a cure. Or claim to have one."

"And so I do."

"Well? We're waiting. And it ought to be obvious we don't have forever."

"Then let me say again, your ailment would be treated through the restoration of balance at all levels—environment, behavior, body, mind, spirit. All concurrently. In short, through the healing arts of homeopathy."

"At least the name's appropriate," one of the gigglers giggled.

Howie neutralized him with the annihilating glare. To Brewster he said, batting the air in a dramatic show of exasperation, "That's not good enough. I'm asking for specifics. Particulars. The focus of your so-called treatment. Is that so difficult to understand?"

"Not at all," said Brewster mildly. "My focus is on process. On the harmonious interaction of biological and spiritual rhythms."

Howie threw up his hands. "Process!" he shrilled. "I don't want to hear any more about process and temples and rhythms and spirits. Can't you see we're dying! Either tell us how you propose to treat our *bodies* or get the fuck out of here."

Little Barry dropped the makeshift fan and laid his head in his hands. "Oh, please, Howie, I can't *stand* this. Let him finish."

Brewster's lips constricted in a tight facsimile of a smile, something short of benign. Hostility pooled in his eyes. Quite evenly he said, "That's right. You're dying. All of you. Not of the alleged disease, but the diagnosis. Because you *believe* you're dying. Because someone with some intimidating initials tacked to his name *told* you you're dying. Because of that, you are indeed dying."

"We don't need some goddam gloating witch doctor to tell us what we already know," Howie screeched back at him.

Brewster drew in a shallow breath and, fixing Howie with a gelid stare, directing his words at him, said, "Don't confuse me with the quacks and charlatans you've consulted in the past. Their approach is dedicated not to healing but to the suppression of pain. How? Through the prescription of massive doses of concentrated poisons—miracle drugs, they like to call them—that may mask the pain but, over time, defile and vitiate the organism. This fraudulent excuse for treatment is an insult to balance, wholeness, the intelligence of Nature."

"And I suppose *you've* got the magic bullet," Howie sneered.

Brewster gathered a fold of underlip in his fingers thoughtfully. The veil of calm descended over him once again, and in an instant all the hostility was suddenly vanished, gone. "There is no magic bullet, my friend."

"Then for Christ's fucking sake stop the dancing around. Just stop it. We came to you for help, not all this muzzy ass gas."

"And help is what I have to offer," Brewster replied, peeling himself languidly out of the chair. Drawn up to his full majesterial height, an easy five or six inches above six feet, he seemed to loom over them, a craggy, spare, almost skeletal man, almost as fleshless in face and frame as his wasted audience. But unlike those four emaciated figures on the beds, stained with their own hopelessness, there was in him that same peculiar radiant energy, like a low banked fire, diffusing life-heat.

"Help in the form of homeopathy," he went on soothingly. "The natural ability of the body to heal itself. The antithesis of what you've subjected yourselves to, that monster that goes under the name allopathic—or drug-based—medicine. Now, in the case of your particular malady—"

"Why don't you say it!" Howie broke in on him, fairly screaming in an agony of frustration. "Are you afraid of the word? *Say* it! AIDS. We've all of us got AIDS. AIDS AIDS AIDS!"

A tremor ran through Barry's spindly shoulders. Head still in his hands, he whimpered wordlessly. The two gigglers, no longer quite so amused, studied the patterns in the carpet.

Brewster gave it a moment. Stroked his blade of a chin. Finally he said, "Very well. AIDS. You think because some allopath imposed the death sentence of AIDS on you, it won't yield to my methods? Wrong. What you and the medical fraternity choose to call AIDS is nothing more than a symptom of a past disease. A lifetime of abuse and neglect. You want to know the source of your present affliction? All those noxious potions you've ingested into your system. Drugs, cytotoxins, poisons—*there's* your true source."

Howie rolled his eyes at the ceiling. "You're saying the medications we're taking are the *cause* of the disease?"

"Exactly."

"Including AZT?"

"Especially AZT. The most insidious of them all."

"And as part of your 'method' you'd take us off this—what did you call it?—cytotoxin?"

"Immediately."

Howie shook his head slowly, wondrously. "This is lunacy. Sheer madness. I can't believe we came halfway across the country to hear this . . . this . . . voodoo doodoo. Well, no more. I don't know about the rest of you, but that's quite enough for me."

He glanced around, searching for support. Barry didn't move. The gigglers kept their eyes locked on the floor. No support forthcoming. Howie lurched to his feet and in a kind of histrionic staggery flounce crossed the room, stepped out onto the deck, and yanked the slider shut behind him.

For an uneasy moment no one had anything to say. Brewster waited, stiffly erect, flinty features set in the cool distancing of moral certitude. And then Barry unlaced his fingers and lifted his trembling head and in a small, frightened voice petitioned the healer: "Please help us. Tell us what to do."

"Gladly," said Brewster, and now his face cracked open in the miniature smile of a noble benefactor with a marvelous surprise in his pocket. "You must first learn to take the enlarged view. To accept the truth that you are the creator of your own body, the programmer, so to say. And as programmer you can write any program you wish."

"Could you show us how?"

"Of course. That's my function. That's what I do."

"This programming," Barry said earnestly. "How would we begin it?"

"Through a daily regimen of meditation, love, and prayer—not to some man-centered god but to the higher cosmic mind within yourself."

The two gigglers exchanged lewd smirks. One of them nudged the other and squealed, "Oh, I like that daily love part. I could get used to that."

"Sure, if you could ever get it airborne anymore," said his friend.

A mournful contempt sifted through Brewster's expression. With an icy dignity he said, "Perhaps it's time for me to leave."

Barry thrust out a stop signal hand. "No, no," he wailed, anguish in his voice. "Don't go. You're our last hope."

"You'd care to hear more?"

"Please. Yes. Please stay."

"For you," Brewster said pointedly, "I'll stay."

A look of immense relief crossed Barry's shriveled face. "Besides the, uh, meditation, what else would I have to do? For my body, I mean."

"Detoxify it at once," Brewster intoned, and on the fingers of one hand he began enumerating a laundry list of salutary measures. "Eliminate all the barbarous allopathic medications and—" his eyes swept distastefully over the liquor bottles on the bureau and the ashtrays heaped with butts on the nightstands and the containers of pills on the table—"all the self-inflicted poisons, the alcohol and nicotine and all the others. Cleanse it with fasting and high-colonic irrigation. Restore its intestinal flora to purity and balance. Nourish it with a special blend of natural herbs and glandular extracts of my own formulation. That, in brief, is what you must do for your corrupted body."

"If I did all that, could you . . . could you cure me?"

"More than merely cure you," Brewster pronounced in the wise windy tones of a schoolmaster who always gives more answer than there is question. "Far more than that." Swirling his hands, he conjured on air a vision of bursting vigor, the message delivered with oracular, hypnotic intensity, a man come like the paraclete bearing not, in this case, the gift of tongues but of abounding physical health and perfect spiritual harmony. Eventually he ran down. Folded his arms across his shallow chest and fastened his audience, reduced now to one, with a probing stare.

"Would I, uh, be staying out here then?" Barry inquired timidly.

"It would be necessary for you to relocate temporarily. Yes."

"How long?"

"Difficult to say. A year, possibly. Certainly no less than six months."

The pair on the other bed squirmed and twittered like naughty children. Around an elaborate sigh one of them said, "Fasting and herbs. Can't you just *imagine!*"

"Oh, I don't know," drawled the other. "That colonic irrigation sounds like fun."

"Depends on who's doing the irrigating."

"What about giving up the sauce and the ciggies?"

"I'm *sure!*"

"And the mother's little helpers. I couldn't *live* without my Prozac."

Brewster's face creased in an attitude of infinite pity. "Then I expect you'll both have to adjust to the minor inconvenience of being dead," he said with a twitch of a smile, as if he had just made an excellent joke comprehensible only to himself and the cosmic mind.

"Oooh! Doctor's getting cranky."

"I think maybe we're souring his scam de jour."

"Worse than that. Peeing in it."

"Oh, shut your filthy mouths, both of you," Barry yipped at them, and he got off the bed and came over and stood next to Brewster. Gazing up, up, up into the healer's placid eyes, he declared, "I'm willing to try."

"You'll not be sorry," Brewster said gravely. "This I promise you."

Acolyte and master beheld each other for a long moment. But the wave of pledge-taking solemnity crested and broke on a spray of jeers:

"Isn't it romantic?"

"Better not turn your back on little Dingle-Barry there. *Doctor*."

"He's liable to pack your fudge for you."

"But *good!*"

Brewster gripped Barry by the shoulders, spun him around, and steered him to the door. "Come along, my friend. We'll find another place to talk. The stench of negativism is much too strong in here."

3

In a cocktail lounge on the ground floor of the same hotel, two men sat easefully in cushy swivel chairs, facing each other across a small table. Smiling warmly, puffing cigarettes, savoring drinks, they were to all appearances engaged in a lively conversation, rich in reminiscence, though for one of them the talk was, in its own circuitous way, most certainly business. The lounge, elevated by three steps, offered a panoramic view of the casino, craps and black-jack and pai gow tables dominating one wing, and gleaming files of slots extending down another. The casino was not heavily trafficked: a scattering of bandit junkies, blank-eyed and rudderless as somnambulists, shuffling in and out among the rows of machines; a few of the tables in action but equally as many idle, their bored dealers glowering into some toke-vacant middle distance like ambushers arrived too late for the kill. And the lounge, known as Mr. Bigs, was itself close to deserted but for some desolate lumpers nursing beer and bruised fortunes in ruined silence at the bar, and of course for the talkative pair sitting off in a corner, purposely distanced from the curdling odors of defeat. One of whom was saying just then:

"Remember the old pigeon drop? We'd size the vic an' then tell him we gonna share all this found loot if he come up with some good faith bones of his own. Remember that?"

"Indeed I do."

"Or that one where you'd smoke your way into a biscuit's house, hang them sacks all around, test it for—I forget what it was you was suppose to be testin'."

"Radon."

"There you go. Radon. Fuck was in them sacks, anyways, Eggs?"

"Beads. Colored beads. That little venture was always good for some quick walking-around money."

"Jesus, all them doughheads. You'd tell 'em down is up and they wanna try walkin' on the ceiling. Or doin' headstands on the floor."

"Fear and greed, Cleanth. The simple application of the tools of our calling. It's a world peopled with believers."

"Yeah, maybe. But nobody had it down like you did. You was a fuckin' artist, them days."

The one called Eggs gave an assured toss of a hand. "Still am, Cleanth. Still am."

He was a wiry, slender-built man, this Eggs, nattily outfitted in apple-green slouch jacket, dust-colored slacks, white linen sport shirt, tasseled loafers. The initials I.L. were stitched into the pocket of the shirt, for Ignatius LaRevere. He came by Eggs not in reference to any dietary predilection but simply as an abridgment of his given name. In a hurry-up town short on time and patience, where all communication was routinely pruned to accommodate the urgent transaction of business, Ignatius telescoped quite nicely into Eggs. Which was fine with him, Ignatius being somewhat out of fashion nowadays.

Similarly was Cleanth Clifton Koontz known to most everyone else as Click, for an unfortunate nervous habit of occasionally punctuating his speech with a curious noise, rather like a sharp grating skirl, produced by a vibration of the tongue against the left molars. This mannerism, a lifelong affliction, had the regrettable effect of tucking back a corner of his mouth in the appearance of a pained grimace regardless of the nature of the foregoing utterance, be it question, declaration, exclamation, or merely an assentive grunt. Among all his acquaintances, Eggs alone, for reasons best understood by himself, perhaps a kind of fussy need for exactness, precision, order, addressed him as Cleanth. To Click this had always seemed a bit odd, though in no way objectionable, for in their past association he had regarded his sometime partner with a veneration approaching awe. As he did yet.

"Seem like just day before yesterday we was runnin' all them good clips," he was saying, basking in the cozy warmth of times gone by. "What's it been? Couple years?"

"Closer to three."

"Live in Vegas, you lose track a minutes, never mind the years."

"That's part of its charm. That and the buzz in the air. Hear it, Cleanth? It's the hum of money."

"Hum a money," Click echoed. "You always could say it just right, Egger. Always got the words."

Eggs gave an insouciant shrug. No disputing the obvious.

"So where all you been, them years?"

"Here and there," Eggs said vaguely.

"Gettin' small, huh."

"Something like that."

"I figured. One day you're around, next it's like you done a Casper. What happened, anyways?"

"Oh, nothing special. Little touchup that got out of hand."

"This touchup, where was it at?"

"The Riv Mark was reluctant to part with his winnings. He may have expired."

"Anybody make you?"

"Difficult to say. There was a certain amount of confusion. Screaming, you know. That sort of thing. Very untidy. I thought I saw a couple of citizens peeking out a door at the far end of the hall, though I might have been mistaken. In any event, it seemed prudent to put some distance between me and this vicinity. Discretion and valor, you remember."

"You shouldn'ta gone at it solo. Clip like that takes two. I'd've been there, we coulda wrapped it up neat and clean."

"*Carpe diem,* Cleanth."

Click looked at him blankly.

"It means seize the day," Eggs explained, a faintly ironic intonation in his cultivated voice. "Or in that particular case, the moment.

You *weren't* there, the circumstances seemed propitious, and so I elected to go ahead on my own."

"And this was out to the Riv?"

"Yes."

"It was the same weenie, think I heard he croaked. Read it someplace, I remember right."

Eggs shook his head ruefully. "Foolish man. As it turned out, there wasn't all that much cash at stake either. Cost him his life. And three of the best years of mine, going to ground. Senseless waste. For both of us."

Click recognized something of his friend's melancholy over the senseless waste, and so to cheer him he said brightly, "Yeah, well, least they never nailed you on it. Three years, steam's for sure gotta be cooled down. You're back in town. And you lookin' real good too, Eggs."

The last observation in this sunshine bulletin was more than empty flattery, for in spite of his forty years Eggs did indeed look remarkably youthful and fit. His face was smooth, uncreased, the peach-pink skin drawn tight over fine chiseled bones. Behind smoke-lens glasses worn so habitually rumor had it he slept and showered and made love in them, the pale blue eyes were clear, perceptive, astute; eyes that, could they be seen, gave away nothing at all. The straw-colored hair was abundant and so meticulously styled and moussed it appeared almost enameled to his skull. The cumulative effect was a face some would call handsome, though on closer inspection they might be inclined to qualify that judgment. For there was a peculiar imbalance to it, like a halved sphere reassembled slightly off-center. Maybe it was the small derisive arch to one brow. Or maybe the mouth, a thin predatory line angled upward ever so slightly in a perpetual ghost of a mirthless smile. It could have been that, the mouth. Whatever the aberration, there was something about the totality of the Ignatius LaRevere features that summoned the disturbing impression of a veiled malevolence thoughtless as a force of nature and utterly unacquainted with remorse or pity or mercy.

"You really think so?" he said in response to Click's generous words.

"Listen, I'm tellin' ya. 'Bout as good as I ever seen you lookin'. Like you put in them years at a health farm."

Eggs ran a careful hand over his contoured hair, smoothing away a wholly imagined irregularity. "Well, I do try to take care of myself."

"Y'know, good health, it's a lot like pussy," Click observed sagely. "Man can't never get too much either one of 'em."

"I suppose you're right," Eggs allowed, no longer much interested in an avenue of conversation broadened beyond himself. Somewhat in afterthought he asked, "What about you?"

"Me? Oh, I'm in pretty good shape. Could maybe drop little lard, but otherwise I'm doin' real fine."

About the excess baggage he was absolutely right. His considerable bulk was exclusively of the acquired variety, for in height and skeletal frame he was almost dwarfish. Yet as if in defiance of genetic law, he had thickened into that most disagreeable manifestation of obesity: the sawed-off, slight, delicate-boned runt fully intended by nature to be skinny but swollen by appetite into the chunky dimensions of a piglet. Sadly, that same porcine quality of torso and limbs extended to his face, its cheeks mushy, skin mottled as a slab of blue cheese, nose flat and wide-nostriled, eyes hog-bright. His hair, sparse, midnight black, salted with moist flakes of dandruff, was slicked back from an abnormally low and protruberant shelf of forehead. Though he was five years younger than Eggs, anyone reckoning their ages would have put him at least that many years senior to his friend, maybe more. Evidently his appearance was not at that moment deeply troubling, for he gave his low-slung orb of belly a contented thump and made a cracked smile and the trademark lingual squeak.

"What I meant, Cleanth," Eggs said, now the patient tutor coaching an especially dull charge, "was how have you been getting by. In my absence."

"Oh, that. Well, y'know, little scufflin' here, little hustlin' there. Sidewalk spittin' stuff, mostly. Couldn't turn up much, after you bailed. Never did have your gift for it. And anyways, things got real slow in town."

"I noticed," Eggs said, taking in the meager casino crowd with a sweep of a hand. "How do you account for that?"

"Nobody know for sure. Some say it's A.C. moochin' all the East Coast action. Some say Laughlin. Tellya my idea, though."

"And what would that be?"

"Slopes. Way they buyin' up the Strip, it's gonna be Yokohama West out here quicker'n you can say bans-eye."

"Oh," Eggs said without inflection.

"Giveya a for instance," Click went on, warming to the topic. "Right now you go in some a them hotel chow houses, order your basic American burger'n fries, they serve you up a fisheye san-wich, side a rice. Eat it or go boff yourself. Ask for a doggie bag and you just as like to find a boiled pooch in it."

The thought of the creeping yellow tide imperiling the community sparked a bitter indignation in his earnest face. Eggs tightened the muscles of his jaws against a yawn. Already he was regretting the question.

"Yeah, it's them goddam zipperheads doin' it. They the ones. You watch. Gonna be Pearl Fuckin' Harbor all over again," Click declared grimly, underscoring his dark prediction with the automatic tongue skirl. He stubbed out his cigarette, lit another. Flicked some wet snow specks from his collar. Scowled at the floor.

Eggs watched him curiously. Genuine moral outrage. And over an issue that had no bearing whatsoever on the advancement of one's personal fortunes. For him it was a phenomenon impossible to comprehend, totally alien to his experience. "Ingenious theory," he said, and then, gently steering the talk along more utilitarian lines, he added, "but it's you I'm interested in, Cleanth. These days, what are you up to?"

"Y'mean lately?"

"Yes. Now."

"Guess y'could say I'm, like, workin' for this fella. Sorta."

"You have a *job?*"

"More like helpin' him out," Click said sheepishly. His eyes were no longer on the floor, but neither did they meet Eggs's steady mocking gaze.

"This person. Anybody I'd know?"

"Nah, you wouldn't know him. Name's Brewster. Use to be a doctor. Not the kind you go to, you're sick, but like them ones make the pills, in a drugstore."

"A pharmacist?"

"That's the ones."

"You say 'used to be.' What happened?"

"It ain't too clear. Way I heard it, he was tellin' people he could cure whatever ailed 'em. You name it, clap to cancer, he got the fix."

"Really. And what is the, ah, nature of this cure?"

"One thing it for sure ain't is your regular drugs. He's real down on drugs. Legal ones, I'm talkin' here. Which is pro'ly why the state come in an' sat on him, yanked his license."

"The cure, Cleanth," Eggs prompted.

"Well, he got this idea he can fix anybody up with, y'know, right thinkin'."

"His cure is right *think*ing?" Eggs said, his own interest picking up considerably now.

"That'n these special foods."

"What kind of foods?"

"Your healthy ones. Like herbs," Click said, sounding the *h*.

"That's pronounced herbs," Eggs corrected. "The *h* is silent."

"Whatever. Anyways, he got a whole line a these foods he's sellin'."

"So it's a little game he has going."

"Kinda yes'n no. See, guy actual' believe it, this curin'. S'pose he's a whackadoo, but he ain't too bad to work for."

Eggs made a prayer steeple of his hands, perched his chin on the thumbs. "Sounds fascinating, this job of yours. Tell me, what exactly are your duties?"

"Drive him around, mostly. He hates to drive. Like tonight, I bring him over to the hotel here so's he can pitch some tail gunners got the package."

"Claims to cure AIDS, does he?"

"Oh yeah. AIDS is big, all the rump-rangers floatin' around. That'n cancer. He got patients all over town, some of 'em dead on their feet. I oughta know, I take him on his rounds."

"Even does house calls. Very enterprising fellow."

"Bet your ass. Hear him tell it, ain't nothin' he can't cure."

Eggs pursed his lips thoughtfully. More and more was he intrigued with all he was hearing. "Besides the driving," he asked, "what else do you do?"

"Oh, y'know, this'n that. Some other things."

"I'm asking what other things, Cleanth. Precisely."

Click's eyes once again sought the floor. Clearly, he was less than happy with the turn these questions were taking. "Well, he got this place over on Spring Mountain, sorta like a health food store. Sometimes I help out there."

"Help out how?" Eggs persisted.

"Packin' orders, shit like that. He does a real good mail order business."

"Terminal patients, mail order, a store. I gather he does quite well, for a defrocked pill pusher."

"Does okay, I s'pose. Can't be that much in it though. Herbs ain't exactly sellin' like Whoppers, y'know."

Again the herbs *h* was vocalized. Eggs sighed but let it go by. There were limits to what a man could do. "You might be surprised," he said.

"All's I know is what I see."

"Anything else you do there?"

"Where's that?"

"The store, Cleanth. We're still talking about the store."

Cornered at last. In a voice scarcely more than a whisper, scarcely audible, Click said, "Yeah, well, sometimes I wait on the customers."

"What's that?"

"Wait on customers."

A sardonic crimp came into Eggs's pinched mouth. "A clerk? A *sales*clerk? Cleanth, Cleanth, how the mighty have fallen."

"Man's gotta eat," Click muttered defensively. As if in evidence, he picked up his glass, sloshed some whiskey around his mouth, gulped noisily. A cloud of hurt passed over his porky face.

Eggs undid the steeple and turned up placating palms. "Just making a little joke, Cleanth."

"Ain't so funny, bein' tapped. You try it."

"I know about that. Better than you may think."

"Hadda do somethin', after you bugged out."

"I understand. But I'm back now. Things will change."

"Yeah, how's that gonna happen?" Click said, still smarting some from what he perceived as a totally uncalled-for taunt. Friends don't go raggin' friends.

"I'm not just certain yet. Have to give it some thought."

Click glanced at his watch, and all the hurt in his face was suddenly gone, displayed by an expression close to panic. "Jesus fuck, I gotta jam outta here. Suppose to meet him in the lot half an hour ago."

He hauled himself out of the chair and extended a parting hand. Eggs rose up simultaneously, took the hand, and gave it a fraternal squeeze.

"Sure glad ya called, Egger. Real good seein' ya again."

"All my pleasure," Eggs said, still gripping the hand. "Oh, yes, one other thing, before you leave. Perhaps you could, ah, advance me a few dollars. Against our next joint venture, say."

"You cashed?"

"Afraid so. You see why I can appreciate your present circumstances."

"Maybe spare you half a yard. Best I can do."

Eggs released the hand. "That would help," he said.

Click got his wallet, counted out some bills, and laid them in the upturned palm. "Gotta shag ass now. Gimme jingle, huh. After you done that heavy thinkin'."

"You'll be hearing from me shortly, Cleanth. Trust me; in matters of this sort, business, there's always a way."

4

At about the same moment Click was scooting toward the Dunes parking lot, Waverly was exiting the Barbary Coast with the magnificent sum of two hundred and forty dollars in his pocket, the rewards of six long hours at the tables. Not one of your more auspicious nights for business. But not over yet either. For as he came through the casino doors and stepped out into the chilly autumn air, there was another, quite unexpected and altogether different bit of business waiting in the person of his freckled friend from the counting fracas. There he sat, slouched on a sidewalk bench, clearly covering the entrance. And just as clearly watching for him.

Waverly glanced about. Flock of pedestrians much too thin at this hour to fade into. No place to duck. So he walked quickly to the intersection of Flamingo and Las Vegas Boulevard, but the light went red and an unbroken stream of traffic surged ahead and whipped on by. No stutter stepping through that. Out of the corner of an eye he saw the squat figure rising off the bench and bearing down on him aggressively, or as aggressively as a wobbly juicer can bear down on anything. From harsh experience he knew, none better, it was just this sort of trifling farcical disturbance that had a way of flaring into something loud and ugly and attention-generating. Attention as in heat. The sort of trouble he could do nicely without.

And so that's what he said as he turned and faced him, putting up a gently restraining hand: "Look, I don't want any trouble."

"Neither do I."

He stared at Waverly a moment, owl-eyed and deeply solemn. Then the red fleshy face opened in a grin and he seized Waverly's hand and pumped it vigorously. "Just wanted to shake the hand of the first genuine counter I've come across in years."

"It's not exactly a distinguished talent. Such as it is."

"No, that's where you're mistaken. It's a rare gift. Freakish maybe, aberrant, but no less a gift."

Waverly recovered his hand. "Thanks. I guess."

"My name's Pettibone. Roger Pettibone."

Waverly wasn't about to bite on that. He volunteered nothing.

"Improbable, right? But then the name's not the man. Any more than the map's the territory."

If a face is its own kind of map, this one, even pushed up close this way, was not easy to read. Drink-pillaged, rubbery, jaded, fiftyish or up, it nonetheless had a certain guileless cast to it, the perpetually startled look of a newborn child. Still had to be selling something. This, after all, was Las Vegas. Waverly was mildly curious, but not enough to stick around and find out. The light turned, the traffic ground to a halt. "Nice talking to you, Mr. Pettibone," he said, and started into the street.

Pettibone fell in beside him. "Where you headed?"

"I've got to meet someone."

"Like to buy you a drink."

"Thanks, I don't think so."

"Come on, you owe me."

Waverly shot him a wary glance but kept right on walking. "Owe you? How's that?"

"That little contretemps back there."

"Afraid I don't see it quite that way."

"Pretty ignominious for me, you've got to admit."

Waverly stepped onto the curb and inspected him narrowly. There was something almost comic in that inflated, self-parodying speech, delivered as it was on a nasalized ripple in the voice. Certainly nothing even faintly menacing in those freckle-washed cherub cheeks. Most singular pitch. "And what is it you figure I owe you?" he asked.

"Company," Pettibone said simply.

"That's it? Company?"

"In this sorry world what's more priceless than good company?"

In spite of himself Waverly had to smile. He held up an index finger. "One."

"One it is." He pointed Waverly toward the entrance to Bally's. "Come along," he said, "this breathtaking, albeit fading monument awaits our pleasure."

A moment later they were seated at the end of an oval-shaped bar strategically located next to the casino floor. To their right the sports book's bank of television screens flashed highlights of the day's games, while a battery of urgent odds-shaping communiqués on future contests snaked across the silent radio. To their left a shimmery wilderness of slots jangled incessantly. Waverly ordered a light beer, Pettibone a double J.D. straight on up. Waverly laid some bills on the bar. "I'll get this."

Pettibone pushed the money aside grandly, went for his wallet. "Absolutely not. It was my idea."

"Also it was you took the fall across the street."

"I'm sure I can lead a reasonably happy, moderately useful, and for the most part socially sanctioned life never setting foot in the Barbary Coast again the remainder of my days."

Waverly gave an acquiescent shrug. The drinks arrived, and Pettibone elevated his glass in a formal toast: "Here's to you, sir. Master of blackman. That confounding game."

"Player," Waverly amended. "Hardly a master."

They clinked glasses. Pettibone took down half his Jack Daniels in a long gurgly swallow. Released a satisfied wheeze. Looked at Waverly shrewdly. "No need for kicking the feet in the sand. You're obviously a professional."

"What makes you say that?"

"The way you were looting those tables."

"*Looting*," Waverly snorted. "That's a pretty heavy word for the loose change I collected tonight."

"The amount is never at issue, it's how you play the game. To put a perverse spin on that old bromide."

This was not a theme Waverly cared to follow too far. "Yeah, well, think what you like."

"Not to worry. Your secret's safe with me."

"And what about you?"

"Me? What is it you'd like to know?"

"Your game."

"I have no game."

"Here I assumed you were a player yourself. Of sorts."

"Your assumption is wrong," Pettibone said testily. "I despise gambling."

"Really. I'd never have guessed. What do you despise about it?"

"The way it rusts a man's soul."

"Soul? There's a quaint notion."

"You think so? I don't. What you're forgetting is that universal credulous trust in things invisible. Consider all the phantoms we accept on faith and yet will never ever see: germs, viruses, molecules, atoms, electrons, neutrinos, quarks. From there it's only a hop and a skip to various other chimera: spirits, souls, God, if you like. And from there to fate, chance, luck."

"That's a novel theory, considering also where we are," Waverly said. "Both of us," he added significantly.

"But that's the point! Look around you," Pettibone directed, steering Waverly's gaze out over the casino. A sudden missionary vehemence came into his voice. Sparks flashed in the rheumy eyes. "We're here because we want to believe in those specters. Listen to the buzz of frantic wants in the air. Look at these people, either side of the table, conniver and victim alike. They want, want, want, but what it is they want they couldn't begin to name. There's a ghastly value at work here."

In a town full of swaggering misfits, moonstruck dreamers, twisted neurotics, cunning predators, this one had to be among your first-order oddballs. Either that, or a most devious scammer, virtuoso of indirection. "Yet you *do* play," Waverly reminded him.

"All of us do things we despise," Pettibone said ruefully, now just as suddenly subdued. "All of us."

He drained off the last of his drink, signaled the bartender for another. When it was set before him, he said to Waverly, as if in afterthought, "Join me?"

Waverly covered his glass. "I'm still good."

The cautious silence that will sometimes settle over strangers settled over them. Lengthened. Waverly finished his beer. "Well, that's my one," he said, bland preface to a departure. But before he could get to his feet, a familiar booming voice hailed him. He looked over his shoulder and there was Bennie. Glowering. Clearly not in the jolliest of tempers.

"Timothy? Where you been, man? We was suppose to connect an hour ago."

"I got sidetracked."

"I notice. Like in sloshin' beer sidetracked."

Waverly ignored the little barb. "How'd you find me?"

"Process of elimination. Don't take no astrophysics diploma, scopin' casinos. So how'd you do?"

Waverly was acutely conscious of Pettibone shifting in his seat and watching both of them, taking it all in. "Roger Pettibone, this is my . . . associate, Bennie."

"Pleased to meet you," Pettibone said affably, hand extended.

Bennie gave the hand a perfunctory clutch, barely looked at him. "Yeah, likewise."

"We were playing the same table," Waverly said by way of explanation.

"Sensational. But what I'm askin' about here is your takeaway, that table."

"Couple bills is all."

"Couple bills," Bennie groaned. "Jesus, more negative numbers."

"I guess that means you didn't have a profitable day."

"Bingo on that zip profit."

"Maybe you'd care for a consolation drink," Pettibone said.

Bennie acknowledged the suggestion with a peevish head toss. "Nah, already I got the hot pipes, all the dog doo dumpin' on me today." He made a short summoning motion at Waverly. "C'mon, let's motor outta here. Catch a cab out front."

"I'm ready."

A hint of distress flickered across Pettibone's boiled features. "Let me give you a lift," he put in quickly. "I'm parked right around the corner."

"Cab will do," Waverly said, rising and starting away.

Bennie, however, didn't move. He looked at Pettibone as if he had just now discovered him there. To Waverly he said, mock reproval, "Hey, hold up. Man offers you something free, it ain't mannerly to turn him down." And to Pettibone, genially: "We be glad to ride with you, uh . . . what's your name again?"

"Call me Roger."

"Roger. Okay, Roger," he said, swinging an arm in a waiterly flourish, "you lead the way."

Pettibone gulped his drink, eased his bulk off the bar stool, and lurched headlong through the casino and out the door and around the corner in the direction of a parking lot fronting a tiny mall just south of Bally's. Bennie caught up with him on the street and they marched along side by side, yammering a mile a minute, perpetual-motion word machines. A pair of ambulatory mouths. And now there were two of them. Waverly stayed a few paces behind, keeping a distance, keeping out of it. From this angle he was struck by their remarkable physical resemblance. They were almost identical in stature and girth, shaped—if shaped it could be called—like two slab-sided rectilinear obelisks crowned by large, neckless heads. There the resemblance ended, for Pettibone's sported the shaggy thatch of flame-red hair, while Bennie's was, but for the scanty wisps drawn like paint streaks over the globe of skull, barren as a moonscape.

"There it is," Pettibone announced, indicating a battered, antiquated Mercury Grand Marquis, big and black and square as a tank.

"Nice vehicle," Bennie said, softening the irony with a judicious nod.

Pettibone swayed toward it, fumbled for his keys. Waverly thought it prudent to ask, "You want me to drive?"

"Thanks, no. I've got everything under control."

Waverly glanced at Bennie. Bennie shrugged. Free is free. They climbed in, Bennie up front, Waverly in the back. Pettibone brought the car to a sputtery start and took it to the parking lot exit. "At your direction," he said. Bennie wagged a thumb northward, Pettibone wedged his tank into the current of traffic, appropriating a lane and exciting a furious squawk of horns, and they were off and wheeling.

Bennie gestured expansively at the gaudy hotels flashing by. "I tellya," he told them, some of the invincible optimism returned to his voice, "bad night or not, you gotta love this town. Ain't noplace like it on God's green earth."

"Absolutely right," Pettibone affirmed. "About that latter, anyway."

"Y'know," Bennie went on, directing his words at Waverly now, "Roger here been livin' in Vegas since before the Flood."

"Really."

"How many years you say, Roger?"

"Eighteen. Exactly one-third of my life."

"Expect you seen a lot a changes, them years."

"My share. I can, for example, recall when where we were just sitting, Bally's, was a grubby little hostelry known as the Bonanza, and before that an arid stretch of sand."

"Go you one better'n that. I did a turn out here in the forties, and in them days all the action was downtown. 'Cept for a couple joints, your whole Strip wasn't nothin' but scrub brush and jackrabbits. Took old Bugsy Siegal, Moe Dalitz, Gus Greenbaum to see the potential. They was some smart Jewboys, them three."

"Giants in their time," Pettibone remarked dryly.

"Hope to shit your statue, giants. Them boys had—" he hesitated, hoisted a seizing hand as if to pluck the precise word from the air—"vision."

"Deep as the oceans," Pettibone said gravely, "boundless as the spheres."

Bennie squinted at him uncertainly. An ironist himself, he was not always quick to spot it in others. "You wouldn't be raggin' me here?"

"Not at all. Only an extraordinary vision could conceive this." He swept an arm the width of the windshield, taking in the kaleidoscopic assault of dancing, twitching, glittering neon on either side of the street. "The same vision, I suppose, that could conceive a place called Hell."

They rode a while in silence. Passed the Sahara Avenue intersection, approached Charleston Boulevard. The traffic thinned some and the glitz of the Strip began to give way to shabby hotbed motels, dreary eateries, taverns, wedding chapels with marquees announcing credit cards cheerfully accepted, pawnshops, palmist and spiritualist parlors, assorted fringe enterprises.

"Okay," Bennie directed, "up there on Garces hang a left. We're couple blocks down."

Pettibone turned at the designated corner and drove through a deserted, dimly lit street flanked by single-story houses, some frame, some stucco, all of them most charitably described as weathered. But even the charity of night could not conceal the neighborhood's unrelieved seediness: yards absent of shrubs or grass, shadowy outlines of vehicles jacked up on cement blocks outside crumbling sheds, here and there an abandoned though as yet undiscarded stove or sofa gracing a porch.

"That's it right there," said Bennie, and Pettibone pulled the Mercury over, cut the engine, and peered around him at a frame structure compact and diminutive as a stunted pillbox. Its dirt-patch lawn was circumscribed by an incongruous waist-high picket fence whose gate dangled precariously from a single hinge and whose symmetry was disturbed by a missing slat or two. Pettibone made a nasal *hmming* sound through locked teeth, followed by the noncommittal observation, "So. You have a house."

"Rent's cheap this part a town."

"I'm sure."

"Beats an apartment. Ones we looked at, be like livin' in a submarine. Here you got your privacy. Two bedrooms, bath, kitchen, living room, even got a little screen porch out back."

"And handy to downtown," Pettibone allowed generously.

"Upkeep ain't much either."

"So I see."

To forestall any more of this rambling real estate colloquy, Waverly said, "Thanks for the lift."

Bennie echoed the thanks and they cracked open respective

doors and stepped out of the car. Simultaneously, Pettibone did the same.

"I, ah, enjoyed your company tonight. Both of you."

Not quite a plea, but plainly fishing for an invitation inside. Waverly and Bennie traded looks. For an instant neither spoke. Finally, assuming the weight of decision, Bennie said, "You wanna come in, pop back a loosener?"

"Are you sure?" Waverly put in quickly. "It's pretty late."

"Yeah, why not. One good turn, y'know. Anyway, ain't no such thing as late or early, Vegas. Whaddya say, Roger?"

"I'd be delighted."

Bennie led the way. They came through the door and the delighted guest paused in the entrance a moment, inspecting a living room whose furnishings, early Goodwill, included lumpy leather couch, a pair of matching vinyl-covered not-so-easy chairs, stepladder coffee table, frayed carpet, and not a thing more. The celery-green plaster walls were empty of adornment. An unshaded overhead bulb supplied the only light. Pettibone produced his all-purpose *hmm*, then drawled, "Spartan."

"In our line," Waverly said, "things don't accumulate."

"Well, maybe not your most prepossessing digs for two gentlemen of your obvious parts. But then, as we all know, those swindlers illusion and reality are seldom quite the same."

"Fuck's he talkin' about, swindlin'?" Bennie called from a doorless galley kitchen opening onto the far end of the room.

"Never mind," Waverly called back.

Pettibone took one of the chairs, Waverly the other. Soon Bennie appeared bearing water glasses filled to the rim with Scotch. He sank onto the couch, fired up a cigar, lifted his glass, and declared, "Here's to better days."

"There's a charming sentiment," Pettibone seconded, and they tossed off manly jolts in mutual celebration of that noble conviction.

Waverly took a small sip. He hated Scotch. He felt burned out, whipped. What was he doing, sitting here listening to all this wandering babble? Where was his head? "Which are those?" he said sourly.

"Ones we keep hearin' about. Ones just around the corner and up the block. Listen, one wormy night don't mean you're spanked permanent. Am I right, Roger?"

Somewhat indulgently, Pettibone averred he was right.

"Take tonight for a for instance. Early games I couldn't pick a winner if I'd had on future goggles. Them pros never play like they suppose to. Can't count on nothin' no more. So anyway, time the late ones roll around I'm down to layin' props an'—"

"Props!" Waverly broke in on him. "Those are knuckle-walker bets. You know better than that."

"Yeah yeah yeah, but I got this hunch, see. More'n a hunch. Vikes'n Bears are playin', and it's like I got this stat sheet in my head, whole game right in back a my eyes. Before it's even played. Y'know what I'm sayin' here?"

"No," Waverly said. Hunches, proposition bets, prophetic stat sheets, premonitions—he couldn't believe he was hearing any of this.

"Rather like the vision you were speaking of earlier," Pettibone offered helpfully.

"There you go. Vision. So they runnin' this prop on who gonna hit the most field goals. Already I know it's gotta be the Bears. I lay down the rest a my roll. One sweet touch is all it takes, get me well for the night. Lock city, right? Wrong. Comes the two-minute buzzer and the Vikes are one goal up. But here come the Bears chargin' down the field, get in the red zone, get stalled. Bring in the kicker. This range it's like a point after, so I figure I'm gonna get a push out of it, least stay even. What happens? Fucker kicks a *whiffer,* is what. You believe it? Fifteen yards out and Mr. Shmuck gotta choke. Vanishes me right down the Chinese pisser."

His shag rug brows soared in disbelief. He took a deep sustaining pull on the cigar, released a gust of smoke, evidently signaling a close to the melancholy tale.

"I seem to be missing a point myself," Waverly said.

"What point's that?"

"The better days one."

"Oh, that. Well, so the kick's wide right," explained this terminally compulsive dreamer, sixty years young and still chasing after fairy dust, "next time it's straight arrow right on through them uprights. Drowned today, doin' the Jesus walk on top the H_2O tomorrow. Point is, Timothy, we gonna make it to the bigs yet. You watch."

Pettibone gazed at him as though he were examining a curious specimen under glass. He shook his head wonderingly, shifted the contemplative gaze onto Waverly. "You remember my theory? About things invisible?"

"I remember it," Waverly said, coolly and with more than a little annoyance riding his voice. He was getting mightily sick of all this smirky bottled in bond ninety-proof wisdom. "You know, Mr. Pettibone, you've never told us what it is *you* do, these eighteen years you've been here."

"And you've never told me your name."

"You heard it. Timothy."

"And I'm a professor. Though most people mistake me for a cab driver."

"Professor. Where?"

"Timothy, what?"

Waverly said his last name, and immediately wondered why he'd said it. First score to his verbal sparring partner.

"Waverly," Pettibone repeated. "All right, Timothy Waverly; I'm employed by that day care center they like to call UNLV. Un-love, if you were to enunciate the acronym."

"Professor, huh," Bennie interjected. "You oughta get on good with Timothy here. He's a college boy too."

"Yes, I took him for an educated man."

"What's your discipline?" Waverly asked, unwilling to let it go.

"History."

"What period?"

"Greeks and Romans. Not, as you might guess, in urgent demand these days. Hotel Management is our flagship curriculum, you know; the conferring of degrees on glorified bellhops. Or chefs. Actually, I'd be better off versed in the culinary arts."

"Or coachin' roundball," Bennie volunteered, "teams they been fieldin' out there lately."

Pettibone suddenly scowled. "No," he said grimly, "even if I were qualified, I've still got a vestige of conscience left, however tarnished."

"Whaddya mean? You don't approve slippin' them slamdunker spades few honeybees under the table? That's how it's done, man, college sports."

"That I understand. It's when they start manipulating the players, corrupting them with their sordid little schemes . . ." He trailed off, staring indignantly into his lap.

"What kinda schemes we talkin' here, Roger?"

"Point shaving."

Bennie regarded him carefully, skeptical yet, but visibly more attentive. "Where'd you hear that?"

"From a reputable source."

"C'mon, that's just street noise."

"It happens I teach one of those players. Very troubled young man, not your average sweaty oaf. He talks to me. Seems to think I have answers, God knows why."

"Aah, he's pro'ly just jivin' you. Boogies always get a hoot outta shuckin' whitey."

Pettibone shrugged. "Have it however you will."

Bennie gave his pouch of secondary chin a ruminant tug. He picked up his glass and bubbled down the rest of the Scotch. Swiped a hand over his lips, magically transforming them into a wide mein host grin. "Who's hungry? Dunno 'bout you boys, but I could eat the ass end of a skunk. Roger?"

"I'll join you for a bite."

"Timothy?"

"I'll pass."

Bennie pushed himself up off the couch and beckoned their guest with a follow-me jab of the head. "C'mon, Rog, let's see what we can rustle up out in the eats factory."

Pettibone came to his feet, a trifle unsteadily. Bennie laid a comradely guiding arm across his shoulders. And as they disappeared into the kitchen, Waverly could hear the smooth, ceaseless B. Epstein rap: "Know we got some ham, cheese, tongue. Oh yeah, my name's Epstein, case I forgot to say. Benjamin Saul Epstein.

Course nobody ever call me Saul 'less I'm holdin' their marker. Now, about that point-shavin' business . . ."

Waverly loosened the knot in his tie. It promised to be a long night.

5

For another Waverly, Valerie by given name, it was proving to be an equally long and, in its own way, arduous night. Stiff, bone-weary, fighting off sleep, she steered an ancient Chevy Impala southwest across terrain stark and cragged and eerie as a lunar wasteland. Jammed haphazardly (for this was not a seasoned voyager) in the trunk and the back were three suitcases and a number of cardboard cartons containing among them the sum total of all the possessions accumulated in forty-one years of living. In the front was the creature dearer to her than perhaps any other in the world, a sleek sinewy Doberman curled up on the seat and lost in a dreamless doggy slumber. Apart from its rhythmic breathing, the only sound was the labored chug of the engine bearing them steadily, behind probing fingers of yellow light, in the direction of Las Vegas.

If a pilgrimage linked with an excursion into a wounded past could be described as business, then for Valerie Waverly this journey surely qualified as just that, an errand of private business. It had begun a little over forty hours ago—no, no, that wasn't right. Thinking about it now, dead of night, she recognized that the seed of the adventure was planted with the phone call from her brother, the strange, tight, circuitous conversation and the news, reluctantly revealed, of his latest whereabouts. *That's* where it began, actually.

Eight weeks the spore lay dormant, germinating in an abandoned vase in a forgotten greenhouse of her mind, until finally it blossomed in the impulsive bold resolve to put behind her forever the speck of a town nudged up against the eastern boundary of South Dakota. Aurora, South Dakota, that remote austere outpost, site of a ten-year self-imposed exile, population half a thousand good and prying souls who knew her simply as the crazy dogs and herbs lady, the hermitess. Aurora, goddess of dawn. Only now did its name seem to augur something mysterious, portentous, renascent. The lifting of a decade of night and the dawning of a new and lustrous morning in her life. A once and for all coming to terms with her brother and, possibly, an audience with the man revered from a distance for longer than she remembered. Two destinations in one.

And so, with a fine feel for the symbolic, on the literal morning of the previous day (Saturday, November 7—mark it well!) at precisely that moment the first band of orange light shimmered on the horizon, she pointed the rust-scabbed Impala—last tangible legacy from her father, gone these many years—south on Highway 29, and the magnificent adventure was under way at last.

Four hours later she turned west on Interstate 80 and followed it across a Nebraska landscape still as a photograph nailed to the windshield, and flat and limitless as the farthest reaches of deep space. Unlike most travelers, the lonely tedium of a protracted journey was never a factor for her. Enchanted as a child, she absorbed everything: the white serpent of highway uncoiling before her; the legions of purple-bellied clouds advancing relentlessly through the leaden sky above her; the wind voices crooning to her from just beyond the window. Oh, look there!—a covey of birds, black as night, feasting on the pulpy polychromatic innards of a mashed rodent. And over there!—a stand of trees, drowning victims, their trunks submerged in a stagnant pool, topmost branches clawing the neutral air. Nothing escaped her; everything spoke to her. And when she tired of extracting covert messages from the abounding spirits of the earth, she dispatched her own spirit on ahead, across the miles, to murmur in the ears of Timothy Waverly and Wyman Brewster, reassurances to her brother, petitions to the healer.

Only infrequently did she stop, and then only to refuel and attend to nature. The Doberman, of course, welcomed the breaks and went romping joyously in ever-widening circles about the car. She was unconcerned. A gentle summons—"Electra, come on, girl, time to go"—brought the dog scampering back obediently, and they were on the road again. By late afternoon her eyes grew heavy, and so she pulled off at some sleepy forgettable hamlet near the Wyoming line and dozed with her head propped against the door. When she woke, the world was shrouded in darkness. She owned no watch; the metronomic rhythms of earth and sky and her own body were clock enough. And one of those rhythms reminded her it was time now for sustenance.

From a large wicker provisions basket on the floor in the back she removed a jug of demineralized water, a saucer, two organic dog biscuits, a packet of Sun-Chlorella, and a bottle of Enervite tablets. Electra was served first. The dog gulped the biscuits greedily and lapped up a saucerful of the purified water. Next herself. She filled a palm with the tiny green Chlorella pellets, masticated them thoroughly, shook out a single Enervite, and took it down on a long, satisfying pull from the jug. The herbal stimulant jolted her like an electric shock, or at least so she imagined. Since thought and reality were for her one and the same, instantly she was revived. She opened the passenger door and let Electra hop out and take care of business. Astonishing how animals, properly cared for, were such efficient machines of digestion and elimination. Another of Nature's masterful wonders. Thus reenergized, both of them, she turned the key in the ignition, swung the Impala back onto the highway, and sped on through the night.

By mid-morning they were in Salt Lake City. She pulled into a truck stop and gassed the car. Once again the feeding ritual was repeated, identical fare. Much as with monotony, food was never an issue for Valerie Waverly. Years of dining exclusively on natural products—seeds, herbs, organically grown fruits and vegetables— had so sensitized hers and the dog's systems that it was inconceivable to consume anything else. Certainly not the charred carcasses of dead creatures and all the other execrable dung served in cafés or purchased off grocery shelves. Perhaps as a result she looked extraordinarily young, late twenties, thirty at most. A mane of long straight hair the color of sun-bleached wheat fell to her shoulders, framing the impeccable geometry of a narrow, sharply planed face. The eyes were large, dusty blue, serene; the skin luminous, uncreased but for some barely perceptible squint lines, and untouched for years by cosmetics of any kind. Glimpsed from some angles it was a lovely face. From others it appeared sad and intensely private, missing beauty only by a certain grim set to the mouth, though that impression could be erased in a fingersnap with a sudden smile. She had a good smile, Valerie did, artless, genuine, and ready whenever there was something to smile about. Under the outfit of men's denim workshirt, off-the-rack jeans, sea snake boots, her body was as lean and hard as one of the Dobermans she had recently bred and trained and sold for a living. Five-ten in the boots, a hundred and sixteen pounds in the raw (fewer now, after the thirty-hour partial fast), she looked rather like a finely tuned athlete, a marathon runner, or, to those less kind, a recovering anorectic.

Nevertheless, for all her stamina, real or apparent, and for all the tonic powers of Enervite, an unaccountable fatigue set in just south of Provo and she was obliged to pull off the road yet again. Immediately she was asleep. The dog's distressed, needful whine wakened her. Other than by the sun's sinking in a fanfare of gorgeous violet light, there was no way of knowing how long she had slept. Too long. For she had hoped to be in Las Vegas at a reasonable hour, find her brother, get by the inevitable explanations and the uneasy tiptoeing around the past, and settle in for the night, refreshed and ready the following morning to seek out Wyman Brewster. That was how she had envisioned it. Clearly, that was not how it was going to fall out. So be it. Years of solitude had taught her patience. She would make do.

Three hours later and here she was, pushing on into a second night. The miles clipped by. Cedar City came and went. Not far now.

An ominous stillness hung in the air. A distant rumble sounded off in the west, drew gradually nearer. Needlebolts flashed on the horizon. The first light spatters peppered the roof. In an instant a shattering rain drilled the earth. Explosive thunder salvos boomed directly overhead. Forky streaks of lightning split the dark. Vendetta lightning, the kind that seems to be stalking you and only you. The dog, normally stoic, laid its wedge of a head in her lap and whimpered piteously. "It's all right, we'll be fine, just fine," she cooed, while the wipers slapped across the windshield, thumping out disaster's heartbeat, and the world outside the window undulated like a film snagged on the frame of a dissolve scene.

Suddenly as it began, the storm broke. As though a strict margin, unseen but no less real, parted the air, fierce rain on one side, perfect tranquility on the other. Passion and harmony. Violence and peace. Yin and yang. A benign sliver of moon peeked through the black clouds. Electra slept. On she drove. An oriental calm descended over her. She feared nothing, welcomed whatever lay ahead. The car toiled up a steep rise, came over its crest, and there, spread out like a velvet tapestry embroidered with glittering jewels, was Las Vegas.

A fter Click's abrupt departure, Eggs lingered awhile in the lounge, turning over everything he had heard, weighing it. Intriguing notion, the terminally ill, potentially quite lucrative, certainly a clientele in plentiful, not to say continuous, supply. Astonishing, it had never occurred to him before. Now that it had, broad new vistas seemed to open out ahead of him, elegant in possibility. But so too were the obstacles, particularly for a man with fifty dollars and change in his pocket. Still, for Ignatius LaRevere all obstacles were merely challenges to the imagination, and so he sat gazing patiently into his glass, a visionary awaiting the arrival of a reliable inner voice murmuring words of guidance, inspiration.

Instead, it was another voice, quite external to himself, intruded on his reveries, enunciating his name on a slight interrogatory lift: "Eggs? Eggs?" He glanced up and discovered a girl standing over the table in the studiedly provocative, hip-cocked pose of the centerfold model brazenly flaunting her wares. This one, high-rise legs poured into feline frenzy pants that fit like shrinkwrap, had a good bit on display. Pure pavement princess, right down—or up, in this case—to warheads bursting out of a deep-cut black top and the aggressive bouquet of some vile Eau de Wal-Mart. He stared at her blankly.

"Eggs?" she persisted. "You don't remember?"

His stare remained vacant, wary, cold.

"It's me, Cool Whip. You *better* remember."

Behind the smoke-lens glasses a glimmer of recognition came into his eyes. All his adult life Eggs had painstakingly cultivated the image of the man impervious to discomposure, and so he allowed a trace of a smile to play across his lips, leaned back, and put a recollective finger in the air. "Dawnette. Of course. What a pleasant surprise." And before she could reply he was up out of the chair, laying a light brushing kiss on her cheek and catching his breath against the assaultive perfume. "Won't you join me?"

"I, uh, dunno if I can. Right now. See, I'm with my, y'know, girlfriends." She nodded in the direction of a tough-looking pair, unmistakable bull dykes, glowering at them from over by the nearest files of slots. "But we got to talk, Eggs," she added, a determined edge to her voice, "you and me."

"Then sit down, please. Invite your friends."

But there was no need for formal invitation, not with this truculent twosome, already fast approaching across the casino floor. Eggs watched them climb the lounge steps and close in around Dawnette, flanking her protectively. Carpet munchers to the rescue. He produced an amused, engaging smile. Neither acknowledged it. One of them, an older, matronly sort, announced herself via the fashion statement—make that proclamation—of an outlandish neon green dress. The other was about Dawnette's age, similar height and generous endowments, identically costumed. A couple of gaudy bookends they made, standing side by side. The confluence of aromas issuing off the three of them advanced like a wall of scented mustard gas. Light a match and the hotel would surely go up in flames.

"This dildo givin' you grief, honey?" said the matriarch of the trio, addressing Dawnette.

"No, no grief. He's . . . just a guy I know."

"We're old friends," Eggs volunteered.

"Nobody's talkin' at you, dickeye," snarled the bookend.

"Hey, look, it's all right," Dawnette put in quickly. "He's cool. We use to do some numbers together." Then, suddenly Miss Manners, she said, "Eggs, like you to meet Velva—" thumb wag at the Mother Inferior—"and this—" reverse wag—"is Gayleen Rae."

Velva, Gayleen—apt names, particularly the latter. Eggs made a courtly half-bow. "Ladies," he said, mock cordial, "would you care to join us?"

The ladies regarded him with frosty, grudging eyes. Their varnished faces wore the nostril-pinched expression of pedestrians narrowly sidestepping a steaming dog turd. The one called Velva, spokesbitch, answered by ignoring him, turning to Dawnette and urging, "C'mon, honey. This place is a tomb. We're goin' over to the Aladdin, see what's shakin'."

Dawnette looked back and forth between her two champions. Then at Eggs, who merely shrugged. Her jaws punished a wad of gum. Clearly, a hard call. Finally she said, "No, you two go on. I'll catch up to you later."

"You sure?"

"Yeah, I'm sure. We got business to talk here," she said, casting a meaningful glance Eggs's way.

For an instant he was the cynosure of all eyes, Velva scowling at him, Gayleen Rae glaring bullets. "Another time, perhaps," he said affably.

The dragon ladies huffed away.

"Guess they're pissed," Dawnette said.

Eggs, all gallantry, helped her into a chair, settled into his own, signaled a cocktail waitress, and remarked, "Charming companions."

"Least they treat me right," she said pointedly.

The appearance of the waitress spared him a reply to that. Dawnette ordered a strawberry Daiquiri, he another brandy and water. They waited in silence till the drinks arrived. Assembling their thoughts, both of them. Eggs was the first to speak.

"Do you know why it took me a moment to recognize you?"

"Why's that?"

"The outfit. The Dawnette I remember wore girlishly demure skirts. And frilly lace blouses, in soft shades of lilac, I seem to recall, to set off that porcelain-doll complexion, the opalescent eyes, the gorgeous cockscomb of platinum hair."

It was a fair enough description and, omitting any mention of the induced streaks of pink staining the hair and the harsh black eyeliner and vampire-blood lipstick tarnishing the lovely virginal face, fairly accurate even yet. And he was pleased with the way it came oiling out. Words seldom failed him.

She, however, was unmoved. "Yeah, well, things change. School-girl look is out. Trade likes it rawer now-days."

"Alas for subtlety."

"Don't talk shit to me, Eggs. All that porcelain, cocks-suck, opa-whatever. This is Cool Whip here. Remember?"

Only too well did he remember. Cool Whip Day, christened Dawnette by Tennessee hillbilly parents of truly execrable taste (Dawnette Day—get it?), the kind who collected beer cans and fretted over bowling averages and decorated the walls of some rude little country shack with prints of adorable saucer-eyed puppies (for that, in fact, is how she had once, in a boozy wash of sentiment, described them). Like Cleanth and every other Vegas scuffler he had ever known (himself included, he supposed), she preferred to go under the shorthand label bestowed by confederates, which in her case carried a variety of connotations: Cool, for the crafted sleety distance in her bearing (which, at the moment, seemed in serious lapse); and Whip, as in the rich sugary dessert topping, for the creamy skin and bottled silver hair (which was still appropriate), but also in veiled reference to her sexual specialties (which, judging by the departed pair, had taken a decidedly deviant turn in his absence). Quite a team they had once been: Eggs and Cool Whip, the epicurean scourge of every sorry mooch luckless enough to stray across their path. Yet in those days, even as with Cleanth, he had always chosen to address her by given name only, however tacky. And, speaking in accents of injury, that's what he did now: "Dawnette, you mistake me. Why would I want to mislead you?"

"Why? Tellya why. You owe me *money!* That's why."

The shrill squawk turned some heads at the bar. So much for her vaunted cool. He put a hushing finger to her lips. "Please, lower your voice."

"Don't go shushin' me," she said, though in a somewhat softened harpy hiss. "You get in the wind with 5K of mine—all I got in the whole world—and now you got the nads to try greasin' me. Spare me the butt butter, Eggs. Won't wash."

Butt butter, grease, nads, talk shit—how coarse her vernacular had become, deprived of his tutelage. Prowling the streets in that tawdry outfit like some common trollop. Not much different from poor Cleanth, really, clerking in a store. Helpless children, both of them; without him and his wise counsel and direction, lost in a tangled, perilous wood. And thinking about them this way, himself as the steady benevolent center in their otherwise spinning universes, he was struck with a flash of insight, still a little blurry yet, but surely a presentiment of the vision he had been awaiting only a moment ago. "It saddens me to see you like this, Dawnette," he said dolefully. "So hard and bitter with an old friend."

"Forget sad. Old friend. I want my loot."

"And of course you'll have it. In good time. Unfortunately, my present cash flow position is not all it might be."

"You sayin' you don't got it?"

"Not just yet. But I do have a project in mind that could be extraordinarily profitable. For both of us."

"Forget that one, too. I heard your big projects before. Just gimme my five dimes. Rest is smoke."

Eggs sighed. This was going to be knottier than he'd expected. The Dawnette of three years back would have been considerably more malleable. About things—and people—changing, that much she had right. But then persuasion was no small part of the burden of leadership. "Dawnette," he said, coming at it from another angle, "do you remember Cleanth?"

"Who?"

"Cleanth Koontz."

"Don't know nobody, that name."

"Very likely you knew him as Click. He used to work with me now and again."

"Oh, yeah. I remember that nasty little oinker, made the weird noise when he talked. Always tryin' to bag a freebie off me." Her face wrinkled in distaste at the memory. "What about him?"

"It happens I was speaking with him earlier. This very evening, as a matter of fact. And it seems he may have stumbled onto something that could lead us to a handsome score."

"Yeah, like what?"

Arranging his features in shrewd dealmaker expression, Eggs explained everything he had gleaned from the conversation with Cleanth, dressing it up here and there, embellishing it, filling in some numbers wholly imagined and almost certainly inflated. Half a lifetime of improvising on the theme of money had taught him you said what must be said, did whatever had to be done. When he was finished he fixed her with a wise patient gaze and said, "So. What do you think?"

She let the question hang in the air between them. Took a sip of Daiquiri. Set the glass down and stroked its stem thoughtfully. Playing at shrewd herself, though way out of her league. He waited. Eventually she allowed, "Could maybe be something to it. Heavy on that *maybe*. Don't sound to me like you got a helluva lot to go on, Eggs."

The inflection was still tough, challenging, skeptical—doubtless the pernicious influence of those two aberrant mattresses she was running with these days. But interested too. He had her snared now, and he knew it. The reeling in, that could be delicate. "Obviously, it will require further investigation," he said. "And of course certain preliminary measures must be taken." And after a nicely timed beat, he added, "Immediately."

"What kind of 'measures' we talkin' here?"

"Well, to begin with, we'll need some venture capital."

Perplexity and suspicion, in equal blend, smudged her eyes.

"A nut," he explained, "operating money. From everything you've indicated, I assume you have none."

"You got that one right," she said waspishly. "You oughta know."

Eggs put a hand to his brow, massaged a temple. The larger view, he reminded himself, saying, "Dawnette, when this project is completed, the five thousand that troubles you so will seem like throwaway change, a paltry toke. But in the meantime we need to focus our attention on raising a stake."

"How you figurin' to do that?"

"As I remember, we were never at a loss for inventive ideas in the past, you and I."

Now a dim cognition shimmered in those cagey eyes. "You mean do a slick?"

"Why not?"

"I gotta tellya, Eggs, I'm way outta practice, that end of things. Velva and Gayleen and me, all's we do is put on a little show. Horizontal bop with some, y'know, kinks to it. We're not into rollin'. 'Less the john's too blitzed to know better, course."

"Ah, Dawnette, not to fear. The moves, once mastered, are never lost. Rather like your horizontal bop."

"Okay, supposin' I was in. And I'm just sayin' suppose here. But if I was, when you lookin' to make this move?"

"What better time than now?"

"Now? Like tonight?"

"The thousand-mile journey, the first step—remember?"

"I dunno, Eggs. Tonight, that's pretty sudden. I got to think on this."

"Look around you," he said, taking in the collection of melancholy juicers at the bar with a sneering glance. "Paralytics. Sunday night losers, the worst kind. All their fervid prayers, devout petitions, pulling at the sky—none of it shields them from disaster. That's not for us, Dawnette. We were meant for better than that."

She shook her head slowly. "You're the same old boy, Eggs. Nobody ever blew the smoke like you can."

It was a signal of resignation, capitulation. Exactly the signal he was waiting for. He got to his feet, motioned to her. "Come along. Let's see what turns up."

They strolled idly through the casino, reconnoitering the tables. One in particular caught Eggs's eye, or, more precisely, one player, a highballer deep into black check action, going at it head to head with the dealer and, judging by the pillars of chips in front of him, riding a streak. His table was located near a line of slots, and his first base seat offered an unobstructed view of the machines. He was, Eggs noted, an obvious tourist, a puny gnome of a man, sixty or better, with a stringy corded neck, the pasty skin of the midnight to dawn player, and a display of teeth big as dominoes whenever he flashed his winner smirk, which was often. A set of circumstances close to ideal. "That's our man," Eggs whispered in Dawnette's ear, and he guided her over behind the machines and spelled out the strategy.

"Here's how we proceed. You make one more pass, casually, taking your time, no great hurry. Stop at the table opposite him and watch the game awhile. Not long, just enough to let him have a good peek. Throw a quick glance his way, nothing bold; remember, you're not firing on him, not yet. Then you come over here and start doing the idiot pull. Put yourself into it; you know, some body English, a squeal or two. Make love to the machine, give him something to think about."

"What if he don't see me?"

"Believe me, Dawnette, in that getup, he'll see you."

"Where you at, all this?"

"A couple of rows back. Monitoring."

Her eyes flickered anxiously, her mouth pummeled a fresh gum wad. "Okay, say he tries to lay on a hit. Then what?"

Eggs was himself beginning to feel the intense gathering energy he always felt going into a score. To contain it, funnel it—and, not incidentally, to keep her steady—he pitched his voice low, serenely confident. "Then you tell him you've got a room in one of those units behind the pool. And then you bring him through the back exit and across the lawn. *Not* down the interior corridor. This is important, Dawnette. If he balks at coming outside, tell him you want some air. Make it sound erotic, like he might catch a little foreplay out in the dark. Use your abundant charms."

"And you be there by the pool?"

"Oh yes. I'll be waiting."

"How you gonna take him down? You're not packin', Eggs?"

"Of course not."

" 'Cuz I don't wanta get involved in nothin' twisted."

"Don't concern yourself. All you have to do is follow the drill. You understand it now?"

"I guess so."

"All right, let's do it. Oh, Dawnette, one more thing."

She looked at him doubtfully. "What's that?"

"Let's lose the gum."

Out it came. She hesitated, but only a moment, just long enough to compose her get-to-business face. Presto! Dawnette into Cool Whip: brow slightly arched; scarlet lips pursed in a pouty half-smile; liquid, fuck-me eyes glistening. Remarkable transformation. Then, without a word, she was gone, sauntered away on an undulant roll. Eggs slipped behind a parallel file of machines. He watched her. All that lush sinuous flesh—turn the Pope into a satyr. This one was going to be a gimme, absolutely.

In under half an hour she had the mark out of his chair, trotting off to the cashier's cage and sidling back to the slots. Leering, clutching a drink, stoking up his courage, narrowing in on her. Dick-driven. Snagged for certain.

Nevertheless, Eggs gave it a moment, just to be sure. Once he heard Dawnette's stagy pealing laugh and the eager echoing bray, he was sure. He walked to the far end of the casino, turned a corner, came to the exit leading to the pool, and ducked through it, out into the perfect silence of a grassy, empty courtyard. He filled his lungs with the crisp night air, bracing as a tonic. The exhilarating, dizzying rush he had felt earlier, inside, was tempered now by a certain indefinable purity of emotion, almost a transcendent joy. He positioned himself in a band of shadows just beyond the pool house. And there, under a halo of neon suspended in the black sky, he waited.

Not for long. Ten minutes later the door swung open and Dawnette led their mark out onto the lawn. One of her hands slithered over his crotch, impelling him along in a tight jiggly gait. Delivering him up on order, this wizened little bundle of goatish appetite, tittering expectantly, probably sporting his first real woody in a decade or more. Good girl. Eggs let them get a few paces ahead, and then he came out of the dark, slipped in behind, tapped a bony shoulder, and said, "What are you looking for, old-timer?"

The mark stopped, turned, froze. His jaw unhinged, baring the outsize teeth. His eyes bugged. "What's goin' on? Who're *you?*"

Eggs, at a couple of inches under six feet himself, still towered over him, outweighed him by forty pounds, easy. "Looking for the Las Vegas total, are you? Little cards, little sauce, little doodah?"

"What do you want?"

"What's your name, old man?" Eggs asked in a tone bland, conversational.

"Duane."

"Well, Duane, this is the part they never tell you about." And for Eggs the part he enjoyed most, the prelude.

"You want my money."

"That's very good, Duane."

Now the bug eyes darted wildly, fell accusingly on Dawnette. "You're in it. You did this."

She faded wordlessly into the shadows.

"Also very observant," Eggs said.

"It's not *fair*. I won it." His voice, elevating to a piping squeak, gave away the quality of his fear. He took a halting step backwards.

Eggs advanced on him. "Fair? Nothing's ever fair. Life's a swindle, Duane."

The seamed, terror-struck face was suddenly all ticks, twitches, tremors. The mouth opened scream-wide, but nothing came out, no pleas, no moans, no cries, nothing but a gurgly strangulated rasp. The knees went rubbery, and he toppled face first onto the damp grass.

"I believe our Duane has swooned," Eggs chuckled.

"Jesus," Dawnette groaned, "freeze dry's havin' a heart attack. We gotta bolt."

"Stay right where you are," Eggs snapped. He stooped down, removed his wallet from a hip pocket, and rolled him over on his back. Bending in close, he put an ear to the gaping hole of a mouth, listened a moment, and then laid two fingers along the grizzled neck. "Hmm, breathing's fairly steady, good strong pulse yet. No, I don't think it's a heart attack. Probably just panic."

"Whatever. Come *on!*"

Eggs ignored her. He straddled the trembly figure, laced his fingers, locked his elbows, placed the heel of a hand squarely in the middle of the frail chest, and pushed down hard. Compression, release, compression—voicing a tempo to the rhythmic strokes: "One, push . . . two, push . . . three, push . . ."

"What're you doin', Eggs? You got the loot."

"It's called CPR—" four, push "—an emergency measure, just in case—" one, push "—an act of mercy, actually—" two, push "—come over here."

"What for?"

"Now!—" three, push.

She came over and stood alongside him. "Aren't you suppose to breathe in his mouth, or somethin'?"

"Not in this version—" four, push "—in this one you cover the mouth—" one, push.

"Cover it? How's he gonna breathe?"

"Just get down here and do it—" two, push.

She dropped to her knees and, gingerly, put a hand over the distended mouth. A thin muffled bleat rose from the pit of the throat.

"Remember that slogan, Dawnette?—" three, push " '—You deserve a break today—' " four, push "—whose was it?"

"For chris' sake, Eggs. He's gonna croak!"

"Whose?" Eggs demanded. Underneath him the scrawny body wriggled powerlessly. With each stroke he bore down harder.

"I don't *know*! Why? Why?"

"No special reason—" one, push "—it just occurred to me—" two, push "—keep your hand tight on his mouth now—" three, push.

Abruptly he stopped. Straightened his back, squared his shoulders, flexed and re-extended his arms, sucked in a huge breath. "Welcome to Vegas, Duane," he said, and on "Four," putting all his weight and all his force behind it, he drove his clasped hands into the chest, collapsing it in a grinding snap of brittle bone.

Duane shuddered. He made some faint indecipherable sounds, diminuendo, receding into silence. He went limp. A tide of drool washed through Dawnette's fingers, spilled over his chin. She yanked her hand away as if it had been singed by molten lava. She swept it furiously across the ground, in widening circles, like some crazed charwoman polishing the grass. "Jesus. You killed him. Jesus."

"Hardly," Eggs said. "But I suspect he won't soon forget this visit."

"Jesus," she chanted, "Jesus Jesus Jesus . . ."

Eggs got to his feet, grasped her by an arm, and hauled her up roughly. "He's not dead. Damaged goods, maybe, but not dead. Now control yourself. You wanted to leave? Now it's time. Our business here is done."

7

Three A.M., Monday, November 9. A night for business, all around.

For Wyman Brewster, swaddled in a bulky terry cloth robe, planted catatonia-stiff in a hardbacked wooden chair, the night had been, he supposed, a modest success. One convert out of four—a better than usual percentage, better by far. Nevertheless, lights out, alone at last, he contemplated it, among many things, glumly and without much satisfaction.

The apartment he called home, one flight up from his natural foods store, was by any standard austere, some might say ascetic: three closet-sized rooms sparely furnished and given over exclusively to the rudimentary functions—feeding, ablution, elimination, sleep. Store and living quarters were housed in a narrow stucco-sided building set in a chain of enterprises fronting Spring Mountain Road a few miles west of the Strip. Brewster's emporium, formerly the site of Sal's Pizza and Sub Shoppe, was announced by an anomalous unelectrified sign and went under a prolix, somewhat immodest and altogether opaque name: The Great Western Center for Quantum Healing and Attitudinal Awareness. Vestigial odors of Sal's cheeses and cooking oils and condiments still clung to its interior walls and filtered through the ceiling, an aromatic contrast to its present wholesome restorative services. For Brewster, an olfactory reminder of the monumental thankless task to which he was passionately committed.

But there were times when the commitment faltered, the passion waned. When it all seemed so fruitless, so overwhelming. When the world's blind jeering ignorance dismayed you, eroded your finest resolution. Wore you down. And tonight, for reasons unclear to him, was he more than ever worn down. Stooped under the full weight of his five and fifty years. Time's remorseless gravity. Also, paradoxically, the unaccountable malaise that always overtook him after a night of missionary pleading, the vague desire for whatever he did not at that moment have. In a crowd he yearned for solitude; alone, as now, he craved an audience, even a hostile one. It was baffling, vexing. It was perverse.

Recognizing the perversity, Brewster was locked just then in a struggle with his own attitudinal awareness. Healer, mend thyself. Restore thyself. Purge the spirit of all base desire, appetite, craving, longing. Release it into that vast ocean of consciousness, that cosmic sea of perfect tranquility, harmony, peace.

Tonight it was not to be. His spirit remained earthbound, his thoughts stubbornly fixated on matters temporal, infected by ambition's viral itch. The nagging sense of things undone. An image of the single, selfless, elusive, goading dream that fired his restless imagination danced behind his eyes. The Wyman Brewster Memorial Clinic—concrete and glass, unstuccoed anyway, certainly unstuccoed, secluded in a quiet wooded grove somewhere, distanced from desert and neon and heat, shaded by towering trees, nourished by gentle rains, touched by the whisper of the wind. And himself a kindly patriarchal figure, beloved by patients, revered by staff, dispensing wisdom, solace, compassion, and universal goodwill. The Wyman Brewster Clinic, last refuge for the allegedly terminal. In a calling dominated by arrogant scoundrels, a last bastion of hope.

The image persisted. He got up heavily and padded over to the scruffy couch that served as a bed. He stretched himself out, stared into the dark. Gradually it blurred, that consoling vision, and after a time he slept.

* * *

Been a fuckin' roller coaster of a night, you wanna ask Click Koontz about it. First comes the buzz from the big B sayin' pick me up half an hour I got a consultation to do over to the Dunes. That's what he calls it—consultation. Anybody else say pitch, call it what it is. Not askin' *can* you, neither. Like if you got any plans—not that he did but if he had—forget it, bag 'em. Nine bells of a Sunday, suppose to be his day off, too. What're you gonna do?

So he scarfs up what he can of his KFC twelve-piece bucket supper, Click does, slops down what's left of a Bud, switches off the chop-socky flick he's watchin' (good part just comin' up, too, splatter part), takes a quick whizzer, sprays his mouth with Binaca on account of Brewster don't approve of beer, and gets halfway out the door and the goddam phone rattles again. Now what the fuck?

Only this time it's the last voice he ever figured to hear—yar! sheesh! word up and lick me hard if it ain't Eggs-natius LafuckinRevere, old Egger sayin' Cleanth this is a voice out of your deep past—like the Clicker here ain't gonna know who it is soon's he hears the name Cleanth (outside of Brewster, only one person in the whole world call him Cleanth anymore)—and sayin' I just got back in town let's meet for a drink, chat. And Click so stoked the nerves under his skin startin' to prickle, like he's about to get himself boinked or somethin', which in a way is how old Egger works on you, gives everybody a mind-boink, Click he goes Hey, man, that'd be cool, Dunes, say, ten, ten-thirty, Mr. Bigs?

So he piles in the Brewstermobile—big Lincoln Town Car, bone white, Signature Series four-door notchback, got all the bells and whistles and got Click Koontz behind the wheel—and swings over to the Center and gets Dr. Cosmic and gets him to the Dunes and up to the north tower room—fucker always talkin' outta the side of his face about the universe but down here in the real world get lost in a phone booth—where the flamers waitin'. Brewster says Meet me at the car, an hour, and Click goes You betcha, and then blazes back downstairs and connects with Eggs and they have this real fine rap, old times and everything, except for when Eggs is zingin' him about his job, that ain't called for, but the rest of it, hintin' about goin' back into business, partnerin' again, that gets you real pumped and time just get away from you.

So when he shows up late Brewster, who's heatin' his heels out by the Abe, got one of the buttboys in tow, he's so hacked he about carves a new Koontz asshole. When he's done with that he says Take us to the Center, and so Click does what he's told and they go inside and he waits in the car also like he's told. And waits. Jesus H. Fuck does he wait, till finally out they come, two of 'em seizin' the digits, all pals, all smiles, 'specially Brewster who's for sure made a sale and who says Take Barry back to the hotel—oh, and Cleanth, I want you here tomorrow ten o'clock sharp, for my rounds. Click does a quick brow-flicking salute and then he wheels the swisher over to the Dunes and drops him off at the door (little faggot says Thank you *so* much, and Click just makes his lingual squeak) and then finally he gets to go home.

Home for Click is a two-room efficiency in a string of fourplex units just off Flamingo, just down the road from Bally's, one room a pisser, the other an all-purpose sleeper (sleep on a hide-a-bed which never seems to get hid, or made), kitchen (eat off a hot plate or out of a mini-fridge), sitter (sit on your ass and watch the teevee in the corner) with a view out the window of a snatch-sized patch of grass and across Fredda Street a bulldozed construction site big as a couple city blocks, maybe bigger. Face it—a VIP suite at Caesar's it ain't. But tonight that's okay by Click. Polishin' off the last chilled chix in the bucket, washin' it down with a cold one, eyeballin' the jiggly twat parade on the MTV channel but mostly thinkin' about Eggs bein' back in town and everything gonna be boss shit again, Click don't feel so bad. Feel real good, in fact, real wired. Yeah, some night she'd been. Some night.

The night had come up aces for Velva and Gayleen, and a relief it was too, seeing as how they'd logged zip in the income department the past week or so, November not being your peak action month. Which didn't mean the bills quit coming in, or Gayleen's heavy habit didn't need to get fed. So while they were both of them, Velva in particular, still steamed over Cool Whip taking off with her breeder buddy (scam man for certain; Velva knew, she could spot one coming the other end of the Strip), they were feeling a whole lot better after they fired on this john at the Aladdin, a world-class Barney but with the deep pockets and a special hankering for discipline. Said his name was Claude. Looked like a Claude.

"That kind of hormone fix cost you four," Velva told him. "For each of us. Be the best eight bills you ever spent in your life, Claude."

He kiked her down to six, final bid, take it or leave it. Doing his Claude Trump. Velva took it. They needed the loot. And anyway, looking at Gayleen's sweet buns wiggling under the tiger pants there, she was ready to get to it. Got her wet just thinking about it (and about Cool Whip too, traitorous little bitch).

The deal struck, they brought him to their three-bedroom apartment (two for sleep, one for games) on Decatur, set him down in the living room with a glass and a bottle of Jim Beam (he hadn't been so cheap they might have broken out the Crown Royal), and directed him to wait while they freshened up and got things ready. "Whatever you say," he mumbled obediently, already shifting into character.

Back in the bath they took some hits off a happy stick, and Gayleen, who always had to have her poppers before showtime, swallowed a couple tooies. They warmed up with a little squirrel stroking and then, giggling like bubblegummers, ducked into the games room and peeled off their clothes and slipped into working outfits: for Gayleen a black G-string with leather V-patch in front and butt floss leather strap in back, topless, to display those gorgeous pouty titties; and for Velva a studded one-piece teddy, also leather, also black, size XL to accommodate the ample hips and buttocks, and with half-cup bra underwired to prop up the drooping hooters. Apart from a footlocker full of ingenious toys, a polyurethane playsheet on the uncarpeted floor, and a massive wooden chair equipped with ankle and wrist restraints and dubbed by Velva (who'd picked it up at an out-county girlie ranch going-out-of-business sale) the "hot seat" for its remarkable resemblance to a death chair, the games room was empty of furnishings. Crimson drapes covered the windows, and four red night-lights, one to a wall, supplied the only illumination.

Velva selected the evening's gear. When Gayleen saw it laid out on the footlocker she said, a little doubtfully, "You sure we oughta go *that* far?"

"Freak wants discipline, we'll give him discipline."

Gayleen snickered and Velva, brandishing a devil's-hand split paddle, marched over to the door and called, "Claude. Get in here. Now! And bring that bottle with you."

This is what happened to Claude.

First he was ordered to strip. Then to drop to his hands and knees, facing the chair where Gayleen sat rubbing her leather pussy patch. "What're you looking at?" Velva snarled. "Head down! Cakes up!" She gave him ten hard ass whacks with the devil's hand, putting her considerable weight into it, an athletic expression of her loathing of all men generally and this one—thick-bodied, hairy as an ape, shivering with delight and anticipation—specifically.

After that they traded places, Velva in the chair fingering herself under the teddy, and Gayleen on her feet, deftly fitting him with a neck collar and chain and leading him around the room on all fours, occasionally commanding him to heel or sit or speak, at which latter injunction he made some falsetto yipping noises. Then she straddled his lower back and rode him awhile, urging him along with a crop slapper. For a reward she put a saucer on the floor, filled it with Beam, and let him lap it up. While Claude slurped greedily, getting deep into his role, she took a jumbo butt plug and a tube of Slippery Stuff off the footlocker and went around behind him and was about to lubricate the furry crevice when Velva said sharply, "No! Do it dry."

"But he's been a pretty good doggy," Gayleen said in mock protest. They'd done this number so many times it was by now perfectly choreographed.

"Dry!"

Gayleen shrugged. "Here comes your rubber duckie, Claude," she said, and plunged it in.

Claude let out a delirious squeal. Velva sprang off the chair and thrashed him furiously, raising raw welts across his quivery haunches. Gayleen got out of her G-string and settled onto the playsheet. Coming up next was the part she liked best.

Abruptly, Velva discarded the paddle and bawled, "Roll over, Fido!" Claude flattened out on his back and she lowered herself over the downside arc of his belly, facing south, and sneered, "You don't like your duckie? Okay, let's try a little digital penetration instead."

She reached down and yanked out the plug and replaced it with first one finger ("That better?"), then two ("Better yet?"), three, four, till finally she was fisting him brutally; and Claude, groaning in raptured agony, surrendered himself to the surgically dispassionate hand probing deep inside him.

When she figured he'd had about enough, Velva removed her hand, helped him to his feet, led him to the chair, and shackled his wrists and ankles. "Gayleen's right," she purred, "you been a good doggy. So now we got a special treat for you."

She went to the footlocker and came back with a cock strap and ball stretcher and, very gently, fitted them over the respective organs. Then she got down beside Gayleen on the playsheet and slathered her with the Slippery Stuff, head to foot. With a practiced tongue, she embarked on a slow, delicious voyage around the honey-sweet Gayleen world, the journey culminating with her head buried in the moist crack of heaven. And while Gayleen squirmed and moaned, Claude, helplessly restrained, looked on with wild inflamed eyes and with the crazed pained pleasured leer of a soul consigned to the innermost circle of hell.

It was almost over, not quite. Velva and Gayleen came up off the floor and approached the chair. Velva said, "Your turn, Claude," and tightened the cock strap while Gayleen simultaneously tugged at the ball stretcher. Claude's eyes bulged. His mouth gaped. The wormy veins in his temples pulsed violently. From her wealth of experience Velva knew the precise moment he was ready. She smirked a signal at Gayleen, and they released his punished genitalia; and then Velva licked the naughty finger of the same hand that had so recently skewered him and laid it on the tip of his member and ran it down the rigid shaft once, which was all it took to bring on the mini-Krakatoa blast. He shuddered, gasped, sagged forward, head lolling on his chest.

Now it was over.

Later, showing him out the door, Velva said tauntingly, "See what six bills buys you, Claude. Imagine what eight would have been like."

Eggs and Dawnette were settled in a room in the Sahara Hotel, prudently removed from the scene of the score by a couple of miles of Strip. Dawnette occupied one of the double beds, Eggs the other. Both of them were naked (though Eggs, faithful to the rumor, had on his trademark smoke-lens glasses). Dawnette lay on her stomach, face buried in a pillow. She was still shaking some, but not so much anymore. Eggs sat with his back braced against the headboard, counting the take, arranging the bills by denomination—hundreds, fifties, twenties, the occasional stray ten—in neat stacks between his outspread legs. In the middle of his tally Dawnette said, "Why'd you do it, Eggs?" Her voice was pillow-suffocated and a little trembly even yet.

He put up a staying hand. "Wait a minute, wait." He continued laying the bills on their appropriate piles. When the last one was down he stroked his chin pensively. His face furrowed. Mostly to himself he said, "This is a bit disappointing. There's under three long here."

"He said he started losin' after he saw me. Couldn't keep his mind on the cards."

As if he were just now fully aware of another presence in the room, Eggs glanced over at her, at the platinum puff of hair, the exquisite architecture of the body, delicate curvature of spine, swell of firm and perfectly cleaved buttocks, sleek coltish legs—and all of it gift-wrapped in skin spotless and smooth as a layer of vanilla icing. Cool Whip, indeed. "I'm not surprised," he said. "Testimony to your manifold charms. Nevertheless, I'd expected five, minimum."

She lifted her head and regarded him with genuinely perplexed eyes. "So why'd you do it?"

"Do what?"

"Hurt that old man. You know what I'm talkin' about here."

"Oh. That. I've no idea. It seemed like a thing to do. At the time."

"But you had the money."

"So I did."

"Why, then?" she persisted.

"An impulse, I suppose." Immediately he recognized that wasn't right. It was more than impulse. Considerably more. "Call it a lesson," he amended. "A kind of divine tutoring."

"What's *that* mean?"

Mean? Eggs wasn't sure himself. Interesting question, one he'd never explored at any length. He thought about it a moment. Finally, in an effort to capture the elusive notion, he said, "You must understand there was no actual cruelty in the transaction. Merely an oblique justice."

"Justice? Damn near killin' him? For no good reason? That's justice?"

"In a way. You see, Dawnette, people like me, we're a necessary antidote to all the world's pious craven wheezing. All its dreamy yea-saying. In that sense we serve a noble function. Agents, you might say, of fate's more savage whims."

"You're talkin' crazy, Eggs. That don't say why."

Evidently it was his own fate to be forever saddled with simpletons. To have his most masterful designs turn on the whims and scruples of the Dawnettes and Cleanths and other like mouthbreathers of this world. So be it. One learned to make do. Very patiently, he said, "Don't trouble yourself. It's late. Get some sleep."

He put the bills in a drawer of the nightstand, removed his glasses (thus dispelling the snide rumor), and switched out the light.

Dawnette was accustomed to drifting into slumber cuddled safely against someone—Velva, Gayleen, a man, someone. In a small, subdued voice she said, "Eggs, you wanta come over here with me?"

"I don't think so."

"You don't have to do anything. Just snuggle a little."

"Some other time, maybe."

"Please?"

"No."

Silence descended over the room. For a while Dawnette tossed fitfully. Then, later, her voice druggy with the onset of sleep, she murmured, "Eggs?"

"Now what?"

"That slogan you was askin' about?"

"Slogan?"

"When you was doin' him."

"Oh. Well, what about it?"

"It's McDonald's."

For Valerie Waverly, finding her brother was nowhere near as easy as she had expected. It had never occurred to her that Las Vegas would be this large. In Aurora there was Main, a few residential blocks, and then open field, far as you could see. Not so here. Coming into town she pulled off at the first likely-looking exit, turned some corners to escape the urgent zooming traffic (where were they all going, middle of the night?), and was immediately lost. Road-stoned, weary beyond anything in recent experience, she drove aimlessly until she spotted an elderly black man shuffling along an otherwise deserted street. She swung the Impala over by the curb, cranked down the window, and asked for directions. He looked at her as if she were an alien materialized suddenly from a distant galaxy, said not a word, kept on walking. She drove farther. Electra was awake now, and skittering anxiously about the seat. "It's all right, girl," Valerie said soothingly. "We'll find it."

Up ahead was a Seven-Eleven. She parked in the small lot, instructed the dog to wait, locked the car, and went inside. The clerk, also black, thumbed idly through the pages of a magazine opened on the counter. "Never heard of it," was his reply to her query. He didn't bother to look up. However, another man, this one young, white, painfully skinny, with a narrow sallow face offset by glimmery spears of eyes, intercepted her at the door, saying, "Maybe I can help you out, ma'am."

"I'd appreciate it if you could."

"What street you say you're lookin' for?"

"Garces."

"Lemme think." He rapped a knuckle on his forehead, got the door, and walked her to the car, chattering amiably. "Where 'bouts you from?"

"South Dakota."

"No kiddin'. You're the only person I ever met outta South Dakota."

"Well, there aren't that many of us."

When he saw Electra peering through the windshield, teeth bared in an ominous rumbly growl, the young man stiffened, shrank back. "Uh, you got a dog, huh."

"Yes."

"That one of them racing kind?"

"She's a Doberman."

"Them's the mean ones, right?"

Unschooled in the ways of the world though she might be, Valerie was nonetheless not a fool. "Only with strangers," she said innocently. "Now, can you tell me how to find Garces?"

He put up surrender hands, flashed a crooked grin. "Okay, lady. You win."

"Win? Win what?"

"Never mind. This Garces, it's in Vegas?"

"Yes. Of course."

"Then for starters you're in the wrong town. This here's North Vegas."

"That's different?"

He rolled his eyes skyward. "Yeah, I'd say different."

"Look, can you help me or not?"

"Guess I dunno the street after all. But if you wanta get into Vegas you go back on this one till you hit Las Vegas Boulevard, 'bout a mile, then go south, left, and you run right into downtown. That's Fremont. You won't miss it. Ask somebody there."

Valerie thanked him and stepped up to the door of the car. She got out her key and fitted it into the lock. Electra lifted a paw and scratched eagerly at the window.

The young man came around behind her, keeping a cautious distance. "Uh, lady, you spare a little toke?"

She turned and faced him. "Toke?"

"Yeah, y'know, some change. Reward, like, for my trouble."

"For directions? Such as they are."

"Ain't nothin' free, this town. It ain't South Dakota."

She reached in a pocket of her jeans, produced a coin, and laid it in the outthrust palm. He looked at it incredulously. "This is a *quarter.*"

"You said change."

He laughed in spite of himself. "Lotsa luck, lady. You gonna need it."

Astonishingly, that was what delivered her: luck in abundance, extravagant improbable luck, though for Valerie Waverly luck was just another way of saying benign guiding Spirit. She made it back to Las Vegas Boulevard, steered left, as directed, and followed it two miles, three, difficult to tell, till it broke onto Fremont Street. On a hunch, nothing more, she turned right and found herself in a canyon of bursting shimmying light, fiendish light, dazzling as a runaway blaze glimpsed from within parallel walls of fire. She and the dog gazed at it dumbstruck, mesmerized, both of them, as their Impala crawled along trailing a furious escalating horn blast from the line of cars backed up behind them. Certainly there was nowhere to park, had she noticed. Fremont simply and suddenly ended at the entrance to a towering hotel, and again she had to choose, left or right. Another hunch said left. Now she was on a street, considerably less illuminated, that went under the familiar reassuring name Main; and while it was unlike any Main ever seen in South Dakota, an instinct told her to stay on it, and she did. Sure enough, in a few short blocks an intersection sign announced, miraculously and out of all the streets in this strange turbulent city, Garces. Instinct—Spirit—never failed you.

But sometimes joy could, as it did when a moment later she pulled in behind a car big and square and ancient as her own, and squinted at the shabby little box of a house, utterly dark, in a neighborhood so squalid even she had to wonder what wicked turns of fortune brought her brother to this. And recognizing that now she was here too, she wondered also what life has in store for all of us, and all our lofty dreams and expectations.

She had, of course, no idea of the time. Late, clearly it was late. She cut the engine, opened the windows just a sliver, secured the doors. From a carton in the back seat she took a coarse woolen blanket and bundled herself and Electra in it. They huddled together against the cold. She comforted the shivering dog with a gentle humming monologue. Electra nuzzled her gratefully, licked her neck. And eventually they both found a measure of solace in sleep.

Inside the house there had been other, more strident, monologues going on the better part of the night. Rambling, propelled by drink, thinly disguised as conversation yet running at weird cross-purposes, they were for Waverly oddly reminiscent of joint babble, the interminable bughouse rap of hard-timers voicing private fanciful visions of a world outside the walls, clinging to the battered remnants of dreams. Fucking the dog, in Jacktown parlance. Not, for him, a sunshine memory.

Mostly it was Pettibone dominated the floor. Quite literally. On his feet and pacing like some caged grizzly, arms flung wide in the expansive gestures of the man habitually given to inebriate oratory, he held forth on whatever topic came into his head. In doing so he soon enough had the briefcase of his life open and all its contents out on display. He was born and raised, they learned, in Thief River Falls, Minnesota. Took three degrees at that state's university: Dr. Pettibone, if you please. Taught at a succession of dismal little colleges across the midwest. Married once, long ago, no longer. Got on with UNLV in the late sixties, just a beat ahead of the collapsing market for undistinguished historians specialized in unfashionable eras. Rooted here ever since.

Of course that was merely the skeleton of the chronicle, emerged patternless from a string of ranting digressions and fleshed out with sardonic pronouncements on the blighted landscape of the human condition. Nor was it delivered in strict chronological order, for Bennie had his own windy observations to interject, one man's story sparking the other's, though in Bennie's case there was always a sure, if circuitous, direction. When, for example, he heard the name of Pettibone's hometown he was moved to remark, "Hey, Thief Falls, no wonder you ended up out here, Roger, city of thieves."

"That's Thief *River* Falls," Pettibone said, somewhat testily.

"Yeah, whatever. Anyway, you tellin' about that reminds me of growin' up out in that part of the world myself, Iowa for me . . ."

And he was off and running with a parallel account of his boyhood, his father, the two alien Jews stranded among the corndogs.

Waverly lit a cigarette. He had heard the story before.

Like most intensely centered monologists, Pettibone was deaf to the speech of anyone else. He stopped pacing, helped himself to another drink from the dwindling bottle, and waited while the Epstein saga, father and son, wore on. His eyes, ignited by Scotch, fell on Waverly's cigarette, and some stray association prompted him to break in with, "My father, you know, was a trucker. Long-distance hauler. Something of a lush. Otherwise a decent man. He smoked too. Always said it would kill him one day, and in a curious way he was right. A prophet. Slammed his rig right into the concrete wall of a bridge trying to get a cigarette lit with a farmer match. The wooden kind, you know. They found the box on the seat beside him. The matchbox, I mean. Also an open fifth. He was forty-two. Relatively young."

For an instant he seemed to wince at this droll fragment culled from the thicket of memory. And then with a singsong whiskey rhythm to his voice, he concluded, "The moral being, I suppose, if you drink and drive, don't smoke."

Bennie, back on course, began to question him about his work at the university, his classes, students, things like that. Mistaking the subtext, Pettibone launched into a wandering tirade on the woeful state of learning ("Contemporary education, as some wise pundit once remarked, Bellow I believe, is 'the casting of artificial pearls before real swine . . .' "). Which led him backward in the unfolding personal history: to his graduate school days ("Collecting my own synthetic pearl, my fud, terminal degree, aptly named . . ."); to an account of the many layovers on his academic odyssey ("Every-where a staggering ignorance, colossal ignorance—what your Catholics call invincible ignorance—a positive lust for it . . ."); and finally, on an oblique tangent, to his faithless wife ("It was a defective toilet spelled the end of the marriage. Ran off with the plumber, she did. No matter. The union was infelicitous, at best. Happily for me—for both of us—there was no issue. Not from those dry loins. Or dry to me, it would seem.").

Bennie chomped impatiently on the moist stub of a cigar. During the lengthy side trip into the ruptured marriage Waverly averted his eyes, studied the floor. No less bitter for its comic rendering, the tale aroused in him too many sleeping ghosts. By now he had taken a reading on their voluble guest and decided this was a desperately lonely man, consumed by disappointments and failures and smoldering resentments, craving an audience as much as he craved the sauce, a sentimentalist barricaded inside an arsenal of irony. Waverly remembered the type, though only dimly.

At a breath-drawing pause in the otherwise nonstop recital, Bennie allowed, "Well now, that's real interesting, Roger, how this crapper jockey dicked you over, but gettin' back to your job out to the brain factory—"

"Speaking of which," a suddenly distressed-looking Pettibone interrupted, "toilets, could you direct me to the facilities?"

Waverly pointed him down the hall. No sooner was he out of earshot than Bennie muttered, "Man's got a serious case a the oral dribble shits."

"So why don't you let it rest?"

Bennie elevated an eyebrow, made a Who, me? face. "Whaddya talkin', rest?"

"You know what I'm talking. I heard you trying to pump him in the kitchen."

"You got somethin' against gettin' a leg up on the competition? Little edge? Ain't no different than you countin'."

"There's a difference, Bennie."

"Yeah, how's that?"

"Casino toy cops are one thing, authentic heat's another. You forgetting Florida? Or Michigan? Or Jacktown?"

"Course I ain't forgettin' them fine locations. But we could maybe be a pussy hair away from strikin' the mother lode here. Don't go gimp on me now."

Waverly looked at him steadily. "You call it gimp," he said, "I call it lunacy, what you're fishing for. A point shaving scam's the heaviest kind of risk. Kind we're in no position to take. You know that."

"C'mon, Timothy. Risk is what we *do*. You wanta put something on your plate besides burgers and beans, you run risks. Anyway, pro'ly nothin' to it, comin' outta that juice sponge."

Just then Pettibone came weaving into the room, tugging at his fly. End of debate. He looked around dazedly, collapsed into a chair. "Where was I?" he said.

"You was tellin' us about this hotdog roundballer you got in your class," Bennie coached.

Waverly sighed. So much for caution.

"Oh yes, the athlete. Very interesting case. Very perplexing moral dilemma facing that young man. Comes from a ghetto, of course, Philadelphia, I think he said. Or was it Chicago? Can't seem to recall . . ."

"So what's his problem?" Bennie asked, gently steering him back.

"Problem is his mother has cancer. No father in the picture. Naturally, no money. If he goes along with the scheme he can help her. Did I mention it, this dirty little scheme?"

"Yeah, you already told us about that part, Roger."

"There's another dimension. You see, he's deeply religious. Raised in one of those black fundamentalist sects. You know, all the old inflexible verities in Bible-thumper dress: right is right, and wrong isn't. So he's not used to dealing with slippery moral distinctions."

"Well, least he got Jesus on his side," Bennie said. He took the bottle off the coffee table and came over and filled Pettibone's glass with the last of the Scotch. "What'd you say this boy's name was?"

"Lafayette Waters. Possibly you've heard of him."

"Oh yeah. Everybody heard of Lafayette. That boy's deadly from three-point land, on the line, downtown, you name it. He sparks 'em out there. Whole team milks his hot-shootin' touch. Rest a them Rebels run, Lafayette, he flys. Got a lock on the pros, for sure."

"In two years. Which is the core of his dilemma. Without proper treatment his mother won't last that long."

"Why don't he just turn pro right now? Be an instant millionaire, solve all his problems."

"As difficult as it may be for you to understand," Pettibone said archly, "he wants an education."

"Y'ask me," Bennie, the easy ethicist, volunteered, "boy oughta look out for his mom. It's a obligation, like."

"True enough. But an obligation squarely in conflict with all his values. For him all the more baffling."

Bennie returned to the couch. Torched his cigar. Around a gust of smoke he inquired innocently, "So you think Lafayette's got his mind made up yet?"

Waverly watched him, fascinated as much by his transparent moves as his unflagging faith in an eternally evolving equation for deliverance, the Big Score.

"I think perhaps he has."

"He, uh, say which games fix gonna be in?"

Pettibone squinted at him, glassy-eyed and stuporous, but nobody's fool, not just yet. "Why do you ask?"

Bennie shrugged. "Curious, is all. Round off the story, s'pose."

"If I knew," Pettibone said, "which I'm not saying I do, you understand, but if I did I'd never reveal it. Ever. There's enough low conniving in this sour little wasteland without me as partner in the corruption."

He spoke with surprising vehemence, hands slicing the air. Bennie lifted a pacifying hand of his own. "Hey, Roger. No offense."

"None taken."

"There's something I'm curious about," Waverly said. "We've heard a lot of talk about morality here. You're the moralist, what did you advise him?"

Pettibone recoiled at the question, startled, snake-bit. "Me? Advise anyone? Out of the botch of my life? No, I'd never be that presumptuous. What would I counsel? The *summum bonum?* Hedonistic calculus? Categorical imperative? What do I know? What do any of us know?"

Nowhere to go with that. For a moment they were silent, all three, staring into private middle distances. Then Pettibone sloshed down his drink, rocked to his feet, and staggered over toward the empty bottle on the coffee table. He contemplated it, saying nothing, swaying dangerously.

"You better sit down here, Rog," Bennie said, patting the leather cushion next to him. "You lookin' a little wobbly."

Pettibone plopped onto the couch. In a voice gone slurry now, booze-blitzed, he intoned, "Consult your Isaiah 24, verse 11, if memory serves: 'There is a crying for wine in the streets; all joy is darkened; the mirth of the land is gone.' "

His head sagged off to one side, then fell to his chest. He slumped forward. Bennie lifted his feet, settled him on the couch. To Waverly he said, "Looks like we got us an overnighter."

"Is he out?"

"Blotto."

"Terrific. That's all we need."

"Cheer up, boy. We just made a new friend."

Bennie stood over the comatose figure, studying him with an expression part pity, part contempt, part even a twinge of affection, but all parts coalesced in cunning. Waverly knew the look.

"Let it be, Bennie."

"He knows."

"I wouldn't bet to that."

"We'll see," Bennie said, and before Waverly could protest he stretched elaborately and added, "Sleep on it, okay? Dunno 'bout you, but I'm zonked." And with that he shambled off to his room.

Waverly sat there awhile, not long. He looked at Pettibone sprawled on the couch, this sodden lump of a guest whose chance remark threatened to erase their thin margin of security and send all they knew of coherence and order spinning wildly out of control. Again. What he wanted to do was sort through everything he'd heard tonight, but he felt too wasted to think about it, any of it. Maybe it would all go away in the night. He got up heavily and went down the hall to his room. He found a blanket in the closet, took it back, and spread it over Pettibone, unconscious and, but for the sputtery breathing, motionless as a cadaver. He switched off all the lights. Bennie's snores resonated through the house. A moment later Waverly was stretched out on his bed, sinking fast toward an exhausted sleep, but with an uneasy sense of something unpleasant awaiting him in the morning, something perilous, and with an equally certain conviction of that waking world swerving off at angles hostile to his own interests. Bennie's too. Both of them.

PART
TWO

Waverly's sleep was agitated, fitful, lashed by bizarre fugitive dreams, unsatisfying, and brief. Especially brief. He surfaced, still in the dark, to a discordant symphony of snores: Bennie's slushy whistling wheezes next door, Pettibone's contrapuntal honks echoing in from the living room. Not exactly your angelic choir. He sat on the edge of the bed, head in his hands. Stiff, groggy, a bundle of assorted aches. His temples thumped. Mouth tasted like the bottom of a leaky boot. Had to be the Scotch; never drink Scotch. And never play at tables with wannabe counters. And never ever take up with strangers, particularly of the flame-haired and freckled variety. Axioms to live by. Starting today, for sure.

He pulled on trousers and shirt, padded into the john, attended to urgent matters, splashed his face with cold water, prudently avoiding the reflection in the smudged glass above the rust-flaked sink. He came down the hall and through the living room and into the kitchen (tread softly, Timothy, softly, else you open yourself to a fresh volley of instant bughouse babble). Mostly by feel he found the coffee makings and plugged in their Mr. DiMaggio, stained and time-worn as the old jolter himself. He waited, smoking a cigarette while the machine sputtered and farted and burped. Gradually his vision adjusted to the dark. Better it hadn't, for the emerging sight—grease-splotched counter; rickety chrome-legged table littered with the remnants of last (or was it this?) night's impromptu feast; basinful of unwashed plates and silver and glasses (cigar butt floating in the bottom of one of the latter); grime-encrusted linoleum floor patterned in clashing chords of color—was not inspiriting. One day soon they'd have to get a cleaning lady in here. Another salutary resolution.

He drank a cup of coffee and then tiptoed carefully, very carefully, out of the kitchen and around the couch. He stood at a front window, peeking through the blinds. Checking the perimeters, out of habit. Under dawn's first feeble light he could make out the grass-vacant patch of lawn. Moldering picket fence. The shadowy outline of Pettibone's tank. And there, parked behind it, another vehicle, just as shadowed, yet vaguely familiar somehow. He peered at it. Thin streaks of light began to fall on the hood, windshield, doors, trunk. Moment by moment it took on contour, form, dimension, color. And for one or more of those moments he felt as if he were hallucinating, hurtling back through the expended years. Chevrolet Impala, his father's car, the very same, driven out of the wilderness of the past by that tall, thoughtful, ascetic man come from halfway across the continent and from the farther distance of the grave to confront him with the stern questions: What have you done, Timothy? Why are you here? What went wrong? Dreadful questions. Unanswerable.

Waverly blinked rapidly, clearing his eyes. Couldn't be. Couldn't. He hurried out the door and down the walk. The dangly gate creaked at his touch. A growly black wedge appeared suddenly in the passenger window. Heaven's hound, or hell's. A figure rose slowly off the seat, a woman. She shook off the daze of sleep, quieted the dog with some murmured words, and stepped out of the car. "Tim?" she said. "Is it you?"

"Valerie?"

For an instant they gazed at each other across the hood of their father's car. For Waverly it was as if he were staring into the depths of a fractured mirror, a solemn distorted reflection of himself staring back. He was rocked by a collision of emotions. Conscious of the disbelief stamped on his face. He came around and clasped both her hands in his. They joined in a quick, stiff, almost formal hug, like two heads of state embracing. Waverly drew back, still inspecting her, still dizzied by the sudden warp of time. "Valerie," he said again, but the rest of his utterances came out stammery, incomplete: "What are you . . . ? How did . . . ? When . . . ?"

"I drove from South Dakota," she said, settling the disjointed questions with the same quiet economy of words he remembered. "Two days on the road. Got in last night. Very late. Your house was dark. We thought it best to wait till morning."

"We?"

She pointed at the dog, who continued to watch Waverly with a look very near to human suspicion on its bladed face. "This is Electra."

"Well, you and Electra should have come in, whatever the hour. Sleeping in the car, you must be beat. And cold. It can get cold here at night."

"No, we're fine. But we'll come in now." She hesitated, tucked back a fluttery wisp of hair fallen over her forehead. "If we're welcome, that is," she added timidly.

"You're welcome, Val. Always have been. It's just . . . I had nothing to offer, all these years." He swept a hand in the direction of the house. "Not much now, as you see."

She gave him a smile purely seraphic. "I'm awfully glad to see you, Tim. It's been a long time."

"I know. When I looked out the window and saw the car I thought I was tranced, dreaming."

"You remember it?"

"Of course."

"Dad gave it to me just before he died. It's half yours, you know."

Waverly didn't care to follow that. There were limits to the tumbling rush of memory he could accommodate. "We can talk about it later," he said. "Come along."

She took a wicker basket off the floor of the car and signaled Electra. The dog bounded out and came up beside her. Waverly led them toward the house. At the entrance Valerie stopped, glanced about and asked, "Does the fence go all the way around?"

"Yes."

"Just a minute, please."

She stooped down, removed two organic biscuits, a saucer, and a water jug from the basket, and laid the meal out on the porch. She whispered something that sounded like instructions in the dog's ear, her inflections kind but firm.

"You can bring her in," Waverly said. "It's all right."

"This will do. She needs to move awhile."

"You're sure you want to leave her out here, this neighborhood?"

"This is a trained Doberman, Tim. Believe me, no one's going to hurt her."

Looking at the sinewy-thewed animal, the contained mindless ferocity in its eyes, Waverly could believe her. He turned, got the door. Then, remembering Pettibone, he paused and said, "Never mind the guy on the couch. He's, uh, just a visitor."

He guided her into the kitchen and opened the blind at the window over the sink. Valerie stood in a frame of light, surveying the room, saying nothing. No need. Her expression said it all.

Waverly made an apologetic shrug. "I know. It's a mess."

"Could use a little tidying," she allowed charitably.

"Without a doubt. Sit down. I'll get you some coffee."

"Oh no," she said, indicating her basket. "I've got everything I need right here."

She took a chair, set the basket on the floor, and produced the Enervite bottle, a packet of Chlorella, and the water jug. Waverly poured himself a cup of coffee, came around the table, and sat opposite her, watching the methodical ritual curiously. Once it was finished he said, "That's your breakfast?"

"When I'm traveling."

"A bit meager, wouldn't you say?"

"It's plenty. Here, try some Chlorella."

"Ah, I don't think so."

"Try it. It's good for you."

She shook a cluster of the tiny green pellets into his palm. Waverly looked at them doubtfully. Looked like the droppings of dwarf mice, dyspeptic ones at that. "Chew or swallow?" he asked.

"Either way. They're assimilated instantly. Instant vitality."

He elected chewing. Major error. It felt as if he had a mouthful of bitter dust.

"There," she said brightly. "Don't you feel better now?"

"Oh yeah. A new man."

"You look tired, Tim," she said, suddenly serious. "Thinner, too. You haven't been taking care of yourself."

Waverly knew how he looked. Casino pallor, two deepening vertical furrows bracketing his nose, horizontal ones creasing his brow, worry gorge between his eyes, hair flecked with silver. Thirty-eight, pushing on ninety. But he'd forgotten her face. Time had blurred the image of its quiet beauty, shaped by good bones and a serene resolution. Three years older, yet she could pass easily for a niece, sitting there fresh as the morning at his vile cluttered table. And that's about what he told her, saying truthfully, "But you have. You look remarkably young, Val. Must be the Dakota air. And the magic green pills."

"That's part of it," she said, innocent either of pride or a fraudulent humility. "But mostly it's an inner peace."

Waverly wasn't sure what to say to that. A quip, maybe. "Well, that makes one of you."

"You should try it yourself."

"Yeah, tomorrow, first thing. Meantime, Val, you want to tell me what brings you to Las Vegas?"

The question startled her. Maybe it was impertinent, or too abrupt. But he needed to know these things. His life was dislocated enough, and her sudden appearance brought an ambiguous new dimension to its already messy tangle.

"Can I use your bathroom?" she asked.

"Look, I don't want you to misunderstand . . ."

"I just have to use the bathroom, Tim."

Waverly forced a smile. "Sure. Around the corner and down the hall. First door to the right. Only one, actually."

As soon as she was gone he got up and went into the living room and lifted the blinds at the front windows. The celebrated Nevada sunshine streamed in. A particularly violent thunderclap snore erupted from the couch. Waverly came over and shook a meaty

Pettibone shoulder. May as well deal with one of those tangles straightaway. "Roger," he said. "Time to get up."

Pettibone groaned, tugged the blanket over his head. Waverly pulled it back. "Roger? Come on. It's time."

Slowly, painfully, resisting all the way, he climbed out of the mire of a sotted sleep. He got himself upright, knuckle-ground at watery bulging eyes. His skin was the color of slate; even the freckles looked bleached. The puffed face wore the bewildered, desolate, gap-jawed expression of a nursing home resident. He was seized by a fit of deep-bellied hacking. It ran its course. His lips moved, generating an inaudible mumble.

"What's that, Roger?"

"I say," he said, voice hoarse with misery, a grating nasal whine, " 'Awake, for Morning in the Bowl of Night,/Hast Flung the Stone that puts the Stars to flight.' *The Rubáiyát,* you remember."

Jesus, a sunup-to-sundown quote machine. Did he never give it a rest? The answer to Waverly's unvoiced question was, evidently, no, for next he was peeling himself off the couch, shuffling over to a window, unlimbering, and addressing, it seemed, the great out of doors. " 'Then I saw the morning sky:/Heigho, the tale was all a lie,' etcetera etcetera, however the rest of it goes."

"Try, 'Nothing now remained to do/But begin the game anew.' "

He turned and regarded Waverly approvingly, or as approvingly as his miseried condition allowed. "Good man. Anyone who knows his Housman—that crabbed buggerer—can't be all bad. Let's trade some more, see who runs down first."

"I concede," Waverly said. "And while this is all very instructive, Roger, I expect you've got someplace to be. Am I right?"

"Absolutely. Everyone has to be someplace." He glanced at his watch. "For me it's a classroom in another hour or so. Today I march the sleepwalkers through Thucydides. Or is it Herodotus?"

"It'll come to you."

Pettibone made a limp motion at the empty bottle on the table. "You wouldn't happen to have any more of that, ah, elixir? A little jump-start, as they like to say?"

"Afraid not. We did it in last night."

"Well, in that case . . ." His voice trailed off dismally.

Waverly sighed. "There's coffee," he said, but without a trace of enthusiasm.

Pettibone ran a deliberative palm over his sandpaper tinge of red beard. Examined his rumpled clothes. Seemed to hesitate. Maybe the message was sinking in. Maybe. But before he could accept or decline, another voice—gentle, quietly confident—asserted, "I could suggest something, if you're not feeling well."

It was Valerie, gliding into the room noiseless as a spirit of the air.

Pettibone squinted at her. "And who might this be?"

Waverly's turn for dismay. This was not how he'd wanted it to go. Too late now. "My sister," he said.

A Pettibone brow lifted skeptically. "Sister?"

"Yes, sister. She got in this morning. Valerie, Roger Pettibone."

She came right up to him and extended a hand. "I'm happy to meet you, Mr. Pettibone."

Pettibone grasped the hand and shook it warmly. Another potential audience. "Roger, please." His smeary eyes shifted back and forth between her and Waverly. "Yes, there's a distant family resemblance. Your name again is?"

She repeated it.

"Valerie Waverly, Timothy Waverly. Euphonic names. Your parents had a fine ear for melody. Tell me, where is it you journeyed from?"

She told him.

"South Dakota," he echoed in the sagacious tones of the worldly traveler, "that pastoral Eden."

"You've been there?"

"Indeed I have. Augustana College, Sioux Falls, South Dakota. A year's sojourn among the godly heavy-breathing Lutherans. About a century ago."

Waverly sensed a monologue in the making. To head it off he said to Valerie, "You had something to recommend to Roger?"

"I'll get it."

She vanished into the kitchen and returned bearing a full glass of water and two Enervite tablets. "Take these," she said to Pettibone.

He looked at the pills dubiously. "May I inquire what they are?"

"An herbal remedy. Take them. You'll feel better shortly."

Pettibone managed a good sport smile, popped the Enervites into his mouth, and took them down on a quick gulp.

"Drink it all," Valerie directed.

"All? This is water, you know."

"Purified water. Your system needs it."

Obediently, he emptied the glass. "And when can I expect these miraculous results?"

"Any minute now. You'll see."

Waverly's interest in the experiment was something less than keen. "You mentioned a class, Roger."

"Class? Oh, yes. Class. Well, I must be off, then. The cretins await." He stepped over and pumped Waverly's hand. "Many thanks for your hospitality." Valerie he favored with a stiff bow. "And to you, kind lady, for your nostrums."

"Let me know how they work for you."

Waverly steered him to the door. "Yeah, you be sure and let us know. Sometime."

No sooner was the door shut behind him than it swung open again, and he poked his head in and said, "There seems to be a beast barring my way."

"Electra," Valerie said. "I forgot." She slipped around him and uttered a sharp command at the snarling dog. "Now it's all right," she assured him.

Pettibone looked unconvinced. "You're, ah, quite sure about that?"

"It's perfectly safe. But I'll walk you to your car if you like."

"That would be most comforting."

Waverly watched them from a window. They stood by the Mercury, Pettibone's mouth running ceaselessly, semaphore arms flagging a dramatic dispatch. Valerie appeared to be listening attentively, patiently. A moment later she was back. She unballed the crumpled blanket, folded it neatly, and settled herself onto the couch, remarking, "Interesting man, your friend."

"He's a drunk, Val. Garrulous drunk. The worst kind. And hardly a friend."

"He told me he's a history professor. Wants to exchange Dakota tales, he said."

"I wouldn't encourage him."

"Oh, I don't know. He seems like a good person. Terribly dissipated, though. You're right about that."

"You've got to be wary of people out here. It's not South Dakota."

"Isn't that curious," she said dreamily. "Someone warned me that very same thing. Just last night, when I was asking directions to your house."

"Good advice."

"But that's not what you want to talk about. Is it, Tim."

"No, I suppose not."

"You want to know why I'm here."

"That would be helpful. You see, my circumstances are—"

"Why don't you sit down. I'll try to explain."

Also good advice. He had no idea what he was about to hear. He took a seat facing her.

"There's an extraordinary man lives here," she said, voice swaying between pitches as if she were not quite certain where to begin, or end, "a healer . . ."

An herbalist, Waverly learned, homeopathic practitioner, but more than that, much more: a selfless visionary, gifted with powers all but divine, dedicated to the creation of a healing sanctuary for the hopelessly ill. A man outside his time, surrendered to an absolute probity of purpose. Gradually and with many fuzzily convoluted side trips, the earnest recital unfolded; and as it did her serene features seemed to take on an almost luminous glow, the unsummoned smile radiant, the eyes inward-turning, abstracted; and as he sat there displaying a listening face, Waverly was once again plunged backward across the gulf of years, against his will remembering her anguished delirium at their mutual betrayal by their faithless spouses, the simultaneous disintegration of their marriages, and (his censors yielding utterly to a flood of appalling images) the rash murderous act that changed his life irreversibly and forever. Hers too, as he recognized now, watching those absent, moonstruck eyes.

Eventually the rambling explanation wound down. "And that's

more or less why I've come," she concluded. She laid her hands in her lap and gazed at him solemnly, waiting a response.

"Let me see if I've got this right," Waverly said. "On the bases of some correspondence, a few phone calls, a couple of flimsy promises, you packed up everything and came out here expecting to go to work for this . . . healer?"

"If he'll have me."

"And you sold your kennels?"

"Not sold, exactly. More like leased."

"What does that mean, 'like leased'? Do you have something in writing?"

"I have an understanding with the fellow who took it over."

"An understanding," Waverly repeated. He was trying to keep his voice steady, even, reasonable. Doing his best, anyway. It wasn't easy. "You believe that?"

"I do," she said quietly. "Back there people trust each other."

"That's just my point. You're not back there. This is Las Vegas, city of scufflers, grifters, scammers."

She looked blank.

"Charlatans, Val. And from everything you've told me, I'm sorry to say this—what's his name?"

"Wyman Brewster."

"This Brewster sounds to me like a world-class predator. Hustling the dying, that's got to take a special brand of meanness."

Her mouth tightened. Sparks flashed in her eyes. "I believe I ought to be the judge of that. You needn't concern yourself."

"But I am concerned. You're asking me to put you up. And by that much I'm contributing to this—" Madness, he wanted to say, but instead put in "ill-advised venture."

"Only for a few days. Till I find a place of my own."

Waverly lit a cigarette. A calmative time-out, to gather his thoughts.

"A week at most," she said, her voice softened now, close to plaintive.

"Look, Val, that's not the issue. I'm trying to protect you against a world I don't think you fully understand."

"Why don't you let me worry about it. I've done a passable job of protecting myself, these many years."

Waverly had no argument for that. He looked at her, this sister of his, this fragile child-woman, a new burden in a life already weighted with the oppressive baggage of the past. "I guess you have at that," he said defeatedly; and, not unmindful of Bennie, yet another factor in the thorny widening tangle, he added, "Of course you can stay. Long as you like."

"I'm grateful, Tim. And I hope you realize I came to see you too. There are, well, things between us that need to be settled."

"I know," he said. "We'll get to them. In good time."

9

C lick was yanked rudely out of sleep that morning by a jangly phone, and a good thing too seeing as how the Timex said quarter past nine, which left him forty-five quick minutes to get himself up and shaved shit showered and etcetera and over to the Center to take old whackadoodle on his zombie rounds, and after last night he fuckin' well better be on time or the dingdong doc gonna get another case a the serious red ass. But first he got to see who's rattlin' the Koontz cage, this hour. "Yeah," he muttered crossly into the speaker.

"Good morning, Cleanth. This is your partner speaking."

"Hey, Egg-a-baby, what's up?"

"A number of things, since we spoke last. All of them quite auspicious, I'd say."

Click was buffeted by a battery of dissonant sensations. There was a tingly excitement over the cool promise in Eggs's voice (he didn't have any idea what that aw-spicious meant, but he knew he'd heard a *partner* in there, which meant for sure they were back in action). But there was anxiety too, over the time ticking away (so far all the action just hard noise, and he got a job to get to, only one he got, for now anyway). And the lingering fog of sleep. And something else, hammering at the outer gates of perception—oh yeah, the tube still squawkin' and the MTV gash still shakin' their sugar booties (which is what he oughta be doin' right now, shaggin' his own bootie), which meant he must've crashed last night with all them wiggle butts dancin' the boogaloo in his eye and which maybe accounted for this blue steeler (speakin' of tube and what's up— haw haw) so stiff and throbbin' it's winkin' at the ceiling and he's lucky he hadn't dreamed a wet one and buttermilked his jockeys, it bein' longer'n he could remember since he bumped any fuzz and—

"Cleanth? Are you there?"

"Huh? Yeah, sure. Still here."

"Good. Now, I've given some thought to what we discussed and—"

"What part you talkin' about," Click put in, "this discussin'?"

"Your employer," Eggs said in a voice honed by annoyance. "The medicine man. And how to relieve him of our fair share of his ill-gotten gains."

Thing about Eggs was he never could say nothin' straight. Or short. Always gotta talk like he's given' a Sunday church sermon. "Look, Egger, I'm runnin' little late," Click said, skirring his tongue over a molar in jittery punctuation. "Maybe you fill me in this afternoon, them thoughts."

"This will take only a moment of your valuable time, Cleanth."

Enough flash-frost in *that* voice to chill a sixer, so Click, knowing Eggs, figured he better sit still and listen up and hope to shit he made it by ten. Thoughts was good but they didn't put chix in your bucket (thinking of which and seeing the empty KFC carton on the floor, all twelve pieces vanished, his stomach began to moil and his bowels to bubble ominously, and he lifted a cheek and cracked a thunderous boomer).

"What was that?" Eggs said.

"Uh, nothin'. The teevee. War show."

"Morning television, Cleanth? Not good for the brain cells, you know. Turns them to mush."

Another thing on Eggs, he always got the needle in you. Needle?—more like drill bit. Mr. Fuckin' Perfect. "C'mon, man," Click said, letting some of the annoyance thicken his own voice, "you gonna get to it or what? I lose that job and all's we're talkin' here's smoke."

"I take it you're on your way to work."

"That's what I'm tryin' to tellya. I turn up late again and Brewster gonna have me jumpin' through my own asshole."

A heavy sigh came floating through the ether. "Easy, Cleanth. Relax. And pay attention now. This is what I want you to do."

Easy. Sure. Easy for him. Took him five more of the rapidly shrinking minutes to spit out what anybody else say in under two (him and Brewster gonna make some matchup, comes to smoke), but Click listened anyway, replying vexedly, "Yeah, I got it, got it," to the final summary query. Then he put up the phone and zoomed into the crapper and got himself purged and *de*turged and zoomed out again and duded up in fresh laundry (rust jacket with a window-pane pattern and wide wide lapels, paisley tie, rust and mustard print shirt, pea-green slacks held up by a yard and a half of belt and a ton of buckle, crocodile leather loafers: rounds days he liked to look spiffy, official); and at exactly one minute shy of ten gongs he brought the Lincoln squealing to a stop outside the Center. Talk about your tight fits.

Tight welcoming smile on Brewster too, standing at the counter with a glass of some mossy goop in his hand when Click came puffing breathlessly through the door. Least he was smiling, or as close as he could ever come to it, that slice of a mouth on him. Got to be a good sign though, so Click rigged out a cheeser of his own and said brightly, "Mornin', Mr. Brewster," underlining it with the molar squeak.

Brewster acknowledged the greeting with a clinical stare. No words. No more smile either.

Click tried another route. "Real nice day out, huh?" He hadn't even noticed on the Indy Five drive over here, but it was an odds-on guess.

"You look tense, Cleanth. Fatigued. Try some Barley Green."

Brewster held out the glass in offering. Looked to Click like somebody zuked in it. "Uh, I ate already," he lied.

"Feeding is not necessarily nourishing. Drink. You'll find it energizing."

Click drank it. Fuck're you gonna do? Holy shit, tasted like butt chowder, go real great on top of last night's Kentucky Fried still churning his gut. But since Brewster was watching him, waiting a response, Click smacked his lips, grinned weakly, and said, "Good stuff," thinking Yeah, good if you like a coat of green sewer sludge on the roof of your mouth.

"A new product. I thought you might enjoy it. Well, let me get my bag and we'll be on our way."

Brewster went into a back room designated as his office, like he was president of General Fuckin' Motors or something, while Click, sucking at his fouled tongue, glanced around the store. Business pretty slow, this early, though the daytime clerk, hippo-hipped broad name of Phoebe Jones, bluehead somebody beat on with the ugly stick, she had a couple sure boneyard recruits down the end of an aisle, pitchin' 'em some other kind of grass clippings. It was his place he'd hire a young foxy-looking cunt dolled out in teeny skirt and peekaboo blouse, give the customers a flash of fern and big brown eyes with their wheat germ. Watch your sales pick up, that idea.

Click's reflections on marketing strategy were abruptly suspended by the reappearance of Brewster. "Let's get started, Cleanth," he said briskly, and over his shoulder he called to the clerk, "Phoebe, we leave the Center in your capable hands."

Course it's Click gets to lug the bag—felt like he got a load of bricks in there—out to the car. Brewster, he carries a clipboard. Bag's midnight black, goes with the suit he always wears for rounds. Nice getup. Like your friendly undertaker come to call, measure you for a pine box. But whatever the reason, Brewster's in a sunshine mood, for him, woofin' about the gorgeous day, breath of autumn in the air, Nature's animating beauty, scheize like that. Okay by Click, who needs some slack anyway to figure when be the best time to slide in the Eggs line (suppose to do it casual, Eggs said, like it's no great shakes, just a guy heard about him and the Center, wants to meet him and some other shit Click's goin' over in his head, got to get it straight), so he just keeps drivin' and sayin', Yeah, right, right, and noddin' till his neck aches. Lookin' for just the exact right minute to spring it.

But that minute don't come till rounds damn near done. First they got to go way the fuck north on Rancho Drive, then clear across town, then down to Henderson and finally back up to Paradise Valley. Some stops Brewster takes a bottle of one miracle weed or another out of the bag and goes in by himself and Click waits in the car. Other times Click comes along, haulin' all the gear and more or less just hangin' in the wings, not sayin' nothin' while Brewster does his fixemup number on the walkin' stiffs, except most of 'em ain't hardly even breathin', never mind walkin'.

Take for instance this one patient out to East Vegas, Mr. Fisher, got the rot in his lungs, the Mighty C. You go in his place and it's like goin' in one of them Egypt tombs you see in the movies, shades down, all dark and gloomy, some weird heavy stink in the air (stink of death, you ask Click). Today there's something else too, that air, and Brewster catches it right off. Soon as they're inside the door his nostrils start pinchin', and he marches over to the couch where Fisher's laid out like a mummy only without the wraps, just his undershirt and pee-stained drawers on, and says, "Delbert—" he always calls 'em by their first name—"you've been *smoking.*"

Poor old Fisher (who looks like he goes all of eighty pounds, healthy fart blow him away, but who ain't all that old actually, maybe got five, six years on Click, which makes Click think he oughta give up the nails or switch to lights) lifts a trembly finger and croaks, "One is all."

Brewster gives him a bone-cold stare, and then in his best (or worst, dependin' on where you standin') Judgment Day voice says, "If you persist in ignoring my instructions I can take no further responsibility for your treatment. You will surely die, Delbert."

"Please," Fisher whimpers. "Help me."

"Have you been taking your Homozone?"

Fisher makes his head go yes.

"And the Organic Medley?"

Another painful yes.

"Well at least you've been doing something right," Brewster says frigidly. "Cleanth will make you a fresh supply while we meditate together on wholeness and balance."

That's Click's signal to go out into the kitchen and brew up a batch of the Organic Medley. By now he's got the recipe down, regular chef. He takes five pounds of carrots, pound of spinach, cucumber, couple celery stalks, four garlic cloves (which maybe got something to do with the stink in here) and shoves 'em all in a food processor, sprinkles in some bee pollen and kelp powder and blends it up. Comes out a thick green mash, and lookin' at it there you gotta wonder if Fisher don't wonder which is worse, gaggin' it down or bein' dead.

When they leave he's bawlin', f'Chrissake, real tears streamin' outta them caved-in eye sockets, makes Click feel even a little sorry for the poor fuck. Don't lighten up Brewster any, though; he just warns him about "introducing any more toxins into your already poisoned system" and that's his good-bye. In the car he says grimly, "I fear we're going to lose that one, Cleanth," and he's scowlin' so hard Click figures now ain't the time to bring up Eggs.

But after a few more stops where everybody followin' the therapy right, doin' what they're told, Brewster's back in happy gear again, almost anyway, good as it ever gets with him; so after the last one Click's thinkin' now or never and on the drive to the Center he starts in, offhand-like, like it just come to him, "Oh yeah, Mr. Brewster, before I forget, I ran into this fella the other night, says he'd really like to meet you."

"And what is the nature of his ailment?"

"Oh, he ain't sick, it's just—"

"If he's not ill," Brewster broke in sharply, "why does he want to see me?"

"Well, he says he heard a lot of things about the Center—all of 'em good, course—and when I told him I work for you he got real excited and asks could I fix it for him and you to talk."

"To what end?"

"Huh?"

Brewster made the long wearied sigh of the seriously burdened man. "The purpose, Cleanth, of this talk. In the life I lead there is no room for idle chatter. As you should certainly know."

Click's thinkin', Jesus, this ain't how it's suppose to go. And he's gettin' rattled now, till he remembers the money part Eggs said be sure and slip in there, and he says, "Yeah, I know how busy you are,

Mr. Brewster, and I told him that. He understands about them things. See, he's a businessman, got a pot of money, I heard. Like a, y'know, investor. So he ain't into that chatter you was sayin' either."

Brewster looked at him carefully. "Are you suggesting this person might be interested in, ah, investing in my work?"

"Dunno for sure about that," Click said, just as careful. "All's I know is he don't have a high opinion on your regular medical doctors. Guess he had a bad experience with 'em, couple years back."

For a while Brewster don't say nothin' and Click's wonderin' if he got it out right, hopin' the fuck he did (that's how Eggs told him to say it: high opinion, bad experience, investor—just plant the seed and leave it at that). He cuts a glance over at Brewster, who's starin' out the window, watchin' the streets glide by, lookin' like he's hypnotized or something. Better not push it, is Click's thought.

Correct thought. Just when they're pullin' up at the Center and Click's thinkin' it's all pissed away and wonderin' now how he's gonna explain it to Eggs, Brewster says, "Perhaps I can find a moment for this gentleman. Why don't you bring him around tonight. Eightish, say."

Bingo! Old Egger, he knows his seed plantin'. Bones talk, every time.

Click kills the engine and goes for the door, but Brewster just sits there a minute, funny light in his eyes, maybe back in spiritland, with him you never know. Finally, voice gone all dreamy, he says, "This is most curious, Cleanth. Earlier this morning I had a call from a woman who has long been sympathetic to our work. Fine woman, very enlightened views. I'll be meeting with her tonight as well."

Click didn't see what the fuck that got to do with anything, but for something to say he said, "Hey, things lookin' up, huh? Two people got their heads right. Some coincidence."

"Coincidence? No, I believe there's more to it than that. More of an omen, I should say."

10

After his brief and not altogether satisfactory conversation with Cleanth, Eggs went into the bathroom and took a long soothing shower (talking with that imbecile, one needed instant soothing), dressed (yesterday's clothes, unfortunately, since they'd left the Dunes rather hastily), came out and put on his glasses (darkness in the room notwithstanding, they helped him think), and settled into a chair. Dawnette was still sleeping, which was fine, one fewer distraction. And for the next two hours he sat there, quietly deliberating on strategies.

With a nut of exactly twenty-eight hundred and change, by his precise tally, it was going to be imperative to move smartly. In Vegas that kind of money didn't go far. Of course he could always raise more simply by repeating last night's action, there being an inexhaustible supply of marks in this town. But that could be hazardous, given his temperament, the curious compulsion to put the unmistakable LaRevere stamp on even the most trifling score. His own art could betray him, and he knew it. No, better to husband the stake, work within their current means. And while he would much prefer living alone, what that came to in practice was finding a temporary place for himself and Dawnette, something inexpensive and, ideally, near to Cleanth. Both of his moronic confederates had a disturbing forgetfulness about the important things in life, and one of his knottier tasks would be to hold this fragile alliance together for the time it took to uncover the pill peddler's weakness and empty his till. After that, well, who could speculate?

In the meantime there were many wrinkles yet to iron out, details to consider, a variety of scenarios to devise and ponder, all of which occupied his thoughts for the remainder of the morning. Was he worried? Not in the slightest. Genius, as someone once observed, is merely the capacity for taking infinite pains, and for Eggs LaRevere such capacity was a natural endowment. A gift, so to say. And a gift unexercised is, as everyone knows, a criminal waste.

Shortly before noon he roused Dawnette. None too soon either, for it required a full hour to get her up and moving and out the door and down to the Caravan coffee shop, grouching all the way. Breakfast did in another hour, and something less than pleasant it was too, enduring all her petulant bitching: "God, I feel like shit. No make-up, some ratty clothes, hardly any sleep. Hope you know this is the middle of the goddam night for me, Eggs. Haven't been up this early since I left the farm." And more in that vein. Her appetite, however, was manifestly unimpaired, for all the whining. With the careless resilience of youth, she packed away a peasant meal of cheese omelet, sausage, hash browns, toast slathered with orange marmalade, and about a gallon of coffee, liberally sugared and creamed. Eggs confined himself to more sensible fare: juice, English muffin, a single cup of coffee, black. He wanted to be alert for whatever lay ahead today. Lean and mean.

A little after two Click appeared in the entrance. He cast his eyes around the room, gaping with the vapid expression of the man perpetually lost. Eggs lifted a beckoning arm, assembled a thin smile, and out of the side of his mouth said to Dawnette, "Here he is. Be nice now."

"Yeah yeah yeah."

"I mean it, Dawnette. Nice."

"What'd I just say?" she snapped. "Said yeah."

Click came threading through the tables in his leisurely fatso waddle, but when he caught sight of Dawnette his step picked up and his piggy face opened in a wide libidinous smirk. Eggs motioned him into a chair. "Cleanth," he said, "you remember Dawnette?"

"Bet your ass," Click affirmed. "Ain't nobody gonna forget *this* lady."

Dawnette acknowledged the tribute with a curt nod.

"She'll be working with us on this project," Eggs said.

"No kiddin'? Hey, shine-o-*la*! Dead-*lee*! Cool!" His jowls shook with pleasure, and on the last joyous exclamation some dim recollection sparked his satyr eyes. "Speakin' of cool, ain't that what you use to go by? Cool somethin'?"

"Whip," she said, popping out the word in vocal italics to the signature name.

"There you go. Cool Whip. Knew it was somethin' like that."

"It's Dawnette to you, Pork Chop."

Click ran a self-conscious hand over his pomaded hair, arousing a small blizzard of dandruff in the process. "Pork Chop?" he said uncertainly. "No, everybody call me Click." As if in evidence, he produced a grating tongue-to-tooth screak.

"Pork Chop fits better."

On the scale of things Eggs needed right now, the venture barely under way, petty bickering was an easy dead last. To sidestep it he put in irrelevantly and with all the habitual irony washed out of his voice, "You're looking very dapper today, Cleanth." He turned to Dawnette and inquired pointedly, "Wouldn't you agree?" Give the ball-breaking bitch a chance to fence mend.

Dawnette lit a cigarette, released a languid puff, ran her eyes over Click's colorful go-to-rounds outfit, and drawled, "Nice linen." And after a theatrically timed beat and through a rising plume of smoke, she added, "If you wanta disguise yourself as an asshole."

Eggs smothered a sigh. My partners. Well, nobody said it was going to be easy. "She's making a joke, Cleanth. A little friendly ragging."

"Yeah, joke," Click muttered, but the lecher smirk faded some and the eyes shimmered with hurt.

"So tell me," Eggs prompted, steering the talk toward the firmer ground of business, "how did things go this morning?"

"Huh? What things is that?"

He seemed fuddled by the question. Evidently still nursing his bruised feelings. Very patiently Eggs said, "Your opening moves, Cleanth. With this Brewster fellow."

"Oh, them. Good. They went good."

"Could you maybe elaborate a bit?"

"Yeah, well, I told him pretty much what you said. Worked it in real slick, kinda back door like. Time I was done he bought it all."

"And the upshot is?"

"Uh, whaddya mean, that upshot?"

"The meeting. Were you able to arrange a meeting?"

"Fuckin-a dog, meeting," Click declared. "How's tonight grab your gonads? Eight bells."

"Tonight? That's better than I'd hoped for. Splendid work, Cleanth."

The praise brought a rich glow to Click's round simple face. He shot a glance at Dawnette, who sat with her head tilted back, blowing smoke rings at the ceiling. Then, furrowing his brows importantly, catching the business spirit, he said, "One thing though, Eggs. Tellin' him you're heeled—which I done, like you said—ain't that gonna be a heavy problem? I remember right, last night you was runnin' on the red E, loot-wise."

The faint Eggs smile went bland, indulgent. "So I was. Last night." He removed a fat wad of bills from a jacket pocket, peeled off a fifty, and laid it on the table. "Before it slips my mind, let me repay your generous loan."

Click's eyes goggled. "Holy fuck! How'd you turn up *that*?"

"Better you don't ask."

Dawnette stubbed out her cigarette and looked at Eggs narrowly. "Yeah, I'd say better."

Eggs elected to ignore it. For now. Talk with her later. He checked his watch. "Let's get started," he said, coming to his feet. "We have a number of routine items to attend to."

Three items, three stops. At the first they secured an apartment in Click's complex, an efficiency identical to his in decor and furnishings, and located just four units down. Perfect. And though his bankroll was lighter by eight bills—a month's rent and deposit—Eggs was nonetheless cheered by the way things were beginning to fall in line. Dawnette was somewhat less enthusiastic. "Jesus, what a dump," she pronounced sourly. Eggs said nothing. His patience was rapidly dwindling.

Next stop, The Dunes. Eggs had been obliged to abandon his bags after last night's messy scuffle and speedy flight. Three bags, all his earthly possessions. Happily for him, that would be changing soon. "Cleanth," he said as they swung into the lot, "perhaps you'd do me the kindness of stepping inside and retrieving my luggage."

Click was visibly irked. "How come I'm the one gets all the spearchucker work, this partnership?"

"Under ordinary circumstances I'd of course take care of it myself. Let's just say it could be unwise for me to be seen in there."

For an instant Click looked puzzled. Only an instant. A low-watt bulb flickered behind his eyes and his lips parted in a sly, knowing grin. "Okay, I get it. You two done a little throwdown number. Which is how you come by that jackwad. That the goods?"

Dawnette, sulking in the back seat, was inspired to remark, "Hey, that's real quick, Pork Chop. You oughta try out for 'Jeopardy.' "

Click's grin fell. Squashed again. Eggs said gently, "You remember what I recommended, Cleanth? About asking. That's all she means."

"Know what she means."

Eggs handed him a claim tag. "You'll find the bags at the bell captain's station. Let's hurry along now. We have another errand yet."

As soon as he was out of the car, Eggs turned to Dawnette, sleet in his eyes. "This is your idea of nice?"

"Whaddya expect?" she fired right back.

"I expect you to be civil. A great deal turns on him. Everything, in fact, at the moment."

"So what am I suppose to do about it?"

"You can start by dropping the Pork Chop. In spite of what you think, it's neither clever nor cute."

"What do I call him then? Like you do? Cleee-aanth," she mimicked, stringing out the vowels in a parrot squawk.

"Call him what he wants. Call him Click."

"Like them spazzy noises he makes with his tongue? Okay, what else? Ball him or something?"

"If it keeps him happy, why not? You've done worse."

"Worse! You're sayin' worse'n that dickweed?" Her face crinkled in an unlovely display of monumental disgust. "Listen, Eggs, I got—I got—"

The precise word escaped her. Eggs supplied it, along with a sneer. "Standards?"

"Yeah, standards. You goddam right, standards."

Enough of diplomacy. In Eggs's experience there were some people in this world on whom the finest blandishments of sweet reason were forever lost. Sadly, it appeared Miss Dawnette Day was among them. He reached over the seat and gripped her head firmly at the temples and forced it backwards, arching her neck at a tortuous angle.

"Fuck're you doin'? Let go me."

Her eyes steepened, then squeezed tightly shut under his lowering thumbs. Calmly and without a trace of rancor in his voice, he said, "They say if you press hard enough the eyeball will pop much like a plump grape. I've never actually seen it done, you understand, but that's what I'm told."

"C'mon, Eggs, I didn't mean nothin'. Lemme go."

Her face, so full of bold disgust only a moment ago, was reduced now to a twitchy mask of fear. That much was gratifying. Still, he thought he detected a certain disbelief in it yet, as though the threat were too extravagant ever to be executed. As though they were merely playing some outrageous game. Couldn't have that. So he planted his thumbs squarely and bore down, applying a controlled pressure alternately between the eyes, right first, then left, then right again. Like a horn player rhythmically pushing the keys of his instrument, in this case producing the agreeable, if staccato, music of her terrified cries: "Jesus God—Eggs—don't—it hurts—please."

"Imagine a one-eyed whore," he said. "That's the stuff ballads are made of."

"Please—hurts—please—"

"Or a blind one," he went on, both thumbs pressing evenly now.

"That could limit your clientele drastically. On the other hand, it could be a novelty, too, as jaded as tricks are these days. Who knows? Business might prosper. What do you think, Dawnette?"

"I'll do what you want," she whimpered. "Anything. Fuck him, you want."

Eggs lifted one thumb. The eye flicked open, blinked wildly, swam in its socket. A violent tic took hold in the purpling skin beneath it. The rest of her face was bloodless, all the color drained away. "That's what I was hoping to hear," he said. "You're sure now?"

Her head made a slight up-and-down motion in the firm vise of his hands.

He lifted the other thumb. In a tone clement, reasonable, he said, "You see, Dawnette, all I really want is civilized behavior. That's not too much to ask, is it?"

No audible response.

"Well, is it?"

Nearly as it was able, her head moved back and forth in his hands.

"Good. I'm glad you understand. Now we can get on with this enterprise."

He released her. She shrank down in the seat, staring at him with a kind of glazed impassivity, or through him (it was difficult to tell), off into some stark and intensely private vision of disaster's dreadful possibilities. Either way, at or through, the point had been made. Enough said.

In a moment Click came wobbling across the lot, clutching a bag in each hand, the third tucked awkwardly under an arm. He loaded them into the trunk and plopped himself behind the wheel, huffing mightily. "Where to now?" he asked.

One last stop, to collect Dawnette's things. At Eggs's prompting, she directed them west on Flamingo, then south on Decatur. Considerably subdued she was, too, he noted with satisfaction. The hands-on lesson carried the day every time. During the short drive he remarked on the burgeoning cityscape, the traffic, the brisk fall weather, whatever popped into his head. General affable chatter. No doubt about it, he was feeling good. Better than good: buoyant, weightless, almost euphoric, the way action, any action, even an abortive piece of work like this last one, always made him feel. Bring on those two punchboard dykes! Eggs LaRevere was ready. Primed and ready. Stoked.

They pulled into a cluster of apartments and came to a stop outside the one Dawnette specified. "So this is Velvaville," Eggs said.

Dawnette hesitated. "Uh, maybe I oughta go in by myself, Eggs."

"Oh no. You'll need help with all your belongings."

"I don't got much, just some clothes and stuff. I can handle it."

"I'll come along anyway. For moral support."

"You want me to come too?" Click asked.

Eggs thought about it. Two very tough ladies in there, capable of anything. Two of them, one of him. And he was walking off with their squeeze. Euphoric didn't have to mean foolhardy. "I think that would be advisable," he said.

"Velva always use the chain lock," Dawnette said. "She might not let you guys in."

"Let's find out."

On the way to the door Eggs drew Click aside and cautioned, "Stay alert now. Cover my back."

"You got 'er."

Dawnette heard it. "I don't want no trouble, Eggs. Please. They been good to me."

"Why should there be trouble? You're free to live wherever you like. It's a free country, you know."

He hit the bell. Waited, humming some spirited unrecognizable tune. Nothing. Hit it again, laying on the buzzer this time. There was a sound of approaching feet, grouchy mumbling, a froggy, "Whoozit?"

"Me, Vel," Dawnette said quickly. "Cool Whip."

"Cool? That you?"

"Yeah. Got a couple people with me here."

The chain unhooked, the knob turned, the door swung open. And there stood Velva, filling the entrance, as well as a floral print duster big as a circus tent, squat and shapeless as a pillar, lumpy face destitute of paint and pale as soured skim milk, eyes pink-rimmed and puffed with sleep and assorted dissipations, hair an electrified frizz. Looking at her, Eggs had to wonder why he'd ever bothered to bring Cleanth along.

"You met Eggs last night," Dawnette said by way of identification, adding in afterthought, "And this one's Click. We come in?"

Velva cranked up a fraudulant smile. "Course you can come in, honey. This is your crib too."

The apartment was cavern dark and redolent with an oppressive blend of odors: stale smoke, whiskey, musky perfume, a lingering flatus, some nameless sweetish aroma. Velva ushered them in and drew the drapes at a window. The splash of sunlight revealed a living room seriously disordered, which condition she addressed cavalierly: "Don't mind the mess. Party hearty time last night." And with just a touch of reproach in her roupy voice, she allowed, "You shoulda been here, Cool."

Dawnette displayed apologetic palms.

"Sit, sit," Velva commanded and they did, Eggs and Click on the couch, Dawnette in a corner chair removed from the brilliant light. "Pour you boys a little tightener?" Velva offered, indicating an uncapped bottle flanked by lipstick-smudged glasses and heaping ashtrays on a coffee table in the center of the room.

"Hey, that'd be—" Click started to say, but Eggs cut him off quickly: "We won't be staying that long."

Velva shrugged, filled a glass for herself, and sank heavily into a chair whose cushion deflated under her bulk. "Know better'n to ask this girl," she said with a head toss at Dawnette and with all the implied intimacy of long-term companions. "She never could drink in the morning—or afternoon—or whatever the fuck time it is."

"It's four o'clock," Eggs said.

"Four's the magic hour." She lifted the glass, took a long swallow, made a wet lip smack, and said, "Dog hair time," winking wisely at no one in particular. And since no one responded she shifted in the chair and, directing words and gaze exclusively at Dawnette, inquired sweetly, "So. What's up, hon?"

Eggs watched her. The motion of leg-crossing had hiked the duster up one mealy thigh, exposing a dollop of plump white fat depending from the underside of the knee. The synthetic smile was still stuck on her face. Still playing at charming hostess, a role worn about as comfortably as a hair shirt. Most transparent strategy. She knew what was up.

"Uh, see, how it is, Vel," Dawnette was saying, or trying to say, "I'm thinkin' about maybe, well . . ."

"She's moving out," Eggs finished for her.

Velva's steady gaze never wavered. Ignoring him, she said, "That true, Cool? That what you want?"

"I guess so," Dawnette said weakly.

"Guess don't cut shit. You, me, Gay, we got something special goin' here. You know that."

"Yeah, I know, Vel. It's just I got this chance to—"

Eggs put a cautionary hand in the air. "That's enough," he said. "No explanations are necessary."

"But I was just gonna—"

"I said that's enough."

Velva's eyes flashed. "Whyn't you butt out, pricklick. Let her talk for herself."

"Nothing more to talk about," Eggs said amiably. "She's leaving with us. And you're going to have to get accustomed to twosomes again. Simple as that."

"That's what you think, huh?"

"Afraid I do."

"Yeah, we'll see about that." She set the glass on the floor, came out of the chair, and marched over to Dawnette, declaring, "You don't gotta do nothing you don't want to, honey."

Dawnette lowered her head.

"You hear what I'm tellin' you?" She laid two fingers under Dawnette's chin, boosted the head, and stooped down for a closer look. "What happen, your eyes?" she demanded, voice shrilling, edging toward fury's upper registers. "He do this? He hurt you?"

Dawnette made some fluttery gestures. "It's okay, Vel. Honest, I'm okay."

Velva wheeled around. "You suckwad," she hissed. "I figured you for a piece of chickenshit girl thrasher minute I seen you."

"Really," said Eggs mildly. "How very perceptive." Behind the glasses a vigilance, expectant but quite unhurried, settled in his eyes. From matured and seasoned experience he recognized that, once set in motion, the tide of events about to unfold would have its own pace, its own rhythm, its own irresistible logic. Finally, its own inevitability.

"I'll give you perceptive, you touch her again."

Presenting an upraised fist as bellicose visual aid, Velva stationed herself between him and Dawnette, a fuming steamy tub of flesh filling the room as easily as she'd filled the entrance, the chair, filling it the way she filled her petunia-festooned Ringling Brothers tent, the way she'd once (in Eggs's keen assessment) filled some sick need in Dawnette's dreary life. No more. "I believe we've heard enough," he said, rising off the couch and signalling Click to do the same. "Dawnette, where are your things?"

"Bedroom back there. Listen—Eggs—lemme do it—please—"

But Eggs had given up listening. To Click he said, "Watch the dyke," and he strode purposefully into the hall and flung open the first door. A shaft of yellow light fell across the otherwise blackened room. He peered in and what he saw was the detritus of good times never celebrated in the glossy pages of tourist brochures: in a corner the shadowy outline of a square forbidding barbarous wooden chair; and littering the floor a grease-lathered playsheet, a crumpled tube of Slippery Stuff, a wicked-looking forked paddle, an obscenely feculent plug, some skimpy studded-leather Frederick's of Hell garments. Talk about sick. And that's essentially what he said, recoiling as much from the noxious cloying stench swelling through the room as from the odious sight itself: "This is very diseased, Dawnette. You'll be well rid of this place." He turned and was about to say more but by then Velva was lunging at him, bawling, "Keep outta there, you cocksuck!"

Click stepped into her path. "Better back off, lady," he warned. "You don't wanna fuck with him." Which well-intentioned advice was received with a fierce growl followed by a hand laid flat in his face and a mighty shove that sent him reeling. "Fuckin' shit," he sputtered and came ricocheting off the wall and wrapped her in a heroic effort at a bear hug, but his stubby arms were much too short to circumscribe this tumid fleshy globe and for an instant they grappled and grunted like two snorting rutting pigs. Eggs looked on, appraising the inexpert contest coolly, taking the measure of both of them, confederate and antagonist alike. Not much to recommend either one. Battle of the blimps. Locked in jiggly embrace, they stumbled into the hall. Click, outweighed and outgunned, clearly was no match for her. His tenuous hold slackened, gave way altogether, and she hauled back a clenched hammy paw and floored him with a roundhouse punch.

Time to intervene, put an end to this low burlesque. Seizing that shard of a moment when Velva stood wheezing triumphantly over her fallen foe, Eggs glided in behind her and drove a fist into the spongy kidneys, staggering her. Then he came around and made a blade of the fist and brought it across the bridge of her nose in a chopping lateral blow, splintering, from the feel of it, the bone.

"My nose!" she screeched in testimony, tottering backwards. "You broke my *nose!*"

"So it appears," Eggs said, "but let's be certain." He advanced on her, grasped the back of her neck with one hand and, with the heel of the other, moving it in a circular motion, rather like kneading bread dough, mashed the pulpy flesh and fractured bone.

Velva crumpled. First to her knees and then, with an effortless assist from Eggs, the floor. She curled herself into a tight fetal ball, or as nearly fetal as her corpulence would accommodate. Her breath came in urgent hawking gasps, and on the exhalation a gusher of blood (actually, more on the order of a trickle or at best an ooze, Eggs observed with a clinician's dispassionate respect for accuracy) squirted from the two pinholes that served her now for nasal cavities. A medley of discordant wails echoed off the walls and ceiling. There was Velva's, of course, a sustained anguished yawp; but also Dawnette's, something of a stricken bleating whinny coming from off to his left where she stood quaking in terror; and yet another strain issuing from the astonished chasmed mouth of a figure clad only in the briefest of panties and appearing suddenly at the other end of the hall, this latter a moan transmuted to a caterwauling howl of rage as the sight of the lumpen toppled Velva registered on her sleep-fogged eyes and she came swooping down on him, arms flailing, hands coiled into vulture talons.

Eggs dodged nimbly. He ducked under one of those arms, the

right, plucked it out of the air, looped it beneath the elbow with his left, grasped the wrist, and forced it back in the deft application of a come-along hold that effectively neutralized her, set her dancing a distressed jig. A bit more wrist pressure and her face kinked up in pain and the howl diminished to a series of stuttery yips. In a way it was almost too easy, scarcely worthy of his talents.

"Gayleen, isn't it?" he said, ever mindful of the amenities, enjoying himself now that the little playlet was all but resolved, its conclusion foregone. "Remember me? Last night? Dunes?"

If she had a reply it was lost in the hysterical sobs of Dawnette and, to a lesser extent, the cautious mumbled counsel of Click. Both were on their feet now, but keeping a wary distance. They knew Eggs.

"For God's sake, Eggs, don't hurt her," Dawnette pleaded, a trembly fist held to her chin. "Let her go."

"Uh, she's maybe right, Egger," Click advised, swaying some, still dazed from big Vel's hammer punch. "Maybe just give the twat a thump, huh. Bugass outta here before we catch some heat."

More histrionics. Eggs sighed. He reflected a moment, doing his best to shape an explanation that might fall within the narrow bounds of their comprehension. It wasn't easy. Nevertheless, partly out of his renewed sense of euphoria and partly out of a curious need to articulate it for himself, snare it with words, he undertook the effort. In tones patiently didactic, professorial, he said, "Neither of you seem to understand the nature of pain. Its majesty, purity. Or its artistry. For example, no one with any imagination needs elaborate gear. The body itself is a vast sphere of potential pain. A vessel of pain. Am I right, Gayleen?"

He bore down harder on the wrist, elevating her onto tiptoes and exciting a confirming scream. Dawnette buried her face in her hands. Click's puckered in an empathetic wince. "C'mon, man," he muttered. "What's the good?"

Eggs shook his head sadly. Their absolute and impenetrable stupidity appalled him. It was truly hopeless. "The good?" he asked rhetorically. "Gayleen knows. What she's about to experience will exceed all her previously understood notions of pain. She'll have been to a place you and I have never known. A transcendent experience. Enviable, one might say."

He delivered this intelligence through a small jeering smile. Somebody had to smile. "Consider the elbow joint," he went on, "a whole undiscovered continent of pain." And in demonstration he pivoted slightly, putting the full weight of his upper body on the wrist, forcing it back and down but with a pressure even and measured and slow, befitting the transcendent experience, until there was first a grating sound, then an unmistakable splintering sound, then a sharp pop, something like a dry twig snapping. And then he released her.

Gayleen's mouth widened in a long piercing siren shriek. Abruptly it stopped and she gawked dumbly at the crooked arm dangling limply at her side. Inspected it as though it were some curious appendage sprouted magically from her shoulder, grotesque and alien to the rest of her. She shuddered. Her legs began to buckle, slow motion. She collapsed.

"I expect she'll remember me now," Eggs chuckled, but without much mirth. "At least when it rains. The other one, too, with every breath she takes."

The euphoria had passed. Vanished as suddenly and inexplicably as it arrived, the way it always did, plunging him to earth in an Icarian fall, back into the profane world of details to arrange, deadlines to meet, witless partners to direct. Remembering them, he said crossly, "I've done all the work today. You two can finish up. Get your things and get them to the car." He started for the door, adding with a dismissive sneer, "See if you can do something useful for a change. And make it quick. I need a nap before tonight's meeting."

11

"Yeah ... sure ... no pro'lum," Bennie was saying between molar probes with the tine of a fork.

"It'll only be for a few days. Week on the outside."

"Good by me."

"She can take my room. I'll sleep on the couch." Waverly shifted nervously in his chair. He had the uncomfortable sense of protesting too much.

"Like I say, no pro'lum."

"The thing of it is, Bennie, I've got to make her see it was a mistake coming out here. This is no town for someone like her."

Bennie extracted a bagel nugget, examined it as though he had come across a tiny precious gem, then flicked it into the Pyrenees of dishes rising from the sink. "Hey, I hearya," he said agreeably. "You gotta watch out for family, Timothy. That's in your Bible someplace."

If there was any irony in this pearl of B. Epstein wisdom, Waverly couldn't detect it. And if there was not, then he was vastly relieved at his partner's tolerant reaction to the sudden and altogether unexpected appearance of Valerie and hound. Had it been the other way around, he wasn't certain he'd have been so generous. Yet there had to be at least a grain of self-interest in the cheery willingness to introduce, however briefly, a troublesome new dimension into their already cluttered lives, and he suspected that interest had something to do with last night's guest and the scheme Bennie was surely hatching. He understood how his mind worked; they'd partnered too long for it to be otherwise. Never hurt to make a little deposit in your Goodwill First National—another Epstein maxim. Which is what he was doing right now, the remnants of the six P.M. breakfast satisfactorily dislodged from his teeth:

"Anyhow, she seems like a real fine lady, your sis. Educated."

"She's a very confused woman, Bennie. Educated or not."

"I dunno, looks pretty straight to me. Some weird feedin' ideas maybe, but we all got our quirks."

"Trust me, she's way out of her element here."

Both of them were speaking in lowered tones, for on the other side of the wall Valerie could be heard humming softly, completing her preparations for the long-awaited audience with the magic healer. And in another moment, preceded by the vigilant dog, she stood in the entrance to the kitchen as though presenting herself for their inspection and inquired shyly, "How do I look?"

Like nothing Waverly had seen yet on the glitzy streets of Las Vegas, where if you wait and watch long enough you finally see it all. But what he said was, "Good, Val. You look good."

"Hey, better'n that," Bennie amended. "Lady looks sensational."

An afternoon of sleep had erased all the fatigue from her finely chiseled face and, framed in the spill of silky hair, it glowed now with the natural cosmetic of praise. She wore a filmy peasant blouse, burnt orange, with a scoop neck and a demure gathering of ruffles over her frail chest. A black patent-leather belt cinched her flat waist. Her skirt was patterned in multicolored shapes: squares, oblongs, hexagons, circles, triangles. A geometer's crazy quilt. It fell to her shins, revealing slender ankles and slightly scuffed sandals. The total effect was anachronous, the sixties revisited, but without a hint of artifice or calculation. What you see is what you get: the tall, gawky, almost fleshlessly lean Great Plains waif she was, or had transformed herself into. Yet somehow, Waverly thought, gazing at her now, miraculously lovely still, with a kind of radiance from within, a peculiar fusion of ageless innocence and grace and melancholy experience and stubborn will. And this time that's what he said, meaning it: "He's right. You look lovely, Val."

The rosy luster deepened in the hollows beneath her cheekbones. She served them each a grateful smile. "Thanks. It's the best outfit I've got. Only one, really, apart from the jeans and work shirts."

"Don't do much honk-a-doodle-doin' out to North Dakota, huh?" Bennie said.

"South."

"North, South—Dakota's Dakota. Good place to be from."

"You may be right about that. And I want you to know I appreciate your putting me up this way, Mr. Epstein."

"Listen, you gonna stay awhile, you gotta call me Bennie."

Her smile widened. "Bennie. Anyway, I do appreciate it, your kindness."

"Hey, ain't nothin'," he said, dismissing his own benevolence with a toss of a hand. "It's like I was tellin' your brother here, be good to have some company around the house."

Waverly glanced at him sharply. All these sunny sentiments. It was not exactly the reinforcement he was looking for. He was about to put in a dampening word but before he could get it out, the dog trotted over to Bennie and stuck its head in his crotch and sniffed noisily.

"Electra!" Val snapped, command voice. "Behave!"

"It's okay," Bennie said. "She been eyeballin' me ever since I got up. Wantin' to get acquainted, ain't you, girl—huh? huh? huh?" He ran a flat hand down the dog's sinewy back, scratched vigorously behind the folded ears.

"I think you made a friend," Val said.

"Yeah, mutts and kids, they just naturally love old Uncle Bennie." As if in confirmation, the dog's backside wiggled joyously.

"I hope she won't be too much trouble."

"No trouble 't'all. More a that company I was sayin'."

He was waltzing around something here, this self-proclaimed object of universal affection, beast and child alike; and so to head him off Waverly asked Val, "When are you supposed to meet this . . . person?"

Her eyes drifted to the softening light at the window. "Oh, any time now," she said vaguely.

"Any time," Waverly repeated. He had the orderly man's meager patience with imprecision. "Nothing more specific than that?"

"He said to come by around seven. Thereabouts."

Bennie checked his watch. "Ain't quite half-past six. You got lots time. Better pull up a chair and pack in some chow."

"No thanks, Mr.—"

He put a reminder finger in the air.

She said his given name.

"You sure? That birdseed you was eatin' before, that wouldn't keep a parakeet airborne."

"Those were sunflower seeds. Raw." Now her eyes strayed over the arc of Epstein belly bulging his plaid sport jacket marvelously. "You should try some."

Bennie leaned forward, balanced his paunch between outspread thighs, and gave it a proprietary thump. "Might at that. Wouldn't hurt none, drop a little this tonnage."

"I could help you with a diet," she said earnestly. "If you're interested, that is."

"There's an idea. Take some meat off me, put it on your brother. Even trade. Whaddya think, Timothy?"

What did he think? They were talking about diets, and they wanted his thoughts? He was thinking how his life, disordered enough, had taken a messy and potentially dangerous fork in the past twenty-four hours. Even as he'd feared. As this bizarre corkscrew conversation testified. Diets. Jesus. He said, "I think we've got a couple of other matters to occupy us. More urgent even than our respective weights."

"Oh, I dunno," Bennie replied, tugging a dewlap judiciously. "It's good health that counts, y'get down to it."

Valerie seconded this salutary opinion. "He's right, you know, Tim. You ought to take better care of yourself. Both of you."

"Which is why company like this girl's best kind to have. Put you onto some right habits, for a change."

Valerie beamed at him. Bennie winked back. The two of them in league, sharing an arcane wisdom. Then, with a studied nonchalance, as though it had just now occurred to him, Bennie said to her, "Speakin' a company, you get a chance to meet our friend Roger this mornin'?"

"Oh yes. But only for a moment. He was leaving when I came in."

"Nice fella, Roger."

"He seems very intelligent."

"He's a professor."

"I know. He told me."

"We had a real interestin' talk last night."

"Which is the first time we ever met him," Waverly interjected. "Last night." Neither of them responded, and for a moment he had the curious sensation of having said nothing at all. He tried again. "So he hardly qualifies as a 'friend.'"

"Still a decent guy, old Rog. Not like your average creepazoid you run up against, this town. I'd've liked to rap some more with 'im, but I was all tweaked out when he left. And he ain't in the phone book."

"He gave me his number," Valerie said brightly.

"No kiddin'?"

Waverly glared at him. So this was what the stutterstep dance was all about. Bennie deliberately avoided his eyes.

"He says it's unlisted," Valerie went on, eager to help. "To keep the students from bothering him. I can give it to you, if you like. I know he enjoyed speaking with you and Tim."

"Hey, that'd be terrific."

"Do you have something to write on?"

"You betcha." He produced pen and small notebook from an inside jacket pocket. She recited the number. He scribbled it down, looked at her with genuine admiration. "Got it by heart, huh."

"I always remember numbers."

"Sorta like Timothy here, that way."

"We're a lot alike," she said, fixing her brother with a fond, ruminative gaze. "In some ways."

Waverly shook his head slowly, wearily. The sensation he was feeling now was that of a man knee-deep in quicksand. Or cornered on the roof of a burning tower. Trapped on a runaway train. Snared in the vortex of a gathering whirlwind. Name your image of impending disaster, that's how he felt. And since it was clearly useless, this time in fact he uttered not a word.

"Well," Valerie said, putting something into the ambiguous silence, "expect I'd better get started."

She summoned the dog, stooped over, and murmured something unintelligible in its ear. Electra's almond-shaped eyes took on an alert expression, remarkably close to cognition, as though the coded commands were perfectly decipherable, a behavioral blueprint.

"Don't you worry none about the pooch," Bennie assured her. "She gonna be just fine."

"I'm sure she will. She has her instructions."

"So you break a leg now, hear?"

"Do my best."

Waverly came to his feet. "I'll walk you to the car."

An indolent breeze stirred the chill desert air. Twilight shadows fell across the Impala, the street, both their faces. A few blocks away a sheen of neon burnished the gradually blackening sky.

"Can you find your way?" Waverly asked, and immediately regretted the question, its heavy-handed phrasing.

"I found my way here, didn't I? Across the country."

"You know what I mean."

"I know. I'll find it."

"You're sure you don't want me to come along? Final offer."

"No, it really wouldn't do for you to be there, Tim."

"Not a true enough believer, huh?"

"Something like that. It's nothing personal."

Waverly shrugged. He handed her a key to the house.

"What's this?"

"So you can get in. Chances are we won't be here when you get back."

"You lock your house?"

Waverly resisted an impulse to spin his eyes heavenward. "Out here we lock," he said.

"Where are you going?"

"To work."

"You have a job?"

With an effort of will he held his eyes steady. "In a manner of speaking."

"What kind?"

"We lay selected wagers, Bennie and I."

She tilted her head, looked at him curiously. "Wagers? Gambling?"

"That's right. That's what we do. I thought you knew."

"You've never said."

"Well, now you know."

She hesitated. Destitute of words.

"It's not a totally dishonorable calling," he said.

"No, no, but it seems so . . . out of character. Nothing like what you were raised to be."

In a voice harsher than he intended, Waverly said, "That was a long time ago. In another life."

"I suppose it was," she said wistfully.

For a moment they stood in silence by the door of their father's time-scored Impala, these two strangers, brother and sister, linked to the misty country of the past by an isthmus of memory dense and bleak, eclipsing even blood. Finally Waverly said, "You'd better get moving."

The spell broken, she gave him a quick hug, slipped behind the wheel, pumped the gas pedal, turned the ignition key, and brought the car to a shuddering start. "Wish me luck," she said.

Luck. The currency of this fantastic blighted city. Here not twenty-four hours and already she was petitioning it. Or him to supply it. And looking into the sober mystery of her face, stitched now with the same hope and doubt and resolution he'd seen on the faces at a thousand tables across a million spreads of cards, Waverly had to wonder at the contagion of luck, the malignancy of chance, and to despair at the weight of this new and unsought obligation thrust upon him. Nevertheless, with a confidence he felt not at all, he said, "You'll be fine, Val. However it comes out."

The car pulled away from the curb, pointed west toward Main Street.

"The other way," Waverly called after her, gesturing in the opposite direction.

She executed an awkward turn in the middle of the deserted street. Driving slowly past him, she poked her head out the window, smiled sheepishly, and said, "I knew that."

"Of course you did," Waverly muttered to himself, flagging her on and thinking how, in the days ahead, they were both of them going to need their full quota of luck.

Back inside, Waverly found his partner heaped easefully on the living room couch, bottle of Blue Ribbon in hand, mouth plugged by a cigar of such obscenely prodigal proportions it seemed to be smoking him. Pampering his bones, a little too contentedly. Electra skittered around him, nipping playfully at his heels.

"Lookit here, Timothy," Bennie said.

He set down the beer and held up a crust of bagel. The dog tensed, ready to lunge. Bennie made a no-no gesture, said in that wheedling purl adults will affect for animals and children, "C'mon, Electric, whaddya do? Show your Uncle Timothy what you can do."

The dog sat back on its haunches, looked at him expectantly.

"Whaddya do? Shake, right?"

Recognizing the promise in his voice, the dog lifted a forepaw and extended it toward him.

"Atta girl. Good girl. Now watch this part, Timothy."

He took the paw in one hand and shook it solemnly. With the other he tossed the crust at the ceiling. The dog lunged and, graceful as a gymnast, snagged it out of the air.

"See that," Bennie said, grinning hugely around the projectile stuck in the hole in his face. "Ain't that somethin'? Bet she jumped six feet off the floor. I oughta get into the mutt-trainin' business myself."

"Or the circus," Waverly suggested.

"Circus be good too."

"Maybe it's the bagel."

"Could be that. Gotta be some Hebe in this hedge-clipper, way she gobble 'em up."

"You're not supposed to feed her that stuff, you know."

"Aah, can't hurt. All you Waverlys too skinny. Even Electric here."

"It's Elec*tra*."

"Whatever. Still ain't healthy."

Waverly settled into a chair facing him. "Tell me, is the performance over now?"

"Performance?"

"The dog show."

"Yeah, that's about all I learned her so far."

"All right. Then let me say it again. One more time. What you're planning here, it's a mistake."

"Huh? What're you talkin', mistake?"

"You called him, didn't you," Waverly said evenly. Flat assertion, no question in it.

Bennie made innocent saucers of his eyes. "Called who?"

"Come on, Bennie."

"I called us a cab, is all."

"You're sure that's all?"

"Okay, okay, so I give him a quick jingle. What's the damage?"

"Why do I get the feeling we've had this conversation before? Florida's the damage. Michigan's the damage. We don't know who could be tracking us."

"Anybody trackin', they'd've found us by now."

"You don't know that."

"Four months, they was lookin', they'd find you."

"What about heat?"

"Particularly heat, all the stiffs you been collectin' lately. Speakin' a damage."

Waverly lit a cigarette. Nothing to say to that barbed zinger. Probably had it coming. But for him and his succession of reckless acts, they wouldn't be here now, playing shuck and dodge, scrambling to put something on their supper plates.

"So what you gotta do," Bennie continued, a little more gently, "is lighten up, boy. We're in the clear. Cashed but clear."

"Say you're right. Which is a pretty heavy assumption, but say you are. What's the good of stepping back into the glue?"

"Where's this glue? All's I'm doin' is meetin' our buddy Rog for a friendly glass of beer. Catch the last half of the game. Lions and Pack playin' tonight and I got five big bills ridin' on our Michigan boys. To lose, 'course."

"Don't change the subject."

"Who's changin' it," he huffed. "Roger and me gonna pop back a few, take in the action. He said be sure and tell you to come too."

"Just a couple of sports fans. Cheering on your team."

"Somethin' wrong with that? If you ain't into your game, you shouldn't bet it."

"Especially roundball, right? Maybe you two boosters will talk a little roundball tonight?"

Bennie swept a hand through the air. Throwaway motion. "Topic could come up," he said.

"In passing, huh."

"Listen, Timothy, I ain't gonna lie to you. Sure, I'm gonna nose around some, see what I can turn up about our superspade Lafayette goin' in the tank. So what? Like I said before, pro'ly ain't nothin' to it anyways."

"Suppose there is?"

"There is, we got us a little extra stroke."

"For Christ's sake," Waverly said, and with a vehemence that surprised even himself, "why can't you leave it alone?"

"Why? Tellya why. Score like this come along—what?—maybe once a lifetime. If then. Hit on it, you could crack the slab. Be on rails, livin' large again. Like you and me just naturally suppose to be. Get you off the five and dime bee jay tables and back into mainline action. Where you belong."

"So this is for my own good, is that it?"

"Yeah, you might say that."

"All right, now you listen. You're going to do what you want. But this one I'm sitting out. You understand that, Bennie?"

"Nobody said you gotta be in it. I say that?"

"That includes my share of our nut."

Bennie's baggy face furrowed thoughtfully. His numbers-crunching expression. By now, all these years, Waverly knew it well. Numbers shading easily into money, and for B. Epstein money was the narrow portal that framed his world and through which he measured all its teeming phenomena and events and inhabitants. A measure exact, reliable, and utterly unclouded by lofty sentiment. The cigar shuttled back and forth in his mouth, will of its own. Eventually it came to rest in one corner, and the other elevated in a shrewd half-smile. "Hey, what're we arguin' here, partner? Handful a zip."

"So far it's zip."

A stiff silence opened between them. The dog, sensing something, went back to nipping Bennie's heels. He gave her an affectionate pat. And since space, any space, without words was to him vaguely discomfiting, he said conversationally, "You get your sis pointed the right way?"

"More or less. I don't know this town that well myself."

"Who's this swami she gonna see?"

"Somebody named Brewster."

"That's one scammer I never heard of."

"He's not in our line."

"Y'know, you ain't never talked much about her, Timothy. Your sis, I mean. How come that is?"

For a lengthening moment Waverly fell silent again. An image, quite unbidden, shaped in his head: the Waverly family gathered in the living room of their tidy home for the ritual Sunday night reading; he and Val, children again, seated on the floor, listening dutifully; their father in a cushy chair, puffing a pipe and nodding wisely; their mother standing by the mantel over the fireplace, text in hand, delivering the lines, in this image, of Cowper's (pathetic mad innocent Cowper) "The Castaway," her melancholy voice trembling on the edge of tears as she closed in on the final desolate stanza, the words of which escaped him; and in this deepening reverie he ransacked his memory for them now, a clue perhaps to the somber fatalism bred into his genes, the very marrow of his bones. Till an Epstein finger snap yanked him back.

"Hey, Timothy, where you at?"

"Uh, nowhere. Here."

"Coulda fooled me. Minute there you looked like you just come off a holiday in the Jacktown hole. All's I'm askin' here's a little family history."

"Yeah, well, it's a long story."

"Could be a long wait. You know them cab jockeys."

"Some other time, Bennie."

But he was wrong, Bennie was, about the wait. A few minutes later a horn sounded in the street. Waverly pulled on a jacket, straightened his tie. His go-to-work outfit. Bennie offered the dog the remainder of the bagel and some parting words of comfort. And to Waverly he said, "You ready to go bust some moves?"

"Ready as I'm going to be," Waverly said, his voice softened now with resignation, as if in obedience to a destiny he was powerless to control. As if at last he understood and accepted the arrival of that moment when his life was about to take a new slant in its relentless progress toward disaster.

Out in the cab Bennie directed the driver: "You know Sneakers? Over by Eastern and Tropicana?"

The driver knew it.

"Drop me off at the D.I.," Waverly said.

"Sure you don't wanna come along? Take a night off?"

"I'm sure."

"Okay, I'll pop by around midnight. See how they slappin' for you."

"Come alone. We've got enough company for now."

12

"Can you feel it, Cleanth?"

"Huh? Feel what?"

"The voltage. The energy. It's very high."

"You mean the lights over there, Strip?"

With only the slightest shade of annoyance Eggs said, "It's our project I'm referring to, Cleanth."

Click didn't know what the fuck he was talking about—voltage, energy—but after seeing that number he done on them two box-lunchers this afternoon, Click figured it was maybe best to agree. "Yeah, she's high all right."

"It's always this way for me at the start of a new venture," Eggs went on ruminantly. "Rather like a fresh infusion of the life force. Almost a resurrection, one might say."

Click's sausage fingers drummed the wheel of the Lincoln impatiently. He sat with his shoulders bunched, head craning back and forth, searching for a break in the flow of traffic hurtling down Flamingo. No break. The sun had fallen like a stone, and a cold glitter of stars streaked the black sky. Already they were running behind time, and the one thing for sure Brewster wasn't large on was late. And here's Eggs woofin' about life forces and resurfuckinrections, lookin' like he swallowed a chill pill, for all that energy gas. So the only thing Click was feeling just then was fried nerves. So he said, though still very cautiously, "Y'know, Egger, over to the Center it's mostly pretty quiet. Ain't a lot a that voltage you was sayin'."

"So much the better," said Eggs, quite unperturbed.

"What I mean is, he ain't exactly your stand-up comedian, Brewster. Fact is, he's most time so goddam sour he make them faces on that mountain out west—forget the name—y'know the one, got them faces on it?—" His own face screwed up in the effort of recollection.

"That's Mt. Rushmore you're thinking of."

"That's the one."

"And it's east of here, by the way."

"Yeah, well, wherever it's at, he'd make 'em look like smile buttons. Them faces, I mean."

"Better still. In my experience it's much easier to work on a sober mark."

"That ain't gonna be no pro'lum. He don't drink. Comes to drinkin', he gets real dicked."

"Sober as in solemn, Cleanth," Eggs said with a small sigh. "Serious men. They have so many secret yearnings and dreads."

A gap opened in the string of cars. Click peeled a leftie out of the apartment complex entrance and headed west, tooling along fast as he dared. But at the Strip intersection the light went red on him. Stalled again. Under his breath he cursed softly.

Eggs appeared untroubled by the momentary delay. He gazed placidly at the dazzle of lights; the pulsating phallus soaring into the air, marking the Dunes; the illuminated fountains of Caesar's; Bally's towering marquee announcing some has-been entertainer. It was the sight of the latter seemed to spark a memory, and he said, indicating the hotel, "Do you recall the fire there, Cleanth? When it was the Grand?"

"Yeah, sure, I remember. Didn't see it, though."

"I saw it. Quite a spectacle."

Click didn't give a shit about the fire. Only fire worrying him was the one got to be scorching Brewster's ass right about now. But he said anyway, for a thing to say, "You seen it, huh."

"I remember it vividly," Eggs replied, his voice mellow with reminiscence. "I was standing on the corner over there, across the street. From that angle you could see all those people at the windows on the upper floors. Trapped, smoke billowing up behind them. You could hear their screams. Hoping someone would arrive to save them. Praying, no doubt."

"When was that again?" Click asked, even though he couldn't care less. He was doing some prayin' himself, fuckin' frozen light would turn. All the good it did.

"Back in '80. You know, Cleanth, it was very instructive, watching it. I was particularly curious to see what choice they'd make: death by fire or fall. Consumed by flames or splattered on the pavement." He paused a moment, tilted his head in thought, and when he resumed his voice dipped, mildly disappointed. "As I recall, no one jumped, or if they did I missed it."

Click snuck a sideways peek at him. Fuck, he didn't know what to say to that. Mercifully, the light turned and so, occupied with steering the car around the corner and nosing it into the left lane, he was spared a reply. But seeing him sitting there wrapped in the memory, kind of a sad dreamy smile on his face, like he was sorry he didn't get to see a leaper, Click was thinking how even though the Egg Man was the best digger in the business, absolutely—hustle the Holy Mother Mary right out of her drawers—how, no getting away from it, he was a little scooters too. Maybe that's how you hadda be, be that good. Still could make a man jumpy, bein' around him too much. Least he was in a better mood tonight than when he snapped that one muff-muncher's arm and flattened the other one's honker for her. Which gotta be worth something.

At Spring Mountain Road he hung another left, and the blaze of the Strip slowly ebbed behind them. Since the Center was coming right up, and since so far Eggs hadn't volunteered a word about how he was looking to take Brewster off, Click inquired guardedly, "Uh, you got any ideas on how we gonna slide into this one?"

"No, nothing specific yet. I think of this initial encounter as purely reconnaissance."

"Re-huh?"

"Sizing him up, Cleanth. It's of first importance to get a sense of the man before one can uncover his blind side."

"I tellya, he got one, I sure as fuck ain't seen it, all'a time I been workin' for him."

"Everyone has one. It's simply a matter of discovery. Perception. Which is no small part of the allure of the game, wouldn't you say?"

"S'pose it is," Click agreed, wishing all the while he had a partner talked American. Forget that. But there was something else, been puzzling him ever since Eggs showed up at the door tonight solo, so he said, "This sizin' up, that how come you didn't bring the fluff along?"

Eggs frowned at the reference to Dawnette. "That, and her semi-hysterical condition after this afternoon's unfortunate . . . commotion. Also those bruises under her eyes. Certainly we want her looking her best. If and when we need her."

Click didn't know how she come by them bruises, but no way was he gonna ask. He could figure. And anyway there was the Center dead ahead, so he swung into the narrow parking area out front and pulled to a stop. "This here's the place," he declared.

Eggs read the sign above the door silently. He shook his head in an ironic way and repeated aloud, "Quantum Healing, Attitudinal Awareness . . . this is a shrewd player, our Wyman Brewster. Either that or a madman."

He leaned over and checked his appearance in the rearview mirror. Patted at his sculpted hair, adjusted the knot in his tie, plucked some imagined lint from a sleeve of his glistening saddle-tan silk suit. And then he did something so startling, so totally out of character, that Click's jaw dropped precipitously. For what Eggs did was remove the opaque glasses worn like a set of primary eyes, and slip them inside his jacket pocket.

Click gawked at him. Couldn't help himself. "Y'know, Egger," he was moved to remark, "fucked if I remember ever seein' you without your shades." And looking into those wintry eyes, the real ones, he wasn't so sure he was glad for the opportunity now.

"In that world back there," Eggs explained patiently, signifying the back there with a nod in the direction of the Strip, "the glasses are functional. They serve a useful purpose. But not among your citizenry. For whatever reason, they seem to inspire a certain mistrust. So this is the Ignatius LaRevere you'll be seeing from now on. Till the successful conclusion of our project."

Another thing Click wasn't so sure about was the wisdom of his partner's decision, going it without the goggles. Not with them two icepicks he got on him. But he knew that wasn't the kind of thing you said to Eggs. So he said nothing, though his tongue produced the involuntary screak.

"How do I look otherwise?"

"Hey, look real fly, Eggo. Like you was one a them citizens yourself."

"Ignatius," Eggs corrected him. "In there you'll address me by my full name, of course."

"Oh, yeah, course. I'll remember."

"Good. Well, let's get on with it, shall we."

And remember Click did, after a fashion. "This is Mr. Ignatius LaRevere," he began in the stiffly formal accents of a schoolboy reciting a piece committed to uncertain memory. "Gentleman I was tellin' you about. Y'know . . . this mornin' . . . on rounds . . ." He trailed off, grinning weakly.

Brewster gave it a moment, but when nothing more was forthcoming he rose and came out from behind an imposing mahogony desk and extended a welcoming hand. "You must forgive Cleanth," he said. "Sometimes he forgets the ordinary graces. I am Wyman Brewster."

Eggs gazed upward into a craggy face whose dominant features were lips so bloodless and mouth so thin it had the appearance of an ancient bleached scar. Also eyes that, in testimony to Click's earlier estimate, seemed to measure the world with a severe and humorless gravity. His height was truly daunting, accentuated as it was by a posture rigid as an I-beam, elevating him above that profane fallen world. His suit, funerary black, further distanced him from the tarnished common clay. A remote man. Eggs grasped the hand and returned the faint squeeze. "Mr. Brewster," he said, striking just the right note of deference, "it's an honor to meet you, sir. I've heard extraordinary things about you and your work."

Brewster nodded tightly, accepting homage as his rightful due.

With the released hand he indicated a woman seated opposite the desk. "Miss Valerie Waverly, may I present Cleanth Koontz, my valued assistant here at the Center, and Mister, ah, your name again—?"

"LaRevere," Eggs supplied for him. The woman's presence added an unforeseen dimension to the meeting, one he hadn't allowed for. Nevertheless, he made a reflex bow, Click flicked a saluting finger off a brow, and she gave them back a sweet, churchy smile.

Introductions complete, Brewster beckoned them into the room, motioned them into chairs. On the desk was an elegant tea service, its surface, pure silver, catching the light off the overhead bulb, sparkling. "Would you care for refreshment?" he asked.

"Please," said Eggs.

Click shook his head. "Think maybe I'll pass tonight."

"This is an Ayur-Veda seasonal tea," Brewster explained in tones lenient, composed, but with a look at his valued assistant that dispatched an unmistakable reproach, just short of warning. "Of the Vata blend, formulated to provide a soothing influence in cool dry weather. Such as now. You owe it to yourself to sample this product, Cleanth."

Eggs caught it, that look, and so evidently did Click, who replied meekly, "Yeah, okay, I'll try a cup. It's gettin' kinda raw outside."

Brewster poured, and while his back was turned Eggs seized the moment for a quick visual sweep of the room, collecting details, processing them. Windowless, it was amply sized but made to appear smallish by all the crammed-in furnishings: the huge desk backed by a row of metal file cabinets, above which hung a pair of execrable prints depicting birds in flight; semicircle of facing chairs, presumably to accommodate a reverent audience; Naugahyde couch along one wall, shelf jammed with books, ponderous-looking volumes, on the other; fleecy mouse-colored carpet covering the floor. Altogether, it had the cluttered feel of a cut-rate furniture showroom: too much to display, too little space. If a man's office is a reflection of his character, then this one bespoke a constricted, claustrophobic personality. Not, in Eggs's experience, among the easiest to pry into. Tread cautiously now, he reminded himself.

Brewster handed him a delicate china cup full of the steamy brew. Another for Click. He stood over them watchfully, awaiting a reaction. Eggs sipped, arranged his face in a judicious expression, allowed, "Very aromatic. Interesting tang to it."

"That would be the touch of asperwillow, included for its cleansing properties."

Click looked down at the murky yellowish liquid, hesitated, then took a heroic gulp, thinking, Yeah, sure, touch a this, tang a that, you ask him tasted like somebody drained his dragon in it. Nobody asked.

Brewster resumed his place behind the desk. "My apologies," he said, sounding not in the least contrite, "for stumbling over your name, Mr. LaRevere."

"Quite all right. It's not as though it were a Smith."

"Coincidentally, Valerie and I were discussing the illuminating quality of the given name just before you arrived."

"Really," said Eggs, noncommittal. He hadn't the vaguest idea what this was about, or where it was leading.

Brewster fastened him with a piercing pedantic stare, and with all the assurance of the man who steers a conversation anywhere he likes said, "Consider hers, for example. Valerie. Valor—ee. The *valor* manifestly emblematic of the courage required to uproot her life and journey across the country in search of a higher wisdom. And the final *ee* syllable plainly resonant with delight at her discovery." He shifted the stare onto her. "Would you say this is an accurate analysis, Valerie?"

"I'm not so sure about the courage," she said modestly, "but the wisdom and the discovery and the joy, all those are right."

Brewster's pale lips stretched open in an effort at a humble smile. She gazed at him worshipfully, her face shining.

"Fascinating theory," Eggs remarked. "Tell me, what would you make of your own name?"

"My name?" Brewster asked rhetorically and, lips pursing now, eyes inward-turning, self-enchanted, furnished the answer. "Wyman. Why-man. I suspect it was ordained, fated. A reference to my lifelong quest for an understanding of that baffling mystery, the why of mankind, and the whither. The universal question, cosmic riddle."

He droned on awhile, tracking the cosmos for them, but Eggs soon gave up listening, though he continued to show an attentive face. He was thinking about himself, his thoughts drawn inevitably to his own name, Ignatius, that quaint anachronism passed on to him from his father's father. Ig-nay-shus, its initial sound identical to the opening syllable in *igneous*, for fire, fiery volcanic rock; its second a resolute negation of all the contemptible strictures and constraints laid on lesser men, a nay in thunder; and the last, what other than a serpentine hiss, a silencing. And astonishingly, he found himself wondering if there could be something to it after all, all this oracular wheeze. No. Preposterous. Absurd.

Eventually, the universe properly charted, Brewster ran down. He squared knob-knuckled hands on the desk, refocused his eyes, and brought them back on Eggs. His get-to-business stare. "Well, I go on interminably. And of course that's not why you're here, to listen to my wandering reflections. How may I be of service, Mr. LaRevere?"

"Quite the contrary," Eggs protested, "I can only wish I'd been privileged to hear these reflections, as you put it, three years ago. When they might have made a difference."

"A difference? In what way?"

"My wife," Eggs said, and he was off and spinning a mournful tale of a cancer-stricken spouse, cold negligent doctors, white hospital worlds, barbarous treatments, unspeakable agonies, the slow creep of death, its stark finality; investing his wholly extemporized account with names, dates, venues, for authenticity, and his voice with a fluttery blend of outrage and sorrow, for effect. He concluded, a little choke of grief catching in his throat.

After a moment's decent doleful silence Brewster said, "This is a melancholy story. I could have saved her, you know."

Eggs produced a sad wry smile. "Unfortunately, we'll never know now, will we."

"It is sufficient for me that I know," Brewster intoned, a slight testiness edging his voice.

"I'd like to believe that. Even though it's much too late for

Amy." (For that was the name he had given the fictitious wife. Why, he wasn't sure. The *aim* in it, possibly, an aside to the fantastic theory. A little joke.)

"Be assured, you *can* believe," Brewster declared stoutly. He reached behind him and ran an arm along the row of cabinets. "These files contain the records of my outreach program. Patients from all over the country, the world, suffering all manner of allegedly terminal ailments. Not unlike your late wife. And routinely restored to vibrant good health. There are cases here you would call miracles, Mr. LaRevere. Testament to the efficacy of my work."

Eggs hesitated just a beat. "You asked why I'm here," he said. "I expect that's the reason. To learn more about your work."

"Very flattering. But to what end, might I ask? You yourself appear to be in sound health."

Eggs pinched his brows together. Earnest perplexity. "I'm not certain. It's unclear to me yet. If this work of yours is everything you say it is, I'd like to, well, contribute. In some small way." He gave it another studied beat and then, gaze lowered, the catch back in his throat, added, "In her memory."

"There are many ways to contribute," Brewster said carefully.

Now it was his turn to invoke the pregnant pause. Masters of timing, both of them, and in this game timing, balance, pacing was all. And when Eggs glanced up again it was into a coolly detached face projecting an aura of bottomless wisdom painfully acquired through the acceptance of awesome responsibility, colossal burden. But an aura flawed by a trace of a spark of eagerness in the eyes, oh so infinitesimal, but enough to give him away.

Before either of them could take it any further, the woman made a move to rise, saying timidly and mostly to Brewster, "I really should be leaving. You have things to discuss."

He put up an arresting hand. "No, please. I'd like you to stay. We're all of us just chatting here, getting acquainted."

Obediently she sank back in the chair, the same impossibly sweet smile stuck on her face, looking as though she existed in another, more rarefied element, a Neptune dweller. Eggs had no idea what to make of her, this courageous Valerie somebody, or where exactly she fit in. Disciple? Protégée? Squeeze? No way to tell.

In partial explanation Brewster said to him and, peripherally, to Click, "Valerie will be joining us in our work. She's an excellent case in point, that matter we were just speaking of. Her contribution will be through her time and effort and dedication."

"Hey, no kiddin'," Click said. "Welcome aboard."

Eggs offered his well-wishes.

She thanked them both. Sweetly, of course, and beaming with joy.

Brewster poured more tea all around, in celebration of the happy moment.

And so it wore on, an hour or better, Brewster and Eggs directing the talk, guiding it warily: probe, advance, fall back, dodge, weave, thrust, parry, the object of the verbal contest being to circle in as close as possible to that incendiary word *money* without getting burned. And when the get-acquainted chat was finished, both were left unsinged.

"Most enjoyable conversation," Brewster said, ushering Eggs and Click to the door, Valerie gliding along at his side. "I do hope we'll have the opportunity to speak again."

"I'm confident we will," said a faintly smiling Eggs, thinking how this was going to be no mean antagonist, this Why-man Brewster, healer; but thinking also how much he was going to enjoy taking him down when the time came, toppling him.

"So whaddya think?" Click wanted to know just as soon as he turned the key in the ignition and swung the car out of the lot.

"About what?"

"What? 'Bout the place. Brewster. Whole setup."

"You want my first impressions?"

"That's what I'm askin' here."

They were a long way from clear yet, that welter of impressions fogging Eggs's head; longer still from crystallizing into a glimpse of a shape of a plan. Solitude was what he needed now, for quiet deliberation, a sorting out. Not likely here, not in the narrow confines of a moving vehicle, a brain-dead sideman yammering puerile questions at you. What did he think? He didn't know. But in the absent voice people will sometimes use to speak to themselves, he said,

"Well, for one thing, the place, this so-called Center, it fairly levitates with sanctimony."

Click sucked in a husky breath, held it an instant, and then let it go on a long vexed sigh. "C'mon, man, you ain't back inside there no more. An' I ain't Brewster. Talk plain, huh."

"Plain," Eggs echoed. "Very well, plain. Plainly, it's difficult to escape the conclusion the man is utterly mad."

There's a hoot, Click was thinking, comin' outta Mr. World-Class Wiggers himself there. Talk about your pot and kettle. Takes one to spot one, he supposed. Also ain't exactly your front page news either, Brewster bein' unzipped upstairs. Fuck, he already told him that. Which is what he repeated now: "What'd I say? Tol' you he was bughouse."

"So you did. But there are all kinds of what you choose to call bughouse, Cleanth. And his is very special, close to unique. More on the order of a gift, I should say. Perhaps the greatest gift known to man: the art of minting money without work."

"Hear him tell it, that's all he does is work. All'a time bustin' ass, savin' the goners."

"You miss the point," Eggs said, uncertain himself precisely what that point was but letting his disjointed thoughts, impressions, ideas, notions, speculations—letting them all unroll now, enlarge on their own. "You see, Cleanth, for all his lunacy—and about that you were right, absolutely—but for all of it, in spite of it, or maybe because of it, he has the native cunning, the venom—call it a lordly flintiness of the heart—to love his fellow man unconditionally, but only in the abstract and—most significant of all—strictly for profit." He laid his hands in his lap, fingers laced. Looked straight ahead. Preoccupied yet, but steadier now, and not displeased with his assessment. Maybe giving voice to your thoughts was of some utility after all.

Click restrained a follow-up sigh. This was his idea, plain? "So you're sayin' he's into scammin' too, Brewster?"

"Not in the sense you use the term."

"How then?" Click persisted.

"It's a kind of schizophrenia, Cleanth. An unshakable faith in his own demented vision, but with a shrewd appreciation of the loot that vision can generate."

Click, thoroughly baffled now, and more than a little exasperated, said, "Okay. Okay. So you got him pegged for a one oar. A maybe scammer jacket on him. So how you figure we gonna nail him?"

Eggs unlaced his fingers and turned up empty palms. "I don't know."

"Got no ideas a'tall? None?"

Eggs considered a moment. "Dawnette," he said finally. "Perhaps we'll put him to the Dawnette Day test."

"Y'mean sic her onto him? Why'd you wanta do that?"

"Why? I should think it would be obvious. Surely you noticed the way he was leering at that Valerie woman. The old lecher."

"That bone bag!" Click exclaimed skeptically. "C'mon, Eggs, all's she'd do is shrink your gear for ya. Anyways he looks at everybody that way. Like he's scopin' what's goin' on inside your head."

"I think you're mistaken. On both counts. The woman has a certain ethereal appeal. And our Mr. Brewster his share of the goatish appetites, however much repressed. Dawnette may be just the instrument for unlocking them. It's a place to begin."

Fuck's he talkin' about now?—ether, goats, appetites, instruments. Click, he could use some a that ether himself, all the gas he'd been listenin' to today. "I dunno," he said, still unconvinced. "Comes to pussy, he's like a preacher. Or a goddam monk. Fuck, he couldn't tell a joy hole from a exhaust pipe."

Eggs had extracted all he could from this coarse and directionless talk. All he wanted. "You know, Cleanth," he said wearily, "there are times when you remind me of Hobbes's definition of life: nasty, brutish, and short. Think about it."

"Huh? Who's this Hobbes?"

"Never mind. Don't trouble your head with any more of it tonight. Trust me, the most mystifying problems have a way of yielding to patience. And experiment. And—" turning his face to the window, signaling conversation's end "—time."

13

For all his cultivated vacancy of expression, the dealer had a readable tell, an ever-so-swift adder flick of the tongue when there was power in the cellar, and a tiny tuck of the underlip when there was none. Not much of either, but you take your edge where you find it. And so in spite of the shifting parade of steamers at the table, cowboys and chumps betting on dreams, Waverly was ahead five bills after as many hours of play. So it was shaping up a decent night's take. Decent, anyway, by the measure he'd grown accustomed to lately. Or resigned to. Nobody ever got rich off red-check action.

Midway into a shoe he was conscious of the air behind him suddenly odorous of beer and cigar smoke. One thing about his partner, he was never going to catch you by surprise. "They comin' your way?" Bennie whispered in his ear.

Waverly lifted a hand and waggled the fingers, a stilling gesture. He had the count secured in his head and it was live and he wasn't in a humor to let it slip away on a current of results chatter. He won the hand, tripled the bet, won again, tripled again, lost, dropped back to the base unit, a lowly five, took that one and then, because the tally was still plus twelve, pushed out ten red chips, caught a fourteen against dealer ace, read the giveaway tell, stood, and waited for the hapless dealer to bust a soft sixteen. Which he did. Waverly gathered in his chips. Bennie gave him a cautioning nudge. The dealer glanced at him narrowly. Not a quick study, but coming around. So he backed off, held his bet flat for the remainder of the shoe, deliberately tanking a couple of hands. He wanted to play here again.

At the shuffle he stood and rotated his neck, slow motion. His shoulders felt starched and tingly, rest of him numb.

"Cramp time, huh," Bennie said in a small commiseration.

"Yeah, you might say."

"How's the backside?"

"Granite."

"You wanna pack it in?"

He did and he didn't. Cards falling right; count under control, or reasonably under control; dealer with a telegraphic tic— conditions like these didn't come along often. Instinct told him to stick around for a second helping, fill up his plate while he could. But then there was also the nagging issue of Val, her meeting with Dr. Bizarro, its outcome. He had a stake in that game too, poten- tially bigger than any plodding five-and-dime play. The table would be here tomorrow night. Maybe even the same dealer. "All right," he said, reaching for his chips, "I'm ready."

The dealer nodded at Waverly's pile of reds. "Color 'em up?"

"That would be good."

He stacked them nimbly, gave Waverly back five blacks, three greens and a throwaway red. Waverly toked him a green, but from the neutral thanks he suspected he hadn't bought all that much goodwill.

On the way to the cashier's cage Bennie said, "You want a word advice?"

Want it or not, Waverly had the feeling he was going to hear it. "What would that be?"

"You gotta watch them wide swings. They gonna make you for sure."

"Betting off reds?"

"Reds, blacks—don't mean dog poop. Countin's countin'. Tagged once, tagged forever."

"Look," Waverly said, "I don't pick your teams for you, maybe you should let me play the cards."

Bennie shrugged. "Do it your way."

"Speaking of which, your teams, dare I ask how you did tonight?"

"You can ask. Sure you wanna know?"

"No, but tell me anyway."

"Well, I beat the spread easy. That part went good."

"Why do I think I hear a *but* in there."

"But is, I only laid half the nickel on the spread. Other half on the over/under. I took under, come in over. By two lame points." He held up two fingers in dramatic visual punctuation. "Two!"

They were at the cage now. Waverly slid his chips through a window and a surly woman converted them into bills. Five fifty-five. Not so bad. Depending, of course, on the balance of the B. Epstein news. "So you broke even," he said.

"Not exactly."

"How, 'not exactly'?"

"Also had a prop goin' on will there be a score, last two minutes."

"You neglected to mention that one."

"Musta slipped my mind."

"Now that it's come back, you want to cut to the bottom line?"

"I take no, right? Them two sandlot clubs, no way they gonna put points on the board after the warning buzzer. So what happens? Sixty seconds on the clock, Pack up by two TD's, sittin' on the ball midfield. Just dickin' around, right? Chewin' up time?"

"Bottom line, Bennie."

"Bottom line is they toss a what-the-fuck pass, scrub receiver—gotta be a hot dog, right?—he picks it outta the ozone, breaks a couple tackles, tap dances down the stripe and takes it in. One play and I'm whacked on the prop and the over/under, both."

"This prop—how much?"

Bennie's eyes drifted away. Under his breath he mumbled, " 'Nother nickel."

Waverly heard it but he said anyway, "You want to give me that again?"

"Nickel."

"Nickel," Waverly said, his voice flat, accusatory. Demanding of an explanation.

"Hey, what can I tellya? They woulda run out the clock—like they shoulda done—we'd be up a dime."

Would of, should of, could of—it occurred to Waverly how thoroughly their lives were governed by the conditional. As though they existed in a province of shimmery might-have-beens. The country of If. "I've got five five five here," he said. "You drop a nickel. Fifty-five net. For five hours' work. Seems five is our lucky number."

"Less the vigorish. You gotta figure that in too."

"Vigorish. Right. Can't forget the vigorish."

"C'mon, Timothy, that's the sportin' life. Sometimes you gonna lose. We ain't drowned yet."

"Let me check for a pulse. To be sure."

Bennie swatted the air. "Aah, you're just tired, boy. Let's bug outta here, go home and sink a brewhaha. Cheer you up."

They started for the entrance, threading through the tables and the crowds swarming the platoons of slots. Like a dim alert flashed behind his eyes, it struck Waverly that his partner was entirely more philosophic than he ought to be, given the night's numbers. And as they neared the door, Bennie remarked casually, "Oh yeah, forgot to tellya, Roger's waitin' out front."

Waverly laid his head in the palm of a hand. Roger. Sure. Why not. The natural perigee of a bottomed-out day.

But he was mistaken. There were depths yet to be plumbed before the evening was over.

"Hazard," Pettibone was declaiming, the battered Mercury his rolling lecture hall, its wheel his makeshift podium, "from the French *hasard*, which in turn may have roots in the Arabic *az-zahr*, meaning dice."

"No kiddin'," said Bennie, doing the gee-whiz number broadly and wide-eyed. Overdoing it, to Waverly's thinking. "That's where craps comes from, huh, them ragheads."

"Not the game," Pettibone corrected him, "whose origins are murky. Old as manunkind. But the word, possibly. Consider it. Hazard. The enigma of chance reduced to a pair of innocuous little cellulose cubes. Remarkable, when you think about it."

"Y'know, that's real interestin', Rog, way you put that. Ain't that interestin', Timothy?"

Waverly, slumped in the back seat, said, "Real."

"Roulette, on the other hand, may be traceable," Pettibone chugged on, following his inebriate chain of association wherever it veered, enraptured of his own slurry voice, the interminable whiplash of words issuing headlong from his mouth. "Did you know it may have been invented—created, more accurately—by none other than Blaise Pascal? Did you know that?"

Neither of them knew it. Or even, in Bennie's case, who the fuck this Pascal dude was. But he did know for sure where they were at, and so in gentle prompting he said, "Uh, Rog, that corner up ahead, that's Garces. You wanta turn there."

Pettibone jerked the wheel abruptly and swung the car into an onrushing stream of traffic, giving motorized definition to his word *hazard*. Brakes screeched. A blast of horns trailed them down the dark street. The monologue, however, skipped not a beat. "Now your blackjack," he continued, secure in the perfect isolation bubble of the God-shielded drunk, "is a cerebral game, unlike those other two. Game with a memory. A player's destiny is—or can be—at least partly in his own hands. As who should know better than you, Timothy."

Waverly ignored the question, if question it was. More likely a breath-catching caesura in the torrent of words. Down the block the Impala took shape in the shadows along the curb. The house was awash in light. "Look like your sis found her way okay," Bennie remarked cheerfully.

Well, literally maybe. Some small relief. The rest remained to be seen. Which is what Waverly said: "We'll see."

But what he saw when he came through the door was enough to render him wordless. There stood Val, clearly waiting for them, dog at her side, uncertain smile on her face. And around her, front to back, the place was scrubbed, swept, mopped, vacuumed, dusted, polished, straightened, deodorized—name your sanitizing procedure, it had been done. Immaculate. Spotless. All but unrecognizable. Even Bennie was dumbstruck. But not, of course, Pettibone, who lurched into the room clutching a jug of V.O., glanced about blearily, and declared, "It appears the excellent Miss Valerie has restored order out of chaos."

"The house needed some cleaning," she said with understated charity, almost apologetic. "I hope you don't mind."

Bennie finally found stammery voice. "Mind?—nah—just we ain't ever—well—seen it like this in here—before. We're real happy you went to all this trouble."

"It was no trouble." She looked at Waverly expectantly. "Tim?"

"You do good work, Val," he said. "Always did."

Her smile enlarged. A pink blush rose in her cheeks. "Please, sit. I've got marvelous news."

Waverly took one of the chairs. Since lately trouble was the certain tidings he could count on with every dispatch, about the marvelous news he could pretty much guess. Bennie and Pettibone settled onto the couch. The dog scampered over and sampled the perfumes of their respective crotches, lingering at Bennie's and wriggling in doggy anticipation of another bagel feast.

"Electra!" Valerie commanded. "No! Sit!"

Reluctantly, the dog obeyed. Valerie remained standing.

"So what's this news?" Bennie asked. "Meetin' go good?"

"Better than good. Better than I'd ever hoped." She paused, gathered her breath. Her face seemed to glow with excitement. "I'm going to be *working with him!*"

"Hey, that's sensational. First day in Vegas and already you got yourself a job."

Pettibone, never to be excluded, inquired, "Working with whom, might I ask?"

"Fella name a Brewster," Bennie said.

"That name is unfamiliar to me."

"Runs one a them, y'know, wheat germ shops, health food stores."

"It's much more than a store," Valerie said. She shut her eyes, and her voice went strong, exultant. "It's a commitment. A cause."

Pettibone hoisted his bottle aloft. "And this, then, is cause for celebration. Drinks all around, I say."

"Hold on a minute," Waverly broke in, a lonely voice of reason in all the merry exuberance. "Is that what it means, Val, 'working with him'? A job?"

"Well," she said evasively, eyes open again but focused on the floor, "the pay's not much, not yet anyway. But, yes, it's a job."

"How much is 'not much'?"

"The amount doesn't matter, Tim."

"Matters to me. Should to you."

"I have some money put aside. Enough to get along. And I've never required much. You know that."

"So I do. Also do I know what it requires to live in this shifty town." He looked to Bennie for support. "Tell her."

"Yeah, well, costs a little, get by out here," Bennie allowed. "Course if you're careful . . ." he added trailing away.

Nice middling act. Some support. And even less from their self-invited juicer guest, who volunteered, unasked, "I would tend to agree with Valerie, Timothy. My thought is that honest work, regardless of wage, is the noblest pursuit of man. And perhaps the rarest, here in our city of hosts. As I'm sure Bennie would agree."

Bennie, Timothy, Valerie—getting to be a snug little family circle here. Everybody on first names, everybody with an opinion. "And I'm not so sure your 'thought' is significant," Waverly said coldly.

Pettibone looked startled. More puzzled than offended. Nobody talks to professors this way. It was Valerie to the defense. "He's right, Tim. Besides, it will get better soon. The money part, I mean."

"Really. And how is it that will happen?"

"Wyman has plans to build a clinic. For natural healing. He told me all about it. He has several potential backers. I even met one of them tonight. Awfully nice man."

Wyman, was it? The circle widening. Clinics, natural healing, potential backers (heavy on that *potential*), plans. Better than many, Waverly understood the treachery of plans. In the face of these fantastic dreams, he could think of not a thing to say.

So Pettibone supplied a response. "There you are," he pronounced in the summary inflections of a wise moderator, the issue satisfactorily resolved. He uncapped the bottle and tilted it toward his lips. "Let the celebration begin."

In the voice she had used on the dog, Valerie stayed him midtilt. "Roger, no. I've made us all some tea. Wait. I'll get it."

She vanished into the kitchen. Two quick trips and they each held a steaming cup. Pettibone looked at his gingerly. "Tea," he said, as though conferring the brew with a name. "Well, why not? Stranger things have been ingested."

"Actually, it's more an herbal beverage, a seasonal blend," Valerie explained, echoing her mentor. "Wyman gave it to me. Its therapeutic properties are truly miraculous, he says."

Pettibone elevated his cup in a stagy toast: "To Valerie Waverly, Las Vegas's latest, and least tarnished, citizen. And to her worthy cause of universal well-being. Welcome to America's adult playground."

Valerie, either innocent of the frosting of irony or willing to overlook it, smiled shyly. Waverly and Bennie lifted dutiful cups. Pettibone took a cautious sip, made a distressed face, set the cup on the floor and washed down the droplet of tea with a swig of V.O.

Valerie winced. "You don't like it, Roger?"

"Miraculous it may be," he said, "but as the proverb has it, one barrel of wine can work more miracles than a church full of saints. Or in this case a pot full of therapeutic tea."

She cast appealing looks at Bennie and Waverly.

Through a sickly grin Bennie lied, "Yeah, not bad. Got a bite to it."

Waverly tried a purgative dose of truth. "The hard fact is, Val, it tastes bitter. Almost acrid. And about the miracles, I think Roger may be right again."

"I'm sorry you don't like the tea," she said, stiffening some. "But you don't seem to understand the power of quantum healing. Herbal remedies, as a part of that healing continuum, can cure any illness."

"Any?"

"Yes."

"You're talking about the big ones? Something heavier than a head cold?"

"Any illness," she repeated. "Including what you call the 'big ones.' "

"You believe what you're saying here?"

"More than believe. I've seen it happen."

"This is delusional, Val."

Try as he might, it was impossible for Waverly to erase the impatience from his voice. Or the incredulity. Or the dismay. He knew his sister was out of balance, had been for years; just how far out he hadn't recognized. Till now. And now she was here. His responsibility. And the full weight of that burden was just now beginning to sink in.

"This time I'm afraid I must agree with your brother," Pettibone said, never at a loss for opinion and always prompt to share it. "Against Lord Death," he intoned with sudden and uncharacteristic somberness, "there are no remedies, for all one's generous sympathies on the side of life."

"No," she said flatly. "You're wrong. Both of you."

Bennie hauled himself off the couch, thumped his belly, and started for the kitchen. "All this sick rap, croakin' talk, it's too deep for me. Makin' me hungry."

"I put some rice cakes in the cupboard over the sink," Valerie said. "Why don't you try one."

"Sounds like just the ticket."

The dog tensed, looked at Valerie quizzically, saw nothing restraining in her face, and fell in behind him. Pettibone was launched on a disquisition on death, and so a moment later Waverly followed them into the kitchen.

Where he discovered his partner seated at the cleared and scrubbed-down table, enveloped in a cloud of cigar smoke, nursing the beer and munching a hunk of salami sandwiched between two of the rice cakes. His abandoned teacup sat on the counter. At his feet the dog gnawed contentedly on a tube of the meat.

"Y'know," Bennie said, "them cakes ain't half bad, you slap a little mayo on 'em."

But Waverly wasn't interested in any more gastronomy dialogues. There were matters to settle more urgent even than food. He pulled up a chair, said, "So what's going on, Bennie?"

"Whaddya mean, what's goin' on? 'Bout what?"

"About our guest in there."

"You talkin' about that roundball game, maybe snaked, maybe not?"

"You know what I'm talking about."

Bennie stuck the cigar in his mouth and batted at the curtain of smoke rising around him. "Aah, that's a clean wash. That one you can forget."

"You're saying you didn't try to pump him?"

"Course I tried. Never said I was gonna do no different. All the good it done me."

"He wouldn't tell you?"

"I put it to him, y'know, reasonable like. I says to him, I says—" and here, reconstructing his speech, he shifted into the fluid melodies of good common sense "—'Look, Rog, you're a professor, right? They can't be payin' you a whole lot, the schoolhousin' racket. Not what you're worth, anyways.' See—" he interjected, a shrewd winking aside "—I gotta grease him a little." And then he resumed, Mr. Horse Sense again, the molasses voice of sweet reason: " 'You know somethin' about a rigged game,' I says, 'here's your chance to ring the big bell, maybe even retire, go back to Thief Falls or wherever, you don't like it here. And you don't gotta *do* nothin',' I tells him, 'I'll handle the wagers, spread 'em around, little here, little there. Gonna go down anyway, nothin' you can do to stop it—what's the damage, pickin' up a few loose coins?' That's what I told him. Know what he said?"

"What did he say?"

"Says there ain't enough loot on God's green earth ever make him profit off a dirty little scam like the one we discussin'. That's what he calls it, dirty. You believe it? Man's on his own planet, musta gone to college at the University of Mars."

"So he told you nothing?"

"Closest I come to any true facts is he says now Lafayette's wafflin', maybe gonna deal himself out, come back to Jesus. Maybe, maybe not—I tellya, Timothy, tryin' to squirrel some straight shit outta Roger, be easier nailin' Jell-O to the wall."

"Does that mean you're going to let it go?"

"Might as well," Bennie said, a voiced shrug. "Can't win 'em all, correct? Besides, I'm comin' around to the thought he don't know dick anyway. Could be just bunghole breeze, make him feel standup, in on the action."

Waverly looked at him skeptically. "So what's he doing here, then?"

Now the shrug animated Bennie's shoulders. "Felt sorry for him, is all. He's lonely. And you gotta like the guy, meshugga or not."

"Just an act of charity, huh."

A slipsliding glance came down the barrel of the cigar. "Yeah, you could call it that."

"Okay. Fine. So long as this big score is back on the shelf. Where it's always belonged."

"Hey, I wash my hands," Bennie declared, presenting them as though in irrefutable evidence. "Anymore, by me it's a snore."

"A snore," Waverly said. It was not reassuring. It was as much as he was going to get.

"Which reminds me," Bennie said through a cavernous yawn, "time to rerack."

"Isn't it a little early for you?"

"Yeah, little, 'cept I gotta see if I can tap into the outlaw line first thing in the morning. Whole new string a games comin' up next weekend. Life goes on, boy, even if you don't win 'em all. 'Specially if you don't."

He came around the table, gave Waverly a comradely slap on the shoulder, and was off to bed. The adoring dog trotted right along with him.

Waverly sat there awhile, turning over everything he'd heard. Something was up. Had to be. It was too easy, too glib, like a man responding to life's manifold insults and disappointments and defeats by enrolling in a bowling league, or joining the Elks, or signing up for dancing lessons. He was many things, B. Epstein was, but one of them was not stoic, not when it came to forfeited money. And yet, perversely, in the face of all his instincts, all his experience, all that was rational, Waverly wanted to believe it. If it was true, he could scratch one acute throb from a head assailed by migraine. If it was true. Serious if.

A murmur of voices seeped in from the next room, Val's predominant, reminder of another sort of distress, less critical maybe, but no less persistent. He got up out of the chair and peered around the corner. Val was sitting beside Pettibone on the couch, a comforting arm draped around his hunched shoulders, ministering to him in tones hushed and gentle.

"Our physical bodies," Waverly could hear her saying, "are simply manifestations of all the attitudes and beliefs we've held about them up to now. By learning to reinterpret those attitudes we can learn how to restore health and balance and peace."

Pettibone, strangely subdued, sat like a penitent, head lowered, mouth heavy in thought. His bottle was on the floor by the teacup. In a slushy voice he said, "Balance, peace—uplifting notions. But for me out of reach. Far too late."

"It's never too late. Everything is possible. I can help you, if you'll let me."

Watching them, eavesdropping, it struck Waverly how everyone, his sister not excepted, has a message to deliver, a line to plug. He cleared his throat, announcement of his presence. They turned. Val's face wore a missionary look of shy triumph. Pettibone blinked at him dumbly.

"Uh, sorry to interrupt you," Waverly said, "but I'm pretty knocked out. Have to call it a night."

"You *should* go to bed," Valerie agreed. "It's been a long day for you. Roger and I are going to talk awhile. You don't mind?"

"Well, the thing of it is," he said, making a little joke of it, "that's my bed you're talking on."

"The couch?"

"Right. You get my room, I'll take the couch."

"Oh, I couldn't do that."

"Those are the arrangements, Val."

"No," she said firmly, "I'll sleep here till I get my own place. Which will be very soon now."

"Come on, Val."

"I won't have it any other way."

Her voice was sweet but stubborn. No margin for debate. Nor was Waverly feeling up to any. About the long and fretful day, she was inarguably right. "Okay," he said, "your way." With a nod at Pettibone, whose head was drooping again, chin bobbing off his chest, he added, "But I might suggest you cut the proselytizing short. Spare yourself."

She favored him with a sad tolerant smile, the smile a votary will inflict on the benighted heathen. "It's not a matter of sparing myself," she said quietly. "This is what I *do*, Tim. From now on, this is my work."

No arguing that either. Waverly crossed the room and started down the hall to his room. But another thought occurred to him, a fragment of a memory sparked by something said or summoned earlier in the day, something elusive, all but forgotten, not quite. He hesitated, turned. "Val, do you remember those Sunday night family gatherings we used to have? Mother reading?"

"Of course I remember them."

"That William Cowper poem, 'The Castaway.' Do you recall that one?"

"Yes I do. It was one of her favorites."

"Do you remember how it ends?"

"The last stanza? I remember it well. Would you like me to say it?"

"Yes."

And with the forthright simplicity of a child unencumbered by the baggage of inhibition, she recited the lines:

> No voice divine the storm allayed,
>   No light propitious shone,
> When, snatched from all effectual aid,
>   We perished, each alone;
> But I beneath a rougher sea,
> And whelmed in deeper gulfs than he.

And listening to them, to the somber roll of those ornate eighteenth-century measures, Waverly had the unsettling sensation of time dissolving around him, the procession of soiled and dam-

aged years, decades, magically reversed, the season of his lost boyhood magically restored; and for an instant he was shaken by an unaccountable charge of remorse and grief and dread he could link to
nothing at all.

She looked at him curiously. "Is something wrong, Tim?"

"No. Nothing's wrong. You said it perfectly."

"It's a lovely passage, isn't it?"

"That it is. Good night, Val."

"Good night, Tim."

He stretched out on his bed. The door was open. The honk of
Bennie's promised snore came to him through the wall, his sister's
serene lunatic chant from down the hall, the occasional responsive
Pettibone burble. He felt himself swirling in a confusion of identities: shrewd player in the casino, pragmatic partner in the kitchen,
wise brother-protector in the living room, and back here . . . ? Back
here he was once more the fragile child of that sudden tour through
time, frightened of the dark and the sullied past and the long prophetic shadow cast backward from the future onto this moment,
this unshakable dread. Gradually, the benediction of sleep released
him, but the last sound in his closing ears was Pettibone's voice, a
muttered echo of his scattering thoughts: "Yes, well, in the long
run, it's time that always tells."

14

B ut in the short run, time told nothing, for none of these several players, in their several games.

Inside of a week, Valerie, faithful to her pledge, moved into a
small furnished apartment on Sierra Vista, about a mile east of the
Strip. There were four units in the complex, rectangular three-story
buildings of grainy red brick, with rusted iron railings running the
length of their upper-level exterior passageways. They were set back
from the street, parallel to each other, barracks fashion, and sepa-
rated by scrub-grass lawns littered with beer cans, deflated con-
doms, cigarette butts, styrofoam coffee cups from the Seven-Eleven
down the block, adult entertainment guides blown in on the wind,
here and there the discarded needle. In the parking lot out front, a
malodorous Dumpster heaped with assorted muck displayed the
somewhat superfluous injunction: NO LOITERING. Signs of one sort or
another seemed to be in vogue here, for the two vehicles that habitually flanked Valerie's Impala were each bedecked with mottos. One,
in the rear window of a pickup whose better days were well behind, declared: MY WIFE, YES; MY DOG, MAYBE; MY GUN—NEVER! The
other, stuck on the back bumper of a Nova about the same vintage as
the Impala, advised: DON'T LIKE MY DRIVING? DIAL 1-800-EAT SHIT.

Valerie's apartment was on the top floor of one of the units. There wasn't much to it: living room, bedroom, tiny kitchen, tinier bath, the ratty furnishings and the enduring aromas—a kind of damp sheets and boiled cabbage stink—of a transient hotel. Certainly nothing like South Dakota, but for now it was satisfactory, it would do. A place to store her scanty possessions, to sleep. Its only real flaw—though a considerable one—was its inflexible edict against pets, which obliged her to leave Electra with Tim and Bennie. No other choice. And while she knew the dog was well treated, she suspected discipline was lax and the strict dietary regimen not rigorously enforced. She took comfort in the certain knowledge that the arrangement was only temporary, short-term.

Most of her waking hours were spent at the Center, mastering the arcana of homeopathic medicine, as well as the routine business of the operation. In the latter she was frequently instructed by Wyman's assistant, Cleanth, who seemed a pleasant enough person though not (she was forced to conclude) terribly bright. Occasionally Mr. LaRevere, accompanied by an attractive young girl identified as his niece, came by to chat with Wyman, and whenever he did he always found time for a genial word with Valerie. Evidently the niece worked for him in some capacity, and she often stayed on after he left.

In her second week of employment, Wyman invited Valerie along on rounds, and she was privileged to witness firsthand the practical applications of that peerless approach to healing, its extraordinary results. Sometimes in the evenings, after the Center closed, she was further privileged to join him in his office, attending raptly and long into the night to his soaring visions of the magnificent clinic, an institution of world renown, a soon-to-be reality somewhere off in an idyllic setting, a green forest possibly, or at the foot of a snow-blanketed mountain, somewhere in Montana, say, or Idaho, somewhere away from here.

Sometimes, when she had a moment free, she stopped by the house on Garces to see to Electra and, if they were awake, to visit with Tim and Bennie. Her other free moments, whatever remained of them, were given over to supporting Roger in his arduous struggle with drink, teaching him the salutary uses of herbs and natural foods, and guiding him in the calmative techniques of deep meditation.

It had been the right decision she made, coming out here. She had everything she could ever want or need. She had a restored tie with her brother; a ready-made circle of friends, many of them like-minded; a profoundly inspiring mentor; meaningful work; a shining future; in Roger, a noble private cause—she had it all. She was content. More than content; for her it was an exhilarating time, easily the happiest in recent memory, maybe even in her entire life.

But for Brewster, for all his outward composure, it was a time of intense anxiety, these past two weeks. So acute, in fact, that his bowels, normally mobile, clogged up on him and he was eventually compelled to unstopper them with a product of his own concoction known as Formula-8 (the eight designating that number of stool-softening minerals, herbs, and spices, a potent blend that never failed to offer gentle relief). But while the impacted colonic sludge was speedily expelled, the persistent vexing apprehensions resolutely refused to pass.

For in spite of all the grandiose plans spun for the benefit of his zealous new disciple (and, not incidentally, for himself), the sorry truth of it was he had not a single backer committed to his dream of a clinic. None, that is, apart from this LaRevere fellow, and so far his guarded expression of interest was a long way from a commitment. In point of fact, in those two weeks following their initial meeting not a word had been volunteered about financial support. Not a hint, not a whisper, nothing.

Well, not quite nothing. When LaRevere first introduced his niece, he described her role in his many enterprises as research analyst and asked Brewster to acquaint her with the workings of the Center. "You can appreciate," he said, "that as a businessman I must research any new undertaking thoroughly." To which Brewster vigorously assented, since that was as near as he had come to any reference to money. Near enough to inspire in Brewster a quickened hope. But after that he had seen very little of the enigmatic Mr. LaRevere. And far too much of Miss Dawnette Day.

The young lady seemed eager to learn, but she was woefully ignorant of the nature of his work and, for all his patient instruction, not particularly intelligent. Something of a dunce, actually. "Fascinating," she kept repeating, as though the word had been programmed for her, but enunciated blankly and with neither comprehension nor much enthusiasm. Once—and only once—he took her with him and Cleanth and Valerie on rounds, and the sight of their withered charges evoked in her a badly concealed revulsion. Once he thought he saw her stubbing out a cigarette behind the car in the parking lot. And another time he was certain he caught a whiff of liquor on her breath (for she had the habit of thrusting herself in close whenever they spoke, batting her eyes and brushing up against him casually, as if by accident). He, of course, maintained a proper clinical detachment. Nonetheless, it was annoying, disconcerting, altogether unseemly.

Now and again LaRevere popped in for a chat, but only briefly, for he made it plain his business ventures kept him occupied (though exactly what they were remained murky). "However, I should have things under control in another week or so," he said vaguely. "Perhaps then we can talk at greater length." Once again Brewster made some assentive noises. But then, with a mischievous little dance in his eyes, LaRevere added, "I'll be especially curious to hear Dawnette's impressions. For me she's always been rather like a weathervane, you might say. Her opinions are uncannily accurate." Fine for him; for Brewster it was something less than inspiriting. Not if he relied on the opinions of the dull-witted niece for his investment decisions. It was baffling, all of it. Energy-depleting. And more than a little unnerving.

Through it all, the one steadying element was Valerie. Calm, capable, keenly intelligent (indeed, her knowledge of herbal healing rivaled his own), perceptive, loyal—a most estimable woman, heaven-sent in this time of distress, trial. If the clinic—no!, he mustn't allow himself to think that way!—*when* the clinic became a reality (to visualize is to actualize), he would surely find a responsible place for her. Director of Homeopathic Medicine, say, or at the very least Executive Assistant to himself. And in the meantime he would stiffen his resolve. Ignatius LaRevere, this strange elusive man, represented the last faint beacon of hope on the inky horizons of what, at age fifty-five and after a lifetime of selfless striving, remained of his future and his vision. And in this spiritually famished material world, sustenance, like gold, was where you found it.

It wasn't much better for Eggs. Experience had taught him that progress in any given scam was seldom linear. Reversals were always to be expected, adjustments made, snags unraveled. That was the way these games were played, and for him no small part of their endless variety and sustaining appeal. Ordinarily. But this one was giving him more grief than he had anticipated.

For reasons quite unclear to him, the Dawnette experiment had come to nothing. It was not as if the role were unfamiliar to her. In the days when they had worked together she had reprised it often, and well. Like all trollops, she was an accomplished, if neurotic, actress. And this time out, in the interests of verisimilitude, he had taken pains to reconstruct the persona for her: outfitted her in elegant but prim skirts and blouses (another drain on the dwindling operating capital); softened the garish makeup by eliminating the red death lipstick and the strumpet eyeshadow; coached her patiently in the appropriate bearing and idiom ("When you don't understand something—and that will be most of the time—simply smile and say *intriguing* or *fascinating*. You can use *exciting* too, but sparingly, just enough to get him thinking."). From pavement princess to demure niece in a few deft strokes.

And all of it for nothing. Not a bite, not so much as a nibble. When it came to seduction, Eggs had yet to see the man impervious to Dawnette's practiced lubricious charms, in whatever guise. That was her special talent, her niche. A rare and precious gift. But this Brewster, this demented fanatic, might just prove to be the rule-confirming exception. And after two weeks of unsuccess Eggs was reluctantly coming around to share her crude assessment, delivered shrilly and with easy lapse into her natural persona: "Look, Eggs, one way or another I been in action since I was eleven. One thing

I know is men. What cranks their engines. And I'm tellin' ya, this windbag got no int'rest in gettin' it wet."

"How do you account for that?" he asked, genuinely puzzled.

"My take on it is he got his head so crammed full with weird ideas he can't get it up anymore. Even if he wanted to, which I don't think he does. All's he wants to do is talk. Y'ask me, only thing fires his tube is words."

"You know, Dawnette, you may be right."

"Goddam right I'm right."

"So what you figurin' to do, Egger?" Click asked.

"It appears we're going to have to find another solution."

They were convened, the three of them, in Click's apartment for another of the late-night meetings Eggs liked to call strategy sessions. Click and Dawnette occupied the unmade hideaway bed, he on one end, she wedged into the opposite corner, keeping a scrupulous distance, the measure of her contempt. A cheesy odor rose from the crumpled sheets between them. Now and again Click snuck a hopeful glance her way, but it was never acknowledged. Eggs stood at the window, his back to them, peering out into the dark, lost in reflection. He knew there was money to be had here. The big Lincoln, the silver tea service, the expensively tailored mortician suit, the outreach cabinets full of mail-order marks and the string of local ones—all the signals were there, all his instincts told him it had to be so. But the full extent of those monies and how to attach them remained a mystery. And the solution, alluded to so glibly, escaped him altogether.

Finally, as though reading his thoughts, Click ventured, "Y'got any ideas, that solution?"

Eggs turned and faced them. "This talk of his, there's something we're missing, something we've overlooked. I want you to call it back up, think about it, both of you. Search your memories."

"What is it we suppose to be searchin' for, Eggo?"

Eggs lifted cupped hands, as if to shape his thoughts on air. "Some . . . aspiration. Some dream. Unlock a man's dreams and without fail you unlock his wallet."

"All he ever talks about to me," Dawnette said, "is that quack grass he got for sale, gonna make the dead dance. It's either that or he's feedin' it to me." Her face knotted in an unlovely attitude of disgust. "Why, just today he hands me this glass of green slime, says—" and here she slipped into a mimicking soprano "—'Oh, Dawnette, you really must try this excellent nectar. It enhances the vibration of energy at the cellular level.' Whatever the fuck *that* means. Stuff damn near gagged me, gettin' it down."

Click, looking for a common bond, any bond, was quick to commiserate. "Hey, I hearya. That'd be his Barley Green. That shit 'bout make you blow the green chunks."

A grating tongue squeal punctuated his sympathy. She ignored him.

"The talk," Eggs prompted.

"Uh, that ass-purr-somethin' you was sayin'. What's that mean?"

"An ambition, Cleanth. A goal."

Click brightened. "Oh, that one's easy. He got this idea to build a big clinic someplace. Put all the wormfooders under one roof."

"A clinic," Eggs said, and then he said it again, pensively. "Clinic. Of course. First a center, next a clinic. A natural progression of the lunatic mind. Why didn't you tell me this before, Cleanth?"

"Fuck, I dunno. It ain't like he's yappin' about it all the time, least not to me. I just figured it for more a his chin juice. Y'know, like a guy cuttin' up a lottery he ain't never gonna win."

"What about you, Dawnette? Has he ever mentioned this dream of a clinic to you?"

"Said nothin' to me."

"And nothing to me. This is most interesting. This could very well be the solution."

Click didn't see how it was any big deal. Everybody got dreams. "I don't get it," he said. "Whaddya think it means?"

By Eggs's reasoning it was a world peopled with predators, some more artful than others. Ergo, what it had to mean was that the old fool was looking to reel him in, hang back, wait for an offer, then spring his own proposition: partners in the grand delusion. Job *him.* Very shrewd, very canny. We'd see who would be doing the jobbing. But for now, in response to the vacuous Cleanth question he said simply, "Difficult to tell."

"What I wanta know," Dawnette demanded, "is how long do I got to do this kissy-face number. It's startin' to wear thin, Eggs."

Eggs turned back to the window. For a moment he gazed at the construction site across the street, the flattened earth dotted here and there with mounds of sand, the shadowed outlines of heavy equipment in repose—bulldozers, graders, a flatbed truck or two, a motorized cement mixer. God knows what they're building now: a theme park? another gaudy palace? a soaring tower? plaster pyramid? ersatz lagoon? In a curious and indefinable way it was comforting, the eternally shifting landscape of the city. Nothing was unlikely, nothing too outrageous, nothing too tacky. Nothing impossible. The comforting permanence of change. Already he felt a little better. He said, "Not long, I think."

Maybe the Egg Man was feelin' better, but Click sure as fuck wasn't. Two weeks gone by and zip in the action department. Any action—loot stackin', pipe layin', you name it. Zippo. He figured by now, by rights, he oughta have a fresh fat wad ridin' his hip. And blastoff on that one steamin' down there between his legs, speakin' a wads. Forget them good ideas. Comes to wads, he was sevened-out big time, downtown, fucked-o-rama.

Okay, the loot part he could handle, he could wait. Old Egger, best scammer in the business, he'd come through, even though Click couldn't remember him ever takin' *this* long to size the mooch and score the hustle. Way he remembered it, they was in and out in a day or so, week on the outside. Maybe Eggs lost his touch, them years he got into the wind. That one Click didn't even want to think about.

But that other pipe, that was nothin' but pure bendover buzz-kill, worst kind. Bein' around a fly girl like Cool Whip all day long and half the night, just achin' to take a dip in that juicy honey pot, and comin' up jack—that could get you all twisted. Give you a lifetime case a the stoners. Make you crazy.

Take tonight. Here she comes wigglin' through the door changed outta her Sunday School outfit into a T-shirt, no boulder-holder underneath it, titties about pokin' airholes in it, big brown bettys winkin' at you. Better'n that (or worse, if you're unlucky enough to be Click Koontz), she got on these knock-me-down-and-fuck-me boots, and jeans stick to her like wallpaper, so fuckin' tight you can see the old vertical smile in the front, and on the backside, right on that apple ass, right over the porthole, there's a heart sewed on, like a goddam *target,* for Chris'sake. That don't make your trouser trout paddle upstream, nothin' will. Does Click's.

He's ordered in a couple pizzas for the strategy session, large, deep dish, pepperoni and anchovy, his favorite. Eggs don't want none but she helps herself to a slice, and watchin' her fit them flute-tootlin' lips around a nibbly bite and inhale them cheese ladders—ooo-wah! swoon! flash! swoop on down and lick my love pump! Watchin' gotta be right in there next to boffin', close second. Till she gotta look over at him just when he got his cheeks puffed with a man-sized wedge, and screw up her nose like she just got downwind a blotcher fart, and go, "You get any fatter you can hire out to General Motors for an airbag." Talk about your instant hard-off. Some people, it just don't pay to be decent to 'em.

Shitlaw, he'd tried everything he could think of (short of money, which he knew he didn't have enough of, play in her parsley patch, least not yet anyways), get her on her back or on her knees, either place do just fine. Nothin' worked. Even tried comin' at it with a little humor, like. Like the other day they're toolin' up the Strip on their way to the Center and he sees a cab got one a them signs for a jumbo pot slot says: ONE PULL CAN CHANGE YOUR LIFE. So Click, he points at it, then points down south, goes, "Dunno 'bout your life, but a little pull on Mr. Wet Burrito here sure do a lot to change the next couple minutes." Kinda cute, right? Kinda sly. What's she say? She makes her eyes round as supper plates and says, real sweet, like it's a real question, "Why don't you pull it yourself and see?"

Turbobitch. What he oughta do is jump her bones, stab the old dagger into her. Make them eyes roll up in their sockets, make her squeal. He got the chance, he'd fuck her brains right outta her head, somebody hadn't beat him to it already.

It was gettin' him seriously tweaked, all'a time thinkin' about it. Startin' to see it in his dreams, that sugar gash, sniff it in his nostrils, taste it on his tongue. Gettin' him pussy-wretched, desperate. Somethin' gotta happen, and soon. Before suddenly. Maybe it would. Maybe after they cracked the Brewster slab, maybe when he got that wad swingin' on his hip, maybe then. Man's gotta hope. He'd pay for a piece, come to that. It ain't fair, being partners and all, oughta be free, but he'd do it. Your dick don't know no difference. Way Click saw it, life's too fuckin' short, gotta suck it up while you can.

If it was distressing for Cleanth Koontz, it was not exactly your sunniest time for Dawnette Day. The way she saw it, they were just spinning their wheels here, going noplace. Going backward. Made you wonder about their genius leader, who you couldn't trust anyway, and all his big strategies, talk, plans. Also about yourself. Two weeks firing on that gonus Brewster, giving him the fuckeye, shoving her Mount Joy up so close it's practically a wall job, doing everything in the trick-and-treat bag but plant her squirrel in his face, and still she can't get the maypole aloft. Two weeks. Not a cheering sign, her line of work. Maybe they were both of them losing the goods, her and Eggs both.

For Dawnette, thoughts of the fleeting rush of time, the corrosive power of the years, life's terrible brevity—thoughts like that had never worried her head. Forty-five by experience, twenty-three by the calendar, eighteen by the mirror, it was inconceivable to her, being dead or, infinitely worse, old. Terrifying. She remembered her Granny, lived with them back home in Tennessee. Remembered how that cranky old woman gummed her grits, peed her drawers, wore glasses thick as thumbs and still stumbled into walls, had a crooked hump looked like a lumpy feed sack growing out of her back. She was doing a lot of that kind of remembering lately, Dawnette was, and not because she wanted to. Images from the past, stark and vivid, like Granny there, came to her unsummoned, no good reason at all, flickered behind her eyes for an instant and then were gone.

Didn't help any, listening to all that gas out of Brewster, came on like those Bible wallopers she use to hear when she was a kid, same wheeze, only with him it's body rot instead of soul. Or seeing up close all those bluehead lungers and chest-clutchers and full-packaged tail gunners that time she went on his zombie rounds with him. Never again. Not for this girl. Too creepy. You ask her, every last one of them ought to be in a hospital someplace, or a vegetable farm, or boxed and buried. Someplace out of sight anyway. Ugh. Of the two, old or dead, dead was better.

Double ugh on what she had to put up with right now, day to day, never mind your dreary past and gloomy future. Got Mr. Groin on her tit all day long, begging and squirming for a cuffo bop. Like she was suppose to comp him because they happen to be working the same side of the street? Scrub that! Nasty little jerkoff worm. She'd sooner diddle a cold Oscar Meyer weenie than bump that porker. Only thing he was going to snag off her was some hard attitude. Look at him there, pig ugly, shoveling pizza into that pit in his face, asking Eggs all those putz questions and doing all those weird wig factory noises every time he talks. For sure, he got all his shit in one sock, and that one got a hole in it. Ugh squared.

How about Eggs, speaking of weird. Every night sleeping in the same fold-out bed, about the size of a baby crib, and he hadn't once laid a hand on her, not once. Came to your basic roto-rooting, he was about as droop-dicked as Brewster, maybe droopier. Pair to draw to, those two. Been two long weeks since she got her drain sanked, longer than she could ever remember being out of action. Well, technically that wasn't quite true, you were to put a fine point on it. One night Eggs let her blow him and she gave him the Coupe De Ville job: rimming the exhaust pipe, tickle-tonguing the engines, deep-shafting the piston rod. Full lube, dyno deluxe. What's she get? Not a hip twitch out of him, not a quiver, not a groan. There was a television on the ceiling, he'd've been tuned into "Meet the Press." Man wasn't human. Being in the life, she didn't think she'd ever miss it; figured the time out be like an overdue vacation, give the beauty spot a rest. But a girl's got needs too.

She wished she'd never run into Eggs, or when she spotted him that night at the Dunes just let it go, bagged the 5K he nicked off her, walked away. Wished she was back with Velva and Gayleen. What he done to them was a terrible thing, awful, pure dog mean. Made you almost sick, thinking about it. Made you feel, like, guilty, an emotion formerly alien to her and which, feeling it now, she didn't much like, not one bit. So tonight, before they come over to piggie's place for the smoke session, while Eggs is in showering (four, five times a day he's got to shower), she cranks up her nerve and gives Velva a quick call, find out how they're getting by.

Not good, is how. News not good. Velva says Gay's arm's in real bad shape, gonna need reconstructive surgery. No money, now they're off the pavement, and no Blue Cross, their work. And nothing free in Vegas, nothing. She don't sound a whole lot better herself, Velva, voice a froggy croak coming down the line, like she's talking underwater (in her mind Dawnette can still see that mashed bloody beak on her); but for all of it she don't seem *too* hacked, asks Dawnette how she's doing, where she's at, things like that. Things you say. Dawnette, she don't dare tell where, not with Eggs in the picture. Got to dance around that one. Says she's doin' good, be in touch when she can and when this score's done and she's collected her cut she'll help out on the money end, make things right again, like they use to be. Which is probably just a feelgood lie since there probably nothing to cut up here anyway, and which Velva, who's nobody's mark, sees right through. She goes, "Yeah, sure, like it use to be"; and then before they ring off she says, sort of by-the-way, like the thought just come to her, "Oh, you better tell that boyfriend yours watch his back. This ain't over."

Velva meant it, too, every fuckin' word. Nobody, least of all a breeder, get away with what that suckhole done to her and Gay. She didn't know the how of it yet, or the where, or the when. But the why, that part came easy. That part she knew.

Seething with barely contained fury, she put up the phone and shambled down the hall to the bedroom. Stood in the doorway a moment. There was a nightlight by the dresser, otherwise the room was dark. Gay was lying on her back, deep in a two-week sniff haze. The arm, right-angled in its plaster sheath, was held above her head, as though to shield her eyes from the glare of a phantom sun. In a feeble stoned voice she asked, "Who's that called, Vel?"

"Nobody. Wrong number."

"It was a trick, I could maybe do a knobber. Mouth still works good."

"It was nobody."

"Nobody?"

"Yeah."

Gay began to weep. "What're we gonna do, Vel? I *gotta* have a steady jolt. You know that. Snow only thing get me through this."

Velva had no ready answer. She came over and sat on the bed, stroked Gay's feverish brow tenderly, crooning, "I know, I know." In the mirror over the dresser she caught a shadow-streaked glimpse of her own face, never lovely, now horribly disfigured, the nose a flattened blue-black smudge, jaw horseshoe-rigid, eyes blazing, the total effect borderline gargoyle. It was startling to see. She thought about their abruptly upended lives. About payback. Somehow, there was a way, and she was going to find it. She said, "Don't you worry, honey. Velva take care of you. Take care of everything."

The reflection greeting Roger Pettibone in the mirror these past two weeks was, in its own way, equally startling, though altogether more agreeable to its beholder. The eyes gazing back at him were alert, clearing; the puffed pomegranate cheeks tightening some; the fiery flush beginning to bleach. Were those fleshy wattles under the chin shrinking a bit? Could be. He was certain he looked taller, not nearly so stout. Even the layer of shellac, lived with so long it had an almost epidermal feel to it, seemed gradually to be peeling from his tongue. For the first time in longer than he cared to remember, his head was unfogged, his thoughts lucid. Fourteen days without a drink. Not one. Fourteen, and counting.

Which is what Saint Valerie persisted in cautioning him against, the counting. "It's a new life you're embarked upon, Roger," she would murmur in that serene purling voice of hers, coaxing him into a velvety somnolence. "To count is to look backward, acknowledge that other life. The past is behind you now, the old Roger gone." But he did it anyway. He kept count. Old habits, and all that.

Though he couldn't recognize it, they were the abiding, obstinate, bred-into-the-bone habits of the dry drunk. The tunnel vision: everything or nothing. The manic mood swings, as unaccountable as they were unpredictable: an Alpine high one moment, through the bottom of defeat's abject pit the next. And in his particular case, the historian's melancholy perception of the fundamental imperma-

nence of things: nothing endures, nothing; and the consequent un-
utterable doubts cloaked, for him, in the bravado of compulsive
talk. Especially the talk. When he wasn't asleep, he talked. If there
was no one to hear, he addressed himself, aloud. Wherever he
went, the orotund peal of his voice preceded him. Announced him.
Shielded him. As if only a wall of words could stay the smoldering,
aching, deep-bellied joyless need.

"Fourteen days off the sauce," he crowed to Waverly and
Bennie (for he was spending the greater part of his not inconsider-
able free time with them, his new—perhaps his only—friends) on
the evening of the landmark occasion. "And I owe it all to your sister, Timothy. A veritable angel of deliverance, that woman."

Waverly made the colossal blunder of inquiring, with only a
pinch of irony, if he were now a convert to the magical Quantum
Healing. The kernel of the answer, had it been extracted from the
shell of a meandering, defensive, quarter-hour drone, was an arch
Certainly not, he had not taken leave of his ratiocinative senses, not
Dr. Pettibone, merely applied the more efficacious features of that
pseudoscience. Waverly, once burned, withheld any further questions.

But not Bennie. Serene optimist, manifestly still trolling after
the Big Tuna, disclaimers notwithstanding, Bennie wanted to know
if he had switched to "that birdseed diet," the answer to which
should have been self-evident since Pettibone was just then disap-
pearing a mustard-varnished liverwurst on rye, the creative Epstein
six P.M. breakfast generously shared with guest and live-in dog alike.
That answer was necessarily delivered via mouth-plugged, negative
toss of the head; and so Bennie allowed, "Myself, I'd sooner nosh
a roadkill hoagie than any that gorp she call food," adding in aside
to Waverly, "No offense, Timothy, your sis."

Waverly gave a none-taken shrug. No disputing that judgment.

Bennie shifted gears. "So what're you doin' with all your time,
Rog, now you booted the demon?"

Ill-advised question. Pettibone swallowed the last of his liverwurst, and in a big confident voice regaled them with an exhaustive
dawn-to-darkness chronicle of his newly disciplined days, his matu-
tinal setting-up exercises (demonstrated, with considerable huffing),

his revitalized classroom performances (dramatically reenacted), his renewed intellectual pursuits (reading list numbingly enumerated), and his projected, soon-to-be-commenced scholarly article on heretofore overlooked nuances in Xenophon's *Anabasis* (suffocatingly explicated).

Doubtless there would have been more had Bennie not appropriated a breath-hitching instant to put in, conversationally, "How 'bout them Runnin' Rebs. Word on the street is they gonna do some serious butt-kickin' this year."

In sudden vocal swing, fortissimo to anomalous piano, Pettibone replied, "I wouldn't know."

"You ain't been keepin' up, your team? Season gonna start any day now."

"No."

No? That was it—no? For a moment Bennie looked perplexed. Only a moment. "Yeah, well, early games don't mean dick anyway," he said, coming at it from another angle. "Your Rebels wax the floor with them scrub teams."

Pettibone said nothing at all.

"Be sorta like Electric here sparrin' with a toy poodle," Bennie continued. The dog's nozzle head was laid lovingly on a hammy Epstein thigh. He fed her a liverwurst scrap and, as if in casual afterthought, remarked, "Course there still be some heavy coin changin' hands, even them calesthentic warm-up games."

Not a syllable from Pettibone.

So Waverly said, "You ready to hit it, Bennie?" What remained of his patience was rapidly running down.

"Hey, no rush," he said to Waverly, "plenty time." Then, innocent of segue, no master of indirection, he asked Pettibone, "How's Lafayette doin' these days?"

Pettibone folded his arms over his torso, high on the chest. A stubborn stance, just shy of belligerent. He looked at Bennie steadily, said, "In class, he's doing fine."

"I'm talkin' ball here, Rog. He healthy?"

"As far as I know."

"He, uh, get his little pro'lum worked out yet?"

In a voice ice-glazed, whispery thin, Pettibone said, "I haven't the slightest idea. And even less interest." Abruptly, he got up and strode to the window. Stared at the falling light and, as though addressing it, countered with a question of his own: "You're wagering on football tonight?"

"That's right. Broncs and Raiders. Oughta be a barnburner."

"Did you know the Olmec Indians played a game not dissimilar to our football? Some say it's a direct ancestor of the sport."

Bennie looked wholly baffled. "Never heard of no Olmec Indians."

"An ancient civilization," Pettibone explained, back to booming voice, "in what is now Mexico. Circa 1500 B.C."

"No kiddin'. They was into football way back then?"

"A version of it."

"Huh. Be go ta shit. Ain't that somethin'."

"And did you know that in their equivalent of postgame ceremonies the losers were routinely decapitated. Did you know that?"

"That dee-cap-tated, that's loppin' off the old noodle, right?"

"Correct."

"Well, that sure gotta get your boys pumped for some major head-bangin' out there," Bennie opined. "While they still got somethin' to bang with," he added, guffawing at his excellent quip.

"I expect it was an incentive," said Pettibone, unsmiling.

"Bet they knew how to give a pep talk, them days. Somethin' real basic. Like, win or croak, huh."

"We do much the same to our athletes," Pettibone said grimly, and with more than a little bitterness. "In a manner of speaking. We serve them no better today."

Waverly and Bennie exchanged eye-rolling glances.

"*Now* are you ready?" Waverly said.

"Yeah, think I'm ready."

Pettibone dropped them off at the Desert Inn. He declined Bennie's invitation to come along, take in the game. No more casinos for him. Begone, temptation!

As it turned out, it might have been better had he accepted. Waiting at the door of his apartment was a towering figure, shuffling restlessly, dark face twitching in an anguish of doubt, desperately needing to talk. They went inside, and for a change Pettibone did the listening. All of it. He had nothing to offer, nothing to recommend. No answers. And when the long, wretched monologue was finished and the young man was gone, Pettibone felt about as desolate as he had ever felt in his life. Certainly as helpless. And for the next seventy-two hours no one saw him—students, colleagues, his new friends, no one. Vanished utterly. As if he had stumbled off the edge of the earth.

"I'm tellin' ya, Timothy," Bennie was grouching as they came through the entrance to the Desert Inn, "if assholes could fly, Roger be one a them Concorde jet airplanes."

"You want me to say I told you so?"

"He maybe ain't a bad guy," Bennie went on, ignoring the question. "Deep down, y'know, y'get past all that smack talk. But he can be a serious haunch pain sometimes, too. Ain't nothin' worse'n a born-again juicer."

Particularly an evasive one, Waverly thought but didn't bother to say. He was not in a commiserative humor. He understood the source of his partner's irritation, but he had no interest in exploring it further. Not tonight. Been enough of that already. More than plenty. What he needed tonight was some space, room. The comforting orderly distance of cards and numbers. So what he said was, "Meet you after the game."

"Yeah, right. I'll come lookin' for ya." He started away, paused, turned, and delivered a nugget of Epstein advice. "You watch them wide swings now, huh."

"I'll do that," Waverly said with a small sigh, "if you'll watch the props."

"Hey, got all my bets down and there ain't a prop in the lot."

"There's a welcome switch."

They parted. Bennie veered off toward the circular bar, Waverly strolled down a file of tables, searching for the dealer with the giveaway tell. Nowhere in evidence. Night off, maybe, or maybe sacked by some Argus-eyed pit boss. An unforgiving vocation, dealing. No margin for error. Worse luck for the both of them, if in fact that's how it had fallen out.

And yet, curiously—more accurately, perversely—his own luck

had been good lately. Better than good, given the measure he was reduced to and all the naggy poison headaches of the past two weeks. Just last night he'd come away six yards winners, night before that four. And all of it off a humble sawbuck base unit. Even Bennie was hitting, holding his own anyway, winning more than he lost, if not by much. Something to be said for that.

He spotted an empty third base, settled in, laid out an innocuous three bills and asked for greens. All this spectacular luck, might as well up the base. The dealer, a pretty girl with a pasty indoor pallor and a tatooed heart on one wrist, skull on the other, called out smartly, "Changin' three hundred," got the sanctioning echo, stacked the chips in front of him, and resumed slinging the cards across the felt. Scarcely a beat lost. Her moves were dexterous, her face expressionless, tight mouth turned down at the corners, eyes perfectly blank. No tells here, no edge.

Only two other players at the table, couple of ruddy-cheeked, strongly made males, one old, one young, both outfitted in jeans and denim shirts and both with seed caps perched on their large square heads. Father and son, by the looks of them: near-identical features but for the ruin of time etched on the old man's face. Mostly they were betting reds, trading advice, bad jokes, condolences on a bust, huzzahs on a win, which wasn't often, for their game was not expert. Didn't seem to matter. They were ragging each other, having fun. The easy camaraderie between them was obvious and genuine. The family that plays together . . .

Coming in mid-shoe, there wasn't a whole lot to be done for the next several hands, so Waverly played a straight, sleepwalking basic and waited. And found himself watching the father-son team. Even after the shuffle, when it was time to empty his head, adjust the emotion-neutral screen behind his eyes, center himself and go to work—even then, he watched them. And against his will, images floated across that screen where there should have been tallies, numbers; and his thoughts went reeling through the years, generation, backward to his own father, forward to his son, both lost to him forever, the one to the earth, the other to the iron consequences of a single rash frenzied irreversible act; and laterally as well, to his sister, Valerie of the wounded moonstruck eyes, tall and graceful as a swan and just as fragile, all that remained of family. Family, the prison of love. And for an instant he was seized by an impulse to bolt from the table, rush to McCarran, catch a plane somewhere. Where? Michigan again? No, he'd been to Michigan. Florida? Certainly not Florida. Where then? Somewhere to . . . what? Do what? Interpret? Explain (you see, this is what happened, and why; it was nothing intentional, you understand, nothing personal)? Apologize? Make atonement for the botch of his life? *Some*where.

But he didn't move from his place at the table. Instead he played cards. Played them badly, the count in his head hopelessly blurred in the swamp of memory. Yet, astonishingly, he won. Won consistently. More of that perverse. Fortune's perversity. And when Bennie came by three hours later his round face was creased in a sunburst winner's grin. "Zapped 'em both," he declared triumphantly, "spread and the over/under both. One large dime up."

Waverly collected his chips, cashed them in at the cage, and took away six bills and change.

"So?" Bennie said, "You?"

"I had a passable night. God knows why. I couldn't focus. Pure dumb luck."

"Listen, in this business it's better to be lucky than smart."

"What if you're neither?"

"Bet 'em anyway. Scared money never wins."

"Ours is courageous?"

"It's gettin' ballsy, boy. We startin' to build some bank here. We're on rails, Timothy, scorchin'. Feel it in my bones."

Waverly felt his mouth shaping a smile. Ballsy money, building bank, scorching, rails—well, why not? It occurred to him that's how they'd gotten along, these many years: his own somber fatalism, confirmed so many times, in teetery balance with the terminal knee-jerk optimism of a Benjamin Saul Epstein. The foundation of their improbable alliance. Maybe Bennie was right after all. Still, he couldn't shake the uneasy feeling, that dark vision peculiar to the Jacktown graduate, of something about to happen, and soon, and whatever it was it augured no good. And as they passed through the door and out into the grip of the chill night air, he said, "Or in your dreams."

＊　＊　＊

Thirty-six hours later, on the morning of the day before Thanksgiving, something did happen. Valerie, in her euphoria, took it in her head to host a holiday dinner for her brother and Bennie and Roger and, as the idea expanded, all her new friends. And from that moment, time, in its steady mindless beat, did at last begin to tell.

PART
THREE

15

Valerie was wide awake at dawn. She got out of bed immediately, pulled on jeans and work shirt, and spent the next two hours scrubbing and cleaning her apartment to an immaculate spit-polish shine. The remainder of the morning was given over to putting together her holiday feast. Because she had no table, it was to be laid out on the counter dividing living room and kitchen, and served buffet style. This was her menu: sesame nut mix; a chilled raw soup consisting of mung beans, alfalfa seeds, and a medley of cruciferous vegetables (all of them carefully oxygenated in a solution of food-grade hydrogen peroxide); sprouted bread with rose-petal conserve; soy-based dumplings; steamed corn on the cob (also properly oxygenated); an herbal fruit concentrate known as Kalash that included such exotic ingredients as Indian gall nut, dried catkins, gooseberry, pennywort, nutgrass, ghee, butterfly pea, and shoeflower, among many others, and that had the color and consistency of congealed tar; vegetable juice cocktails and chamomile tea as beverages of choice; and as concession to certain of her guests, an organic turkey and organic pumpkin pie (sweetened with a touch of raw cane sugar) baking in the oven. It was, after all, Thanksgiving.

By noon her preparations were more or less complete. She

showered and changed into the peasant blouse and skirt worn the night of her first meeting with Brewster—her good luck outfit. She was bursting with excitement, and so to calm herself she put on a tape of Gandharva-Veda instrumental music (cassette and player both generously loaned by Brewster) and stretched out on the spotless carpet and allowed the thrumming melodies to waft over her, restoring a harmonic balance of body, mind, and spirit. It was the same tape she used as part of Roger's therapy, and to profound effect, though the thought of him now, his mysterious absence the past couple of days, excited a troubling ripple in the pacific sea of tranquility settling through her. But she dismissed it, put it in the hands of Cosmic Spirit, and within an hour she was refreshed, her serene self once again.

At three o'clock the arrival of her first guests was announced by a rap on the door. She swung it open and there stood Brewster and Click. They were dressed for the occasion, Brewster in customary black suit, Click in slacks and sport jacket, the dandruff-salted collar of which he flicked at nervously. Both were smiling, Brewster's suitably grave, Click's a little tight, but smiles all the same. From behind his back Brewster produced a bottle that looked much like a fifth of liquor. "Wakassa," he said, "the liquid extract of Chlorella. An excellent predinner cocktail. I thought your guests might enjoy it."

Valerie made some flustered oh-you-shouldn't-have noises. Even after two weeks, the presence of the great man still inspired a certain deferential awe. She ushered them in, motioned them to seats. Her living room came furnished with a couch scarcely larger than a love seat and two easy chairs. To accommodate everyone invited today, she had borrowed three folding chairs from the Center and positioned them strategically around the room. As though by divine mandate, Brewster settled into one of the easy chairs. Click took the couch. Valerie remained on her feet, clutching the gift bottle uncertainly. "Would you care for some of the Wakassa now?" she asked, the question naturally directed at Brewster.

"I suggest we wait until all of your party is here. For a celebrative toast."

"Some nut mix, then?"

"That would be fine."

"Cleanth?"

Click hesitated, but only long enough for a furtive glance at Brewster. "Uh, sure, I'll try some."

Valerie went to the counter, filled two fruit dishes from the sesame nut bowl, and brought them over. One to each. She took a folding chair opposite Brewster and said, a trifle worriedly, "Mr. LaRevere and his niece . . . they are coming?"

"Oh yeah," Click put in quickly, saying it like Eggs told him to, or as best he remembered how Eggs told him. "I called up Eg—Mr. LaRevere this mornin' and he said he had some business he gotta get done today but they be here for sure. Oughta be along any minute now."

"Business? On a holiday?"

"Yeah, well, he's a pretty busy guy. Got all them, y'know, investments. To watch out for."

Brewster, not to be upstaged, sighed wearily. "For some of us, there are no holidays."

Didn't Click know it. He's on his way out the door last night, headin' home to chug a brewbie, an' Dr. Dead Battery says be sure and turn in tomorrow for rounds. Turkey day, and they gonna do rounds. So when he tells Eggs he gotta work Eggs goes, Oh, that'll do just fine, him and Cool Whip catch a cab, he don't want Brewster seein' where they cribbed anyway, bad for the image. Which ain't exactly the point. He ain't the one doin' the rollin' out this mornin'. Fine? Yeah, right. Easy for him.

"Cleanth and I had rounds to do today," Brewster was explaining in the enervated inflections of the man committed to a severe and, in the eyes of ordinary mortals, lonely calling. "Human suffering knows no holidays."

Valerie's brows were creased in an attitude of earnest concern. "I do hope all your patients were well."

"Reasonably well, given their histories of body insult. All but one. Hubert. Perhaps you remember him."

"The elderly gentleman with the heart condition? Mr. Jessup?"

"That's the person. Sorry, deluded man, Hubert. I have reason to suspect he's gone back to his doctor-prescribed toxic drugs."

"That would be tragic," Valerie said.

"Fatal, in his case," Brewster affirmed through a mouthful of sesame nut mix. For a moment he chewed thoughtfully. Then, as if to dispel the melancholy thoughts of the doomed Hubert, he said, "But enough of work. Now is a time for respite, renewal. Did you say your brother was coming?"

"Around four. With one of his friends. And possibly another, the man I told you about."

Brewster frowned. "With the drinking problem?"

"Yes."

"Well, I look forward impatiently to meeting them all."

Thirty minutes later his taxed patience was at least partially rewarded by the appearance of Eggs and Dawnette. Like Brewster, Eggs came bearing a gift concealed behind his back, a dozen long-stemmed roses whisked out and presented to the hostess with a flourish and an exaggeratedly formal bow. "Perhaps these will add a dash of color to your festive board," he said. Today was the day he intended to open fire on the windbag healer, first serious volley anyway, and he was tuning up, getting into the rhythm of it.

"They're beautiful," said Valerie, beaming gratitude.

Brewster had come to his feet. Likewise Click. Holiday well wishes were exchanged all around, hands pumped. Valerie took the flowers into the kitchen, snipped off their stems, and arranged them in a vase filled with demineralized water. Eggs and Dawnette joined Click on the couch, Dawnette squeezed between the two of them, thinking If they want to make a sandwich they sure as shit got a head start on it, but saying nothing, her face stuck on a smile, the way Eggs had warned her to do. Lots of grinning going on here: Eggs at Brewster; Brewster to himself, like he got some secret nasty joke; the fuckstrated pork chop at nothing at all, unless it was the freebie feel he was getting off her hip and thigh nudged up against him, entirely against her will; and Snow White, back in the room now and gushing directly at her, "I love your necklace." Dawnette mustered a laconic thanks. In the few times they'd spoken at the Center, the dimbo struck her as so gooey sweet it had to be either natural or the best ho hustle going. Probably natural. Probably came as loose-wrapped as Brewster.

Along with the shoulder-skimming crystal drop earrings, the gold-link (well, gold-plated, anyway) necklace, both gifts from Velva, helped set off her outfit: frilly white blouse, short black skirt, black hose, black spike heels. Except for the blouse, which Eggs had insisted on (though without much force, for him, seeing as how his latest strategy, near as she could tell, no longer turned exclusively on her, which got to make you wonder some too, your rung on this greased ladder), the rest of it was all belly ride fashion statement, the skirt equipped with fore and aft slut cuts revealing a generous peek of thigh, the killer heels designed to spark all manner of deviant carnal fantasy. Add to that the get-to-grips war paint, the crimson lip gloss and violent lavender eye shadow, and the expertly feathered, pink-streaked bottle-blond hair, and it was pure Cool Whip, gloves off and down and dirty all the way.

For himself, Eggs wore a pastel peach linen suit, summer weight and expensive, but a little out of season. Under the circumstances, the bankroll's perilous shrinkage, it was the best he could do. He had been chatting with Brewster, trading aimless pleasantries, but now, so as not to appear too driven, he turned his attention to Valerie and remarked favorably on her apartment.

"It's very basic," Valerie said. "There's not much to it."

"Yet you've done wonders with it," Eggs said, meaning it, too, for he had always admired antiseptic cleanliness.

"Yeah, real homey," Click seconded, largely for something to say, having uttered scarcely a word ever since he arrived. But nobody seemed to be listening, so he went back to nibbling the squirrel nuts. Better'n nothin'. He hadn't grubbed anything but a couple creme curls (maybe it was three) since before rounds, and he was feeling hungry for some real chow, normal chow, though he figured he probably wasn't gonna get any here, probably gonna have to go scarf a Double Whopper after they bugged outta this place. Fishwich be good too. Also was he feeling a slow rising heat down in weenie world, what with his ass practically spliced to Cool's and her leg bumpin' up against him. Tellya, he told himself, y'sit there long enough, think about it hard enough, that sugar ass and them python

thighs locked around you, squeezin' the spooch right outta you—
y'do that a while and the ol' pood likely go over the mountain all by
its lonesome. Dedicate one without even a spank on the monkey.

The conversation stalled. To jump-start it, Eggs told a long, convoluted, cunningly fabricated tale of an investment transaction that
had occupied his every waking hour the past weeks, the subtext of
which was the oppressive weight of his work. Brewster, never to be
bested, responded with an anecdote of his own, its message underlining the equally punishing nature of his vocation. Their chronicles
of arduous labor delivered, Eggs steered the faltering talk to the
broader topic of economic development, the explosive growth of
the city and the manifold opportunities that expansion promised.
Brewster agreed heartily. A couple of venturous pioneers, judiciously forecasting the climates of their respective callings.

Dawnette crossed and recrossed her legs. Only her frosted smile
bridled a yawn. Let go that smile and she'd have a hole in her face
big as a cave.

Click looked back and forth between Eggs and Brewster, nodding sagely, like he was in on the dialogue, understood what the
fuck it was all about, but thinkin' how they both of 'em sounded like
actors talkin', them afternoon soaps he watched whenever he got
the chance.

Valerie was listening too, or showing the rapt expression that
said she was. But some of the nervousness, the jittery agitation she
had experienced earlier in the day, was overtaking her once again.
Sitting, as she was, on a folding chair next to Cleanth and the flashy
(if somewhat sulky, certainly uncommunicative) niece, she felt
gawky, graceless, empty of words. Maybe it had been a mistake,
hosting a gathering like this after all those years of solitude. So
many people, crammed into so tight a space. She wished Tim and
Bennie were here. Where were they? What about Roger? If only
they were here all this stiff conversation would surely loosen. If she
had a phone she could call, urge them to hurry, salvage the party.
No phone. Nobody to the rescue.

Not until well after four, when help, of sorts, arrived at last in
the persons of Waverly and Bennie. Also, and to her dismay, Elec-

tra, tugging excitedly at the leash grasped by Bennie in one hand, bag full of foodstuffs in the other. "Couldn't leave the pooch at home, party time," he explained.

"But you know dogs aren't allowed here," Valerie protested.

"Aah, one afternoon ain't gonna hurt. Listen, anybody give you grief, you tell 'em talk to B. Epstein." He reined in the dog, handed her the bag. "Brought you some munchies."

Valerie peered into it doubtfully.

"Y'got your Fritos in there, onion dip, Swiss cheese, liver paste, some a your cold cuts, tongue, jar a kosher dills—what else we got, Timothy?"

"Beats me. It was your idea."

Valerie's plaintive eyes shifted to her brother.

Waverly made a helpless shrug. "I tried to tell him."

Recovering some, she said, "It's very thoughtful, Bennie. But you really shouldn't have."

Bennie waved away her thanks. "Hey, that's how your Pilgrims done it, everybody pitchin' in." The Epstein interpretation of history.

"Well, I'm sure someone will . . . enjoy it."

"There ain't, I'll hog it up myself. Hungry enough to eat a—" he searched his imagination for a suitable metaphor, settled on the inoffensive "—horse. Don't you worry, won't none go to waste."

She led them inside. Introductions went around the room, more of the hand pumping, though a little less vigorous this time, the guarded grips of strangers. Valerie took the bag into the kitchen. She had no idea what to do with all this processed, devitalized, chemical-polluted junk food. Certainly she didn't want to hurt Bennie's feelings. But what would Wyman think? A terrible dilemma. Finally, she laid it out on a back corner of the counter, as nearly out of sight as possible. Best she could do.

In the living room Bennie was uncinching Electra's collar and leash and, both his burdens lifted now, collapsing heavily into the unoccupied easy chair. Waverly took one of the folders. The suddenly freed dog made straight for Dawnette's perfumed crotch. She recoiled fearfully.

"C'mon, Electric," Bennie said, gentlest of scolds, "behave yourself."

Eggs leaned over and placed himself between Dawnette and the sniffing dog. He stroked it behind the ears, produced some soothing sounds. Remarkably, Electra settled down at once, nuzzled up against his leg, her backside twitching. A new friend. To Bennie he said, "Magnificent specimen. Is she yours?"

"Belongs to Val. We're keepin' her at our place on account of they don't let dogs in here. 'Fraid she lost her manners, boardin' with a couple sofa rats like me'n Timothy."

"I've always admired Dobermans," Eggs allowed. "Most intelligent breed. To say nothing of their brute strength."

"Look like you're pretty good with the mutts yourself."

"I used to raise Weimaraners. When I was young. Another excellent breed."

"The extraordinary sensory perception of the dog," Brewster said enigmatically, reclaiming center stage, "can be quite instructive. We have much to learn from them."

Eggs couldn't agree more, and for the next several minutes the mystical capacities of animals supplied a handy conversation piece. Bennie wasn't sure what the fuck they were talking about, but he joined right in anyway. Dawnette and Click had no opinions on the matter. Neither did Waverly, who watched and listened, taking silent measure of the assembled company. What he saw and heard was not cheering.

In the kitchen Valerie was putting the final touches on her dinner. Disappointed though she was by Roger's nonappearance, she couldn't delay any longer. Meticulously she arranged food platters, plates, soup bowls, tea cups, juice tumblers, silver, napkins, Mr. LaRevere's roses on the counter. When she was satisfied everything was in order, she opened the Wakassa bottle, filled seven cordial glasses, set them on a tray, and carried it into the living room. "Dinner is ready," she announced. "But first we must have a toast."

A glass of the sustaining nectar to everyone. It fell of course to Brewster to deliver the pithy sentiment. He rose out of his chair and drew himself up to his full Lincolnesque height, signal for the others to stand and come together in the middle of the room. He hoisted his glass. His craggy face seemed almost to liquify in a mushy smile. "To the blessings of vigorous good health, spiritual harmony, and—" fleeting glance at Eggs "—abundant prosperity, for all of us, not only on this day of ritual thanks-offering, but in all the days ahead."

"Well said," Eggs declared.

Glasses were clinked. Brewster drained his, savoring every drop-let of the pea-green liquid. Valerie did the same. Everyone else sipped cautiously. Everyone but Click, who tossed his back in a sin-gle heroic gulp, figuring better to take your poison in one quick slug, and stifling the dyspeptic burp elevating through his chest and throat.

"Please," Valerie said, indicating the lavish spread. "Help your-selves."

Dinner was served. A line formed at the counter, plates were heaped (some more than others). Electra, emboldened by two weeks of Epstein tutelege, bounded across the room and scuttled through the forest of legs, wriggling expectantly, pleading with beg-garly eyes. A chagrined Valerie hustled the dog, resisting all the way, into the bedroom and in tones more than usually severe com-manded her to stay. She recognized something would have to be done about the seriously undermined discipline, and soon. But not today. Today she had enough to occupy her attention. She stood there a moment, eyes closed, limbs slackened, breath steadied; and once her composure was restored she returned to her guests, glid-ing about the room, seeing to their every need.

Waverly watched her, this lissome figure, delicate as lace yet with a density of beauty and grace that was all inner light and soul. And the others as well, he watched them, wondering how it was she had gotten herself entangled with this bunch, about as sinister a col-lection of freaks and misfits and predators as he'd seen outside the walls of Jacktown. And potentially just as vicious.

Maybe not the one introduced as Cleanth. Dwarfish, barrel-shaped, fat as a blowfish, he sat at one end of the couch, bent to a plate held in precarious balance on a pudgy knee. Evidently his tastes and appetite ran along lines similar to Bennie's, for the plate spilled over with an assortment of Epstein munchies and he vacuumed them up with a purity of focus ardent and intense. Lot of big eating going on there. No, maybe not that one.

But certainly the girl sitting next to him on the couch, picking gingerly at a near-empty plate. The niece with the improbable name. Niece. Sure. Whory-lipped, painted see-pure-evil eyes, skin white as chalk dust, face framed in a corona of silvery hair, gorgeous sumptuous body flagrantly on display (Sunday services blouse not-withstanding), manner remote as an ice floe and just as deadly— your prototypical niece. Curiously, she looked vaguely familiar somehow; from where, when, Waverly couldn't place. Didn't matter. No mistaking, there was sleeping pill of the high-rent, lowdown, name-your-nasty variety written all over this one.

It got worse. Consider Val's mentor, idol, the master healer there, his dinner fare confined exclusively to the cuisine bizarre, his small precise mouth, when it wasn't busy masticating, running tire-lessly, triathlon mouth, taking up all the air in the room. In a the-atrically whispery voice, the kind meant to be overheard, he was explicating to a bedazzled Val some muddy metaphysic of time, the eternal Now, weaving it cannily, if none too subtly, into a paean to himself and his noble life mission. His face, gaunt and bloodless, seemed corroded by ambition, the bones sharp in the hollow cheeks, socketing bird-bright eyes that looked permanently fam-ished and only partly sane. A harmless zealot? Not likely.

Worse still was the one in the peach suit, Mr. Ignatius LaRevere (speaking of your improbable names), who occupied that end of the couch nearest Brewster and who was plainly tuned into every con-versational hum in the room, listening out of both ears (for in ad-dition to the healer's monologue, Bennie was chattering away at the fatso and the hooker, regaling them with tales of large dollars won and lost, adventures in the world of wagering). But if eyes were the touchstone here, the tell, then his were easily the most alarming of all, no contest. A cool mineral blue, they were languidly vigilant, street-seasoned, but with a pathology fierce as Brewster's in them, though of an altogether different nature and scale. The difference between Jacktown eyes and the kind you saw at Ypsi's Forensic Center, dumping ground for the criminally insane. And when they slid over Waverly, as now and again they did, a dead smile creased

LaRevere's thin slash of mouth, and a look rather like a code seemed to pass between them, as though each recognized in the other something of himself, each privy to the darkest secrets of the other's heart. The barest flicker of a glance was all it ever was, but enough to raise in Waverly a slow chill, a warning in the blood.

At a juncture in the Brewster monologue, Valerie excused herself and sailed over by her brother. She asked if he were enjoying the dinner.

Awkward question. It was her party, her day. What do you do? You lie. "It's very good," Waverly said. "All of it."

"Have you tried the Kalash?"

A lump of it, dark as coal, sat on his plate. "Not yet," he said. "But I'm getting to it."

"I think you'll like it. It's marvelous for the immune system. Delicious too."

Double threat, this Kalash. "I'm sure I will," Waverly agreed.

A sudden troubled cloud skimmed across her face. "Tim, have you seen Roger lately?"

"Not for a few days."

"Neither have I. He was invited, of course. I called from the Center and left a message on his machine."

"Maybe he's out of town. One of those professor meetings."

"I'm sure he would have mentioned it. I do hope nothing has happened to him."

Waverly had an idea on what might have happened to the missing Pettibone, but it wasn't the sort to share with her. Instead he said, "I wouldn't worry too much about Roger. I expect he can take care of himself."

"But I do worry. He was making such good progress with his . . . problem. I wish he'd come today."

A glance across the room revealed a more immediate problem: Brewster silently telegraphing a need with his empty cordial glass. She hurried into the kitchen and returned bearing the Wakassa bottle. Brewster was served first, then the wholesome palate-numbing tonic offered all around. No takers.

Which didn't in the least discourage him from lifting his glass and pronouncing in an organ-peal, call-to-order voice, "I propose another toast. To our gracious hostess, whose efforts in preparing this bounteous feast are, in this as in everything she undertakes, masterly and without parallel."

The fulsome praise brought a pleasured glow to Valerie's cheeks. Her face was wreathed in a madly innocent smile. And just then there came an urgent pounding on the door, and her last wish of the day was granted.

For Eggs, it was becoming increasingly difficult, attending to the many murky cross-currents, voiced and otherwise, eddying through this cramped little room. More so than he had anticipated. More than accounted for in his painstakingly crafted scenario. To his right, Brewster, sparked by a leading question or two, was launched on a rambling exegesis of the Quantum Paradigm, bedrock of his healing art. That much was manageable, that had purpose, a calculated direction. Opening move in the overhauled and polished game plan.

But over to his left, on the other side of Dawnette and Cleanth (the one about as animated as a car crash dummy, the other fidgety as a child, a pair of cumbrous anchors, both of them), the latecomer drunk and the hail-fellow Jew were engaged in an intense dialogue, fragments of which came to him (". . . you'll doubtless be pleased to learn . . ."; ". . . you're sayin' he's for sure in the tank . . ."; ". . . in his mind the only choice open to . . ."; ". . . talkin' whole season or just the swing games . . . ?"; ". . . mentioned only one but I suspect for him there's no . . .") and which triggered an alert in a distant chamber of his head. The drunk's voice was sloshy, bitter-edged; the Jew's low-toned, guarded, studiedly casual. Something was going on over there, entirely unexpected, coming out of those two buffoons. Something demanding of his attention. He strained to pick up more of their muffled words, but it wasn't easy, tracking both conversations. Too many distractions.

For one thing, there was the loopy hostess flitting about, a stricken look on her face ever since her juiced guest came lurching into the room, pouchy-cheeked, rheumy-eyed, stubble of beard the color of rusted pig iron, a sweaty stink rising off his slept-in clothes and unwashed person. For another, and infinitely more disturbing, was the brother, silently contemplating him with a steady assaying gaze. And from out of another time in his life, long since past, Eggs understood the peculiar defining qualities locked in that gaze: isolate, brooding, wary, yet demon-driven behind all the tight control. Understood them well. And he understood, instinctively, if there was one player in the room to be reckoned with, this was the one.

". . . consciousness, purpose, function, matter," Brewster was droning at him. "These, then, are the four stages of the Quantum Paradigm."

Summary inflection in there. His turn to speak. Caught only half-listening, Eggs parried with a stalling remark. "Intriguing theory. But I'm not certain I fully understand its application in your work. The day-to-day treatment of the terminally ill, that is."

"Allegedly terminal," Brewster corrected with a tolerant speck of a smile. "It's really quite simple. That matter we call our bodies is merely the place memory calls home. It is the aim of homeopathic medicine to evoke memory at the cellular level."

Since that dust mote of bogus profundity was deliberately left drifting, Eggs felt obliged to do the straight man number. Whatever had to be done, you do. "Which memory is that, may I ask?"

Clearly gladdened by the question, Brewster hauled in a deep breath and, in a voice so low and portentous it seemed to resonate from the bottom of a well, delivered his answer. "Each of us carries within himself a microcosm of the universe. The distances between the numberless billions of cells in the body are comparable, in miniature, to the vast distances of intergalactic space. And each of those cells has an identity, thoughts, emotions, dreams. And memory. A memory of the Cosmic Spirit that conceives, infuses, binds, governs, and ultimately holds the key to restored harmony and perfect health. The search for that memory, *that* is the foundation of my treatment. The rest is ornament."

A moment's time-out while the lofty notions floated up into the air around him. His smile enlarged slightly, but a contrapuntal frown pinched the paired vertical clefts, symmetrical as quote marks, between his eyes, as though the two halves of his face, top and bottom, were in contradiction. His rope-veined hands sought each other, clasped, and he rocked back and forth slowly, like a venerable old bell tolling a call to mourning. "If only the resources were available," he said sadly, "there is no limit to the suffering that might be lifted, the good done."

So at last they were getting to it. Madman or not, you had to admire his moves. "By resources," Eggs said, "you mean a site, a central location, a . . ." He hesitated an instant, a man groping after an elusive concept, narrowing in on the pitch word (he had a few moves, too). Now. Let it be said now. "A clinic, say?"

"Exactly."

"Something larger in scope than your present facility?"

"Much larger," said Brewster, rocking no longer.

Eggs gave his chin a thoughtful tug. Thoughtful entrepreneur. "That would, of course, be costly," he said. "And would involve enormous responsibility on your part."

"The man who aspires to greatness," Brewster intoned with as much humility as he could summon, eyes piously lowered, "must draw a wider circle around the commonly accepted idea of the possible."

From across the room came a jeering nasal bray: "Emerson!"

Brewster's eyes lifted and fastened on the drunk. "I beg your pardon?" he said, a chilly distancing in his voice.

"That line you filched," Pettibone said. "It's Emerson. Or maybe Thoreau. One of them. Doesn't matter, couple of flyweight clones. And you've got it garbled, by the way. If you're going to steal, at least get it right."

All this was dispatched through a bulging mouth, for he was the only one still eating, forking in the food with the mindless ravenous ferocity of a famine victim, bits of it lost in transit, staining his already filthy shirt, or lodging between his teeth. His flame-colored hair flew in every direction, wild dance of a grease fire. The freckles seemed to boil beneath his skin.

Brewster drew himself up in an attitude of frosty dignity. A share of the piety was gone out of his eyes. He trimmed what little remained of the smile, said, "I hardly think you're in a condition to question my integrity."

An expectant hush settled over the room. Eggs leaned back on the couch, suppressing a smile of his own, watching carefully, both of them. He was curious to see just where this smoldering exchange might lead.

"So that's what you hardly think, is it," Pettibone said, jaws grinding the last morsels in his mouth, and then setting in a challenging thrust. His brows soared belligerently. A man itching for trouble. "Well, let me tell you what I think of all your recycled bargain-basement mysticism. Make that know. Even skunked—as, sad to say, I most assuredly am—but even still, I know there's deeper thinkers than you been over all this tired ground before. Back to the books of the wise, old boy. Study them by day, ponder them by night."

"And who might these wise 'thinkers' be?" Brewster asked, the question voiced around a patronizing sneer. "Apart from yourself, of course."

Pettibone looked blank. He set his plate on the floor and knuckle-thumped a temple, as if to shake loose a retort from his fogged head. None seemed to come to him.

Valerie fluttered over and picked up the discarded plate. Stood there, hovering anxiously. "Wouldn't you care for some more, Roger? Some Kalash?"

The thumping hand made a negative swipe through the air.

"Some tea, then? It would do you a world of good."

"World!" Pettibone bawled, triumphant yawp of the aphasic suddenly reinvested with the power of speech. He leaned forward in his chair, stabbed a finger at Brewster. "Blake! William Blake! Another of you world-in-a-grain-of-sand simpletons, got the key to the universe gift-wrapped in some muddled occult theory. He was mad too, incidentally."

Brewster's scowly face tightened, but he replied without hesitation and in the smugger-than-thou tones of the morally superior, God, or some deputy of equal weight, squarely on his side. "Mock that theory if you like. Nevertheless, this very earth you stand on, the air you breathe, calcium in your bones, iron in your blood—all are simply elements in a cosmic physiology obviously beyond your shallow comprehension. Like it or not, you are a particle of that collective consciousness, my friend. A mere cinder of a star, for all your ignorant scoffing."

"So now it's stars we're back to."

"Roger," Valerie said quickly, "all Wyman is saying—"

Not quick enough. "Oh, I hear what he's saying," Pettibone cut in. A wicked leer sifted into his eyes. "Stars. The starman. Did you know, sir, that bovine flatus, in the form of methane gas, is detectable across those vast stellar reaches you speak of so glibly? Were you aware of that? Friend? And all man's frantic bustle, all the mean acts and paradigms and philosophies, yours included, go utterly unobserved. So it's cow farts may be the only means of announcing our poisoned presence in this cosmos you're on such familiar terms with. Think about it. Cow tooters. There's a lesson in there somewhere."

A nervous titter rippled through the room. At what, nobody seemed certain. Or willing to acknowledge.

Except perhaps for Eggs, who was enjoying himself thoroughly (though his coolly detached features betrayed nothing of the amusement), thinking how the lush had an admirable verve, skewering Brewster this way, turning him over a spit and letting him pop and sizzle and burn. Barbecued fraud. All that inflated wheeze, healer had it coming. Cow farts indeed.

Brewster, not among the titterers, was clearly unamused. His face wore a nostril-pinched, dung-sniffing expression of monumental disgust. His eyes flashed. And in a voice landscaped by contempt, to no one in particular, himself maybe, or his Cosmic Guide, or maybe just the silent witnesses in the room, he said, "What could a stupified sot ever hope to understand of my work."

"One thing I do understand," Pettibone shot right back. "You're no different from or better than all the other imposters and cheats infesting this moral sinkhole. Same pond-slime ethics. Same swindle. Dupe the dying, corrupt the innocent—"

Sudden stop. Dead stop. Thirty seconds or more. For him, a lengthy silence. A look of whipped misery worked its way into his booze-bloated face, as though a nagging bitter memory, momentarily buried by the acrimonious debate, had surfaced once again. And when he resumed, it was in the sluggish disconnections of a man worn down by a helpless indignation. "Innocent," he repeated. "I know about innocent. Young man. Athlete. Fundamentally decent.

Till the vultures got to him. Found his weakness. Tell you about him."

Eggs was attending closely now, taking it all in. Smell of confessional in the air. Smell of score. Whatever had been going on over there between those two, drunk and Jew (who looked none too cheered himself just then), *this* was what it was about. All his finely tuned senses told him so.

But before it could be spilled, another voice intruded, the taciturn brother, warning, "Wait a minute, Roger. This isn't anything you want to be talking about. Even to friends." And with a glance Eggs's way, he added, "And these people are not your friends."

"Doesn't matter anymore," Pettibone slurred. "Point to be made here. Cautionary tale."

The brother shook his head slowly, came to his feet. "I need a cigarette," he said.

And Eggs heard, or thought he heard, him muttering something else as he went through the door, something that sounded like, "I want no part of this"; and he recognized he had stumbled, or was about to stumble, quite by chance, the benign gift of chance, onto something heavy.

A fat yellow moon punched a hole round and symmetrical as a smile button in the black sky. An occasional cloud sailed across its surface. Closer to earth, a gray fuzz of smog hung motionless over the lights of the Strip in the near distance. Waverly puffed at a cigarette, contributing his tiny share to the smirched halo, thinking maybe Pettibone, skulled or not, was right after all. Maybe it was its own kind of sinkhole, this city of slippery hosts. Maybe it was time to move on. Yet even down here, far end of the exterior corridor, the low rumble of quarrelsome voices reached him. Sensational idea, moving on. On to where?

He went down a flight. A faint bellicose echo still trailed him. Down another, ground level, and out into the silent parking lot. He strolled over by the Dumpster and, heedless of both its loitering injunction and the sour stench rising from its open top, stood there surveying the street, neighborhood, foursome of dingy apartment buildings grim as cell blocks and just about as inviting. First time he'd seen them, couple of weeks back, it was all he could do to hold off a groan (he had, though, out of deference to his sister, her child-like joy: "I found a place, Tim, no trouble at all."). A long way—in miles and years and fortune—from the green, elm-flanked, slice-of-Americana street they'd grown up on. Long way from Grand Rapids, Michigan. For both of them. And gazing at it now, the whole ugly scene, its ugliness not much softened even by the charity of night, he had to wonder what would become of her, and to wonder, equally, at the murky frontiers of brotherly responsibility.

And so, these vexing dismal thoughts chasing through his head, he was something less than kindly disposed when a rattly pickup swung into the lot and two six-pack-lugging louts hopped out and, spotting him, traded first some whispered remarks followed by, from one of them, the harsh barked query: "Nobody ever fillya in on the rules, this place?"

With exaggerated deliberation, taking his time, Waverly looked to his right, left, over his shoulder, then back at them. "You talking to me?" he said.

"Don't see nobody else in the lot. You, Buck?"

"Nope, he's the only dude out here."

That fact established, the other one, interrogator, said, "So? We're waitin'."

"You want to repeat the question?" Waverly said.

They advanced on him. Two large square men, beefy chests, drum bellies, lots of hip flesh curling over their belts. The kind of body molded by the wrong end of a shovel. Made for bullying. Both were clad in grease-spattered chamois shirts, jeans, shit-kicking biker boots. Tufts of wiry hair sprouted from under seed caps fashionably worn backwards. The one called Buck had a face the shape of the moon overhead, but absent of even a hint of a smile. Interrogator's was flat, fissured, the lower jaw aggressively underslung. He wasn't smiling either. "Question is rules," he said. "We got rules here."

"That's comforting. No rules, no civilization."

For a moment he regarded Waverly with a squinty, not-quite-certain stare. Long moment. Broken at last by a snarly, "What them

---

rules say, wise fuck, is there ain't no dogs allowed in these apartments. An' it was you we seen bringin' one in. Am I right, Buck?"

"Absolutely," said the compliant Buck. "Up on three. Crazy twat got the pad down on the end."

Waverly could feel himself stiffen. Feel a slow heat gathering in the pit of his stomach, elevating through his torso. He cleared his throat, said mildly, "Let me see if I've got it straight. You're asking me to get the dog out of the crazy twat's apartment. Is that it?"

"Half. You got half. Dog part's right. Only we ain't askin'."

"But I have to ask you something."

"What'd that be?"

"You the owner? Manager?"

"We live here."

"Concerned citizens, then."

"Said we live here, asshole. You got the shitear?"

"The dog bothering you?"

"Ain't a matter a botherin'. Matter a, like, hygiene."

"Yours?" Waverly said, still mild, eminently reasonable, but knowing all along it was foolhardy, what he was doing here, worse than dumb, its own kind of madness. He finished anyway. "Or the dog's?"

The interrogator, losing not a beat this time, said, "Y'know, I was hopin' you'd say somethin' cute like that. Whaddya think, Buck? Ain't that cute?"

"Oh yeah. Real cute."

"Maybe we oughta show him cute, huh."

Simultaneously, drill-team precision, they set their six packs on the ground, fanned out, Buck to the right, nameless interrogator left, and closed in on him. Waverly took one step back, reached up behind him, and yanked a trash bag out of the Dumpster. Gripping it at the knotted end, he swung it like an oversized bat and caught the charging figure left full in the face, staggered him. The bag split. Cans and bottles clattered across the parking lot tar, dissonant harmony to the furious howl. Waverly pivoted right, shred of an instant too late to dodge a spearing, head-butting lunge that slammed him into the iron wall of the Dumpster, whacked the wind out of him. Buck was all over him, swatting wildly, the punches missing as often as they connected, but bruising when they did. The other one stepped in and laid a restraining hand on Buck's shoulder. Evidently he was recovered now, swaying a little but howling no more. Instead he made some wordless growly noises, set himself in a wide-legged stance, balled a hammy fist, drew it back like an archer taking punctilious aim, and drove it dead at Waverly's jaw.

Waverly, chest heaving, still gasping for air, watched it coming. He bobbed his head off to one side. Not far enough. It struck him alongside the ear, force of a falling sledge. A seismic boom thundered through his skull. He sank to his knees, first stop in a numb, chuteless fall. Plunge any further and it's the stomping ground, for sure. A blind instinct told him to hold his balance, and he did, but only barely. From some vast distance, like those stars they were talking about a while ago, upstairs, he heard a directive voice saying, "Gimme one a them longnecks, Buck." Heard a shattering of glass. A mongrel laugh, part cackle, part squeal. Felt his helplessly dangling arms wrenched up behind him, pinned securely. Saw the blurred outline of a face—peppered with coffee grounds, sliver of orange peel comically ornamenting the chin, trickle of blood leaking from the mouth—stuck in close to his own. Also a jagged green cylinder weaving like a cobra head before his eyes. More distinctly now, at this narrow range, he heard the words, "Now you gonna get to eat the big bun, boy. Shame. Waste of a good beer." And, miraculously, some other words as well, coming from somewhere off beyond that eager glowery face and enunciated in a cultivated voice the very model of stately calm: "I think you'd better let him go now."

Waverly's eyes fluttered. Some of the focus came back into them. He saw a figure approaching unhurriedly from out of the shadows in the stairwell. Mr. Peach Suit, name he couldn't seem to recall just then, something odd. Abruptly, his arms were released, and a wall of lout formed between him and the peach suit.

"You with him?"

It was the interrogator speaking, tireless questioner. Buck stood with his hands planted belligerently on his hips.

"You might say that."

"You lookin' for a piece a this?"

"No. I'm simply recommending you let him go." Casually, it was said, a casually tendered suggestion, but italicized by a confident mockery. Nervy guy, this peach suit.

"That's what you're recommendin', huh. See this?" *This* was identified by the jag-edged bottle describing a circle in the air.

"I see it."

"Know what it is?"

"Looks remarkably like a broken beer bottle."

"Wrong. Y'got that wrong. This here's a recommender. An' it's recommendin' you butt the fuck out. While you still got all the skin on your face."

"Really. Appears our recommendations are in conflict, then. How do you suppose we're going to resolve them?"

"Oh, I got an idea on that. Buck, cover the dog-fucker."

Waverly had wobbled to his feet. His head was clearing some, not much. Still felt full of buzzing flies. That would be me, he concluded, dog-fucker.

As if in confirmation, the interrogator wagged the bottle-clutching hand in his direction. Serious blunder. Buck started to turn, but Waverly, sensing this was the moment, now, and it wouldn't come again, spiked a shoulder into the back of Buck's knees, toppling him. At the same time, the peach suit slid inside and under the upraised bottle arm, seized it at the wrist, chopped a bladed hand across the throat, and delivered a knee to the crotch—all these moves executed with a kind of balletic grace, a rhythmic pounce, nothing flashy, nothing wasted. The bottle fell, shattering completely. So did the interrogator. No more questions out of him, only a thin reedy squawk.

Waverly scrambled out from under Buck, who lay on his back, momentarily dazed. Mr. Peach Suit stepped over and lifted a tasselled shoe and drove it squarely, though with a slight twisting motion at the heel, like a man squashing a particularly odious bug, into Buck's throat. Poor Buck. His buttocks and shoulders seemed almost to bounce off the ground, as though he were being dribbled by some enormous unseen hand. His limbs twitched. What began as a scream mutated into some dry croaky sounds.

"Sensitive part of the anatomy, the throat," the peach suit remarked. "Very vulnerable."

He looked back and forth between the two fallen antagonists. Both were gagging, both writhing. He passed a tip of a finger along his upper lip thoughtfully, the thoughtful gesture of a man searching for inspiration. Something seemed to occur to him. He stooped down by Buck and recovered a splinter of the broken glass.

Waverly recognized what was coming next. "Wait," he said. "That's not necessary."

"You think not? I can't agree. What's a brawl without a memento?"

He clapped a hand over Buck's mouth, forced his head back, and carved the figure of a cross into his cheek. And then he went over to the other one and did the same thing. Two piercing wails ascended up, up into the night, spiraling through the air, trailing away gradually in piteous whimpery moans. To Waverly he said, "Religious symbolism is always in vogue. Who knows? They may become converts yet."

He helped them, each in turn, to their feet, all solicitude now and generous concern. They stood rocking dumbly, mouths gaping, eyes full of the stunned vacancy of shock victims, hands tacked to cheeks. Blood oozed between the fingers.

He pointed at the pickup. "Can you drive?"

One of them nodded.

"Better get to an emergency room. You'll want to see to those lacerations. Could require stitches."

Obediently, they started for the truck, moving in a lock-legged shuffle. Stiffly, painfully, they climbed in. The engine turned. Gears ground. The pickup lurched backwards, then rolled out of the lot and vanished down the street, taillights winking a farewell.

He smoothed the rumples out of his peach suit and sauntered over by Waverly, who stood with his back braced against the Dumpster, stroking a throbbing temple. "Anything broken?" he asked.

"I don't think so."

"Pleased to hear that, Mr. Waverly."

"So am I. Seems I owe you one."

He merely shrugged.

"Sorry to say I've forgotten your name."

"Ignatius. Some people call me Eggs."

"Eggs. Many thanks, Eggs."

"It was nothing, actually. At bottom, all bullies are cowards."

"Maybe. But one of those cowards got a punch like a wrecking ball."

"Still," Eggs said with a little chuckle, "leaving, they didn't seem nearly as combative as when they first arrived."

Waverly lowered the stroking hand. Looked at him narrowly. "You saw them pull in?"

"I did."

"Then you saw the whole thing. All of it."

"That's right."

"Any special reason why you didn't step in sooner?"

"The truth is, I was curious to see how you'd handle it."

"Little scientific observation? Behavioral study?"

"Something like that. I like to think of myself as a student of human behavior."

"And what did you conclude?"

"That it was very foolish of you, provoking them that way."

"Yeah, well, we all play the fool now and then."

"So we do. Fortunately, this time the ending was happy."

"Can't fault a happy ending," Waverly said. "So I guess I still owe you. Half, anyway."

"Half's a start."

Waverly took the cigarette pack out of his shirt pocket, extended it in offering. "Care for one?"

Eggs glanced over at the stairs. Quick glance. "Not just now," he said.

Waverly shook one loose, lit it, and inhaled deeply, or deep as his achy lungs allowed. "You know," he said, "speaking of behavior, curiosity, that sort of thing, there's something I'm curious about, too."

"What might that be?"

"Those moves of yours. Where'd you pick them up?"

"Moves?" Eggs said, his expression carefully empty.

"In the scuffle."

"Oh. Those. Well, you see, in my youth I practiced the martial arts. But not very seriously, I'm afraid. I was an indifferent pupil."

"Martial arts, dogs—sounds like a busy youth."

"It was full."

"How about the cutting? You learn that in your youth too?"

A slow smile crawled across the empty face. Same dead smile Waverly had seen earlier, upstairs. "That was learned elsewhere," Eggs said evenly.

"Elsewhere," Waverly repeated, and he might have said more, followed it further, but for the sound of heavy footsteps banging on the stairs.

"That would be my companions," Eggs said.

He was right. A fraction of a moment later three figures emerged from the dark stairwell, Brewster in the lead, Click and Dawnette close behind, but pushing to keep pace with him. Brewster marched toward the Lincoln parked at the opposite end of the lot, his eyes locked on the ground, baleful glare in them, and a stony set to his jaw. Astonishingly, not a word escaped his tightly constricted lips. Clearly not a happy healer.

"Three blind mice," Eggs chuckled, and then, lifting a beckoning arm, he called out, "Cleanth, over here."

Click wheeled around and, catching sight of him, trotted to the Dumpster. Brewster kept right on walking. Dawnette just stood there tapping a heel, peevish look on her face.

"Jesus, Egger," Click said breathlessly, his anxiety displaying itself in the twittery motions of his hands, "where you been?"

"Taking the air," said the ever-imperturbable Eggs and with an our-little-joke glance at Waverly.

"He's really steamed."

"Is he now. And about what?"

"*What!*" Click exclaimed, spittle-winging the word and punctuating it with a raspy tongue skirl. " 'Bout that juicehead up there raggin' on him. Callin' him fake, scammer. Givin' him the barb-wire enema. That's what. You seen it."

"So I gather the party's over."

"Hope to shit a slot fulla silver, over."

As though not to exclude him from the conversation, Eggs

turned to Waverly and remarked offhandedly, "Interesting fellow, your friend."

"He's a professor," Waverly said. Like that was supposed to explain everything. Some explanation.

"I should have guessed. Anyone that garrulous. Cleanth's right, of course; he is something of a bully. Of the verbal variety."

"But no coward." Why he was defending him, Waverly hadn't the dimmest idea.

"Tell me, is he a gambler too?"

No way was he going to bite on that. Not with this psycho. Been enough damage, probably irreparable, already.

It was Click, anxiety fairly exploding now, spared him a reply. "F'Chris'sake, Eggs, c'mon. We gotta blaze outta here. 'Fore he blows his cork. I ain't seen him this hacked in—ever."

"Easy, Cleanth. Relax. You go on ahead. Dawnette and I can catch a cab."

"That ain't gonna wash. He said be sure an' find you, tellya ride along. Said you two gotta talk."

Eggs sighed. He adjusted the knot in his tie, said, "Very well. But we drop him off first, you remember."

"Whatever. C'mon."

"Him first, Cleanth."

"Awright, awright. But let's get toolin', okay?"

"Mr. Waverly," Eggs said, "it's been a pleasure meeting you. My warmest regards to your sister. And apologies for the hasty departure."

His voice, Waverly noticed, had a way of curling up at the close of a phrase, investing even formal well wishes with a ring of scorn. Or was it menace? Blend of both, maybe. "I'll tell her," Waverly said.

"Perhaps you and I will talk again sometime."

"We could do that. Anything in particular?"

"Oh, I'm certain we'll not be at a loss for a topic. Couple of gladiators like ourselves."

He started away, same easy saunter, striking contrast to the jittery sidekick scooting along out in front of him. And over his shoulder, coolly nonchalant, he took the time to add, "Let's make it soon."

Waverly climbed the stairs and slogged down the open passageway, moving stiffly, stiff as those two thoroughly punished (no thanks to him, punished) louts had moved. Coming through the apartment door, he lowered his head and made straight for the kitchen, got a cube of ice from the refrigerator, and rubbed it along the side of his face. Out in the living room Valerie knelt by the couch, ministering to a sprawled and still ranting (though, from the sound of it, rapidly running down) Pettibone. Bennie stood at the counter, scooping up the last of his munchies. "Fuck happen to *you?*" he blurted out, midchomp on an obscenely huge pickle.

Waverly pushed a flat palm through the air, silencing gesture. For all the good it did.

Bennie stepped in for a closer look. "Holy horse apples, Timothy. What happen?"

"Nothing. A little dispute. It was nothing."

"Dispute!" he boomed, big booming voice. "Look like somebody done the jail house tango, your face."

Waverly glanced into the living room, made what he hoped was a significant nod. "You want to hold it down?"

Too late. Valerie, hearing them, rose and rushed across the room and around the counter and, seeing the purplish splotch on her brother's face, suddenly stopped. "Tim, you're hurt? What happened?"

Waverly flipped what remained of the ice into the sink. The question was getting tedious. Irksome. Everybody fretting over the status of his health. "There was a small disagreement," he said. "Downstairs. Nothing serious."

"Disagreement over what?"

"Dogs."

"Dogs? I don't understand."

"Seems some of your neighbors aren't so fond of them."

"Someone did this to you because of Electra? Someone *here?* In the apartments?"

"This is not your Elegance Arms, Val. No genteel folk here."

"We should call the police."

"That's not a good idea," he said.

Bennie was quick to second him. "Timothy's right. Heat ain't got no time for a little pooch squabble."

"But look what they did to him."

"I took a thump, is all," Waverly said. "Sometimes you do. Let it go."

From out in the living room a feeble summoning voice called his name. Pettibone, arm in the air, flagging him. Nice timing, for a change. "We better see what he wants," he said, and the three of them went in and stood over the couch.

"Waverly? That you?"

"It's me, Roger."

"I."

"What?"

"It's I. Speak grammatically."

"Okay. I, then."

"Democritus."

"What are you talking about, Roger?"

"Atomism of Democritus. Just now remembered. Should've told him. That ignorant scoundrel."

"Next time."

"World full of scoundrels, Waverly. *Vade retro, Satanas.* Know that one?"

"Get thee gone, Satan."

"Hence, strictly. Get thee hence."

"I'm a little rusty."

" 's okay," Pettibone mumbled, "it'll come back to you." His eyes glazed over. His head lolled. The flagging arm fell like an axed tree.

"I'm afraid he's gone for the night," Valerie said.

"Afraid you're right. Maybe we can get him out of here. What do you think, Bennie?"

"Give 'er a try, anyway," Bennie said doubtfully.

"No. Leave him. He's going to need help in the morning."

"You're sure?" Waverly said.

"I'm sure."

His head was pounding. Whole body ached. Stand there much longer and he'd be doing a Pettibone himself. "We'll be going, then," he said. "Been a long day."

She gazed at his battered face. "That's a terrible bruise, Tim. At least let me get you some aloe vera lotion for it."

"How about you spare me the aloe vera," he snapped, not meaning it to come out quite as harsh as it did.

A gauzy film of tears welled in her eyes. Her mouth trembled. "I did so want things to go right today," she said in a desolate, baffled voice, as though nothing in her experience had prepared her for this shambles of a party. "And everything went wrong. Everything."

And seeing her this way, this sister of his, so innocent of heart and full of a goodwill nobody wanted, the curtain of years seemed to part once again, and Waverly seemed to see in her face a faint vestige of the melancholy beauty and dignity he remembered in the face of their mother, that gaunt sad unlucky woman vanished by death's curt fingersnap when they both were children. Nothing ever went right for her either, and it occurred to him to wonder if a share of her evil luck infested their genes, poisoned their blood, and lurked in their bones. He came over and wrapped an arm around her quivery shoulders and guided her to a chair, murmuring, "It's all right, Val. It'll be all right." The empty words you put in the air.

She swiped at her damp eyes. "I'm sorry, Tim."

"Nothing to be sorry for."

"I never cry. It's just that it's all so . . . melancholy."

More even than melancholy, he thought but didn't say. But he knew, and knew with the laggard gloomy insight that needs no blinding flashes, no thunderbolts descending from a placid sky, the limits of his duty were boundless, borderless; and if there was a way to shield her from this world of predatory scoundrels, it was up to him and him alone to find it. But not just then. Tomorrow was soon enough. Tomorrow would do. So that's about what he said: "Call me tomorrow if you need any help with Roger."

"If I do, I'll call."

"And I want you to lock your door tonight, Val. Use the chain."

"I will."

He signaled Bennie. "Why don't you get the dog."

Bennie went into the bedroom and brought Electra out on a leash. "You don't wanna feel bad," he said to Val. "That was a sensational feed you fixed."

She managed a game smile. "Thanks, Bennie."

"Hey, it's us doin' the thankin'. Am I right, Timothy?"

"Right again," Waverly said.

Bennie phoned for a cab from the Seven-Eleven on the corner. They waited under a streetlight at the curb. A trio of badass blacks came out of the store and swaggered toward them. Bennie slackened the leash slightly, and at the dog's deep-throated growl the blacks went bango-eyed and veered off across the street. "Don't hurt none havin' ol' Electric around, this vicinity," he said. "Them night fighters don't want no part a her."

Waverly nodded, to show he agreed. About that, his infallible partner was right too.

"You shoulda had her along, you took that little stroll tonight."

"Yeah, well, too late now."

"So you gonna tell me what really went down?"

"It was about like I said."

"C'mon, Timothy. This is Saul Epstein's boy you're talkin' at here."

"And what would Saul Epstein's boy's scenario be?"

"I seen that thrasher tail you outside. My money says it was him play the smash-mouth on you."

"Actually, he was the one saved the day."

"You sayin' *he* bailed *you*?"

"He did."

Bennie gave him a skeptical look. "That don't compute, Timothy."

"I know. Tell me, what's your take on him?"

"Real mean. Calls to mind some a them Five-Blockers, Jacktown. That kinda mean."

Waverly was thinking about the crosses embroidered on the cheeks of the two luckless louts. "Maybe even worse," he said.

"Don't come no worse'n Five Block."

"I'm not so sure. How about the rest of them? What do you think?"

"Pure twilight zone up there. Swami's straight outta your twitch house. Little porker ain't far off, all them squealy noises he makes. An' the bambi, she got south Strip mattress all over her. No missin' that."

"So you'd have to call it a pretty sketchy crew?"

"Sketchy's bein' nice. Freaky come closer."

"How about deadly?"

"Deadly's little strong, that bunch."

"Even the one in the peach suit? Your Five-Blocker?"

"Maybe that one."

Waverly looked at him steadily. For a moment he said nothing, but when finally he did there was an unmistakable accusatory pitch in his voice. "And now they all know."

"What's that, know?"

"This is your partner you're talking to now, Bennie. Martin Waverly's boy. Remember?"

"You referrin' to Roger's roundball game?"

"That's a clean bingo."

"That's where you're wrong. One letter shy a the big bingo."

"What are you saying?"

"Sayin' Roger's still holdin' his mud. Still ain't tellin' *which* game's in the tank. Or how many."

"But they know at least one is. That much he spilled, right?"

" 'Fraid so. I tried to get him to stuff a sock in it. Done what I could. How you gonna talk to a sponge?"

Waverly massaged his bruised face gently. It didn't help. "They're not going to leave this alone, Bennie. You know that."

"It ain't escaped me."

"And Val's right in the middle."

"Don't I know."

"When's the next game?"

"Saturday night. Playin' LSU, over to Baton Rouge. Be on the TV."

"Saturday night. Jesus. Clock's ticking."

Bennie shook his head ruefully. "Hey, I hearya. Better we'd just gone to work tonight."

"Or stayed home."

16

"The higher good," Eggs was saying in a voice oiled and suasive and careful. Very, very careful. "At issue here is that fundamental ethical question: ends and means." He hesitated, shook his head slowly, a small gesture meant to convey the impression of a man not untroubled by doubts of his own. "I wouldn't presume to have the answer," he added humbly.

"But what you're proposing," Brewster said. "Isn't it . . . illegal?"

"I expect it is, strictly speaking. At the same time, the offense, if indeed it can be called such, is all but inconsequential. Certainly victimless."

"I suppose what you're saying is true. No one would actually be hurt."

"No one."

"Still, it *is* a violation of the law."

Eggs swallowed an exasperated sigh. "In this particular instance," he said, "I'm inclined to believe an infraction so trifling is fully exculpated, measured against that higher good."

They sat facing each other across Brewster's massive desk, two thinkers wrestling with the riddle of moral absolutes. This higher good Eggs kept alluding to was, of course, the preposterous chimera of a clinic, swing point of a conversation begun (and by Eggs prudently terminated) the night before. Driving away from the aborted dinner party, Brewster, still steaming from the drunk's taunts, had tried to get it out in the open, nail down a commitment. Eggs, however, had sidestepped deftly, suggested they consider the matter in a calmer and more appropriate setting. Cooler heads, and all that. Tomorrow? Your office at the Center? Noonish, say?

Grudgingly agreed.

A stalling tactic, to be sure, but not without its merits. Let the windbag stew awhile, do some sweating. Also, and from Eggs's perspective vastly more significant, it bought him the time to engineer what might just be his boldest design yet: the yoking together of two discrete scams into a single cohesive package whose potential exceeded even his wildest fancies. If it could be timed and executed properly, proper surgical precision. If.

So what he did when he got back to the apartment was retire early and without a word to his bungling confederates (appendages now anyway, essentially worthless). But he didn't sleep much. All night long the jag-edged fragments of an inspired idea gathered behind his eyelids, and by morning they had smoothed and coalesced into a finished, symmetrical plan.

And so now, Friday, half-past noon, he sat listening to the craven healer's skittish whine: "I don't know . . . all these messy tangles, unsavory people . . . I just don't know . . ." Playing out his sanctimonious little charade. Disgusting to witness, repellant. Patience, Eggs reminded himself, but, reminders notwithstanding, it was dwindling fast. There were other urgent matters to attend to. He didn't have all day. "Look at it this way," he said. "The clinic is within our grasp now. Not some indeterminate time in the future. Now."

"I understand that," Brewster said, eyes averted, a trace of censure in his voice. "But I had assumed you were in a position to support the undertaking through more, well, conventional means."

Eggs eased back in his chair, steepled his fingers. The wise banker pose. "You must also understand the nature of my investments," he said evenly but with a little frost in it. This was the sort of challenge you met head-on. "I have associates to answer to, shareholders. My assets are far from liquid. They could be tied up for months. Years, even, in these uncertain times."

"Years?"

"Years. And what we have here, Wyman, is a unique opportunity to raise a goodly share of the required monies instantly." He dissolved the steeple and punctuated the *instantly* with a smart finger snap that reverberated through the claustrophobic room. Then, softening his tone somewhat, he added, "Of course, a certain amount of venture capital would be required."

"This, uh, venture capital. How much did you have in mind?"

"How much could you lay your hands on?"

"By when?"

"Oh, the next twenty-four hours, say."

Brewster removed a ledger from a drawer, opened it on the desk, and scanned the columns of figures. He turned the pages rapidly, lips moving in silent tally. Finally, aloud he said, "Something in the neighborhood of ninety thousand dollars. Maybe a bit more."

"If we could produce that amount," Eggs said, careful to keep everything in the plural, a joint effort, partnership, "we could double it overnight. Within a month, six weeks, multiply it ten times over."

"A *million* dollars?" Brewster said, as much exclamation as question. A fevered light came into his eyes. His hands coiled and slithered like snakes. Greedy eyes, giveaway hands.

"Possibly more. Enough, certainly, to get the project under way."

"A million dollars," Brewster repeated, dreamily this time.

"But only if we act now. An opportunity like this may never present itself again."

"How, exactly, would you go about it?"

"Perhaps you know that gambling on the local university's teams is strictly prohibited in this city. Entire state, for that matter."

"I know nothing of gambling," Brewster said archly. "Never approved of it."

"Well, trust me, such is in fact the case. Which would seem to be something of a major hurdle. However, there are people who can help us place the wagers."

"But there must be serious risks involved."

"All opportunity comes saddled with risk. Ordinarily. But this one appears to have the compelling virtue of certitude."

"How can you be so sure? I didn't hear that sotted oaf mention any specific games last night."

Eggs generated a small, slow smile. "Perhaps he could be persuaded," he said. "He, or someone else."

"Persuaded? How?"

"You wouldn't want to trouble yourself with that. That would be up to me. It's what I do, you know. Persuasion."

An anxious frown played across Brewster's seamed face. His mouth moved in desperate twists, as though searching for words that obstinately refused to come. Then, head lowered, eyes closed to the appalling truth, he said, "What would be expected of me?"

"Absolutely nothing. All you need do is wait here for my call."

"I have my rounds this afternoon."

"But you can secure the cash?"

"Yes."

"Today?"

"It could take till tomorrow."

"That's not a problem. Most likely it will be tomorrow before I contact you. Tonight, at the very earliest."

A silence opened between them. Brewster kneaded his temples, a display of agonized soul-searching, saintly scruples. Eggs understood. He waited it out. And after a prolonged and fervent reflection, Brewster said, "In the grander scheme of things, a dishonest athletic contest is, I suppose, finally meaningless. Weighed against all the good that might be accomplished."

"So it's done, then?"

"Done."

Simultaneously, they came to their feet and clutched palms. Done.

Eggs left Brewster to his own guilty ruminations. He shut the office door behind him, paused, glanced about. Apart from a few browsers wandering the aisles, the Center was empty. Click stood at the counter, absently sucking a toothpick. Eggs hurried over and said, "The woman, is she here?"

"Which one's that?"

"The Waverly woman, Cleanth."

"Ain't seen her around."

"Isn't she working today?"

"Far as I know. She's usually here to open up."

"Well, where is she then?" Eggs demanded, a thread of irritation stitching his voice.

Click gave a slack-limbed shrug. "Beats shit outta me. How come you wanta see her? What's goin' on, Egger?"

Eggs didn't reply. He deliberated a moment. "All right," he said, "get her on the phone."

"Can't."

"What do you mean, can't?"

"She ain't got no phone."

Eggs drew in a shallow breath, held it. No phone. Not here. This was exactly the kind of petty hitch he didn't need just now. The unaccounted-for kind. He let the breath escape slowly. Can't get rattled. Got to think.

But as it happened, there was no need for further thought. Through the front window he saw a rust-scored Impala pulling up outside and the very lady in question sprinting across the lot. Eggs intercepted her at the door, smiling his counterfeit smile and saying, "Valerie, what a happy coincidence. I was hoping to see you today."

She gave him back a twittery little smile. "I'm awfully late."

"Wyman will understand."

"I hope so."

"I want to apologize for leaving last night without properly thanking you. Your dinner was superb."

"I'm the one who should be apologizing," she said wistfully.

"Nonsense. What happened was none of your doing."

"It was a terrible embarrassment. I just can't imagine why Roger was so vicious to Wyman. He's not like that."

"It was the drink speaking, not the man," Eggs said wisely.

"I know. He'd been doing so well, too. After you left he passed out."

"Really? And how is he today?"

"Better, I think. He was starting to come around some when I left."

"And your brother? No serious injuries from the little, ah, disagreement with the neighbors, I hope."

"You knew about that?"

"Oh yes. I was there. Even able to help out a bit."

"He's got a very bad bruise on his face. Otherwise, he seemed all right."

"I'm relieved to hear that."

Valerie's eyes darted nervously over his shoulder. "Yes, well, it's been nice talking with you, Mr. LaRevere, but I really must get to work now."

Eggs was standing in the doorway, blocking it. "Of course," he said, but he didn't move. Not quite yet. "By the way, would he be home at this hour, your brother?"

"He's usually home during the day. Why?"

"After that unfortunate misunderstanding was corrected, we had a most pleasant chat. But all too brief. Seems we have a great deal in common. So I thought I might stop by, time permitting. Perhaps you could give me his address."

And with that open, perfect trust in universal goodwill, she did. Gave him the address and unlisted phone, both. And they stepped inside and at his direction Click phoned for a cab. And in a flash it arrived. And as the car nosed into the traffic zooming down Spring Mountain Road, Eggs found himself thinking about chance and destiny and fate, and how all three were always divinely ordered when they were going your way.

17

While Eggs's cab was turning onto Las Vegas Boulevard and heading north, another taxi bearing B. Epstein was at that same moment pointing south on the same street. Inside the house on Garces, Waverly was examining his discolored face in the bathroom mirror. Overnight, the bruise seemed to have splayed out across his left cheek and taken on a vivid magenta hue. Not good. At the tables, any kind of attention-grabber was never good. But it was going to be with him awhile, nothing to be done. So he went to the kitchen, poured a cup of coffee, took it to the living room, and settled into a chair. He lit a cigarette. A buttery-soft November sunlight sifted through the window. He could see the dog scampering about in the front yard.

Earlier, Bennie had poked his head around the bedroom door and asked the gratuitous question: "You sleepin', Timothy?"

Not anymore.

"Gonna buzz over to Little C's, see what the line on Sunday's football doin'."

Fine by Waverly.

"Electric's out takin' her dump. Gonna let her run the yard awhile. Maybe you check on her, huh?"

Waverly could do that.

"Seeya all of a sudden."

That he would.

The outer door banged shut behind him.

By then Waverly was wide awake. No more hiding in sleep. So he'd gotten out of bed and showered and shaved (very gingerly) and dressed and stared long at his punished reflection in the mirror. And now as he sat sipping the bitter coffee and smoking and gazing around the room returned to its familiar clutter in Val's absence, it came back to him that today was the tomorrow deferred from last night. For most people, he thought idly, time was linear, a progress of sorts, an advance; for him it seemed more on the order of a circle, a continuous loop, ending where it first began. Idle thoughts, profitless. There were quandaries to address, decisions to be made. Mazes yet to be run. What he knew he should be doing was reviewing his options (which he knew already were not many) and plotting his next moves (fewer still).

But when his eyes fell again on the window he saw a man kneeling by the dog, stroking her gently behind the ears. The man wore slacks and sport jacket and open-necked shirt: no peach suit today, but that didn't matter, Waverly recognized him all the same. He went to the door and swung it open.

"Mr. LaRevere."

"Mr. Waverly."

A noncommittal trading of names, acknowledgment of identities.

Eggs rose and came across the yard, Electra nipping joyously at his heels. As he approached, his head tilted slightly and his features pinched in an expression of solicitous concern. "That's a pretty serious bruise you've got there."

"I like to think it adds some character to the face."

Eggs produced his narrow smile. "Giving you any discomfort, is it?"

"Smarts a little."

"Well, it doesn't look as if it should leave any scarring."

"So far, so-so. Is that why you stopped by, Mr. LaRevere? Check my pulse?"

"Please, call me Eggs."

"Question's the same. Eggs."

"Actually, I was hoping we might talk. Do you have a moment?"

"Sure."

"May I come in?"

Waverly swept a hand at the door. To Electra he said firmly, "Not you," and got a desolate whimper in response. And to Eggs, "Dog seems to like you."

"Most animals do," Eggs said, not so much boast as simple assertion of fact.

They stepped inside. Waverly watched him glance around the room, clearly picking up details, cataloging them. "Get you some coffee?" he said, motioning him to a chair.

"Coffee would be welcome."

Waverly got the coffee. He took a seat opposite him. Waited.

"I gather smoking is permitted here," Eggs said, indicating one of the many heaped and blackened ashtrays.

"It's permitted."

"So many fanatics nowadays, one always feels the obligation to ask."

They both lit up. Eggs inhaled deeply, expelled a satisfied gust. He swallowed some coffee. Smacked his lips. With his thin, relentless smile and contented noises, he projected an air of almost drowsy congeniality.

"Cigarettes, coffee," Waverly said. "I don't think your friend Brewster would approve."

The smile enlarged a little, not much. "Something of a fatuous fool, isn't he."

"Fatuous, yes. Fool, I'm not so sure."

Eggs elevated a brow. "Not a fool? How would you describe him, then?"

"Cunning, maybe. Maybe a low, animal cunning."

"That may be," said Eggs, ever agreeable. "Still, anyone with so stubborn a faith in his own tunnel—some might even say lunatic—vision has to be a bit of a fool, don't you think?"

"That might describe us all."

Eggs chuckled softly. "It might at that," he allowed.

It was getting on Waverly's nerves, all this mannerly sparring. To move things along he said, "Is that why you're here? Dissect the character of Wyman Brewster?"

"No. Well, only peripherally."

"Not that, not my health. What, then?"

"You have no idea?"

"I think I do, but why don't you fill me in anyway."

"Last night I believe I heard you say you owed me."

"I said I owed you half."

"That's the half I've come to collect. Figuratively speaking, of course."

"Figuratively," Waverly said after him. A tail of ash dangled from his cigarette. He stubbed it out. "Maybe you ought to explain how I can repay this debt. Literally."

"Take a guess."

"The basketball game."

"There you are. Very good."

"And you want to know which ones are rigged."

"That would be most helpful."

"Why ask me? Why not Roger?"

"I'm sorry to say my impression of him is much the same as with Brewster. Another of your fools. More of the sentimental variety, perhaps. Even a bit hysterical. In any case, he didn't strike me as a reasonable man."

"But I do."

"Oh yes. Eminently reasonable."

"And you just naturally assumed I'd know."

Eggs set his cup on the coffee table. With a slow circular motion he ground his cigarette in an ashtray. He leaned back in his chair, widened his smile by a microspeck, turned over his palms, and said, "It seemed a not unreasonable assumption."

Waverly watched him carefully. Watched the expressions, gestures, deliberate stagy moves. But mostly he watched the eyes: somnolent, impenetrable, wholly self-sufficient; and some of the code he'd detected, or thought he'd detected, last night flashed from them now; and he said, bluntly, without transition and not as a question, "You've done time, haven't you."

"Time?"

"Joint time."

"By joint, you mean prison?"

"Right. Prison."

"As a matter of fact, I've never been incarcerated. At least not in that sense."

"What sense, then?"

Eggs moved his head slowly, side to side. In a voice affable, mild, he said, "You know, I rather expected we'd get to this. Sooner or later."

"So here we are. Tell me, what sense?"

"The medical, you could say. I spent a few years in a hospital."

"I thought so. State or private?"

"Sadly for me, it was a state institution."

"How'd you earn your ticket?"

"Ticket? I'm not sure I understand."

"I think maybe you do."

For a long moment Eggs was silent. His eyes were almost shut, as if an image were shaping behind them. Finally he said, "You're of an age to remember the gas shortages. The early seventies."

"I remember them."

"Do you recall those interminable lines at the stations?"

"I remember them, too."

"I was in such a line once. Engine idling, patiently waiting my turn. When it came, my car—it was a Porsche, I remember, beautiful machine—anyway, it stalled momentarily. Must have overheated. Odd, when you think about it, how a simple mechanical failure can alter the course of one's life. Maybe it only proves there's a larger truth locked somewhere inside every small mystery."

This calm insight was delivered in a musing tone, slight interrogatory lift at the end. The closed eyes were lifted now too, and fixed on Waverly, who said nothing, continued to wait. Eggs resumed.

"Another driver pulled in front of me. I suggested—quite civilly, I might add—he was in violation of accepted behavior. To say nothing of common courtesy. But he was a contentious sort, you've seen the type: always looking for a quarrel, and usually finding it. He made the familiar rude gesture, shouted an obscenity or two. Go fuck yourself, I believe it was. Something like that, something uninspired. The word *fuck* has been so tiresomely overworked it's lost all its shock value, don't you think?"

"I've never given it much thought."

"If you will, I'm sure you'll agree."

"So what did you do?"

"At the station?"

"That's what we were talking about, if I'm not mistaken."

"Why, run him down, of course."

"For cutting in line you ran him down?"

Eggs seemed genuinely puzzled by the question. "Of course," he said.

"This was when?"

"Let's see, must have been fall of seventy-three. Thereabouts. I was studying for a master's degree at the time. Philosophy. University of Chicago."

"Graduate student with a Porsche?"

"My father's an investment banker. The family is, well, comfortable."

"What were you charged with? Second degree?"

"I honestly don't remember," Eggs said with a dismissive toss of a hand. "It's not important. Justice is for sale in America. I was acquitted."

"NGRI, right?"

"They chose to call it insanity. But we know better, don't we. You and I."

"Why do you say that?"

Eggs ran a finger along the side of his nose thoughtfully. Like all his gestures, it looked rehearsed, timed. "Come now, Mr. Waverly. If we're going to be working together we have to be candid with each other. That's only fair."

"What makes you think we'll be working together?"

"Call it a hunch."

"So what is it you want to know?"

"Well, among other things, I'd be interested to hear how you, as you put it, earned *your* ticket."

"Same as you," Waverly said. "Murder."

"Really. And who was your victim?"

"My wife's attorney. It was a messy divorce."

Eggs clapped his hands together exuberantly. "Good man! There's a profession whose ranks can always use some thinning."

"But I wasn't as lucky as you. Most of my time was done in-house."

"You know," Eggs said, the pensive philosopher again, "I've always discounted the notion of luck. Never believed in it. I prefer to think of it more as fate, or destiny. And now that a benign destiny has brought us to the same crossing, perhaps it will change for the better. What you call luck, I mean."

"That's what you think?"

"Can't see why not," Eggs said. He let his eyes wander over the shabby room. "I'm guessing you're a little down on that luck just now. Purely a guess, you understand."

"Oh, I understand."

"But you do have some extremely valuable information. And thanks to the maleable Wyman Brewster, I have access to a substantial sum of money. By pooling our resources we could both realize a handsome profit."

"So all you really want from me is information."

"That's all."

Waverly considered a moment. Not what he was going to say—he knew that. But how he was going to phrase it. He wanted to get it right. It was important to get it right. "Let me tell you something," he began. Stopped. Started over. "No, strike that, let me *not* tell you something. Tell you why, too. One, because I don't have it, that information you're after. And two, because even if I did you'd never get it out of me. Not in light years."

Eggs looked at him skeptically. "You're saying you don't know."

"That's right."

"I find that awfully hard to believe."

"Believe the flip side of it, then: If I knew, I wouldn't tell you."

Now he looked thoroughly baffled. "Why is that?" he asked.

"Maybe I'm more like Roger than you'd counted on. Sentimentalist, maybe. My own kind of fool."

"I can't believe I'm hearing this."

"Believe it."

Eggs shook his head sadly, the sad rueful motion of the man witness to a natural disaster, but from a safe distance, helpless to intervene. His smile was long since gone. He said, "I confess I'm disappointed in you, Mr. Waverly. More than that, I pity you. The way you'd pity a cripple, or a mongoloid, or the village idiot."

"Pity's a lot like contempt," Waverly said. "Just a shade of a difference. So maybe it's a standoff. Mr. LaRevere."

Eggs opened his mouth as though to reply, seemed to think better of it, got up out of the chair instead, and unlimbered himself and started for the door. But he paused with his hand on the knob, looked over his shoulder. "By the way," he said, and a twist of the elastic smile was back on his lips. "Aren't you just a little curious how I was able to find your place?"

"Why don't you tell me."

"Your sister. I spoke with her earlier today. At the Center. She was very helpful."

"I see," Waverly said flatly.

"Fine woman, your sister. You're fortunate to have her. My family disowned me after the little . . . incident. Didn't matter, though. I've always been able to make my own way in the world."

"Bet you have."

"Well, I must be off. You take good care, now."

"I'll do that," Waverly said. "Extra special."

18

Out where Dawnette grew up, Bristol, Tennessee, they had a saying, went: I been to see the elephant. Meaning not just you been to the circus but once you been there you was a little wiser now, shrewder, like, nobody's fool no more. Which in a way was what she was trying to tell Velva that afternoon. Because she was getting scared, as in megascared, and she had to talk to somebody and Velva was the only one she could really trust. She had a pretty live idea on what Eggs was up to, and if she was even half-right what it come to was like five miles of dead-end corduroy road for your Cool Whip Day, dead ahead. She knew him. Seen that elephant before. And that's more or less what she was saying now, in desperate summation: "He got a game goin', Vel. I can smell it comin'. And it don't include me in the players."

"Whyn't you just duck out?" Velva said sullenly. "You're good at that. Got plenty practice lately."

"Nobody duck on him. Fucker's couple dots short on the dice he's rollin' with. Real twisted."

"Took you better'n two weeks to figure that one out?" Velva sneered.

Dawnette didn't answer. She gazed at the floor, made as contrite a face as she was capable of.

"I'm talkin' at you, Cool."

"I hear you."

"Look at me when I'm talkin'."

Obediently, Dawnette lifted her eyes.

"Whaddya see?"

"See you, Vel."

"See this face?" Velva demanded, voice rising.

"I see it," Dawnette affirmed meekly. But it wasn't easy, looking square into that whacked boiled face, nose all raw and squishy, like a ripe plum somebody stepped on. She did it anyway. She understood what was going on here. Velva needed to see some squirming, little dirt-grubbing. Okay, she could do that. Whatever it took to get herself out of this, she could do it.

Velva jabbed a finger at her. "It's on account a you it looks how it does. Also on account a you that poor sweet girl's layin' back there zoned outta her head all day long so's not to feel the pain. That arm hers never gonna be the same."

"Who we got to thank for this?" she asked, rhetorically and somewhat redundantly, voice a strident trumpet blast now; and without pause she answered her own furious question: "You is who. You and that hemorrhoid boyfriend yours. An' you got the smack to sit there and tell *me* he's twisted. Gayleen and me, we learned twisted real good. Real quick. Didn't take us no two weeks either."

"Jesus, Vel, I'm so sorry," Dawnette said, putting a plaintive little twitch in it, little tremble in the mouth. "Can't tell you how sorry. I didn't know what was gonna happen."

By working at it, keeping her eyes on that mashed nose, and by picturing in her mind Gay's splintered arm, the white bone peeking out at the elbow, and mostly by imagining all that could maybe happen to her, Dawnette was able to generate some actual tears.

Tears did it every time.

"So now you come sneakin' back home," Velva said, scowling yet, but the voice softening some, leveling off to a surly growl. "Expect Velva bail you out, fix things up again."

Sneak part she got right. Eggs ever found out where she was at right now, she'd be history, dust. Good-bye Cool Whip. When he left this morning he told her to wait at the apartment, not to go noplace, he maybe need her later. Said he got business to tend to. Yeah, right. She could put a pretty good figure on what kind of business. One thing she knew was men, and while Eggs was a special breed, one of a kind, he was still a man. Got that same look in the eye they all get thirty seconds after the parallel parkin's done, look that slides over you sideways like you're not there no more, while they're hitching up their jeans and edging for the door.

So what she done was give it about an hour, see was it a test or something; and when he didn't come back or phone she scooted over to Flamingo and hailed the first passing cab and told the driver take her to the apartment on Decatur. And now here she was in the scuzzy, murky living room, drapes pulled shut, looked and felt like a fucking tomb in here except for the stale smell of booze and smoke and Vel's stinkwater perfume; sitting across from her, big old bashed Vel still in the same feed sack duster (speaking of your elephants) from the last time, probably hadn't changed in them two weeks; and lubing her best she could, trying to make peace, saying in her best quivery voice, "I was hopin' maybe you'd have some ideas, Vel."

"Okay," Velva said, "lemme see I got it right. Starts out he's runnin' a slick on this Brewster weirdo, usin' you as bait only the mark ain't into goodies so that don't fly. Then he hears about this— what's it again?—some kinda game?"

"Basketball game. Last night when this lush says he knows about a fix bein' in, Eggs, he damn near fires a wad. I was watchin'. I seen it."

"Who's the lush?"

"Never seen him before."

"You think he knows what he's sayin', slosher like that?"

"Dunno that either. Point is, Eggs thinks so. He got the money eye."

"So you figure he's lookin' to roll the two scams into a package deal."

"That's how I see it."

"Why both? He got a sure thing goin', why even fuck with the weirdo?"

"It's like I told you, Vel," Dawnette told her again, muffling the sigh in her voice. They'd been over all this before, and it wasn't like she had the whole goddam day to talk shit. "Nut's almost gone. See, when we took down that mooch out to the Dunes, that first night back there, he didn't come away with much loot. He gotta be about cashed. Awful close anyway. Which is why he got to make a move soon."

"So you think he's gonna try chump this Brewster into springin' for a stake, get the straight goods on the maybe wired games, and if he scores 'em, cut you loose and bug out the back door. That about it?"

"It's that cuttin' loose part got me tweaked," Dawnette said. And without thinking, she added, "I already seen what he can do." Big mistake. As soon as she said it she wished she hadn't.

"*You* seen!" Velva bawled at her. "Whadda *you* know?"

Dawnette shrank back in her chair, truly awed by the sudden burst of wrath. "I didn't mean it like that, Vel."

"Shit's what you know. Me and Gay, *we're* the ones knows."

"Hey, I'm sorry."

"Watch what you say, then."

"Sorry."

Velva rubbed cautiously at what was left of the bridge of her nose. Pondering a moment, or cooling down, or both. "What about that sideman his?" she asked, considerably calmer now.

"You mean the little worm?"

"Yeah, that one."

"Nothin' about him. He got his head glued to his asshole. All he ever thinks about is feedin' his oinker face and dippin' his wick."

"But they teamed together before, right?"

"Yeah."

"And he's close to the other one, right?"

"Close as anybody get to Eggs. Which is about as close as your South Pole."

Velva deliberated a while longer. At last she said, "Okay, here's what you do. Give the worm the freebie he's after. Find out where he fits in this, what he knows. Pump for a pump. And then you get back to me with whatever buzz you got."

"Aah, Jesus, Vel," Dawnette groaned. "That's sick city. Super gross. Besides, he won't know nothin'. Too stupid."

"You don't know that for a fact. If he don't, what's lost? It ain't like your cherry's at risk here."

"Say I was to do it, which is not what I'm sayin', but just say I was. Comes up zip. Like I know it will. Then what?"

"Then we got to think of something else."

"Easy for you," Dawnette said miserably. "It's me the time's runnin' out on. That's what I'm tryin' to tell you."

"That's what you shoulda thought of before you got yourself into this. An' drag me and Gay right along with you. Seein' you did, we got a little bonus comin' too. Settlement, like. Breeder makes that score, we're talkin' the big banana; he don't, there's still the stake. Either way, it's a nice piece a change to cut up. Plus a heavy payback in the bargain."

"All's I want is out of this, Vel. Payback's something else."

"No," Velva said grimly, "you got that wrong. Payback's what it's all about."

Click don't know for sure what's goin' on, but he ain't about to ask. You fill an inside straight, you ask? You don't ask. Don't never want to fuck with the old gift horse, is what he always say.

And it's a real world-class thoroughbred shows up at his place maybe—what?—ten minutes?—quarter hour?—no more'n that after he gets back from callin' it a day at the Center. She got on this shirt, kind that ties in the front, so thin you can see the warheads right through it, and them same spray-on jeans with the target in the back. In between the two there's this patch a bare white skin, little round belly button square in the middle. Shit, he be happy poke the johnnie into that. On her, that'd be close enough to a joy hole.

She asks can he spare a beer and you can bet your ass he gonna find her one he gotta brew it himself. One each.

In she comes and plunks that sweet back door on the couch and smokes a cigarette and sips at her beer and says, So how you doin'? Even makes a crooked little smile when she's sayin' it.

Doin' good, Click says.

Workin' hard?

More like hardly workin'. Haw haw.

She pats the cushion next to her and says, Why don't you sit down, take a load off.

Click, he sits. Them words *hard, load,* they got him thinkin'.

You seen Eggs today? she asks him, and he tells her how Eggs was over to the Center earlier but he ain't seen him since. She says she ain't either, not since he left this morning.

Ain't noplace to go with that so Click asks her how she been doin' and she goes, Fine. That's it—fine. Like she don't wanta talk about that no more. Usually she dumpin' all over him, so when she bein' half-friendly like this it's hard (there's that word again) to think up what to say.

But he don't have to because she asks him how he thinks the scam's goin'.

He just shrugs, says, Okay, I s'pose. Little slow maybe.

See, that's what I'm thinkin', she says. Been over two weeks now and still nothin' happening.

Well, Click says, doin' a Mr. Thoughtful (which ain't easy, all that creamy flesh right next to you, perfume comin' off it so rich and thick and spicy-sweet he's startin' to feel dizzy, like he maybe gonna blast off on the spot, or faint), Brewster ain't your ordinary mark. Eggs gotta take it slow.

But we got to be gettin' low on cash, she says.

Click says, Yeah, he tol' me he was runnin' short (which wasn't true, course, seein' Eggs never told him nothin' 'cept what to do. But it sounded good, like he was in on the action).

Don't that worry you? she asks him.

Click just shows a tough face, goes, Nah, nothin' to worry about. We got it under control.

I hope so, she says, but she's lookin' worried anyway, and for a couple minutes they don't neither of 'em say nothin', just sit there shockin' their brewbies, Click wonderin' how to turn all this talk into a hide the salami game, but he got no good thoughts there.

Finally she says, real serious, Can I ask you something, Click?

Ask away.

What do you think about him?

You mean Eggs?

Yeah, Eggs.

Think what?

You think he's, like, dealin' straight up with us?

What Click's really thinkin' is she gotta be tellin' him something, puttin' it that way, *straight up*. But what he says is, Eggs?—course he is—why wouldn't he?

You notice we ain't had any them strategy sessions lately?

Yeah, been a couple nights.

Also how he ain't talkin' about his big plans for takin' Brewster down no more. You notice that?

That don't mean nothin'.

You sure?

Click, he ain't sure he's sure about nothin'. Got him all bent, mind goin' one way, dick another. So he says it flat out, What're you sayin' here? You sayin' he's lookin' to stiff us? (Word stiff just pops right outta his mouth, but he got a pretty good idea where it come from.)

Sayin' nothin'. Just askin' your take on it.

Aah, Eggs stiff us? That couldn't be.

But if it was?

It was, we gotta do something, is what Click tells her. He's startin' to get a little stressed now himself, thinkin' maybe she onto something he missed.

Like what?

Dunno. I got to think on that.

Like maybe keep a close scope on him, both of us?

Yeah, that. Could do that.

Watch to see is he gonna try and shine on us? Listen to what he says? Pass along any buzz?

That too.

Like stick together, say?

Yeah, right, absolutely.

So we got a deal? You and me watchin' out for each other?

You betcha, Click says, but it comes out husky and kinda gummy, like he got a Polish brown trout in his throat from thinkin' not about Eggs but about him and her stuck together.

Then, like she's readin' his fuckin' mind, she turns and looks him dead in the eye and goes, Because you know, Click, sometimes that stickin' together part can be fun.

Holy mother of fuck, Click's thinkin', if I'm dreamin' don't nobody wake me. Real cool though (even though dickie boy down there scorchin' a hole in his pants), he goes, How's that, fun?

You ever had a butt job?

You mean do a reamer? Sure, everybody done that. (Which wasn't true in his case, but you don't got to tell everything. Anyway, any hole she wanna offer, he's first up in line.)

Maybe not exactly the way I do it. Want me to show you how?

She askin' does he want her to show him how? Pope got an ass? Cat Catholic? Or the other way around, however it goes, ain't easy to think straight right about now. What he says, supercool, is, Yeah, that'd be good.

So what she does is set her beer on the floor and get up off the couch and sashay over to the TV and switch it on to the MTV channel where they got some half-naked boogie ladies doin' the jungle stomp. But Click, he ain't even seein' the spooks, he got his buggy eyes locked on that swingin' target, which is backin' up toward him, rollin' and swayin' right in his face, movin' in time to the music. And then she starts lowerin' it, but slow, slow, bendin' at the knees like she's easin' down to drop a load, till pretty soon it's brushin' the head of Big Daddy, teasin' the old boy till he about pop right through the fly. Click trys to get his hands around and onto them sugar nubbies, but she shakes 'em off, sayin', No, only two contact points here, that's how this game's played. Fuck, that's okay, target's grindin' away on Daddy now and he can feel the weirdest sensation, kind of like a tuggin' motion in the muscles of her asshole, almost like it's a quicksand suckin' him under (or up, in this case, world turned upside down on him), like one a them snappin' pussies he's heard about (but also never experienced), only in the back door; and if there wasn't no clothes in between, ol' one-eye be deep into the chocolate speedway; and the music starts goin' faster and gettin' louder—boogies really beltin' now—and them bung muscles gettin' tighter; and before Click know it his tongue's gallopin' over his teeth, back, front, all of 'em, making the squeaky sounds he's famous for, got him his name; and then them sounds turn into a rushing whinny and then a long shrill squeal, and he bucks forward and up, and then he shudders and sags back and it's all over, all she wrote.

While he's catchin' his breath, she picks up her beer and finishes off what's left of it. When he's back to earth she says to him, You like that?

Click, he's still too groggy to do anything but make his head go up and down.

You gonna remember our bargain now? Stick together?

Oh yeah.

So you gonna pay real close attention, he talks to you tonight. Tomorrow too. Whenever. Anything you hear, you let me know. Right?

Right, absolutely.

You won't forget?

I won't forget, Click says. (Forget?—fuck—she tell him to fly, he'd put on a fuckin' cape, take a leap off the Landmark, do a Superman for her.)

Because there's lots more where that came from, Click. Who knows? Next time you might even get a shot at the front end. Bottom *and* top.

That last part she says runnin' her tongue over her lips, wettin' 'em down. Then she turns, and the last thing Click sees is that target swingin' out the door, thinkin' proudly, I scored a bullseye on that, but still not positively sure he ain't dreamin' (the evidence of the damp stain on his trousers notwithstanding). Didn't matter none. He was to croak in his sleep, they'd find him in the morning with a shiteater all over his face.

After Eggs left the house on Garces he walked over to the Strip and caught a cab to Valerie's apartment. He climbed the two flights of stairs and went down the exterior passageway to her place at the end. Tried the door. It was locked. He knocked, waited, knocked again, nothing, banged at it, more of the nothing. No response, no luck there.

So he walked to the Seven-Eleven on the corner and at the pay phone checked the directory under *P's*. No Roger Pettibone listed. He considered calling the Center, trying to squirrel the number and address out of the compliant Ms. Waverly. But that wouldn't do either; very likely the brother (who was hardly a fool, for all his righteous dissembling) had got to her by now, alerted her. Very frustrating. Till it occurred to him that last night he'd heard it said the lush was a professor. Nobody's said where, but UNLV was the logical assumption. He started to dial for yet another cab, thought about the shrinking roll of bills in his wallet (to call it a wad anymore would be delusory), and decided against it. Economy, and all that. Besides, the exercise and the air might do him good, clear the head, help sort the thoughts.

He walked over to Maryland and all the way down past Flamingo and turned in at a campus entrance. The grounds were unfamiliar to him; he'd never been here before, no occasion. So he wound through an empty parking lot and around an uncommonly ugly sculpture in the shape of an upended flashlight (their tasteless symbol of the beacon of knowledge, no doubt) and down a grassy, tree-studded mall flanked by buildings designed by an architect trained on Lego blocks and whose style could, in his considered judgment, most charitably be described as contemporary-hideous and therefore perfectly suited to this community.

The mall was deserted. He tested the doors on a couple of the buildings. They were locked. It was beginning to seem as though every door he approached today, figurative and otherwise, was bolted. And he was getting seriously annoyed. Where the fuck was everybody? What's going on? Then it came back to him: Thanksgiving, goddam holiday. Nobody supping at the fount of wisdom today. So he was not going to find the elusive drunk here. So now what?

Apart from the vile Waverly coffee, he'd had nothing to eat or drink all day long. He supposed he was hungry. Certainly weary, all this foot-shagging across town. Maybe what he needed was a brief respite, sustenance. A place to get off his feet, to think. There were some bars opposite the campus on Maryland, so he walked that way and stopped in at the first one he came to. It was crammed full of raucous, tacky-looking kids, doubtless a watering hole for the university's finer scholarly minds. He found a seat at the bar, ordered a brandy and water, and asked to see a menu, both of which were rudely slapped in front of him. For a dump like this, the prices (not to speak of the service) were outrageous, bordering on brazen. But he spotted a free snacks table over along a wall, so he elbowed his way through the crush of bodies, filled a paper plate, and brought it back to his seat. And as he picked at the stale chips and mousetrap cheese chunks and wilted celery stalks and meatballs puddled in a greasy red sauce, the accelerating downward spiral of his fortunes did not escape him. Reduced to scrambling again, no different from the lowliest, scruffiest hustler in the house. His mood, so elevated this morning, so sanguine, was rapidly souring. It had not been the productive day he'd anticipated. He shoved the plate aside, finished the brandy, and marched out.

And so it was that by the time he got back to the apartments (half an hour and something over two long miles later) he was understandably not in the best of humors. He went directly to Click's place, pounded on the door. This one opened. Revealing the occupant standing there, beer in hand, wide vapid grin splitting the moronic face.

"Hey, Egger, whereya been all day?"

"Here and there."

"Whaddya been up to?"

Eggs pushed past him and flopped onto the couch. "Working on our project, Cleanth," he said irritably. "What else?"

"You look kinda whipped. Wanna brew?"

"No."

Click came over and sat next to him. "So how's she look?" he asked. "Project, I mean."

"At the moment, rather dismal."

"Yeah? Brewster ain't doin' no nibblin' yet?"

"Brewster's not the problem."

"I don't follow. He ain't, who is?"

Eggs glowered at him. "Were you at all listening last night?"

"To what?"

"To that juicer. The basketball talk."

"Sure, I heard him. Sounded like smoke to me."

"I don't think so."

"I dunno," Click said doubtfully. "Fucker was shitfaced. Coulda been the sauce talkin'."

"No, you're mistaken."

"Why's that?"

"It's the other two, Cleanth. The brother and the Jew. They're too clever by half not to be in on this. The brother, anyway. Of that, I'm certain."

"How come you so sure?"

"Call it an instinct."

"Okay, say they are," Click said, underlining his hypothesis with an urgent tongue screak. "What's it got to do with us?"

"I should think that would be obvious."

"Ain't to me."

Eggs laid his forehead in the palm of a hand. Problems to address, puzzles to solve, tactics to revise, time growing short—what was he doing here? "All right," he said. "What we're going to have to do is persuade them to cut us a share of their score. Share the wealth. That plain enough for you?"

Click's eyes narrowed, tightened. A baffled squint. "I gotta tellya, Eggs, I don't get it. Even if we was to do that, we ain't got no stake money. And anyways, you ain't never been into the wagerin' life before. You ain't got the fever, do you?"

"Of course not," Eggs snapped. "Gambling's for imbeciles. Unless it's a sure thing. Which is what we're looking at here. Certainty."

"This mean now we ain't gonna fire on Brewster?"

"Compared to this, Brewster's pocket change, shortcake. However, we still need him. Temporarily."

Now Click looked totally mystified. "For what?" he asked. "Sound to me like you got a whole different scam in mind to run."

"For that stake money, Cleanth," Eggs said with an enervated sigh. Speaking of imbeciles.

"So what're you figurin' to do?"

" 'Disorder is merely an order we cannot see,' " Eggs said ruminantly. "It was Bergson said that, I believe."

"Fuck's *that* mean?"

"What it means for us," Eggs explained, gentler now, more patient, "is that probability is not the same as certainty. The next game is tomorrow night. It may be on ice. Or it may not be. And that's our problem. That's what we have to determine." Curiously, out of the fog behind his eyes, a plan of sorts was taking dim shape. It wasn't much, but it was more than he had when he first came through the door. So maybe this puerile dialogue wasn't utterly wasted after all.

"How we gonna do that?" Click wanted to know.

"The persuasion, Cleanth. I'm confident we'll be able to convince one of those three."

"Which one?"

"Whichever is the most pliant."

"Huh?"

"Don't worry about it," Eggs said. "That's a happy problem." He stood, rose onto tiptoes, and stretched his arms overhead like a man coming out of a deep slumber. "Let's get some rest now. We've got some serious stalking to do, first thing in the morning. Tomorrow, Cleanth, promises to be a lively day."

19

A s soon as his guest was out the door, Waverly phoned the Center and asked to speak with Val. "Not here," he was told, and it took another question to extract the intelligence she was off with Brewster "on rounds." Still another to get a vague estimate of "three, four hours, hard to say" before they'd be back. Male voice on the other end of the line, sounded like it could be the big appetite from last night, so he decided against leaving a message. He put down the phone, checked his watch. A little after two. Long afternoon ahead.

For a while he paced, sorting through his anxieties. The dangers were real but maybe not imminent, not just yet, and for the moment there was absolutely nothing he could do. Nothing but wait. At waiting, he had plenty of practice. He took a chair and, to accelerate time, played a couple of games of chess in his head, severing himself, move by countermove, into two distinct identities: Timothy Waverly on one side of the phantom board, an anonymous but equally skilled opponent on the other. A kind of managed schizophrenia. Prison had taught him how to do that. Both games were long and bitterly contested. Both Waverly lost.

Around four he remembered he'd forgotten the dog. He went to the door and beckoned her in. She was tired and hungry from all the unaccustomed open-air romping. Also perplexed by the absence of the chummy Bennie. So he led her into the kitchen, filled a saucer from the jug of Val's demineralized water, and fed her some of the organic biscuits. Then back to Bennie's room where she curled up by the bed and promptly fell asleep. That consumed maybe ten minutes.

At five he tried the Center again. Learned from the same voice (abrupt now, almost surly), No, not back yet. So he waited some more, filling an ashtray with an ascending mound of butts, watching the house across the street blacken in the slow-motion creep of night, and seething at the wicked joke of fate that appointed him (of all the unlikely people—bungling steward of his own life) guardian of his fragile, vulnerable sister.

He gave it until half-past six. Then he picked up the phone and called again. This time it was a different voice: amiable, accommodating, determinedly chipper, female. But not Val. He repeated his question.

"Sorry, not here."

Had she and Brewster returned from their rounds?

"Oh yes. An hour ago, at least."

Could he speak with Brewster?

" 'Fraid not. He went straight to his place upstairs. Said he didn't want to be disturbed."

And Val?

"She left soon's they got back."

Alone?

"Didn't see anybody with her. She just drove away in that funny old car of hers. Is there some kind of, uh, problem?"

No problem.

"You want to leave a message, she'll probably be in tomorrow."

No message.

He thanked the cheery voice, rung off. Okay, got to think now, got to act. But for a moment he merely stood there, barren of ideas, iced in a zone of paralytic dread. Okay, okay—not at the Center, had to be home then. Where else? She didn't know anyplace else. Except for the one he'd overlooked, and three digits into an urgent summons of a taxi two fingers of yellow light appeared beyond the window, suddenly extinguished. He sprinted to the door. She was coming through the sagging gate and up the walk. Alone. Apparently unharmed, though with a tight distressed look on her face.

"Val. You all right?"

"I think so," she said.

He bolted and chain-locked the door behind them. She sat, Waverly remained on his feet. "What happened?" he said. "Where've you been?"

"We had the most terrible experience on rounds today," she said, striking a mournful note.

Waverly brushed the air impatiently. "First tell me where you've been."

"Like I said. On rounds."

"After that."

"I went back to the apartment. To see how Roger was doing."

"Was he there?"

"No."

"Anyone else?"

"At the apartment?"

Waverly drew in an agitated breath. "Right," he said. "The apartment."

"No."

"Nobody else? Nobody giving you grief?"

"Grief?"

"Trouble."

"Of course not. Why?"

"Never mind. Roger leave a note?"

"No, but that's not unusual for him. What's wrong, Tim?"

"I'd better call. You got his number?"

She recited the number.

Waverly tapped it out, waited through ten rings, got no answer, gave it another ten, still no answer. Nobody home at Pettibone manor. Or nobody tending the phone. He recradled his. Nothing he could do. What could he do? He couldn't be everybody's keeper. One helpless charge was enough. There were limits. He took a chair facing her.

"What's wrong?" she asked again.

He answered with a question. "This terrible experience—what happened?"

"One of our patients, Mr. Jessup, passed over today."

"Passed over, as in died?"

"Yes. He had a serious heart condition. He'd been in Wyman's care for about two months and we thought he was making progress. But he'd also been taking these drugs."

"By drugs, you mean medicine?"

"I mean drugs," she said stiffly.

"Okay, drugs. Go on."

"When we got there he looked just awful. Very pale, ashen almost. Trembling. Could barely speak. The poor man, if only he'd followed the treatment program . . ." She trailed away, eyes misting over at the what-might-have-been thought.

"So what did you do?" Waverly prompted.

"We fixed him a liquid herbal stimulant, but he couldn't get it down. He was getting worse. Convulsive. So Wyman gave him an injection of ozonized water and—"

"What's that?" Waverly broke in on her.

With a kind of forthright, stainless innocence she said, "It's a therapy we use sometimes. Raises the oxygen level in the blood. Wyman believes it's particularly helpful for heart patients. He's convinced—"

Waverly interrupted again. "Wait a minute. This man is having a heart attack and you two squirt voodoo water into his veins?"

"*Ozonized* water."

"What about his medications? Those drugs?"

"He was asking for them. Trying to ask. But Wyman knew they'd only hurt him, so he, well, decided against administering them."

"You mean he withheld them."

"It was a choice someone had to make."

"So to spare him all this hurt, your healer friend killed him instead. Some choice."

"That's not true!" she said hotly. "It's unfair for you to say that!"

"Tell your stiff about fair."

The mist in her eyes had gone drizzly now. She made a move to rise, murmuring, "I thought maybe you'd understand. Evidently I was wrong."

"Sit down, Val."

It tumbled out harsh, exasperated, closer to threat than command. She looked startled. She sat down.

"What I understand," he said, "is Brewster could be held accountable for this guy's death. You too, since you were there. But that's an altogether different problem. I suppose it's a small relief to know that's the extent of your 'terrible experience.' "

She gazed at him. Shook her head slowly, sadly.

"What?" he said.

"You never used to be this way, Tim."

"Which way is that?"

"So . . . callous. Insensitive."

"Yeah, well, a Jacktown holiday will do that to you."

"What was it like?"

"You're asking about prison?"

"Yes. You've never told me."

"This is not the time, Val. There are other matters to attend to. Urgent ones."

"No," she said gravely, "it's always been there. Like a gulf between us. You know that. And ever since I've been here you've avoided it. This is the time."

"You want to know what it was like? Not exactly a stay at a resort hotel. Nothing to recommend it. Does that explain it for you?"

"That lawyer. Why did you kill him?" The question was delivered in the accents of genuine curiosity, not a trace of censure in it.

"How can I answer that? If I knew, I'd tell you."

"But why him?"

Waverly remembered his scornful remark of only a moment ago, on the subject of choices. In a life defined by ruinous choices, the mockery seemed suddenly hollow. "Better it had been nobody," he said, "but if it had to be someone it should have been—" He hesitated. After all those years the name of the man who'd triggered the first of those calamitous choices, first of many, still stuck in his throat. "Your ex," he finished. "Or mine."

She supplied the names for him: "Arthur and Annetta. What they did was wrong. But you and I need to understand what happened. To understand is to forgive, Tim."

"Nothing to understand. What happened was we both married the wrong people. Two cheaters who found each other. At our expense."

"But nobody deserved to die for it."

Again Waverly hesitated, and when he spoke it was impossible for him to erase the bitterness from his voice. "We all of us get just about what we deserve. All of us. Including their lawyer."

"Even Dad? It killed him too."

"You're asking me questions for which I have no answers. What is it you want from me? Remorse? Guilt? Fresh out of both."

"I want you to forgive yourself. So you can be what you really are. Not what you've become."

For a flash of an instant Waverly's censors deserted him, and in a spurt of visual, visceral memory he saw the lengthening trail of victims, some blameless, some not, left behind in the run of years. "After an act like that," he said, "a killing, you put on a mask. In the beginning it's loose, floppy. A bad fit. But in time your face grows to fill it."

"He loved you, Tim."

She was speaking of their father again, one of the blameless ones. "I suppose he did," Waverly said. "Truth is, I try not to think about him anymore."

"You should, though. Because he's here, you know. In the earth, sky, the air. Everywhere. Walk through a field sometime, you'll feel his heartbeat under your feet."

"There are no fields here, Val."

"That doesn't matter. Let me show you something."

She foraged through her worn bag, came up with a small photograph and handed it to him. Waverly stared at it: a color snapshot of his father in academic gown, rigidly erect, square-shouldered, square-jawed, solemn, imperious, as secure as Wyman Brewster in his faith in his own rectitude, but with mortarboard perched on his head at a perilous, almost rakish angle as if to confound the austere expression with a nervy little gesture of defiance. As if the tilt of

---

that preposterous piece of headgear said, I understand the absurdity of it all and I accept it, but I don't approve.

"You remember how much he disliked graduation ceremonies?" she said.

"I remember. But he always went. Felt it was an obligation to his students."

"This was taken the year before everything . . . went wrong. It was the last one he ever attended. Three years later he was gone. But if you listen, Tim, you can still hear his voice in the wind. Which is what I'm trying to tell you."

Waverly said nothing. He continued to stare at the picture. In the background was a grove of trees, elms mostly, a few stately evergreens, couple of white birch. He didn't recognize the spot, though he'd doubtless been there himself once. And holding it, this framed and colorized wink of time, he was struck by the peculiar alchemy of a photograph, invested with the substance of reality only by common assent; and by the sleight-of-hand that vanishes the man and leaves the trees behind. It occurred to him that a man— any man, his father, say, himself—is more than the sum of his experiences, is as much a product of his geography, the groves and streets and landscapes of his past, and the slow rhythms and patterns of place that mold his character until it's set like plaster. And in this replica of a departed father, this sorcerer's illusion, he seemed to see a blurry trace of himself and an even blurrier likeness of his lost son. So maybe she was right, Val. What did he know of the overarching, desolate offices of love? He knew nothing. Only that in this swirl of memory, this backstroking through the toxic currents of time, no conviction was reliable anymore, no axiom absolute, no truth true. All that was certain was the obligation to stand, endure, like those specters of trees in the photo he held in his hand.

And which he returned to her now, saying gently, "I'm afraid we'll have to finish this another time. I've got to go out now. Some things to be done."

"I think maybe we have finished, Tim. I know I feel a whole lot better for it, this little talk. And I hope you do too."

"Much better," Waverly said, as absent of irony as he could pitch it. One of the many lies you tell, the loving variety.

In the moment of awkward silence that will follow any surgical probe of the secrets of the heart, they averted their eyes, gazed into private distances. Finally, as though the thought had just come to her, she said, "Where's Electra?"

"In the back. Sleeping."

"She's not sick?"

"She's fine. Worn out, is all. She was running in the yard most of the day."

"I hope you're feeding her properly."

"She's doing fine, Val. Go see for yourself, if you like."

"No," she said, coming to her feet, "it only confuses her when I'm here. And I really must be going."

Waverly rose quickly out of his chair, positioned himself between her and the door. "Going where?"

"I've got things to do too," she said with a labored airiness. "Same as you."

"What things?"

"We have this patient who's suffering from lung cancer," she said, her tone gone somber. "I don't think he has much time left, and he's all alone. I'm going to sit with him awhile."

"One corpse a day isn't enough?"

She looked stunned, truly hurt. "That's a terrible thing to say, Tim. I'd hoped that now you'd be more . . ."

"More what?"

"Compassionate."

"Okay," he said, tempering his voice, "sorry I said that. Sorry. But I want you not to go anywhere tonight, Val. I want you to stay here. You can take my room."

Now she looked at him quizzically. "Why would I do that?"

"Because you're in danger."

"Danger? What kind of danger?"

"You don't know?"

"Surely not because of Mr. Jessup's death? That was nobody's fault, in spite of what you may think."

"No, not that," he said. "Deeper even than that."

"I don't understand what you're talking about, Tim."

She didn't either. That much was painfully clear. From inside the bubble of sublime innocence, perfect trust, she hadn't the slightest glimpse of the storm gathering around her. Around both of them. And he had neither time nor patience to explain. May as well try explaining evil gone unpunished to a child. "Then just do it because I'm asking," Waverly said.

"I can't."

"You can't. Why is that?"

"Because I promised the poor man I'd stop by tonight. I don't know what it is that's upsetting you, Tim, but I'm not going to fail him. He needs me."

Waverly knew his sister, recognized the willful sheen in her eyes, stubborn set to her chin. Only too well did he know her. All his feeble protests, nettled pleading—less than worthless, all of it. Time squandering. And time was closing in on him now. "Anyone else know you're going back there?" he asked.

"No."

"Brewster?"

"No."

"You're sure?"

"Of course I'm sure. He'd already gone out to the car when I spoke with this man. You see, he'd been smoking again, and Wyman's pretty much given up on him."

"All right. You made one promise. Make another. Promise me you'll come straight back here after you've seen this patient of yours."

"Well, we'll see."

Waverly threw up his hands. "That's not *good* enough, Val. You've got to do what I'm telling you here. You've got to trust me on this."

She made a vague and puttering reply, on the order of another *We'll see.* Best he was going to get. He walked her to the car. And watching her leave, the look on her face, at once obstinate and serene; her fluttery farewell gesture; the Impala sputtering off into the darkness, leaving the acrid stench of its exhaust hanging in the air—watching all that he felt a slow chill overtaking him, more than just the chill of night.

He hurried back into the house and went directly to the wicker laundry basket at the end of the narrow hallway between bedrooms and bath. He dropped to his knees and rummaged through it, flinging his and Bennie's soiled clothes over a shoulder. At the very bottom, folded into a pair of his partner's stained shorts—mute testimony to perpetually tormented and unquiet bowels—was an envelope full of bills (the B. Epstein theory on security: "Any booster gonna paw through my Hershey squirt drawers lookin' for the gelt, he need it worse'n we do").

Waverly counted the money. Came to slightly over twelve long. Not an abundant stake. He took exactly half, replaced the rest (very gingerly; Bennie's theory, he'd decided, held up). He went into the bathroom and scrubbed his hands. Then he phoned for a cab and stood at the window, waiting.

From melancholy experience he knew money, of itself, solved nothing. But he knew also, better than most, that it bestowed the powers of option, alternative, choice. None of which were open to him now. If he could assemble all his energies one more time, conjure all his skills and all his craft, focus all his attention, move nimbly enough—maybe, just maybe, he could iron out a share of all the messy wrinkles life had dealt him lately, restore some small measure of order. A little luck wouldn't hurt either.

20

If you wanted to believe the guidebooks (the ones with words like *bare* and *sin* and *jungle* and *exposed* in their titles), all the smart bee jay action went on in certain selected dust joints downtown. Single-deck play; double down on any two, three, or four cards; split and resplit any pairs; dodge a bust on a six-card run and you're automatic winners; surrender and hold on to half the bet on your first two if you have to—rules made in counter heaven. And didn't they just love to see them coming, all those sorry witless wannabees. Kind of chump who reads a "make big money playing blackjack" book; speeds home after a day's work at the P.O. or the gas company or some such and practices faithfully at the kitchen table couple of hours a night, couple of months running; faithfully squirrels away a puny stake—pound here, sawbuck there—in a Christmas Club account at the local First National; puts himself to the test at an Elks Club Las Vegas Nite; then heads out here on a week's vacation with a gut full of confidence (albeit churning anxiously) and a head full of dreams. Man with a mission. Going to nail those casinos right to the wall with his flashdazzle. Look out, Chapter Eleven!

While the fool killers, patient as spiders, stand behind their tables and smile their thin chilly smiles and wait. Welcome to the web.

Waverly didn't believe the guidebooks. Placed no faith in printed words, spoken buzz, considered opinions, wise counsel, shrewd advice. Not out here. Out here even simple signs, signals, directions were calculated to confuse, the architecture of deception. (Looking for the john?—Sure, buddy, right over there, other side of the craps tables, can't miss it. Want a bite to eat?—No problem, my man, coffee shop's down at the end of that battery of bandits. Lotsa luck.) Everything was suspect, everything bait, tugging you deeper into a world of light and shadow, angles and agendas, a world of pathological darkness framed in the radiant beguiling drapery of violent neon.

No, if he believed in anything at all it was the elegant symmetry of numbers, their cold austerity, stable precision. And against that kind of bare-bones beauty, all the words and signs and symbols were merely a stained blotch. Rise by the numbers, sink by them—either consequence was scrupulously grounded in a dispassionate equity. Which is more than could be said for most of life.

So it didn't much matter where he played, guidebooks and sly insider wisdom notwithstanding. Mattered even less, given the course he was launched on, for a Vegas scuffler like himself (face it, Mr. Waverly, that's what you are) about as suicidal as a spin at Russian roulette.

Accordingly, he began down near the south end of the Strip, at the Dunes, with the intention of working his way northward up the street. Dunes was a disappointment: traffic much too thin, dealers cooling their heels at idle tables or going heads up against obvious shills, pit bosses with nothing to do but pace and scowl. Far too risky for what he had in mind.

So he went outside and stood at the corner a moment, considering his next move. The jostling Friday night crowds, a swirling surging lemming mass, spectacular in its directionless urgency, migrated from hotel to hotel, Caesar's and Bally's on opposite corners, Barbary Coast diagonally across the street. Caesar's was no good, Bally's not much better. Too many watchful eyes. Get walked either place and chances are The Word would precede you with the velocity of a runaway brushfire. Came to counters, the one thing rival casinos were eager to share was buzz, data (or so he'd been told often enough, and who should know better than your B. Epstein?). At the same time, he was something less than keen on the B.C. For while he was certainly no Jonah, carried no amulets or talismans, he was also not unmindful of the fact it was the very spot where he'd first encountered Pettibone and where his luck first began to turn on him, led him inexorably to tonight's rash, not to say foolhardy, scheme. If you were in the habit of tracing such things. For which profitless investigations he hadn't, just now, the luxury of time. Couldn't plot your moves on vague apprehensions, dubious omens of disaster. So at the next walk signal he fell in with the wave of lemmings, crossed one street, then another, and came through the doors of the Barbary Coast Casino.

Place was jammed. Which was good. Not so good was the faintly arched brow on the money lady at the cashier's cage. He'd almost forgotten the purpled splotch worn like an ID on his cheek. Smiling a foolish, innocent, corndog smile, he asked her to convert two long into chips: Blacks only, please; well, maybe a hundred of it in greens. Unsmiling and without comment, she counted the bills and pushed over the chips. Nineteen blacks, four greens. Didn't look like a whole lot.

Waverly put them in a pocket of his sport jacket, adjusted his tie, and made a slow circuit of the floor, shouldering through the crowd and zoning in on a table. All the seats were taken but that was all right, there was bound to be turnover. He planted himself behind third base, far enough back to blend in with the baggage but near enough to scrutinize all the cards. Just another weenie railbird. He waited for the shuffle. And then he emptied his head and began to count.

He waited through two shoes. On neither of them did the count ever exceed a plus four, and mostly it was running in the negative. One of the players pocketed his dwindling pile of chips and moved on. Deep into the next shoe the count finally rose to a positive thirteen. Time to strike.

Waverly took the unoccupied seat (two down from first base, hardly your position of choice, but doing what he was doing you couldn't afford to be fussy) and stacked five blacks in his wager square. Dealer gave him a neutral look and fired out the cards. Waverly caught a hard fourteen, dealer showed a nine. When it came his turn Waverly declined a hit. Four players to his left all took hits, all went bust. Dealer flipped over his hole card, revealing a five. And sure enough, he dropped a paint on it.

In the blink of an eye Waverly was up a nickel. A quick scan of the cards on the table established a count soared to sixteen. He left the original five blacks in the square. It didn't get much better than this.

A judgment certified by his next hand. Ace and a face, genuine snapper. Waverly produced his best slightly fuddled, Oh lucky me expression. Dealer said congratulations, but dryly and without an ounce of goodwill. Didn't matter. Seven-fifty in bankable bones was civility enough. But the count had dropped a few points and the hand after that came up a push, his ace seven against dealer eighteen.

Midway into the next deal the red cut card flashed across the felt, signalling the last hand in the shoe. Waverly caught paired tens. Dealer got an ace, peeked at his hole card, then turned a studiedly vacant, inquiring gaze on first base. A small relieved sigh went around the table. No dealer natural this time. What remained of the deck was still fat with paint and, by Waverly's tally, three more spoilers. He had a sliver of a second to decide.

At his turn he laid out five more blacks and said mildly, "Split 'em."

"Ye gods and little fishes," muttered the cipher to his right, a smoothly corpulent man who'd been playing a methodical basic, and losing steadily.

Third base groaned.

"*Split* 'em?" the dealer echoed. A glint of suspicion illuminated his otherwise perfectly blank eyes.

"Split 'em," Waverly repeated.

First hit was one of the aces (which evoked an incredulous gasp all around), second an eight. And when the dealer rolled over his down card, it showed a powerless six.

Waverly scooped up his chips, left a green as toke and made

straight for the cage. The money lady, same one as before, re-marked, "That didn't take you long."

Waverly produced his hay-shaker grin. "That's what all you la-dies say. Nothing but complaints."

Her eyes traveled over him skeptically. "I'm sure."

She counted out his take. Two dimes and change. Not bad. Off four hands, not half bad. So much for omens.

Nevertheless, he got out of there fast.

It was called shadow counting, what he was doing, and for a Vegas player it was hazardous in the extreme. Because it was diffi-cult to neutralize, the casinos were not kindly disposed toward its practitioners. Be closer to say they despised them. Not that there were all that many who could execute it with any degree of success. It wasn't as if it were among your easier tactics to master. First you had to be a seamless counter, hurdle enough for anyone. Add to that the matter of timing, which was particularly tricky, had to be exact, dead-on. There'd be times you'd hang back behind a table, playing at geek and running your count and it never came anywhere near the friendly zone. Total wash. Other times, when it did, you could pop into a seat, zing in your bets, and still get blitzed. Cards came with no ironclad guarantees, for all your pinpoint reckonings. And you could never linger too long at a table. Get made and the one guarantee you could bank on, the one Vegas sure thing, was an escort to the door by a brace of bull-necked troglodytes, and a com-plimentary unwelcome mat for a keepsake. But if you were cen-tered enough and agile enough, and if the gods (never mind the little fishes) were even partly smiling, you could swoop in, score a sudden take, and bolt. Like a Panzer strike. Search and destroy. Hit and run. Apt imagery. For it was a very real kind of war you were waging, and against a durable enemy who never blinked, never low-ered his guard, and never ever surrendered.

All this, Waverly was learning rapidly, the accelerated course in shadow counting. Before tonight he'd never risked it. Never had to. Critical times, critical measures. And as he made his way up the Strip, moving from casino to casino, polishing the drill, dodging hostile fire and minting money at each stop, his confidence, shaky to begin with, ripened into a mild, controlled exuberance.

He came out of the Flamingo Hilton 4K ahead. O'Shea's wasn't quite as cooperative and it took a while to get a solid lock on a table, but he still walked away with a dime. Imperial Palace and Holiday, between them, contributed a most generous six more. The Sands he skipped. Too iffy. No sense jamming your luck. Frontier, though, that ought to be a primo target, so he crossed the street and went inside. He was right. By pushing it, hitting three different tables (two more than was prudent for any one casino), he emerged ninety minutes later an astonishing, inspiriting seven long to the good.

Exuberance?—make that exaltation. For a moment he stood mesmerized by the miles and miles of neon tubing exploding against the black sky. A biting wind came in off the desert, swept the street. Rushing clouds dusted the moon. The raw night air stung his smoke-scored lungs, turned his breath to ghostly vapor. He glanced at his watch. Amazingly, it was half-past one. Your time–fun equation at work. He had no clear idea how far he was ahead, but it had to be upwards of twenty thou. Caution, reason—to say nothing of a number-numbed head—dictated a break. But he was on wheels now, steaming. Mr. Invisible, elusive as the wind penetrating his clothes and chilling his bones. Catch me if you can. And as though tugged by some irresistible lunar pull, he set out walking. Stardust, next stop.

Traffic was thinner in here, but not so sparse you couldn't do a quick drive-by. He bought his chips and strolled around the loop of tables, casually, taking his time, settling finally on the most promising one. Dealer was a callow kid with a permanent wised-up sneer that looked to be mirror-rehearsed. Two players: a withered, smoke-dried little man, hollow-eyed and blade-thin, holding down third base; and next to him a plump elderly lady, somebody's prodigal granny, squeezed into stretch stirrup pants, droopy dog face weighted with pancake makeup, lipstick the color of charred bacon, halo of orange-tinted hair. They had the feverish mark of grinds, both of them, humanoid blips on the radar screen of greed, the warranties on their souls long since expired. Watching them, for

Waverly, was like peering down the rutted road of his own future, a spyglass glimpse across the quickening years. Preview of coming attractions.

But now was not the time for such gloomy reflections, and so he assumed his station a couple of feet behind and slightly to the right of third base. On the shuffle he picked up the count. It hovered around neutral through the entire shoe, made it only into the low positives, and then only briefly. But the opening hands of the next one displayed an almost freakish disproportion of low cards, and the count climbed abruptly to plus eleven. Now.

He took first base and pushed in his uniform five blacks. Cards came whizzing through the air. Waverly a seven-three, ten the hard way. Dealer ace up. Carefully shielding his hole card, just like they'd taught him at Dealer U., the sneery young man took a peek. Evidently no cigar. Waverly added five blacks to his original bet, said, "One card." Three nines fallen, it was a reasonable risk. And anyway, he was in a hurry. Dealer made a little sniffing sound, and when he dropped a dirty duck on the ten his lip curled up a notch. He dealt the grinds their hands and then turned over his holer, a limp four, and spanked it with back to back spots. Nice hits, if you were playing twenty-five.

Waverly's next two hands were sorry stiffs, sixteen and fourteen up against eight and ten, respectively. But the count, still balling, said stand, and he did, and in neither case did the dealer have his seventeen or better and in both he got drowned in the plentiful paints left in the deck. Three hands, 2K. A hat trick, handsome lift.

The dealer gathered the spent cards. His upper lip had flattened out some, and the look he cast at Waverly was measured and narrow. "How'd you get that dinger on your face?" he asked conversationally.

Uh-oh. Waverly suspected the country-boy gee whiz wasn't going to play here, so he said cryptically, "Ran into the proverbial door."

"That a fact?"

"True fact."

Momentary standoff. The faces of the two grinds registered a dull impatience at the stalled action, about as close as they could come to genuine expression.

The dealer leaned over to Waverly and in a snarly, side-of-the-mouth whisper said, "Y'know, friend, eye's gotta be givin' you a serious scope 'long about now. I was you, I'd go count the spots on the dice."

"That's what you'd do?"

"Absolutely. Even better idea'd be take a hike. Before you bang into another one a them doors."

Waverly collected his chips and eased out of the chair. Kid was keener than he'd thought. Either that, or he was getting careless. "Thanks for the advice," he said. "You're a standup guy, I don't care what the rest of the world says."

And he sauntered away, leaving no toke behind. He cashed out and started for the door, same easy saunter, but with the disquieting sense of multiple hostile eyes—behind, overhead, either side—drilling into him. Maybe he wasn't quite so invisible after all.

Once he was beyond the door and safely on the street, he picked up the pace. He wasn't sure where he was going. Away from here. A nerve in his eyelid fluttered wildly. The Vegas tic. The attic of his brain was crammed to the rafters with shimmery images of cards, numbers, tallies, totals; with an oscillating blur of players, dealers, pit bosses, security goons, every one of them occupied with the enormous busy task of acquisition. The libidinous waltz of piggish appetite. The whole psychotic vaudeville. Or maybe it was just the thud in the head that always comes with counting too long. Blackjack, played for keeps, was a game so hot-wire charged it made poker, his real calling, seem almost torpid by contrast.

He arrived at the north end of the Frontier parking lot. Stood there with his shoulders hunched against the cold. Crowds, deterred by the bitter gusting wind not in the least, weaved around him. Cars streaked by. If his figures were anywhere near accurate (and this was certainly no place or time to confirm them), he should be about twenty-two big dimes ahead. Tack on the stake and it approached thirty. Now was when he ought to hang it up, call it a night. But directly across the street was the Desert Inn, and he'd not forgotten that was the spot had the dealer with the tell. Who just might be working tonight. Nice round figure, thirty. Why not?

He walked that way.

Unlike the Stardust, this casino was mobbed. The legions of slot addicts gyrated and moaned, dice freaks whooped it up, glassy-eyed roulette druggies gazed into the hypnotic twirling wheel as though in anticipation of an augury from the angels heavenly. Over it all was a steady, resonant, money-factory hum.

Waverly secured his chips and wandered idly through the floor, searching for the philanthropic dealer. Eventually he found him, and manning a big 5K max table with a couple of empty seats at that. He took his position aft of third base and studied the dealer's face while he waited for the next shuffle. Same giveaway tongue flick when the hole card was mighty, lip tuck when it wasn't. Must be you live right, Mr. Waverly. Tonight, anyway.

Fresh shoe. Get to grips time. Summoning his absolute last erg of counting energy, Waverly locked onto a tally and watched it sway from minus to plus and back again with the rhythmic fall of the cards. Much too erratic to risk. He waited through another shoe. Same story. It was vexing to come this close, with these impeccable conditions, only to be braked by the stubborn perversity of chance. Worse than vexing—maddening. But he couldn't hang there much longer. Out on a thread as it was. Maybe one more.

About halfway into the next shoe the count elevated to a positive seven. Not exactly your juggernaut total, but he was weary of waiting. Three, four fast scores and he'd be out of there. He grabbed a seat and set his five blacks in the square. Dealer gave him an oddly wintry look and rolled the cards. Waverly got a fifteen against dealer nine and, following the dictate of the count, rejected a hit and let the dealer dump all over his own sixteen. Next hand was even better: two paints chasing dealer's skimpy four. Waverly's inclination was to split them, but the count had tumbled some so he resisted, sat back and watched the dealer turn over a hole ten and whack it with an eight. Numbers could sometimes betray you, but not often.

Now the dealer's telltale lips went tight. He glanced at a pit boss roving the floor, a round keg of a man with a styled swag of charcoal hair and complexion a uremic yellow. Boss caught the glance and strode over, seemingly towed along behind an opulent belly and the half-foot cigar projecting from his mouth. Two of them exchanged muffled whispers, granite-eyed looks, not a few of which slid over Waverly. Dealer nodded, turned back to the players, and announced, "Shufflin' up."

Midshoe shuffle? Ominous looks? Definitely not good. Waverly raked in his chips, left a hopeful pacifier green, and edged away. Make it to the cash cage and out the door and you're home free.

No such luck. The pit boss intercepted him at the end of the file of tables, stood squarely in his path, arms laid in a belligerent fold across a downslope of chest. A squat, glowering roadblock reeking of cigar fumes and garlic and impotent Tic Tacs. He stuck his piss-colored face into Waverly's, and without preface and in a voice a whiskey-coated growl said, "Myron says you been doin' a shadow on his table."

"Myron?"

"Myron's the dealer."

Waverly flashed a disarming grin. "Nobody's named Myron," he said. Try a little levity.

"He is."

Levity, clearly, wasn't going to work. So he fashioned a puzzled look and said, "What do you mean, 'shadow'?"

"How come is it I think you already know?"

"I was trying to clock the aces, is all. The way the books tell you to do."

The boss grunted contemptuously. "Read the books, do you?"

"Sure. I'm a student of the game. Like every other player in here."

"Deep thinker, huh."

"Semideep."

"You know what I think?"

"Bet I'm going to hear."

"Think you ain't like every other player. Think Myron's right. Think you're a fuckbucket counter. Shadower. Lookin' to chump us."

Waverly shrugged. "Well," he said, "everybody's entitled to his opinion. This is America."

"No, you got that part wrong. This is the D.I. Here we ain't partial to counters. 'Specially your kind."

"What'd I win? A thou? I got a hunch you'll still be in business tomorrow."

"See, you ain't got the words right either. You say win, we say boost. You didn't win that thou off us, you boosted it."

"You know," Waverly said, "this is real educational, talking with you. Semantics, geography—lot of good instruction here. But if the lesson's over I've got to be moving along."

"Ain't quite over."

"So what is it you want? Want your dime back?"

"No, you get to keep the dime," the boss said clemently. His mouth shaped a mirthless smirk. His eyes, pure venom, drifted to a point above and just beyond Waverly's left shoulder. "What I want is for you to meet another one a our employees."

Waverly turned and looked up, far up, into the rock-jawed face of a mountainous man, Frankenstein in a three-piece suit.

"This here's Einar," said the boss. "He's from Sweden."

Einar was not smiling.

"Worthy people, your Swedes," Waverly said.

The boss, evidently uninterested in ethnic evaluation, said, "He's gonna walk you down to the cage, see you get your dime okay. An' then he's gonna help you find the door."

"That's very thoughtful. But I know the way."

"No trouble. Einar be glad to help out. That right, Einar?"

Einar allowed he'd be glad.

"So," Waverly said. "We finished?"

"Hey, that's real good!" the boss declared with a hand-clap show of mock approval. "Now you learnin' the words right. *Finished* is deadass right."

"Yeah, well, I'm a quick study."

"That's good too. Cuz you got a schmuck jacket on you now. An' you gonna be wearin' it up and down this street. You follow what I'm sayin' here?"

"More or less."

"Your sake, I sure hope it's more. 'Stead a that less. Whyn't you try Laughlin. Rap is they got a soft spot for you number thrashers."

"I'll give it some thought."

"You do that."

"Expect I'd better get going," Waverly said. "I've always hated good-byes."

The boss stepped aside and with a sweep of a hand but no farewell motioned him on. Waverly and the attentive Einar walked to the cash cage, then to the exit. Einar didn't say good-bye either.

It was going on 3:00 A.M. when he came through the door of the house and discovered his partner sitting feet propped on the coffee table, beer in one hand, slab of gorgonzola in the other. But no Val.

"Hey, Timothy, whereya been?"

"Has Val been here?"

"No, but she called. Said she was stayin' over at some patient's place. Said tellya not to worry, she's doin' just fine."

"This call, when did it come?"

"Oh, 'bout an hour back, maybe a little more."

"She say who this patient is? Where he lives?"

"Nope, didn't say. Why?"

It was too much to hope that anything could ever go right. Waverly dropped into a chair. A vicious headache assailed the outermost boundaries of his skull. His stomach, unfed since morning, pitched and yawed. His bones felt ossified, his mouth nicotine-shellacked. Even his hands trembled a bit as he lit yet another cigarette. Legacy of a long night's count.

"So what's kickin' here?" Bennie asked, mildly puzzled.

"I'm not sure," Waverly said. "Maybe nothing."

But even as he said it he recognized the words for what they were: another of the numberless lies you tell yourself, hope's treacheries, the habitual little betrayals committed so routinely they cancel all you ever thought you knew of trust, accountability, connection. What he should be doing was hauling himself back onto his feet and heading back out there and tracking down his sister. Instead he remained rooted to the chair, too exhausted to move. She'd told him nobody knew where she was going tonight. He had no reason to doubt that. And anyway, where would he begin to look? Maybe it would keep till morning.

He was conscious of Bennie talking at him, but he hadn't been listening. "What?"

"Said you wanta beer? Cheese?"

Waverly brushed the air negatively.

"You gotta eat, boy. You lookin' like leftover dog plop."

"Kind of you to notice. Speaking of dogs, where's Electra?"

"In the back. Zonked. She scarfed about a pound a this cheese. Only mutt I ever seen with a taste for your gorgonzola." Through a mouthful of it he added, "I tellya, tryin' to pick winners builds an appetite. Got all my Sunday bets down, though. What you been up to tonight?"

"Plying my trade."

"Huh?"

"Cards, Bennie. Same as always."

"So how'd you make out?"

For answer, Waverly produced a roll of bills from his jacket pocket and set it on the coffee table. "You tell me," he said.

Bennie's eyes bulged. He put his feet and his beer on the floor, picked up the roll, and with that ardor of concentration only money can generate, began to count it. At the last smartly snapped bill he pursed his lips in a low whistle, looked up, and said, "Holy golem. You got twenty-nine large and some cab coin here. This is dancin' money, Timothy. More'n we had on our hip in a good long while."

"Six of it's stake. I had to tap our nut."

"Fuck, you bring home this kind a plunder, you can tap it any night of the week. How'd you do it, anyways? Musta hit a happy storm, huh?"

"It was a storm, all right. How happy, I'm not so sure."

"Well, how you come by it don't matter none. This ain't bean curd we're lookin' at here. Got enough to get you off them bee jay tables and set you down in a poker room. Where you rightfully be-long, boy. Utilize your natural talents."

"Afraid not."

Bennie squinted at him. "What're you sayin', not?"

"For one thing, I got made tonight."

"Made!" he shouted out. "Aah, Jesus. Whereabouts, made?"

"D.I. Probably the Stardust too. Which is to say everywhere."

"You doin' them wide swings again? What'd I tellya?"

"Worse than that. I was running a shadow count."

"*Shadowin'*," Bennie groaned miserably. "That's pure death wish. Where's your head at, Timothy?"

"Who knows? Buried in sand maybe. Point is, I'm scrubbed in this town. They aren't going to let me near a nickel slot in a laundromat now."

Bennie was silent a moment. His nostrils seemed to twitch. His forehead crinkled under the burden of plans hastily patched and amended. "Okay," he muttered, "okay." Then he looked over at Waverly, and with the indomitable yea-sayer's enduring capacity for adjustment, repair, said, "Shame, all settled in here. But we gotta move on, we move on. S'pose we could head up to Reno. Maybe Laughlin." He indicated the neatly stacked bills on the table, and in an effort at a reconciled grin (which came on more as grimace) added, "Least we ain't under the shotgun barrel, like in Florida. Blazin' bareass out the back door middle a the night, grabbin' onto our socks. This time we got us a healthy nut."

"Well, that's the other thing, Bennie."

"Which other?"

"That's not what it's for."

The labored grimace-grin faded slowly. In its place was a look at once impatient and wary. "Look, Timothy," he said, "riddles ain't never been my strong suit. You wanna spare me the smoke?"

Waverly butted out his cigarette. Sooner or later it had to be said. May as well be now. "I'm going to use this money to get Val out of here."

"Outta here where?"

"I don't know. Back to heartland country. One of those Dakotas. Somewhere safe. Buy her a kennel. Herb farm. Something."

"You gonna tell me why?"

"After what you saw last night, that gang of street muggers at her place, you're asking why?"

"Fill me in anyway."

Waverly expelled a sigh. In the wasted condition he was in, a little bit of this slick Socratic dialectic went an awfully long way. "Because she's in serious jeopardy," he said. "So are we. Pettibone too. Remember the one with the five-block stamp on him? He paid me a visit today."

"He was *here*?"

"This very chair I'm sitting in now."

"What'd he want?"

"Wants the inside line on the tanked—or not tanked, whatever they are—games. And he's convinced we've got it."

"So? We don't. Least you and me don't."

"Come on, Bennie. You know better. No way is he going to buy that."

Bennie shrugged. "So what's he gonna do? Solo hustler. It ain't like he's connected."

"Solo or not, he's trouble. And that's the last thing we need. Which is why I've got to get Val into the wind. You should do the same."

"Think you got your work cut out for you, boy. Look to me like your sis found a home here, her swami and all."

"Then I guess I'll just have to find a way."

Bennie fell silent again. No more furrowed brows or twitchy nostrils, though he did pull thoughtfully at an underchin. Finally he said, "Okay, loot's yours. You earned it fair. But I ain't gonna front you, Timothy. Don't make me sleep easy, you goin' off on trips. Last one, Michigan, is the one what got us into this poop, first place."

Waverly started to say something but Bennie forestalled him with an upraised palm. "Lemme finish here. Okay, you got your mind made up. Lookin' out for family, that's good too. Can't nobody fault that. So you scoot her off to North Dakota. Take you a week or so, outside. I'll hang in here till you get back. Then we figure our next move."

Steady as he was able, Waverly looked at him, at the baggy, canny, resilient face of his partner, remembering their shared history, generous fund of common experience. Now came the hard part. Had to be done. "Thing of it is," he said, "I don't think I'll be coming back."

Bennie cocked his head slightly, as though he'd missed a fragment of the words, or misinterpreted them. "What're you talkin'? You don't come back, where you gonna go?"

"No idea," Waverly said truthfully.

"What're you thinkin' to do?"

"I haven't thought about it."

"See, that's it right there. You ain't thinkin' straight. Face it, Timothy. You're a Jacktown grad-u-ate, same as me. Ain't no place in the citizen's world for people like us."

"Could be I'll find something."

"Like what?" Bennie snorted. "Baggin' groceries? Raisin' herbs and pooches, like your sis?"

"I don't know, Bennie. Don't know."

"You wanna know why it is you don't know? Tellya why. Cards is what you know, boy. *All* you know anymore. Cards and numbers. What you got is like a genius for 'em. Gift."

"Gift, is it? More like a curse. Witness tonight."

Now Bennie shook his head slowly. A battery of expressions sifted across his face: doubt, dismay, exasperation, disbelief, alarm. After a moment of dead air he said, "Tell me somethin', Timothy. When'd this good idea come to you?"

When? How do you pinpoint when? Waverly had no ready answer. "Maybe I've played one hand too many," he said. Best he could do.

"So you dissolvin' the partnership? Just like that? All them years?"

Waverly could no longer meet the sober watchful reproach in his friend's eyes. Couldn't think about it, or examine or debate or explain it anymore. He said, "Look, I've got to sleep now. Few hours anyway."

"Yeah, you oughta sleep. Get your head right again. We can talk in the morning."

"Be the same then," Waverly said. He hoisted himself out of the chair and started down the hall.

"You forgettin' your take," Bennie called after him.

He came back and picked up the stacked bills. "Your half of the nut's still in the basket," he said. "I didn't touch it, you know."

"I know."

"Listen, Bennie, I'm sorry."

Bennie stared glumly at the floor. "Know that too," he said.

Back in his room Waverly laid the bills alongside the clock on the nightstand. Clock said quarter past three. He set the alarm for eight. Just in case. He peeled off his jacket, removed his tie, shoes. But nothing else. Too trashed for anything else. He sank onto the bed. Instantly, he slept.

21

The slumber of B. Epstein, normally placid, was riddled by fractured dreams, one of which featured a particularly harsh background clangor, rather like a discordant bell banging in his head. It
took a while for him to emerge from sleep's shadowland, but when
he did, the banging, though diminished some and externalized, still
sounded in his ears. He got up off the couch, his bed of choice for
the night, and shuffled across the room muttering, "Yeah yeah yeah
yeah." He cracked the door open a notch and peered into a face
veiled in the gray murk of dawn. "Yeah, whozit?"

"Bennie?"

"Roger? That you?"

Commencing midthought, as though he and any auditor would
naturally be tuned to the identical frequency, Pettibone said excitedly, "I believe I've arrived at a decision at last."

"That's real interestin' news, Roger. You think it could maybe
keep couple hours?"

In a voice charged with high drama Pettibone boomed, "No. It
must be shared with someone. Now."

"Guess that means you wanna come in, huh."

"I'd be in your debt."

Bennie dug at his bleary eyes with the flats of his hands. It was coming back to him, all that had gone on last night, everything that had been said. He slapped the air in half a beckoning motion. "Okay. But you gotta hold it down. Timothy's crashed. Had a long night here."

Pettibone came in and took a chair. Bennie went to the window and opened the blind. Needles of pale light slanted through the room. "Fuck time's it, anyways?" he said grouchily, flopping back onto the couch.

"Sixish. Thereabouts."

"Middle a the goddam night."

"Apologies. But this is significant. This is urgent."

Bennie regarded him dubiously. Threads looked like they been twice around the tumble dryer, hair a wild greasy tangle, scrub of beard, bughouse glint in the eyes. Talk about your basic gimps. But then he glanced down at his own slept-in clothes. Ran a hand over a whiskered cheek. Caught a whiff of his lingering nocturnal flatus. Made a perfect pair a ducks, the two of 'em. And right about now somebody else's urgency was an easy dead last on the Epstein priority list. Got troubles of his own right now. So he said obliquely, hoping to head him off, "Whereya been keepin' yourself? Ain't seen you since the big feed over to Val's."

"You were there?"

"You don't remember? Musta really been feelin' no pain."

"Depends on your definition of pain."

"Pain's pain, Roger," Bennie said with a shrug. He wasn't into any six a-fuckin'-m hair-splitting.

"Driving."

"Huh?"

"In answer to your original question. Where have I been since the day before yesterday? Driving."

"Well, drivin's good. Mellows a man out. Whereabouts you drive to?"

"The Valley of Fire."

"Yeah? Heard it's real pretty up there. Myself, I never seen it."

" 'Pretty' hardly does it justice. More eerie, I should say. More like a voyage to the moon. All that jagged rock, mountains of sandstone. The vast emptiness. Silence. A lesson in the erosion of time."

For Bennie, it wasn't exactly a joy, listening to this dribbleshit before you even got your eyes peeled open and your head screwed on straight. What're you gonna do? "Have to take me a spin up that way," he said absently. "One a these days."

"Everything is isolate out there," Pettibone went on with an air of profound gravity. "There's no confusion of objects clouding the vision. One can see things clearly. Think clearly. And that's what I did. Pulled off the road and spent the day and the night. Fasting and deliberating."

Yeah and that's the problem right there, Bennie was thinking, your college boys, every goddam one of 'em (including his partner, if he still had a partner): too much deliberatin', too little action. An' total zip in the kickin' back and enjoyin' department. Like somebody hand 'em a ticket to heaven, first place they gotta visit is the sewage plant. But he said, "So what'd you come up with, all this deliberatin'?" Not really givin' a rat's red ass, and wonderin' when it was he got his shrink license and how come nobody compensatin' him for all his grief.

"I'm going to resign my position at the grammar school. And then I'm leaving this sorry wasteland for good."

"Quit your job? Why'd you wanta do that?"

"To salvage what's left of my soul," Pettibone said solemnly.

Jesus, first Timothy, now this one. Everybody got a worry finger on his soul pulse. Whole world gone crackers. Must be somethin' in the water. "You maybe wanta give it some thought," Bennie said, "that salvagin'. Leave here, where you gonna go?" Seemed to him like he just been over this same ground.

"Back to my roots."

"You talkin' about that home town yours? Thief somethin'?"

"Thief River Falls."

"Yeah, okay, whatever. Fuck you do back there?"

"Start over. If it's not too late. And if it is, well, what better place for a journey to end than where it first began."

Up to now Bennie had been paying this wiggy conversation only the scantiest attention. Most of his remarks and queries were pure reflex, words to say. But an airy wisp of a thought stowed somewhere in his head was taking on a kind of willful substance. Not a plot or a scheme, nothing like that; merely a notion, unpolished and quite without design. "Lemme ask you somethin', Roger," he said carefully. "You ain't on the sauce again?"

"Absolutely not," Pettibone declared. "I've consumed enough booze for one lifetime. No more for me. From this day forward. From yesterday, actually."

"Well, you don't object I pop back a chug. Could use a little tightener, get the ol' head bolted down."

"Not at all," said Pettibone stoutly, but with the barest trace of uncertainty rippling through his voice.

Bennie padded into the kitchen and returned with a bottle of Johnnie Walker Red and two water glasses. He set them on the coffee table, filled one of the glasses and nodded casually at the other. "Case you change your mind."

Pettibone said nothing.

Bennie hoisted his glass in a toast. "Here's wishin' you a run a aces, Rog."

"Thank you."

Bennie took a long gurgly swallow. Made some wet smacky-lip noises. Blew a contented burp. "So," he said. "When you leavin'?"

"Immediately. Well, by Monday anyway. No later than that. Every day spent here grows more intolerable for me."

"Hey, take a number. Ain't like me'n Timothy been livin' in the sugar doo ourselves lately."

"You're referring to your gambling?"

"That, yeah. That's part of it. But we got some other heavy pro'lums too. 'Specially Timothy."

"Timothy? What sort of problems could he have?"

Bennie shook his head sadly. "It's his sis. He's real worried about her." As though moved by the melancholy thought, he took another, conspicuously loud swallow.

Pettibone squirmed in his chair, but he kept his eyes resolutely off the bottle and empty glass on the table. "Why would he be worried about Valerie?" he asked. "She seems quite capable to me. In her own way."

"Why?" Bennie sputtered, warming to the role now, getting into the theatrics of it. "Jesus, Rog, you was out to her place the other night. You seen that crew a scammers."

"All I remember is some ignorant dunce babbling about the nature of the universe."

"Yeah, you two was goin' at it like a couple pit bulls."

"Who was he?"

"That's Brewster. Y'know, fella she's workin' for. Gonna cure whatever ails you."

"Then Timothy has reason to be worried. The man's transparently a charlatan."

"Bet your ass, he's worried. Only that ain't the half of it. Brewster, he's a one-bagger. It's them other clippers got Timothy all tweaked."

"Which others are those?"

"You don't remember 'em?"

"I'm sorry to say most of that night's a fog. Most of the week, in point of fact."

"Yeah, well, they're your badass variety. 'Bout as bad as I ever seen, and that's goin' some."

"Bad in what sense?"

"Mean bad. Touch you up for the loose change in your pocket. I tellya, Rog, Val, she's way outta her league, runnin' with that bunch. She could get herself burned big-time. Or worse."

Bennie brought the glass to his lips and emptied it in a single agitated gulp. He glanced over at Pettibone, whose eyes had strayed now to the table, empty glass, bottle. "Sure you won't have one?" he said.

Pettibone jerked his head negatively.

Bennie shrugged, poured himself another.

And in a thin constricted voice, almost a whisper, Pettibone said, "Maybe one. Short one."

"Short one can't hurt."

Across the street and halfway down the block a white Lincoln, incongruous for this neighborhood, was parked along the curb and faced in the direction of the house on Garces. It had been there since shortly after five that morning. Click sat behind the wheel,

Eggs in the seat next to him. It was cold in the car, and so periodically Click switched the key in the ignition and let the engine idle
and the heater run to chase the chill from the air. At best it was a
temporary measure, and for the most part they sat there shivering
in the dark. Neither of them had much to say, particularly Eggs,
who watched the house with a peculiar manic intensity, chaining
cigarettes and, when he wasn't doing that, chewing at his underlip
and flexing his fingers. He had his shades back on, first time in over
two weeks; and for Click that signaled something coming down, and
quick-time.

The first faint streaks of light fell on the street. Objects began
to separate themselves from their shadows. A car pulled around the
corner and came to a lurching stop in front of the house. A figure
emerged and hurried toward the door. Eggs leaned into the dash
and hissed, "Who is it, Cleanth? Can you see?"

Click squinted. "Look like some guy," he said.

"Who? Can you make him?"

Click stuck his face up against the windshield. "Hard to tell.
Could be that juicehead, the other night."

"Are you sure?"

"Yeah, that's him."

"I *knew* it!" Eggs exclaimed triumphantly. "I knew they were all
in this together. This confirms it."

The figure disappeared behind the door.

"So now whadda we do, Egger?"

"Wait. I predict we'll be seeing some action. Any minute now."
But his prediction was wrong. Half an hour went by. No action.
Now and again Click gave his partner a sideways peek, but even
though he was baffled at what they were doing—make that *not*
doing—he knew better than to ask. Anyway, he was feeling like dog
shit himself, Click was. Unracked at five bells, empty gut
groaning—who wouldn't? Also was he still stewing some over what
Cool Whip told him last night, and when he wasn't picturing in his
mind that sweet targeted back door grinding away on Mr. Lovesteak
down there (which was a good share of the time) he was wondering
could there be anything to it, but mostly thinking Nah, not Eggs, no
way, two of 'em, they go back too far. What she said, though, it was

like a bad fart fouling the air between them. Stink just didn't want to go away. So while he remained uncharacteristically silent, Click was keeping a close eye on his partner, too.

Another thirty minutes passed. More of that nothing. The morning sun flooded the street. A flock of birds dropped out of the sky and marched across a vacant lot, savaging worms. Finally Eggs, whose own eyes had never once left the house, said, "What time is it?"

Click glanced at his watch. "Little after seven."

Eggs seemed to frown slightly, but he didn't reply. He sat with his shoulders bunched, a hard set to his jaw, hands clenching and unclenching, as though he were squeezing knots of air.

"I dunno," Click ventured. "He's been in there over an hour. You think maybe it's a wash?"

"Patience, Cleanth. It won't be long now."

This time he was right. Within a quarter of an hour the door of the house swung open, and their patience was at last rewarded.

Inside the house there had been a long, rambling, Pettibone-dominated conversation going on for the past hour or more. Fueled by three fast hits of the J.W. (maybe it was four, he'd lost count), he reflected philosophically on his past and whatever might remain of a future, shuttling back and forth between them, the bright promise of youth sent spinning through the rush of years, time's quiet larceny, the ruin of age. There was so much to say, so many luminous ideas to share. Occasionally, though, he broke off midsentence, midword even, thought engine hopelessly derailed, and gazed mutely into his glass.

Bennie still nursed his second drink, sipping it slowly, displaying a listening face but tracking his own agenda. At one of the protracted pauses he brought the talk back to gambling, specifically his theory of sports betting.

"You take your football," he explained, "now there's a wagerin' man's game. Game a distances: yards, feet, right down to inches sometimes. Distances is solid, real. Y'can see 'em, measure 'em. Which is why it's an easier game to get a handle on, you want my opinion."

A lazy warmth settled through the Pettibone limbs, slackening them. He was feeling smoothed out, unstrung, magnanimous toward his pathetically obvious friend. "Easier than what?" he asked, secure in the certain knowledge of the answer long before it was delivered or, for that matter, the question ever posed.

"Oh, hockey, say. Never did understand that game. Or maybe somethin' like roundball. Yeah, roundball's better for the point I'm makin' here. See, that's a game a seconds, split-seconds even. Y'get a pass or a shot too soon or too late, or a foul at the wrong time, or some crazy swisher comin' outta downtown in the stretch—anything like that an' your spread get kinked on you quicker'n a New York minute. Can take a serious floggin', your roundball."

The spirit of Roger Pettibone, miraculously disembodied from the sodden clay slumped in the chair, drifted to the ceiling and hovered there, suspended in air. With a kind of Boethian sweep of vision, it seemed to see the whole soiled swirling panorama of human existence and human event, all of it, all the storms and furies and strivings and conflicts and bumbling pitiful acts and foreordained choices and puny fists shaken defiantly against the laughing gods, all of it long since laid out, predestined, sealed. His own included. And while that umbral essence looked on with resigned sardonic amusement, the historian below said, "Yet the clock is a means of measure too, no less counterfeit and no more real than those distances you put your faith in."

"S'pose you're right," Bennie conceded. "Still a nervous game, all that dancin' and leapin' and flyin'. First they down one end a the court, then they at the other. Give ya the sweats, just watchin'. I seen games you think is in the can, wrapped up and put to bed. What happen? You bat an eye and your money's gone right down the toilet hole. 'Specially now the boogies got a lock on it, that rat ball they play. Can't count on nothin' no more."

"Boogies?" said the man in the chair. "Such as Lafayette?"

"Yeah, he'd be a good for instance, all them moves he got. Way he can double-pump, switch hands and make a reverse jam, float on air—boy ain't human."

The floating spirit heard the man ask, "Less than human? More?"

Bennie seemed puzzled by the question. "Y'got me, Rog. Less?—more?—different'n your white boys, is all. Nothin' against him, y'understand."

"Oh, I understand."

"See, you livin' life on the off ramp, like me'n Timothy been doin' lately—bets goin' sour, all them other headaches—it get you spooked—that ain't no little pun, by the way—how you gonna lay your money. That's all I'm sayin' here."

"By 'other headaches' you mean Valerie. Is that correct?"

"Well, that's the big one," Bennie said glumly. "We had the loot, we could get her outta here. Before them spivs put the heavy hurts to her."

"And you believe she's in danger?"

"Listen, I'm tellin' ya, one a that crew—you was too blitzed, you wouldn't remember him—anyway, he looks like he on loan from the twitch house. Kinda guy take you out for sport, piss on your grave for bad measure."

"But you have no money to rescue her."

"That's the pro'lum right there. Timothy been gettin' creamed at the tables, an' myself, I ain't been ridin' no fat streak neither. Comes to winner pickin', be better off stayin' with my nose. Our luck don't turn soon, we gonna be havin' more mealtimes'n meals. Worst of it is, ain't nothin' we can do, help out Val."

Finally the man in the chair got to it. Very calmly, very evenly, he said, "And you would like me to tell you what I know of the fixed games. That's it, isn't it?"

In accents humble, eyes averted, Bennie said, "You gotta do what's right for you, Rog."

"I know less than you think. But you might try tonight's game. The un-lovers not to make the spread."

Now Bennie looked at him steadily, carefully. "That the straight skinny, Roger? If it ain't, we're cashed."

"Straight as I know," affirmed the man in the chair; and at just that moment the hovering spirit sank from the ceiling and melded again with the lumpish meat of the man, and he wobbled to his feet, and Bennie also stood, and a dog came trotting into the room, eyes wide, mouth open, tongue projecting like a flat lavender spoon.

"You remember Electric," Bennie said. "Val's mutt."

"Of course I remember," Pettibone said. The dog licked his hand expectantly. "Excellent animal. Perhaps I'll take her along."

"Along where? Where you headed?"

"To Valerie's."

"Don't think you're gonna find her home. She was stayin' with one a them patients hers last night."

"Nevertheless, I'm going there. She's provided me with a key. I'll wait. Possibly the dog and I can be of some small assistance."

"There's a good thought. Listen, I got another. Maybe you could drop me off over on the Strip."

"My pleasure."

"Sensational. Whyn't you take the pooch outside for her mornin' squat-down. Be right with you."

Once they were past the door, Bennie tiptoed back to Waverly's room. He stood in the entrance a moment, watching the figure of his friend sprawled facedown on the bed, thinking I'm doin' this for you, partner. And then he edged over to the nightstand, lifted and pocketed the wad of bills, and switched off the alarm. Out in the hall he dug through the laundry basket and came up with the rest of their nut. He didn't have time to count it, but he knew it had to total somewhere near 35K. Be a big seven-o by tonight, loaf in everybody's oven, and all their problems smoke in the breeze.

As Pettibone swung the Mercury into the street, Bennie said to him, "You want, I could lay some cush for you too, Roger."

"No," Pettibone snapped.

Bennie put up an appeasing hand. "Just a thought. Help you out a little with your trip. Y'know, get you started on your new life there."

Pettibone turned south on Las Vegas Boulevard. An infinitesimal glimmer of the vast and sweeping foreknowledge granted him back at the house seemed to flicker behind his eyes, and he said, much more gently now, "I may not be leaving quite so soon after all."

"Change your mind, did ya?"

"You might put it that way."

Traffic was thin at this hour. Here and there a few scruffy, washed-out hustlers huddled in doorways or prowled the otherwise empty street. Electra, mystified by the morning journey, poked her head over the seat, whined piteously. They passed Charleston Boulevard. At the next major intersection Bennie pointed in the direction of the Sahara Hotel and said, "You can leave me off over there." Pettibone pulled up in the lot.

Bennie was in a hurry, but not so much that he couldn't take time to say gratefully, genuine gratitude warming his voice, "Rog, old buddy, me'n Timothy thank you. We owe ya one, both of us."

Pettibone smiled at him. A wan, boozy, forgiving smile. "Don't thank me yet," he said. "Remember what Kipling says."

"Yeah, what's that?"

He recited the words, emending them slightly for this occasion, this cast: " 'The sins we do by two and two, we must pay for one by one.' "

Neither of them had noticed the white Lincoln trailing along a block or so behind and idling now at the other end of the lot. When the Jew got out of the car and strode purposefully into the hotel, Click said, "Look like they splittin' up. Which one we stay with?"

"That's a hard call," Eggs said. And only an instant to decide. He was perplexed by the absence of the brother, the missing piece in this puzzle. The Mercury slid away, heading for the Paradise Road exit. "We'll follow him," he said.

"You sure?"

"Drive, Cleanth."

They drove south for a little over a mile. At Sierra Vista the Mercury hung a left, and Click said, "He for sure gotta be goin' to the cunt's place."

"I thought as much."

"Don't see how that's gonna do us no good."

"Just stay with him, Cleanth. I'll attend to the details."

The Mercury turned in at the apartment complex lot. Out came the lush and the dog. They started for the stairs, the man weaving some, the dog bounding playfully at his side.

Across the street Eggs and Click watched from the car. "As soon as he gets to the top floor you can go on in and park," Eggs said.

"We goin' up there?"

"Why else would we be here?"

"How 'bout that dog?"

"You needn't worry about the dog, Cleanth. I have a way with animals."

Click made his agitated tongue squawk. "Jesus, Eggs, I dunno. There's any, y'know, scuffle, that hound tear ya up real bad."

Eggs gave him a look compounded of pity and contempt. He reached into an inside pocket of his sport jacket and removed a .25 caliber pistol and a silencer, held them up in reassuring display. "This should give us the necessary edge. Should there be any of what you choose to call a 'scuffle.'"

Click's jaw dropped. More of the tongue activity. Then he blurted, "Holy fuck, Egger, I didn't know you was strapped."

"Ordinarily I'm not."

"Didn't know you even owned a piece."

"A little insurance."

Click didn't like this part. Not one bit. Years back he done a short-change stretch in the keep, for hanging paper. Was just an overnighter, fourteen months, but that was plenty. Never again. "You ain't, uh, thinkin' to use that?" he said with a worried nod at the weapon.

"Certainly not. I should think by now you'd know I have more imagination than that."

"Cuz anything go wrong and we're caught packin', we lookin' at a serious jolt."

"Nothing will go wrong, Cleanth," Eggs said, putting gun and silencer back in the pocket. "Now pull over there. It's time we had a friendly chat with the professor and the lady."

Outside Valerie's apartment Eggs paused and arranged his mouth in a smile. Once it was securely in place he knocked on the door. No immediate response.

"Could be they doin' a nasty," Click opined. "Maybe we oughta come back later."

Eggs ignored him, knocked again, harder. There was a sound of approaching footsteps. A voice, muffled, upwardly inflected, said, "Yes?" But the door didn't budge.

"Valerie?"

"Who is it?"

"Ignatius. Cleanth is with me."

The door opened, ever so slightly.

"Mr. Pettibone," said the smiling Eggs. "What a pleasant surprise. Good morning."

Pettibone stared at him cautiously. "Do I know you?"

"We met just the other night. Right here, in fact."

"What is it you want?"

"To speak with Valerie. May we come in?"

"She's not here."

"Well, that's all right too," said Eggs, shoving back the door and stepping into the room. "You'll do just fine." His bright, tinny smile had never once waned. It was, without a doubt, a morning for smiling.

PART
FOUR

22

Waverly's first sensations, drifting up out of a dreamless sleep, were warm and altogether pleasant, and his first conscious thought was to wonder why it was he felt so rested, so restored, better than he'd felt in a long time. A glance at the clock on the nightstand told him why. Clock said three-thirty, and from the band of light filtering through the blind at the window and falling across his face he realized, suddenly and with a rush of alarm, it could only be the P.M. reading. He jerked upright and sprang off the bed and raced through the house, searching every room. House was empty. Utterly silent. No Bennie, no dog, nobody. And, as he discovered when he returned to his own room, no money. The stack of bills laid carefully alongside the clock was surely gone.

For an instant he felt dazed, almost lightheaded. Nowhere near so good anymore. A bewildering welter of thoughts, emotions, speculations, doubts assailed him. Then, remembering his sister and everything gone on the night before, alarm escalated into something not all that far off panic. Certainly dread. Whatever the connection between Val and his absent partner and the missing money—and connection there had to be—he hadn't the charity of time to puzzle it through. The money was one thing, her safety quite another. He pulled on shoes and jacket, stopped in the bathroom just long enough to splash his sleep-puffed face with cold water, bolted out the door, and sprinted the two blocks to Las Vegas Boulevard. At the corner he stood flagging an arm at passing cabs. Several of them zoomed by, ignoring him. He cursed softly. Eventually one pulled over and he directed the driver to the Sierra Vista address, adding, "Look, I'm in a hurry, healthy toke in it if you get me there fast." For all the good it did. The streets were clotted with midday traffic, the stoplights seemingly interminable. Now he cursed aloud. The gum-popping driver said, "Doin' the best I can, friend." Waverly didn't reply.

And so it was a little after four o'clock when the cab nosed off the street and into the apartment complex lot. Waverly spotted Pettibone's Mercury parked down at one end alongside a battered pickup (same one, he recognized, driven by the two luckless louts from the other night). The Impala was nowhere in sight. Maybe a good sign, maybe not. Impossible to tell.

He paid the driver, hopped out, clambered up the stairs, taking them three at a time, and dashed down the exterior corridor and charged through the unlocked door to Val's apartment, calling her name between panting gasps. To be greeted only by a silence dense and ominous and, curiously, a heavy noxious stench, rather like charred meat, thickening the vacant air. He crossed the living room and came around the counter into the narrow kitchen. Nothing in his experience—not Jacktown, not Ypsi, not the savage violent acts of recent years—none of it had prepared him for what he saw: Pettibone lying on his back at the foot of the electric stove, one of its burners glowing cherry red; his arms outflung in supplicating pose; his mouth wide open, as though in silent scream; and the skin on his face and the palms of his hands raw and gummy, scorched away completely in spots, exposing bone, chalk-white, set in blackened bubbling pockets of blood. His head was framed in a swamp of crusted blood, last thin trickle of it oozing from the gash carved like a crimson toothless auxiliary mouth beneath his chin.

Waverly turned away and went through the door to Val's bedroom, moving deliberately now, bracing himself against what he was sure he would find. But he was wrong. No Val. Nowhere in evidence. He returned to the kitchen, stood for a moment gazing at the grotesquely disfigured Pettibone face. Roger Pettibone, Ph.D., historian, moralist, drunk. Friend, of sorts. Motionless, and thoroughly dead. An odd choking sensation, part nameless grief but as much a kind of raw and basic rage, gripped Waverly's throat. A single elemental thought took possession of him.

He inhaled slowly, deeply. Deep measured breaths. What he had to do now was focus that thought, contain it, compartmentalize it. There was still a chance Val might be alive. Outside chance. Better than none. Find her and then, after that, if there was time, find the one accountable for all this. There'd be time. He'd make time.

First he needed transportation. He stooped down, went through Pettibone's pockets, and came up with the keys to the Mercury. Now a weapon. As if in answer to that urgent need, there came a scratching noise on the bathroom door directly behind him. He yanked it open and Electra, trailing her leash, slipped around him and ambled over to Pettibone. In that peculiar doggy posture, hindquarters elevated, forelegs dropped, she sniffed at the lifeless feet. Waverly grasped the leash and, tugging a bit, coaxed her away, murmuring, "Come on, girl, nothing we can do here."

But something remaining to be done elsewhere. And while he had no conventional weapon to do it with, he had the dog. That, and the single consuming thought, grown vivid now, and seething in a private space behind his eyes. Weapons enough.

Earlier that day, at approximately 10:00 A.M., Eggs, Click, and Dawnette were convened in Click's apartment on Flamingo Road for another of the strategy sessions. Summary one, the last. Dawnette and Click sat on the couch, now and again trading furtive glances, hers anxious, fretful, his deeply distressed. Eggs stood with his back to them, phone pressed to an ear, fingers of his free hand drumming the wall. Though his face was expressionless, his eyes, could they be seen behind the opaque lenses, were animated by a peculiar manic sheen. On the third ring a lordly voice came down the line: "Wyman Brewster here."

"This is Ignatius, Wyman."

"I've been waiting for your call," said the voice, a little irk in it now.

"And I'm happy to report that everything's fallen neatly into place."

"In place?"

"Our project, Wyman," Eggs sighed. "You remember our chat yesterday?"

"Of course."

"Good. Now, about that venture capital. I trust you were able to secure it."

"Most of it."

"Most? What exactly does that mean?"

"It may take a few hours yet to put it all together."

Eggs was not cheered by what he was hearing. He'd come too far to be balked by a skittish quack, amateur at that. Nevertheless, he said evenly, "Not many hours, I hope. Time is crucial here."

"I should have it by three."

"It can't be any later than that, Wyman. Not if we want to take advantage of this unique opportunity."

"It won't."

"Excellent. And what, ah, sum will we be looking at?"

"It should come to about a hundred and three thousand dollars. Everything I could raise on such short notice. The Center's assets, like your own, are not easily convertible into cash."

Eggs suppressed an urge to whistle. A balloon and change. In this respect, at least, things were turning up better than he'd expected. He said, "You've done a superlative job, Wyman. Under the circumstances."

"You're sure it will be safe?"

"You have my guarantee. By tonight we'll have that first installment on the clinic."

"But what do I do now?"

"Now you wait. We'll pick you up sometime this afternoon."

"When?"

"Difficult to say. Very likely around that three o'clock hour you mention. Possibly earlier. In any case," Eggs added, putting just the barest trace of menace in it, "you're to stay there at the Center till we arrive. You understand that, Wyman?"

A silence filled the line.

"Wyman?"

The voice, its natural pomposity wilted a bit by a craven tremor, inquired faintly, a faint whisper, "There wasn't anything, uh, messy, I hope."

"Oh no. Nothing to worry yourself over. Everyone's been most helpful."

They rang off. Eggs began to chuckle softly. Soon he was laughing out loud. Couldn't help himself. Messy. No, nothing too messy. Not just yet.

"You gonna let us in on the joke?" Dawnette said pettishly.

It was enough to bring his mirth under control. Back to business. He turned and cast a long, measuring gaze on his partners, who represented in their persons another of those hurdles some might call messy, and one to be dealt with before the day was out. A minor aggravation. All in good time. He said, "It seems our crusading healer has come up with the money."

"That's a joke?"

"Now then," Eggs said, fixing the gaze on Click, ignoring her, "we must arrange to place the bet. That's your department, Cleanth. What do you recommend?"

"How much we talkin'?"

"It's a jumbo, Cleanth. Full balloon."

"Jesus, that's a lotta scratch. Dunno no out-state book take that big an order. Not this late."

"What about here in town?"

"Only guy I know could spread that kinda gelt around is Zippy. You remember Zippy?"

"Dimly. Runt? Wears a hat?"

"That's the one. He got all them under-the-counter connections. He could maybe lay it for us."

"Phone him."

"I can't."

"I don't want to hear any more *can'ts*, Cleanth."

"I dunno his number."

"Look it up."

"See, that's the thing," Click said miserably, his eyes slipsliding about the room, unable to meet the veiled relentless stare leveled on him. "Far as I know, he always go by just Zippy. He got a last name, I ain't never heard it."

Throughout this exchange Dawnette's head had been swiveling back and forth between them. Now she put in, "Somebody wanta tell me what the fuck's going on?"

"Shut up, Dawnette," Eggs snapped. Evidently it was his lot to be forever stalled by bunglers and imbeciles and squeamish cowards. In a just and orderly world that's not the way it was meant to be. But an orderly man defines his own fate, sets his own boundaries. And Eggs LaRevere, by his own assessment, was nothing if not orderly. So he deliberated a moment. And eventually, as it always did, a thought came to him. His address book, carefully compiled and updated over the years, was in one of the bags in the other apartment. And years ago he'd had some small transactions, unmemorable, with the elusive Zippy. Whose name and number might still be recorded in that book. In a voice chilly and decidedly thin he said, "Wait here. Both of you. I'll be right back."

The door banged shut behind him. Immediately Dawnette turned to Click and demanded once again, "Okay, what's goin' on?"

Click put up a fluttery hand. "You don't wanna know."

Dawnette figured she better come at it another direction. She slid over beside him and plucked the quivering hand out of the air and brought it down into her lap, perilously near the joycrack. Perilous times—and it didn't take no deep thinker to see that's what these was—you do what you got to do. "What did we say last night, Click? About stickin' together? You can tell me."

Click's slippery eyes moved from floor to wall to ceiling, back again. Anywhere but her.

"Click?" she said in accents dewy, wheedling. "C'mon."

"He iced him!" Click blurted out wretchedly.

"Iced? Who, iced?"

"The juicer. One was raggin' on Brewster the other night. Over to that crazy Valerie's place."

"The moonbeam lady, he do her too?"

"Unh-unh. He woulda though, she'd been there. Way he was steamin'."

"Why'd he do it?"

"Why? Fucked if I know why. He geeked. Just plain geeked. You seen how he gets."

"Yeah, I seen," Dawnette said ruefully. Better than most, had she seen.

"It's *how* he done it, that's the worst part. Turned up the stove red hot and stuck a gag in his mouth and then he laid the poor fucker's hands on it till he told."

"Told?"

"What he knew about them wired games. Then Eggs, he shoves his face on it, burner, till you could smell the meat sizzlin'. Hear it poppin', too. And then he takes a butcher knife and unzips him at the neck. Opens him right up, ear to ear."

Click's tongue had been going mile a minute, filling the junctures in his tumbling confessional with a fierce squawk. Dawnette watched him. His porky cheeks were ashen, piggy eyes shell-shocked. Little oinker was seriously tripped. And she wasn't feeling so fresh herself, this line of news.

The hand in her lap twitched violently. She returned it to him. Had to think quick now, Eggs be back any minute. She said, "Okay. Okay. It's done. Nothin' change that. But he got what he needed on them games, right?"

"Got what the juicer told him. Which wasn't all that much anyways."

"How much?"

"Sound like tonight's game maybe tanked. Maybe not too, way I heard it."

"Not? What's that mean?"

"Juicer said he *thought*. Never said for sure, all that squealin' he was doin' every time Eggs took the gag out."

"So it's just this one game. Maybe one, at that."

"Tonight or nothin'. Least that's Eggs's take on it."

"And he got a hundred long off Brewster?"

"*Gonna* get. You heard him on the phone there."

A hundred long. Dawnette had never seen that kind of money in her life. Dreamed about it though, more times than plenty. And here it was, about to drop right into their sweaty palms—*her* palms—and that schizo gonna flush it right down the crapper. Not to say what he got in mind for the bumblefuck and her, after. She seen that empty wicked smile work across his face, way the veins in his throat filled when things weren't going how he wanted. Hadn't missed any of it. Eggs she knew. So she said, "Okay, what we gotta do, Click, you'n me, is—"

Ill-formed though it was, the thought went unfinished, for just then Eggs came through the door, smiling, but only by half, maybe less, the telltale veins big as garden hoses. Not a happy man. "His name is Petrello," he announced, absent of introduction. "Tony Petrello."

"That's Zippy's name?" Click said. "Didn't know he was a wop."

"His ethnic origins are immaterial, Cleanth. Come on. We have to find him."

Click hesitated just a beat. "You got his name, whyn't you call?"

"I've already done that. Some woman answered, sulky bitch. Said he wasn't there, didn't know when he'd be back. However, she did volunteer he'd be downtown somewhere. So let's move it. Time's running short."

"How 'bout me?" Dawnette wanted to know. "What am I suppose to do?"

"You're to wait right here," Eggs said, giving her the merest edge of his attention. He made an impatient whisking motion at Click.

By a process of reasoning not unlike Dawnette's, Click was arriving, independently, slowly, at a somewhat similar conclusion. He got to his feet, stood staring at them, and in a feeble mumble said, "Uh, I was thinkin', Egger, maybe we oughta just, well, bag it. Balloon's a nice store. We could lift it off Brewster easy, skate on outta here. Before anything else go, y'know, dank on us."

Eggs looked at him carefully. "Why would we want to do that, Cleanth? Come this far."

"Bet end, is all I'm sayin'. That sponge, he didn't sound too positive. 'Bout tonight, I mean."

Now Eggs looked at both of them, both his partners. His face darkened some, but the mordant smile, in curious contrast, widened a bit. "No, I believe you're mistaken. I'm confident we can rely on his testimony. A hot stove does much to concentrate the mind. As you witnessed. Come along now."

And on their way out the door he said to Dawnette, elaborately casual, "We have a stove here too, you know. Well, a hot plate, same thing. And we'll be back. Very shortly. So you be sure to wait now."

Only thing Dawnette was sure about anymore was she needed the wise counsel of Velva, and needed it sooner than suddenly. And so the minute she was sure—or pretty sure, nothing sure no more—they were out of there she was on the phone, spilling everything she'd heard and seen the last half-hour.

Once the frantic recital finally ran down, Velva said, "Want you to chill out now. Lemme see I understand what I'm hearin' here."

"He's gonna kill me, Vel, you don't help."

"What'd I just say? Said suck it easy, minute, I got to think."

Dawnette said nothing, but she put a little whimper into the moment's silence. Easy enough to do, she was scared batshit.

"Okay," Velva said, "they're out now lookin' to find some guy lay the bet on. That right?"

"Right, yeah."

"And there's 100K in it?"

"That's what they said."

"But you ain't seen any green yet."

"No."

"When you think it's comin'?"

"I dunno for sure. Got to be some time this afternoon, though, if the game's tonight. I heard a three o'clock in there somewhere."

"And this mark, he's bringin' it over to where you're at?"

"Sounded that way. Hard to tell."

Another space of silence. Dawnette waited as long as her ragged nerves would allow, then filled it with a desperate plea: "What am I gonna *do*, Vel?"

"I'm thinkin' on it."

"I got to bolt outta here. While I still can."

"Oh no," Velva said sharply. "You stay put."

"But what about that stiff? He's gone whackadoo, totally bent. You can see it in his face. Like he's enjoyin' himself."

"Yeah, stiff puts a whole different figure on it," Velva agreed, but in a drawl with a kind of wary neutral distancing in it.

Now Dawnette was truly tweaked. "Help me, Vel. Please. I'll make it up to you. I promise."

"Don't worry, I'm gonna help. You say you're in them apartments on Flamingo? Right down the road from Bally's?"

"Right."

"Two apartments?"

"Yeah. Me'n Eggs in one, yutz in the other."

"Okay, here's what you do. Wait till they all get back there. All of 'em, mark too. Be sure they got the cash. Then you gimme call."

"Fuck'm I gonna do that," Dawnette moaned, "him eye-ballin' me?"

"Use that butt-lick sideman you leadin' around by the dick. Get him to make some shade. Think of something. Find a way. Everything comin' down, you gonna be low on the priority list."

"Jesus, Vel, that's walkin' a high wire in a cyclone, what you're sayin'."

"You want to come outta this with a piece of that balloon?"

"Can't spend it dead."

"You ain't gonna be dead. Trust me."

Yeah, sure. Trust big Vel. But who else you gonna trust? Answer is nobody, nobody left. And no running from Eggs, not now. That much she knew for absolute sure. "Say I can," Dawnette said. "Make the call, I mean. Then what?"

"We know they got to wait on that game. Soon's I hear, I'll be over there. Bail you out, lift the loot, and lay on some real special hurts I got in mind for your breeder. Triple score, all rolled up in one."

Dawnette delivered a long, heavy, despairing sigh. Genuine sigh, no more playacting. "He's gonna kill me. I just know it."

"No he's not. Any killin' gets done, he's the one booked a first-class ticket to the worm farm. You'll see."

◦ ◦ ◦

It seemed strange somehow, gripping the same wheel Roger had so recently gripped, steering the rattly Mercury down a busy street in a busy desert town under a bright, unblemished desert sky. Yet he felt remarkably centered too, almost detached, the way he sometimes felt at the tables, going into a game. Ready to get on with it, regardless of outcome, get it done.

Until the Mercury began to sputter and lurch and, finally, at the next intersection, roll to a dead stop. He pumped the pedal, ground the engine. Resolutely, it refused to turn over. His eyes fell on the fuel gauge. And of course it read empty. And in a sudden explosion of pent-up, impotent fury, Waverly banged his fists on the wheel, thundering, "Goddam goddam goddam god*dam!*"

Electra, startled, and with a doggy need for human coherence and order, put up an entreating paw. About as much as he was going to get in the way of commiseration. Cars roared up behind and swooped on by, horns blasting. A blue-haired lady flipped him a passing bird, in afterjeer. Through the windshield he saw some gas pumps in the near distance. "You stay here," he instructed the fretting dog, addressing it as though it were a person, or as though he were offering a pledge to himself. "Don't worry, I'm coming back." He took off running.

It was one of those glass-walled party store stations, glittery under a flood of natural and fluorescent light. A long queue of customers trailed back from the counter. Waverly skirted around them, inciting some scowls and dark mutterings, and stepped up to the clerk dinging the cash register keys and said breathlessly, "My car's out of gas. Few blocks from here. Can you help me out?"

"Maybe, you wanta wait your turn."

"This is an emergency."

The clerk regarded him with a mixture of indifference and derision, but not an ounce of pity. "Yeah, and this is Vegas. Everybody got an emergency."

Waverly's jaws tightened. Again the rage swept through him. But this was not the place or time to ventilate it. Or the person. Without a word he went to the back of the line.

It inched forward. At last he stood facing the clerk, who leaned into the register and drawled, "Now, what's the problem?"

"I need gas."

"You could try some beans," said the clerk, chortling at his excellent wit.

Waverly was not amused. "Look, are you going to loan me a can or not?"

"Loan, no. Rent, maybe."

"*Rent* a gas can?"

"Remember what I told ya? This is Vegas."

He was a stout young man, this clerk, slack of mouth, slick of hair, eyes full of an indiscriminate spite. A regular Johnnie Vegas, charmed to be exactly who he was.

Waverly got out his wallet. Opened, it revealed a perilously thin store of bills, couple of yards, a fifty, some singles. "How much," he said, "this rent?"

"Cost you ten. Plus the five gallons gas it holds, course."

Waverly handed over the fifty.

The clerk gave him back a smile pure mockery and produced a can from under the counter. He rang up the charge, counted out the change, and said, "Use pump eight. Soon's you bring in the can, you get your sawbuck back."

"That's gladdening."

Twenty minutes later Waverly came through the station door lugging the empty can. No line this time. He set the can on the counter and said, "I'll take the ten in gas."

The clerk wagged his head at the Mercury pulled up outside. "Smart move," he snorted, "that guzzle-bucket you're drivin'. You oughta get it in that antique show the slopes got over to the I.P."

A man with an indisputable opinion on every fragment of the passing scene. Waverly squashed an impulse to reply. He went out to the car and engaged hose and gas portal. Stood watching the slow creep of numbers across the pump's dials, anxiety sweat beading on his forehead and rilling down his chest and back. Electra scratched worriedly at a window. The sun dipped in the sky, lifting a fireworks of color off the jagged mountain profile on the horizon. It occurred to Waverly that darkness would be settling in, and soon. Also that he'd never actually driven a car out here and, apart from the Strip and downtown, margins of his stunted universe, knew it scarcely at all. He was going to need directions. And like it or not, there was only one place to ask.

The sale total dial arrived finally at ten. He recradled the nozzle and entered the store.

The clerk followed his approach, moist toothpick dangling from a mouth shaped in a loose, nasty grin. "Now what? More problems?"

"Can you tell me the quickest way to get from here to Spring Mountain Road?"

"Nope, can't helpya."

"You don't know Spring Mountain?"

"Be on a city map. Whyn't you look it up?"

"Where's the map?"

A glint came into the spiteful eyes. The grin opened in a crafty smirk. "I could sellya one," the clerk allowed.

"You rent me a can, now you're going to sell me a map?"

"That's how it works in—"

"Yeah, I know. I know where we are."

"That one you got right. You're learnin'."

It was rising again, the storm in his head. Will of its own. To forestall it, Waverly said, "All right, where's the manager?"

"You're lookin' at him."

"*You're* the manager?"

"I'm your man. What's your beef?"

No containing it anymore. He'd tried. Comes now the whirlwind. Waverly reached across the counter and seized him at the collar, jerked his head toward the front of the store.

"Fuck you think you're—"

"Don't talk. Listen. See that dog out there? That's a Doberman pinscher. Female, meanest kind. Rip you open in a fingersnap."

"Whaddya want off me?"

"Want you to give me that goddam map before I bring her in here and set her loose. Believe me when I tell you there's nowhere you can run she won't get to you."

The clerk's face went chalky. All his bullying instincts deserted him. Looking back and forth between dog and the wild eyes on the man clutching his collar, he elected to believe. "Rack," he said, voice stippled with fear, "behind me . . . lemme go."

Waverly released him. "Get it."

The clerk backed away, lifted a map from the rack, and slung it on the counter.

Waverly spread it out and pinpointed where he was. Where else but Paradise Road. They had a real flair for names here. Inspired. He traced the fastest route to Spring Mountain, secured it in his head. Then, glancing up at the cowering clerk, he said in parting, "Thanks for all the generous help. Have to nominate you for Jaycee young businessman of the year."

On his way through the door he thought he heard a muffled "Fuck you, asshole."

He swung the Mercury into the street and sped away. And in under a quarter of an hour his eyes picked out from among a confusion of signs fading in the softening light the one that announced The Great Western Center for Quantum Healing and Attitudinal Awareness.

Things hadn't been going any smoother for Eggs that afternoon and, like Waverly, he was doing his best to throttle the storm gathering in his head. Starting at the El Cortez, he and Click had worked their way up Fremont to the dead end of the Union Plaza. With supreme unsuccess. Everybody had seen Zippy, nobody knew where he was.

At the Golden Nugget a cocktail waitress said, "He was in here while back. You try the coffee shop?" They'd already been there. At the Las Vegas Club a dealer told them he'd just spoken with Zippy: "Couldn'ta been five minutes ago. Said he was headed to Binion's." So they doubled back to the Horseshoe and found a player Click knew who reported, "The Zip? Yeah, he's here someplace. Think he went to take a leak." In the john they discovered two men, one jabbering earnestly at his reflection in a mirror, the other vomiting into a sink. Neither was Zippy.

They searched every corner of every casino and bar and coffee shop on the street. No Zippy. From Fremont they hurried over to Ogden, scouted the California and the Lady Luck. No luck. Like some ghostly taunting specter, he seemed to dissolve into a mist just a step ahead of them. Reach out and he was vanished. The phantom hustler.

At last Click felt compelled to remark, "Y'know, we ain't exactly steppin' up big, Eggs. Whaddya think?"

"We know he's down here somewhere," Eggs said grimly. "We'll find him."

"Where's there left to look?"

"We're going to start over. Cover Fremont again. There's still time."

But when they came out of The Four Queens the sun was slipping behind the Union Plaza tower, and Eggs was no longer quite so confident of the clemency of time. "None of this would be happening," he said bitterly and in a mounting agony of frustration, "if you'd held up your end."

"You never *tol'* me nothin'! How was I suppose to know it was comin' down so sudden? You'd've gimme some lead, I mighta been able to make some calls."

Click's voice rose in a hurt, defensive, tongue-screaming whine. And it was true, of course, everything the worthless little turd was saying, but no less infuriating for being the truth. Eggs pulled at his lower lip. Steadied himself. Nothing to be gained from recrimination. No percentage in it. "Never mind," he said. "Let's keep going."

"One place we ain't checked out is Leroy's," Click volunteered. "Y'know, sports book? He could be there."

"I've heard of it. Where's it located?"

"Over on First. Just down the block and around the corner."

They went that way.

And there, slouched against a wall under a No Loitering sign, gaze fixed on the odds board, anachronous Panama hat—possibly white once, now the color of soot—perched on his oblong head, pinch of a cigarette stuck in his mouth, notepad in his hand—there stood a sallow spidery man with a face pocked and cratered as the face of the moon and the wrinkle-nested eyes of a wily old rodent. Zippy.

"I'll do the talking," Eggs said under his breath as they approached him. And to Zippy he said, "You're a hard man to find," forcing as much jocularity into it as he could manage.

Zippy took his eyes off the board and ran them over Eggs. An annoyed, cigarette squint. "I know you?"

Eggs opened his palms in the air, a gesture of astonishment, injured feelings. "You don't remember? Eggs? My partner, Cleanth?"

A dim recollection flickered in the pink-streaked eyes. "Oh. Yeah. Eggs. Been a while."

"That it has."

"So how's it by you?"

"Good."

"Glad to hear," Zippy said. His squinty gaze began to stray back to the board.

"Better than good, actually. Which is why I need to speak with you."

"Yeah? What about?"

"Business."

"What kinda business?"

"Buzz is you've got the contacts to lay a UNLV bet. Locally."

"Where'd you hear that?"

"It's in the air."

"You'n me must be sniffin' different air," Zippy said, twitching his nostrils as though to test it. "That's against the law, y'know."

"So is jaywalking. But we do it anyway, don't we, Zippy. Both of us."

"You wanna wager on our Rebs, whyn't you ring up an out-state book? Country's full of 'em. Spare yourself the grief."

"It's tonight's game I want to bet."

"Tonight? That'd be cuttin' it close."

"And that's why I've come to you."

All that remained of Zippy's cigarette was a glow of ash. He removed the tiny stub and ground it under his heel. "Supposin' I could," he said cautiously. "Just supposin', now. What kinda action we be talkin'?"

"A hundred large."

Zippy shook his head slowly. "Don't know I could spread that kinda money around, this late. Game starts at seven, our time."

"I've got faith in you, Zippy."

"Say I was to get through to some people. Which way you callin' it?"

"Louisiana."

Zippy made a lemony face. "Line is Rebs, give seven. Too light, my thinkin'. Rebs gonna stomp 'em. And you want the Tigers?"

"My bet, my call."

He had to think a minute, Zippy did. But not long. "Might be I could help you out," he said. "But I gotta see some green first."

"Surely you don't think I'd have it on me."

"Still gotta see it. These people I'd be talkin' to, they don't fuck around. Wager go toes on you, you gotta come up with them soldiers. Every last one of 'em. I'm just a middleman here, and I ain't lookin' to get caught in no squeeze. You understand what I'm tellin' you?"

"I believe I can follow it."

"That's good, you followin'. Cuz them's the conditions."

Now it was Eggs's turn to think. He looked at his watch. Considered the timing and everything yet to be done. It did get complicated. Finally he said, "What's the latest you could place the bet?"

"Hard to say. I'd hafta make some feeler calls first."

"Six-thirty?"

"That'd be the outside, absolutely. An' that's gettin' right down to the short hairs."

"But it could be done?"

Zippy shrugged. "Could give 'er a twirl. No promises."

"All right. Be at my place at six-thirty and you'll see the money."

"Where you at?"

Eggs gave him the address.

"Okay," Zippy said, "but the vig's gonna be twenty points, this tricky a deal."

"That's certainly fair," Eggs told him. Why not? Tell him anything. After tonight it wouldn't matter in the slightest.

Zippy watched him narrowly now. A lifetime of shifty experience kindled his eyes and stained his corroded features the way dye will color a fabric. "Y'know, Eggs," he said carefully, "I don't remember you ever bein' into wagerin'. Wouldn't be you know somethin' rest of us don't?"

Eggs produced a twist of a smile. But the smile said one thing, his words quite another. "Don't ask."

And on the drive to the Center it loosened some, that dead smile, and an expression almost dreamy came into his face as he contemplated the upcoming score. Though it was of course disappointing that things hadn't worked out quite as he'd hoped—a string of scores lasting well into the season—nevertheless, he took solace in the knowledge he'd done his best. And 200K would be a nice take, certainly enough to keep him comfortably while he crafted his next venture. What that might be wasn't clear yet. Possibly an adaptation of the Brewster scam. In Florida, say, or Arizona, wherever the walking stiffs congregated. An intriguing notion, healing. He could do as well with it, or better. He had all the words. His thoughts glided forward in time; tantalizing visions unspooled in his head.

Until a querulous voice returned him to the there and then. Some inane Cleanth question. "What was that?" he said.

"Said what you, uh, got in mind for Brewster? After we strip the loot off him."

"Oh, I'm sure we'll think of something," Eggs said absently. "We did this morning, you recall."

If it was possible to feel at once charged and serene, galvanized and almost at peace, that's how Eggs felt. The Center was just ahead. Let the healing begin.

"I expected you sooner than this. You said three o'clock."

"Yes, well, we were delayed. A small snag."

"Snag?"

"Nothing to alarm yourself over. Everything's under control. Now, you do have the money, Wyman?"

Brewster indicated the briefcase clutched tightly in his lap.

"May I see?"

"It's all in here."

"Let's have a look anyway," Eggs said, no longer quite so deferential.

Brewster opened the case, revealing stacks of banded bills.

Eggs leaned over the seat and examined them with his eyes. Most inspiriting sight. He said, "Splendid," and then to Click, who sat hunched over the wheel, stork-shouldered, beating a jittery tattoo on the dash, "I believe we can get started now, Cleanth."

Click took the Lincoln out of the Center lot and pointed it east on Spring Mountain. To avoid the Saturday night Strip traffic, he turned south on Arville and followed it to Flamingo, then east again. They rode in silence. Each was much too occupied with his own tangled emotions—for Brewster, a peculiar mix of aversion and expectancy, jubilance and dread; for Click, the twitchy rising panic of a lab rat hopelessly lost in a confounding maze; and for Eggs, a kind of manic yet thoroughly contained exhilaration—to take any notice of the vehicle that emerged from the lengthening shadows in the lot and trailed along behind them now, keeping a prudent distance, but keeping them carefully in view.

Click pulled up by his apartment and he and Eggs stepped out of the car. Brewster didn't budge. "What is *this* place?" he demanded.

"This is where we're to meet our contact man," Eggs explained. "He'll be here very shortly."

Still he hesitated.

"It's perfectly safe, Wyman," Eggs said soothingly. "Come along now."

Brewster tucked the briefcase under an arm and climbed out of the back seat. He glanced about uncertainly. Various shades of doubt played across his anxious face.

"Go right on in," Eggs said. "Dawnette's waiting for us."

"You're coming?"

"Be right there."

Brewster turned and started for the door. And in a whispered aside to Click, Eggs said, "There's a roll of duct tape, my place, small bag. Go get it."

"What for?"

"Just get it."

"Jesus, Eggs, you ain't gonna—"

"Get the tape, Cleanth."

Inside the apartment Dawnette was pacing frantically, smoking furiously, a riot of nerves. But when she saw Brewster in the doorway, Eggs right behind him, no Click, she froze, stiffened, petrified as a doe locked in the headlights glare of an onrushing sixteen-wheeler.

"You seem startled," Eggs said innocently. "Is something wrong?"

"No, no . . . nothing wrong . . . it was gettin' late . . . I was startin' to . . ."

"Worry?" Eggs finished for her.

"Yeah. Worry."

"Well, we're back now. As you see. Oh, let's mind our manners. Say hello to Wyman."

She stammered out a greeting, got a curt acknowledgment in reply.

Eggs ushered Brewster over to the couch. "Please, Wyman, have a seat."

Brewster surveyed the tiny cluttered room with a look of infinite distaste, but he sat anyway, rigidly erect, alert, briefcase secured in his lap. He wore the predictable black suit, somber silk tie, black spit-polished shoes. A prophetic study in funereal gloom. With some difficulty, Eggs restrained his wayward willful smile. Apt wardrobe, he was thinking; seasonable, one might say, though of course he didn't.

"Where's Click?" Dawnette wanted to know.

"Why do you ask?" Eggs said.

"No reason. Just wonderin'."

"Did you think something had happened to him?"

"No."

"Your concern is touching, Dawnette. But again, not to worry. He'll be along directly."

He went over and stood at the window. Beyond it, a globe of moon hung in a sky filling with dark. Across the street the construction site, utterly deserted, blackened against the night. It would do. As serviceable a venue as any, he concluded, but without a spark of his usual zest. For while it was absolutely essential to move smartly now, vault this last pesky hurdle, still he felt an urgent need, a passionate compulsion, to put the unmistakable LaRevere seal on it, even as he'd done this morning. Recklessness it was certainly not. Rather more a matter of pride in craftsmanship. Exactitude. Symmetry. Artistry, finally.

A cement truck turned off Flamingo Road and came rumbling down the street, candy-striped drum revolving slowly, hypnotically. It pulled to a stop behind a towering mound of sand at the extreme south end of the site. Tranced, inspired, Eggs watched it pass. Like a divinely ordained vision, it seemed almost to float before his eyes. There are some men for whom, strive as they might, plod as they will, the whimsical gifts of imagination and fancy are forever fugitive, forever out of reach. He was many things, was Eggs LaRevere, but one that he knew he was surely not was one of them.

Waverly had spotted it just in time to pull off the street and into a band of shadow at the opposite end of the lot. Same bone-white Lincoln he'd seen leaving Val's two nights ago, parked now directly in front of the door to the Center; Brewster in the back; diminutive fatty—name escaped him—behind the wheel; and in the seat next to him the man whose name gave Waverly no recall problem whatsoever: Mr. Call Me Eggs LaRevere. Man he was looking for. The Center was dark, shuttered, a sorry we're closed sign stuck in a window. Scattering of cars in the lot. None of them Val's Impala. Nothing he could do but watch and wait.

In a moment the Lincoln wheeled into the street. Waverly followed along, but well behind, always with a vehicle or two between them. He had no idea where they were headed. It didn't matter. Eventually they had to stop.

And eventually they did. Waverly drove on by the two parallel files of shabby apartments reaching back off Flamingo Road, hung a hard right at the next corner, went down a long block, and came in the rear entrance of the complex. The Lincoln was parked outside one of the units, maybe forty yards away, no more than that. He killed his headlights and pulled over.

The sudden chill of desert night seeped into the car. His breath steamed the air. The dog's, too, for she was panting now, growling, sensing something was up. Waverly hushed her, stroked the bladed head swaying rhythmically in the dark. But he kept his eyes on the Lincoln and the faint yellow glow behind the drawn curtain at the apartment window. Before long a figure crossed his line of vision, moving in an urgent waddly trot. Could be the fatty, hard to tell. Whoever he was, he made straight for the apartment, straight through the door. Soon it swung open again and now four people emerged, one at a time, each silhouetted for a fraction of an instant in the rectangular frame of light. The first was a woman. Val? He couldn't be sure. Next the waddler; followed by a towering lanky figure—had to be Brewster—whose head bobbed agitatedly; and bringing up the rear, unmistakably, Mr. Eggs LaRevere, prodding Brewster along with the source of all that agitation, the elongated barrel of a handgun shoved up against the small of his back.

The gun brought a whole new dimension to this deadly game. Particularly if the woman was in fact Val. Waverly waited until they passed behind one of the apartments and then he eased open the door, gripped Electra's leash, and ducked between the two units directly across from the car. Slowly, cautiously, he threaded through a patch of grass and came out on a street flanking an enormous empty lot, barren as a moonscape. Already the foursome was halfway across it, marching along in a steady purposeful column, skirting the small hillocks of sand and clearly bearing toward a much larger one at the far corner of the lot.

Electra was tugging at the leash, blowing her breath and growling again, trembly with a kind of baffled, intuited anticipation. Waverly restrained her. "Not yet," he murmured. "Soon, but not yet." He waited until the column disappeared behind the mound of sand in the distance. "Now," he said, and simultaneously dog and man took off running.

"When can we expect this . . . person?" Brewster had asked after a stagy prefatory throat-clearing, addressing Eggs's back, putting his question into the ominous silence of the room.

Eggs turned away from the window. His face was carefully blank. From behind the opaque lenses that looked remarkably like a pair of polished metal eyes, he regarded the healer for a long moment. "Oh, very soon now," he said. "In the meantime, there's something I'd like you to see. I think you'll find it fascinating. Given your calling."

Brewster's bony fingers tightened around the briefcase. "What could that be?" he said guardedly.

"Just as soon as Cleanth gets back I'll show you."

Dawnette began to drift toward the door. Eggs caught the movement out of the corner of one of the metal eyes. "Where are *you* going?"

"Gonna run over to the other place, minute."

"Whatever for?"

"Outta cigs." In evidence, she held up a crumpled pack.

"You can have one of mine," Eggs said, positioning himself between her and the door.

"Not my brand."

"One cigarette's like another, Dawnette. Equally hazardous. Am I right, Wyman?"

Before Brewster could remark on the perils of nicotine, Click came chugging through the door. A hypertensive flush scalded his chubby cheeks, distress flooded the piggy eyes. One of his hands was held crooked behind his back.

"You found it?" Eggs asked him.

"Yeah."

"Very good," Eggs said, and with a playful finger wag at Brewster, "Now then, Wyman, let's go have a look at that, ah, point of interest I was telling you about."

Squaring his shoulders, summoning all that was left of his lofty dignity, Brewster said, "I prefer to wait here until our business is completed."

"There's plenty of time yet. And I'd very much like you to see this."

"I'd rather not."

"It's just across the street," Eggs said in wheedling tones. He was enjoying himself thoroughly now, all these preliminaries. Rather like a voluptuous, tingly foreplay. But he recognized also, in spite of the fraudulent assurance, that time was indeed growing short.

Brewster remained anchored to the couch. "No," he said firmly, but the slightest of tremors betrayed the resolution in his voice.

Something on the order of a smile crossed Eggs's face. He reached into an inner pocket of his jacket and removed the gun. Next he took the silencer from another pocket and methodically attached it to the muzzle. And then he leveled the weapon on Brewster. "I really must insist, Wyman."

Brewster shook his head back and forth vigorously. He didn't move.

"You must understand," said Eggs, eminently reasonable, "a bullet in the hand, say, or worse yet, the knee, can be incapacitating. And terribly painful."

Brewster clamped his lips together and shut his eyes and moaned softly, as if to ward off everything he was hearing and seeing. As if to flee into some remote and inaccessible chamber of himself.

"Stand up, Wyman."

Brewster tottered to his feet, clutching the briefcase as though it were a last tenuous lifeline in a storm-swept sea. He looked stringy, withered, suddenly very old.

"The briefcase you can leave here. It'll be quite safe."

Obediently, he set it on the couch. His eyes were open now, blinking wildly, pooled with terror. He tried to say something, but the words seemed to catch in his throat, came out a stuttery choking sob.

"Wyman Brewster, destitute of speech. There's a first. Apply the tape, Cleanth."

"We gotta do this, Eggs?"

"Oh, absolutely. The success of our venture turns on it. You know that, Cleanth."

"Yeah, but maybe we could just—"

"Let's don't argue."

One thing Click knew for a fact, you don't argue with the man packing the piece. Especially when that man was Eggs. He unrolled a wide swatch of duct tape, stepped up to Brewster and elevated himself onto tiptoes. To accommodate his efforts, the healer lowered his head, but he found voice enough to whimper, "Cleanth . . . for God's sake . . . please . . ."

"Sorry," Click mumbled, "sorry," and he stuck the tape across a mouth damp with spittle. Mercifully, the difference in their heights was such that he didn't have to meet those pleading eyes.

Dawnette had shrunk back against the wall. Eggs turned to her and said, "I'd like you to join us."

"This got nothin' to do with me. I'll wait for you guys here."

"No, this is something you wouldn't want to miss." He made a beckoning motion with the gun, ever so slight, but pronounced enough to propel her stiffly toward the door. To Click he said, "Oh yes, one more thing. I'll take the car keys."

Click looked bewildered. "How come? Drivin', that's my job."

"Merely a precaution," Eggs said. "I'll explain later." He extended the open palm of his free hand. The gun hand swayed gently.

Click searched his pockets, came up empty. He shrugged helplessly. "Musta left 'em in the car."

"You're sure?"

"Gotta be there."

"Well, that's fine too," Eggs said affably. "That will do. Let's hurry along now. We mustn't be late for the redoubtable Zippy."

As much as anything—no, face it, more than anything (Eggs reflected philosophically as he marched them single-file, his platoon of walking dead, across the street and into the deserted site, occasionally thrusting the gun up against Brewster's back, to keep him moving, keep the flabby craven sag out of his knees: poor Wyman, a lifelong thanaphobe, even as he'd suspected), more than the intellectual challenge of crafting a score, more than the galvanizing rush of its execution, more even than the satisfaction of reward—more than any or all of these was the seductive enchantment of the ritual, the ceremony, the words. And so it seemed somehow fitting that the moon laid a wash of silvery light over the steep mound of sand, almost like a celestial benediction, while the racket of the truck's engine and the deep rumble of its revolving drum supplied a suitably rhythmic, atonal dirge.

The driver, in silhouette a blocky, fleshy-hipped man, stood on the metal running board outside the cab, his back to them. He held some indistinguishable tool in his hands, doubtless a screwdriver, for he appeared to be tightening the brackets that secured the rear-view mirror in place. Eggs shoved Brewster up next to Click and Dawnette. With his eyes and a significant jabbing motion of the gun, he signaled them to stay put. Then he slipped the gun inside a fold of his jacket and came up alongside the driver. "Having trouble?" he called out. It was necessary to shout to be heard.

The driver paused, looked down at him irritably, scowled. "Goddam mirror come loose."

"How'd it happen?"

"Fucked if I know. Somebody dickin' around, pro'ly. Suppose to be clocked out an hour ago."

"Shame."

The driver turned back to his labors, no longer interested in this profitless dialogue.

"What's your name?"

"Smitty," he bellowed over his shoulder. "Who's askin'?"

Mostly for his own gratification, Eggs murmured, "Well, Smitty, I'm afraid you just drew the bad-luck bean"; and he lifted the gun, aimed, squeezed the trigger, and took off the top of his head; and the ill-starred Smitty spun crazily, like a marionette on suddenly slackened strings, and plunged face—or what remained of face—first into the sand. His screwdriver clattered across the running board as he fell.

So much for lesser obstacles. But the ladder leading to the catwalk and the lowered cement chute above the cab, that could present a serious hurdle, that could be dicey. Eggs realized he was going to need help, albeit of the temporary variety. And, turning his attention to the threesome cowering against the wheel well of the truck, that's what he said: "Cleanth, pull yourself together. I need your help now."

Dawnette's head was buried in her hands. From behind the tape Brewster produced a curious sound, rather like the insistent buzzing of an angered hornet. Click fetched his breath in short, ragged gasps. "What for?" he said.

Eggs indicated the ladder. "To get him up there."

"You ain't really gonna—"

"Yes."

"Why?"

Dawnette jerked her head up out of her hands and screeched, "He's gonna kill us!"

Click hesitated.

"Don't listen to this foolish hysterical woman," Eggs said. "We're partners, you and I. We need each other."

"He don't need nobody. He got the money, car, he don't need us."

Dawnette again, some grating harpy screech, rising over the din of the steadily rolling drum. Eggs glared at her, but for the benefit of Click he fashioned a thin comradely smile. "Partners, Cleanth. Remember?"

Still Click hesitated.

"Cleanth?"

Click shook his head slowly, negatively.

"You're saying no?"

"Ain't no need for this, Eggs. You gotta whack him, use the piece."

"*You're* telling *me* how to conduct business?" It was impossible for Eggs to contain the astonishment in his voice.

"Sayin' it's bughouse, what you're doin' here."

Eggs looked hard at him. All the smile was gone out of his face. The swelling veins in his throat pulsed dangerously. In this deceitful world there was no one to depend on, finally, but oneself. "This is most disappointing, Cleanth," he said. "But if that's your choice, so be it."

He took two steps back, trained the gun on them. Click crossed his arms over his chest. His pudgy frame shook uncontrollably, a jellied quiver, head to foot. Dawnette covered her eyes with clenched fists, wailing, "Oh God oh God oh God oh God . . ."

"It was a mistake from the outset, you know, your pitiable little scheme to chump me. On the ground now, both of you."

They sank to their knees.

"All the way. Facedown."

They flattened themselves out on the sand. Brewster made a move as if to join them.

"Not you," Eggs barked, freezing him midstoop. The compliant healer. Maybe this would be easier than he'd thought. He came over and straddled the two trembling figures. "I want you to remain in exactly this position," he said. "Should any bolting notions cross your peanut brains, remember I'm right here. Right above you. Watching. And I've got an uncommonly steady hand." And then to Brewster, nudging him along with the gun, he said, "Time to go, Wyman."

Brewster stepped onto the running board and climbed the ladder. Eggs scrambled up behind him. He glanced down at his two earth-bound charges. Neither had moved. It was remarkable, all this docility, all three of them. Extraordinary. Perhaps none of them understood clearly what was happening. Clinging, doubtless, to some wispy hope of prolonging their miserable lives for another infinitesimal nanosecond. Counting, possibly, on mercy.

But for Eggs, mercy had always been a commodity in short supply. And now he and Brewster stood side by side on the tiny platform, gazing into a chute black as a cave, its fins coiling hypnotically, sensuously, gazing together as though into the pumping heart of the supreme mystery. "There's your cosmos, Wyman," Eggs said solemnly. "All there ever was of it."

He studied the healer's face for a reaction to this somber pronouncement. Most singular reaction. The head contracted, turtlelike, into the neck and shoulders, while the eyes widened in stunned, anguished wonder. He seemed at last to understand.

"Surprised, are you? Surely you didn't think we came up here for the view."

The peculiar buzzing started up again behind the swatch of tape.

"You must try to be positive, Wyman. Look at it this way. Today is the last day of the rest of your life."

Brewster's torso began to sway, a slow undulating motion, as if he were mimicking the action of the revolving drum. Suddenly he lifted his arms and flailed the air like a man batting at a swarm of marauding bees, like a man possessed. He made a desperate lunge for the ladder. Eggs swung the gun in as wide an arc as he could negotiate, given the narrow confines of the platform, and slammed it into the back of the retreating head. Brewster slumped over the chute.

Now the difficult part. Now was when he could have used that help. But he hadn't come this far only to settle for something drab and colorless and mundane. Not Eggs LaRevere, not with his soaring imagination. He boosted the limp body up and over the chute; and with a mighty heave delivered it headfirst, down, down, into that churning chasm; and the last he saw was a pair of long, spindly legs, tangled in the coiling fins and vanishing into the black maw of the drum. He would have preferred, of course, for him to be conscious, but there was only so much a man could do.

He checked his erstwhile partners. Still motionless. Still tractable. He squinted at his watch. Still two opportunities to get it right. But only if he moved quickly. And that's how he came down the ladder: a man with no tolerance anymore for squeamish supplications or hysterical pleadings. A man in a hurry.

Waverly was crouched behind the diesel engine at the rear of the truck. Standing in a splash of moonlight less than twenty feet away were the fatty and, on the other side of him, the woman (*still* no way to tell who she was), backed up against the wheel well. Eggs was stabbing at them with the barrel of the gun. Another figure lay motionless at the foot of the running board. It wasn't Brewster. Waverly glanced up at the slowly spinning drum. He didn't know what had happened to Brewster in the time it had taken to cross the lot, but he could guess.

The engine's deafening rat-a-tat assaulted his ears, but it also served to muffle the fierce growl rising in Electra's throat. With considerable effort, yanking on the leash, he restrained her. Twenty feet was a slender margin, but it was more than he could hope to cover. In competition with a bullet, he was a sure second runner. He and the dog both. What he needed was an opening. He watched them.

Eggs seemed to be shouting something, impossible to hear what, and with his free hand he made quick agitated gestures at the ladder. When neither of the two moved, he stepped over and swatted the woman with the back of the gesturing hand. Waverly stiffened. Eggs was turned now, only slightly, but enough so the gun was angled toward the front of the truck. Now was the moment, as good as it would get.

Waverly unsnapped the leash and hissed, "Get him, Electra!—Get him, girl!—Take him down!"; and it was as if the sudden freedom and the sharp commands combined to unloose in the dog some savage lupine urge; and she came whirling around the engine, a snarling pounding laser streak of black tearing across the sand. And Waverly was right behind her.

But by the purest whim of chance, it was Click who saw them first. A terror, primal as the memory bred into blood and bone, took him completely, and he broke into a frantic scuttling dash, legs pumping madly, arms wildly swinging. Eggs, mistaking the panicked flight, lifted the gun; but before he could squeeze off a shot an inky blur of dog, also mistaking her quarry, flashed in front of him and pounced on the scampering Click and brought him tumbling to the ground. With the born predator's sure instinct for peril, Eggs spun around and seized Dawnette by the arm and shoved her onto the running board. Waverly was four strides short of him. Four too many. He launched himself in a diving, spearing tackle, but Eggs pivoted gracefully, graceful as a matador, and in a short hammering motion drove the butt of the gun into the base of his skull. A lightning bolt of pain fired through him. A thunderclap boomed in his head. A medley of screams, Click's predominant among them, sounded in his closing ears. And in that shred of an instant before the darkness settled behind his eyes, he saw, too late, the woman was not Val.

His first sensation was the gritty taste of sand in his mouth. Next, a foot prodding him at the hip. Finally, a mock solicitous voice from somewhere high above him: "Can you stand, Mr. Waverly?"

He wasn't sure. Had to try. He got to his hands and knees. Took a series of quick breaths. Wobbled to his feet. His legs felt buttery. The thunder still echoed in his head. And he was staring down the barrel of a gun held shooter fashion, arms extended, elbows locked. Eggs moved back a step, braced himself against the truck. Directly to his right Dawnette rocked back and forth on the running board.

A trickle of blood oozed from a corner of her mouth. She whimpered softly.

"Did you seriously believe you could get the better of me?" Eggs said. "With a *dog*?"

Waverly shrugged. Give him nothing.

"Look over there."

Waverly looked in the direction indicated by a toss of the head. Electra and Click lay side by side, sprawled, both of them, in an attitude of exhausted sleep. Companions in sleep.

"In Las Vegas," Eggs said pedantically, "the one mistake you must never make—the fatal one—is misjudging the landscape. And of course its occupants. Figuratively speaking, you understand."

"I understand what you mean."

"You said it yourself: dogs like me."

"So I did."

"Too bad she had to be disposed of. Fine animal."

"Also too bad for your friend there."

"Oh, that was an act of compassion. Poor Cleanth, he was in cruel pain."

"And my sister?" Waverly said bitterly. "What about her? More of that compassionate impulse?" The words, carried along on the crest of a powerless fury surging through him, spilled out in spite of himself, in spite of his pledge, a Jacktown legacy, to give up nothing. Ever.

"Your sister?" For a trace of a moment Eggs looked puzzled. Only a trace. "Of course. That's what brings you here." A small, taunting smile spread across his face. Moonlight glinted off the metallic facsimiles of eyes. "Sadly, now you'll never know, will you." He pointed the gun at the center of Waverly's chest. "I tried to persuade you to accept the wisdom of the reasoned choice. Remember?"

Waverly steadied himself. "Yeah," he said. "I remember."

Dawnette's fingers found the screwdriver, and she sprang off the running board and buried it deep in the fleshy portion of Eggs's back, just below the neck. His jaws dropped, but he didn't scream. Rather, an incredulous grunt escaped the gaping mouth. His arms fell. Miraculously, one hand still clutched the gun. He elevated it enough to fire blindly, first in the general direction of Waverly sprinting for the back of the truck, then at Dawnette ducking around the cab. Fired till the chamber cylinder was empty. Discarded the useless weapon, flung it away. Then, exercising a supreme will, he reached up behind him, gripped the screwdriver handle, and, tightening his sagged jaws against the rush of pain, pried it loose.

For a moment the world seemed to pitch and sway beneath him. He reeled a bit, shuddered convulsively, but he stayed on his feet. He was all right. He was going to make it. He was Eggs LaRevere. Maybe his imagination had betrayed him this time. Maybe not. It wasn't over yet. Heedless of the current of blood flowing south along his arm and trailing from his sleeve, he set out in a tottery run. She had a start on him, but not all that much. And he knew exactly where she'd be headed.

Very cautiously, Waverly peered around a corner of the engine box. Two dead men, one dead dog. Nobody else in sight.

Just as cautiously, he came down the length of the truck. The gun, trained only a moment ago on his chest, lay in the sand by the tire. He stooped down and picked it up. Empty of slugs. He kept it anyway. Something in the hand.

He poked his head around the front of the cab. Still nobody. Which proved nothing. He darted over by the steeply sloped edge of the towering mound of sand. In the distance he could make out a figure crossing the lot, moving in a curious hitching trot, like a hobbled animal. That would be Eggs. A starting gun exploded in Waverly's head and, as though fired out of sprinter's blocks, he took off after him.

But at the apartments he stopped abruptly, flattened out and crawled through the grass along the side of a unit. Hobbled or not, injured or not, this was still a slick, dangerous man. As he'd just discovered. He glanced to his left. The Lincoln was gone. He looked right. A van came speeding down the drive between the two rows of buildings. Eggs at the wheel. It passed directly in front of him. And he held an empty gun. A prominent sticker on the back bumper invited other motorists to HONK IF YOU LOVE JESUS.

The van peeled out of the drive, turned west on Flamingo. Waverly bounded to his feet, ran across the road, hopped into the Mercury, tossed the gun on the seat, and drove in the same direction.

Eggs was slowing down some. He could feel it. A burning sensation streaked across his shoulder blades. Tendrils of pain coiled through his arm. The fingers of his right hand tingled. Nevertheless, he slogged on.

The first thing he did was check Click's apartment. He knew what to expect. He did it anyway. No surprises: the briefcase gone, car gone. She was terrified—as well she should be—and she was stupid, but not so stupid as to overlook the loot.

So the next thing he had to do was commandeer a vehicle. He looked up and down the drive. At the far end a woman was unloading groceries from a junkyard van. It wasn't his vehicle of choice. It would have to do.

He approached her. A hefty, matronly lady, round and innocent of face, plump of tummy. Grocery bag tucked under each arm. Watching him coming toward her in a kind of lopsided shuffling roll. "My Lord!" she exclaimed. "What happened to *you?*"

"A small mishap," Eggs said, or did his best to enunciate, for the syllables seemed to clot on his thickening tongue. He held out a hand, the tingly one, palm up. "The keys, please."

"Huh?"

"I need this van. Give me the keys."

"Lookit your hand there. It's all bloody."

So it was. He hadn't really noticed before. He balled it into a fist and punched her in the suety pit of the stomach. It was not as forceful a blow as he would have liked and it sent a fiery sting up the length of his arm and across his back, but it was solid enough to double her over. The bags fell. She made some gagging noises.

"The keys," Eggs said.

She managed to raise a pointer finger at the van. "In there."

Eggs climbed into the van and sped away. And while he was conscious now of his shirt, moist and sticky, clinging to his back; and a certain clamminess rising to the surface of his skin; and a peculiar shimmery light filtering through the lenses of his glasses (the moon?—neon?—the oncoming traffic?—difficult to tell) and clouding his vision, it was nonetheless comforting to have tested himself (on a lumpish woman, to be sure, but test enough for what lay ahead) and discovered all his parts in reasonably sound working order, his mind still alert, keen. Which is all that would be required.

Ten minutes later he spotted the white Lincoln pulled up outside the dykes' apartment. His instincts never failed him. There were still some things yet to be salvaged from this ruinous score.

He parked the van. Removed the screwdriver from a jacket pocket. He hadn't forgotten the screwdriver. There were how many orifices on the female body? Seven, was it? Ears, nostrils, mouth, anal and vaginal cavities. Seven. Nine if you included the eyes. God's plenty.

He stepped out of the van. Swayed a little. Hauled in a mighty gulp of the bracing night air. And then, reinvigorated, fueled by a righteous vengeful fury, he charged up the walk and through the unbolted door at a velocity that seemed to him very near to ramming speed.

But for a thin crease of light falling across the floor at the end of the hall, the apartment was utterly dark. The silence absolute. Games they wanted? He'd introduce them to another version of hide-and-seek. Deadly one. He crept down the hall, arm outthrust, makeshift weapon at the ready. The hand that gripped it fluttered slightly.

The guiding principle in this game was never to expose your back. Accordingly, he tried the first door on the right. Eased it open carefully and peeked inside, into a room dimly illuminated by four tiny crimson bulbs, and also into the flat side of a devil's hand split paddle that came whooshing through the air and struck him full in the chest with the force of a home run swing, staggered him, buckled his knees. It whooshed again, this time in an axe chop across the back of his neck. He crumpled onto the floor. And the last thing he saw before he passed out was a mashed face, indelibly ugly, stuck in close and grinning at him; and the last he heard was a hoarse croaky voice announcing triumphantly, "Now it's our turn."

❊ ❊ ❊

Waverly's heart clubbed. His mouth felt parched, his throat tight, constricted. If he'd had to speak, a wordless, toneless growl was the most he could have managed.

He'd lost him. Couldn't believe it. Come this close, and now he'd surely lost him.

The Mercury had stalled again—perversely, maddeningly, and without warning—at the Decatur intersection, and by the time he got it rolling the van was nowhere in sight. That might have been its taillights turning in at the entrance to an apartment complex half a mile south. Might not. Nothing up ahead, no other options. He turned too. Steered the traitorous sputtering Mercury, rattled by speed bumps, down the narrow streets of a vast sprawl of buildings, each of them identical, a hall of mirrors. Scanned the long files of parked vehicles, either side. Unsure even of what he searched for. The van had flashed by so suddenly, he had no clear image of its make or color. All he remembered was something boxy, square. And the pious injunction tacked to its bumper.

And that's what finally delivered him. He arrived at the end of a street. He'd lost all sense of direction, where he was, where he had been. Go right? Left? A toss-up. He went left. And midway down the next block he saw first the Lincoln. Then a van. And then the redeeming giveaway message on its back bumper. He pulled in beside it. But he didn't honk.

Instead, he sat for a moment inspecting the dark apartment and considering the moves open to him. There weren't many. What he didn't need was a repeat of the action at the construction site. He'd been lucky back there. Fool's luck. It seldom happened twice.

Or did it? The door suddenly burst open and three women came tearing through it. He scooped up the gun, hopped out of the car, came around the front of the van, and planted himself in their path.

Waverly recognized the girl who had neutralized Eggs, effectively, if incidentally, saving his life. Another girl, equally young, sported an arm sheathed in plaster and bent at a grotesque angle. Both of them looked dazed. Both cringed behind a ponderous dreadnought of a woman, much older, with a hard, disfigured face, eyes full of grievance. "Fuck're you?" she demanded.

"Man with a zapper in his hand," Waverly said, giving the impotent weapon a little display wiggle.

"So whaddya want with us?"

"I'm looking for Eggs LaRevere."

"You a shooter?"

"Is he in there?" Question for a question.

"Yeah, he's in there all right," she sneered. "What's left of him." Her voice was guttural, harsh, a nothing-more-to-lose defiance in it.

"What exactly does that mean?"

"Means what it says."

"Is he alive?"

"Go see for yourself."

"Oh, I'm going to do that. But you're coming along. All of you. Quick-step now."

Waverly made an urgent motion at the door with the leveled gun. One of the girls, the one who'd more or less saved him, balked. "I *can't* go back in there, Vel," she moaned wretchedly. "Let him have—"

"Shut the fuck up, Cool," the dreadnought barked at her. "Move your ass. You too, Gay." She shoved them out ahead of her.

"Get the light first," Waverly said.

She flipped a switch on the wall inside the entrance. Waverly came up behind her. Glanced about warily. Nobody in the living room. Empty hall. He poked the gun barrel into a billowy cushion of fat at the not-so-small of her back. "Okay. No more games. Where is he?"

"Look, you got something to settle with that dickeye, that's your business. Leave us out of it."

"I think you'd better tell me where he is."

"Maybe we already done your work for you," she said, adopting a sly bargaining tone.

Waverly sighed. "I'm asking you where he is. Polite as I know how. Don't make me ask again."

She nodded at a door off the hallway.

"Ladies first," he said.

"Uh, what you got in mind for after, that piece?"

"We'll see."

"Maybe we can work something out, huh?"

"We'll see," he said again.

Single file, ladies in the lead, as gunpoint directed, they entered the room.

If Waverly had been unprepared earlier for the sight of Roger, he was no less wonderstruck by what he gazed at now. The figure of Eggs LaRevere, strapped into an imposing wooden chair, emerged in the dim light. Stripped of all his clothing. Even the trademark glasses gone. The light reflected upwards from the four corners of the room cast an eerie ruby glow over his head, lowered as if in prayer. His chest rose and fell. Under the restraints, his fingers and toes moved in a puzzled way. Blood welled up out of his groin, out of the central core of himself, gouged and rent and fissured like the exposed innards of a rotted scrap of roadkill. A glistening metal ring encircled what remained of his mangled organ.

Waverly looked at the three women. "You did this?"

Two of them, the girls, stared at the floor. Volunteered nothing. The big one glared at him fiercely. "Goddam right," she declared, her voice full of a prideful belligerence. "He had it comin'."

"I suppose he did."

"So now what?"

"Now you can get down on the floor. Facedown."

He smothered their rising protests with a jab of the gun. They got down.

"Which one of you's got the keys to that Lincoln out there?"

"I do."

It was the girl who had rescued him once; perhaps, by another impish joke of fate, rescuing him again. "I'll take them," he said.

She reached into a pocket of her jeans, slid the keys across the floor.

Waverly stooped down and recovered them. "All right," he said to her. "I don't know who you are or how you figure in this. Don't really care. I've got just one question for you, and if you want to live you'd better answer it right. Where's my sister?"

"I dunno," she wailed. "Honest. I did, I'd tell you."

"He kill her?"

"Dunno that either. Not for sure. Don't think so. The other one, Click, he said she wasn't at her place when they did that guy. I wasn't there. That's all I know. I swear. You gotta believe me."

There was just enough raw terror in her voice to invest the words with the ring of truth. As nearly as Waverly could believe anything anymore, he believed her. "Okay," he said, "blink an eye, twitch a nerve, and you're whacked. All three of you."

He started for the door. But then, on an impulse he could neither comprehend nor justify, he came over and stood in front of the chair. Eggs seemed to sense a presence near to him. He made an odd gurgling sound. Very slowly, he lifted his head. Shadows danced across his face. His teeth were bared in a ghastly, incongruous smile. Skull smile. His eyes were bright with calamity. He fixed them on Waverly. Drew a long shuddering breath. "Kill me," he said.

Waverly strained to find a voice. When he did it was flat, expressionless, empty of rage, venom, animus, spite, malice. Vacant of pity, remorse, grief. Exhausted of feeling. "No."

He backed through the door. Went into the kitchen and with a damp towel wiped the gun clean of his prints. Left it on the counter. A token of his benevolence. Then, still clutching the towel, he went out to the Mercury and hurriedly wiped down the wheel, dash, seat, window, door handles, everything. A moment later he was gone.

23

Bennie was pacing the living room of the house on Garces, chewing up the carpet. Streamers of blue smoke trailed from the torpedo of a cigar clenched between his teeth. Sweat slicked his bald pate. "You ain't gonna believe what I'm tellin' ya here," he launched right in telling him.

Waverly stood in the doorway. He put up a silencing hand. "Not now. No time now. Come on."

Bennie stopped pacing. Looked at him narrowly. "Huh? Come on where?"

"I'll tell you in the car."

"You got wheels?"

"Yes. Now come on."

"What's goin' on, Timothy?"

On the drive to Val's Waverly told him what was going on. In abundant, graphic detail he told him all the events of the past four hours (only four, was it, since he'd wakened?—remarkable!), all of them, everything he could call back to mind—sights, sounds, smells, sensations—as if the avalanche of detail could impose a meaning, restore an order, hold disaster at bay.

Bennie watched his partner steadily. Listened. And as the sorry account unfolded, his wise canny old face puckered in the solemn gravity of a newborn infant cautiously inspecting an alien and hostile world. And when it was finished he said, "They're dead? Roger, the mutt, rest of 'em—all dead?" His voice was hollow, incredulous.

"All dead," Waverly confirmed.

Bennie shook his head ruefully. "Poor old Rog. Dead. Jesus, Timothy, what can I say?"

"Don't say you're sorry. It wasn't your fault."

"Whose, then?"

Waverly shrugged in a baffled sort of way. "Mine, I suppose. Must be mine. I saw trouble coming the day Val got here. Waited too long."

"But you think she's maybe okay?"

"That I don't know yet. That's what we've got to find out."

"What is it with you and trouble?" Bennie said, genuine curiosity in his voice. "Stick to you like flypaper."

"I don't know what it is. What I've done. Or not done. I'll have to think about it. First we've got to find her."

"Soon's we do, we gotta blaze outta here. You know that."

"I know."

"You can think about it later."

"Right. Later."

The apartments came into view up ahead. Bennie hunched forward in his seat, squinted through the windshield, pointed. "Ain't that her car?"

Waverly craned his neck. "Which one? Where?"

"By that pickup there."

Sure enough, there it was, the Impala, parked in the identical spot Roger's Mercury had recently occupied. Waverly turned into the lot and pulled up beside it.

"Car's here, means she for sure gotta be okay," Bennie said confidently.

Waverly couldn't share his confidence. Not yet. Too much had happened today for the treacherous swindle of hope. "Let's go see," he said.

She sat with her hands gripping the arms of the chair, silent and staring. Her face wore the stamp of a blank, bewildered melancholy.

Her eyes were glazed with shock, inward turning, as though she had retreated into some distant narrowing corridors of her head. But unharmed. To all appearances, unharmed.

Waverly felt an immense surge of relief. He kneeled down in front of her. "Val?" he said gently.

She didn't reply.

He said her name again, gentle still, but with a greater urgency this time.

A flicker of recognition crossed those stunned eyes. "Tim? It's you?"

"Yes. I'm here now. Bennie's with me."

"Bennie?"

"Yes."

"You're all right? Both of you?"

Bennie, hanging back in a corner of the room, answered for them. "Doin' just fine, Val."

"Roger's dead."

"I know," Waverly said.

"Someone killed him."

"I know."

"*Why?*"

"Listen to me, Val. Listen. You don't want to know why. Or who. Any of it. Anyway, there isn't time. I need your help here."

"Help? How?"

"What I want you to do is stand up now and go back into the bedroom and pack a bag. Then I want you to wait there for us. Don't come out till we're back. Can you do that?"

"I think so."

He got her to her feet and led her across the room and through the door. She moved slowly, stiffly, like a shuffling sleepwalker entranced in some fantastic dream. Waverly made certain the door was securely shut behind her. She didn't need to see any of what had to be done.

Bennie had gone into the kitchen, and he stood there now, gazing at the floor, eyes bulging, mouth agape, lips twitching. "Ah, Jesus," he moaned. "Poor fucker. Look what they done to him. Jesus."

"What'd I just tell her," Waverly said harshly. "No time for this. Don't gimp on me, Bennie."

"Who's gimpin'. Nobody's gimpin'."

"Good. Because we've got to get him out of here. Ourselves too."

"Get him where? Where we gonna get him to?"

Waverly didn't immediately answer. Instead he went over to the front door, cracked it open, and peered down the corridor. Empty. The parking lot, as much as he could see of it, appeared to be empty too. The three vehicles—Lincoln, Impala, pickup—were visible from this angle, but only barely, shrouded in the dark. A thought occurred to him. And that's what he said when he came back into the kitchen: "I've got a thought on that. Might just work."

"You gonna fill me in, this good thought?"

"Just trust me."

They squatted down on either side of the body. The once ruddy face of the man who had once been Roger Pettibone was turned ice blue. Clotted blood striped the lacerated throat like some gaudy crimson necklace. The limbs were growing rigid. But most of the charred smell was dissipated, gone. Most of it.

Each of them grasped an arm. Simultaneously, and with a mighty tug, they hauled the body up, braced it between them, and maneuvered it around the counter and over to the door.

"What if there's somebody out in the hall there?" Bennie said.

"It's clear."

"Yeah, but what if somebody shows?"

"We make like drunks."

"How?"

"I don't know. Sing."

"Sing what?"

"Something will come to you. Ready?"

"Ready as I'm gonna get."

Waverly shoved the door open with his foot and they edged through it sideways. Corridor was still empty. They tottered down it, paused in the stairwell to catch their breath. Bennie looked at the two flights of stairs beneath them, then at Waverly. "Fuck, I dunno, Timothy," he said doubtfully.

"We can do it. Got to do it."

Grunting, both of them, under the weight of their burden, they staggered down the stairs. Roger's dangly feet made clomping noises on each step. When finally they arrived at the last one, Bennie, chest heaving, voice a wheezy gasp, said, "Okay, we got him this far. Now where?"

Waverly, panting just as heavily as his partner, wagged his head in the direction of the pickup.

"There? You gonna dump him there?"

"Yes."

"But I figured we'd—"

"No. There. Don't argue."

They dragged the body across the lot and propped it against the side of the truck. Bennie supported it while Waverly got the tailgate. Then, yanking and tugging, they hoisted it up and onto the bed. There was a filthy tarp heaped in a corner. Waverly climbed in, shook it out, and draped it over Roger, covering him completely, head to foot. He hopped to the ground, lifted the tailgate.

"You sure you know what you're doin' here?" Bennie said.

Waverly nodded affirmatively. He was sure. Let the two louts catch some heat. Let them do some explaining. Buy some time, anyway.

"Seem like a helluva way to leave him."

Waverly stared at the outline of the crumpled body under the grease-stained tarp. As a winding sheet, it wasn't much. Best he could do. He felt an odd stinging sensation in his eyes. Why, he couldn't tell. He'd known Pettibone for—what?—a couple of weeks?—three? Maybe that was why: touch my life for three weeks and this is what it comes to. "Rest in peace, Roger" was all he could think to say.

Back in the apartment he went directly to the bedroom to check on Val. She was sitting on the edge of the bed, bag at her feet, eyes still vacant, face empty of expression. "Are you packed?" he said.

She moved her head up and down.

"That's good. Stay here now. Just be another minute."

He started for the door but before he could get through it she pronounced his name, voice toneless and thin, scarcely a whisper.

"Yes?"

"Electra, she's dead too, isn't she."

It was not so much question as appeal for verity, confirmation. "I'm afraid so," Waverly said. "I'm sorry."

"Did she suffer?"

Not like some others suffered tonight, he thought, but he said, "No. It was very quick."

"Are you telling me the truth?"

"It's the truth, Val." And it was, too, or as nearly as he understood the slippery notion of truth anymore.

Bennie was waiting for him in the living room. Both of them knew what remained to be done, and so without a word they set to work. Waverly found a mop in a tiny closet off the kitchen, and he scrubbed the linoleum floor until it was clear of the sticky crust of blood. Bennie got a wet towel and wiped off the knife, unceremoniously dropped in the sink, and the stove and the cupboards and everything else he could think of, everything in the apartment he could remember they'd touched. When he was finished he came around the counter and said, "Now what?"

Waverly took the towel from him, ran it over the handle, and replaced the mop in the closet. And then he turned and faced him. "Now we've got to talk about money, Bennie."

"Money?"

"The money from last night. Money I won. Where is it?"

A look of supreme discomfort clouded the B. Epstein features. The eyes darted back and forth in the troubled fleshy face. "See, that's what I was tryin' to tellya. Back at the house."

"Tell me now. But make it fast."

"Well, plain fact is, I laid it on tonight's game. And I'm over to the Sahara, see, suckin' a cold one, just hangin' out, y'know, and an hour before the whistle they come on the TV with this special bulletin. Guy readin' it look like he gonna drop a load right on camera. I tellya, Timothy, I heard it, I 'bout done the same."

"Fast, Bennie."

"Fast. Okay, fast. What he says is Lafayette's spilled his guts 'bout a points-shavin' scam. Crazy spade gets the Jesus call, last minute, and comes to the window. Says he's the only one involved so they got him in protective custody, gonna play the game without him. Big investigation, startin' tomorrow. Am I lyin'? Fucker *rolled* on 'em! You *believe* it?"

"You bet it all?"

"I was throwin' long," Bennie said. He considered mentioning Roger's early-morning visit. Thought better of it. Nothing served by that admission. Changed nothing. "Seemed like the thing to do," he added vaguely.

"So we're running on empty again."

"C'mon, man, it's only money. We can always make it back." He opened his hands in a conciliatory gesture. "Okay, sure, I shoulda told you what I was doin'. But my thought was good. I was gonna split it right down the middle with you. Besides, it ain't for absolute certain lost yet. Bets is still on. I checked. What's it now?—'bout eight bells? Like they say, game ain't over till it's over."

"This one's over, I think."

Bennie had nothing to say to that. He studied the damp floor. "You got *any*thing left?"

"Some pocket change. Maybe five, six yards."

"Let's have it."

Bennie produced five bills and laid them in his outstretched hand. Waverly looked at them. Five bills. Along with the two in his wallet, came to seven hundred dollars. Sum total of thirty-eight years of living. Make that scrambling. Another of those things to think about later. But for right now he said, "Okay, here's the rest of the drill."

They drove through a series of back streets utterly unfamiliar to him, Bennie in the Lincoln up ahead, leading the way, he and Val following along in the Impala. At his insistence she was the one behind the wheel. The simple mechanical acts of driving—steering the car, hitting the turn signal, obeying traffic signs, keeping the Lincoln in view—seemed to bring her around some, steady her. And after a few blocks she said quietly, "Where are we going, Tim?"

"You're going back to Dakota."

"And you? Where for you?"

Where? Beyond this moment he had given it not the slightest thought. Now, with her question, he was thrust back into that twisted warp of risks and perils and choices and shifting realities and ambushed dreams that shaped the flimsy contours of his life. Hostage to the immutable laws of cause and effect. It was not the sort of thing he could explain to her, but because he had to say something he said, "Another direction."

"Will I ever see you again?"

"That's impossible to say."

She seemed to accept the note of finality in his voice. In the words. "You're not going to tell me what happened," she said.

"It's better you don't know, Val. But there's something I need to know."

"What's that?"

"Where you were today."

"Why?"

"Just tell me, okay?"

"With Mr. Fisher."

"Fisher? Who's he?"

"The man I mentioned to you. With the lung cancer. He got worse during the night. I couldn't leave him."

"So you were there all day?"

"Most of it. Then I went to the Center, to get Wyman's advice. It was closed so I came on home. That's when I found Roger."

"Anybody see you at this Fisher's place?"

"I don't think so. He lives alone."

"But he's still alive?"

"Oh yes. He was even feeling a little better when I left. Why?"

"No reason," Waverly said, but his nerves were strung tight as piano wire and his mind was racing, calculating. If the lunger could only hang on a while longer she might have a story that stood up. If the heat ever put it all together, and if they traced it as far as her. A tangle of very iffy ifs. Nothing to count on.

"What about Wyman?" Valerie asked him. "Is he dead?"

"I don't know. For sure. But I have to tell you I'd be surprised if he weren't."

If she was surprised, she didn't let on. They drove a few more blocks without speaking. Then, in a voice etched with sorrow, she said, "You were right. I should never have come here."

Waverly thought a moment before replying. He could tell her the truth, or what he believed was the truth. He could do that. As a kind of reality therapy. But to what end? Instead he served up another in the endless string of lies that spilled so effortlessly from his lips. "What happened would have happened anyway, Val. It was inevitable. A chain of unlucky coincidences. Your being here had nothing to do with it."

"I wish I could believe that."

"You can. It's the way it is."

The Lincoln slowed and, at the next corner, swung over by the curb. Waverly directed her to pull in behind it. Just beyond where they were parked, both vehicles idling, was a ramp leading to the expressway. "That'll get you onto 15," he said. "Pointed north to Salt Lake. You remember the way?"

"I remember."

He fumbled in his pocket and removed seven crumpled bills. "Here. Take this."

"I don't need money, Tim. I have some."

"How much is 'some'?"

"About five thousand dollars. Maybe a little more."

"On you? You're carrying that much on you?"

"Yes."

"You kept it in the apartment?"

"I've never been, well, comfortable with banks."

Waverly looked at her wonderingly, this sister of his, this vulnerable castaway, transplanted from another sphere. He pressed the bills into her hand. "Take it anyway," he said. "Make me feel better."

She took them absently, saying, "You could come with me, Tim."

"Afraid not. Not this time."

"You don't have to live this way. You could be what you were again."

"It's too late, Val. I'm too full of my own confusions. End product of what I've made myself."

"It grieves me to see that product. It grieves Dad."

"He's gone, Val. Dad's gone."

She shook her head vigorously. "No, you're wrong. He's with us. He's here. All you have to do is listen for him."

"I'll do that," he said gently. "I'll listen. But now I have to leave. You too."

Tears approached her eyes, but by some force of will she held them off. "You'll be all right?"

"I'll be just fine."

It seemed as though something still remained to be said, but he didn't know precisely what it was, or, had he known, how it could be said. He stepped out of the car, waved her on. And as he watched the Impala chugging up the ramp and vanishing in the swirl of traffic, he was overtaken by a powerless desolation too ambiguous even for him to name.

24

On the road again. On the run again. The lights of the roaring gaudy city feathering away behind them, black wall of night ahead. It occurred to Waverly their lives were not altogether different from birds' lives: aimless twittery flights, the briefest of perchings. "Where this time?" he asked incuriously.

"Fucked if I know. Runnin' outta places."

They lapsed into silence.

Bennie, for his part of it, could think of not a word to say. After a while, though, he cleared his throat and ventured tentatively, "Uh, you mind if I flip on the radio there?"

"I don't mind."

"Might as well catch the score, huh?"

"Might as well."

The radio produced a disjointed series of grating squawks as he searched the dial for a news station. Eventually he found one. And after the standard litany of the day's commonplace catastrophes, the score was reported. Rebs by seventeen, the breathless voice announced, a thorough drubbing, testimony to the team's grit and determination to prove itself in the wake of the Lafayette Waters scandal.

Bennie groaned at the numbers. "Aah, God bugger it. I figured that'd happen. Scratch thirty-five big bones."

"It's only money. Remember who it was said that?"

"Guess that'd be me."

"That's right. It was you."

Bennie switched off the radio. "Yeah, well, don't worry," he said, putting as much of a buoyant lilt into it as he could muster. "We'll think of something. Always do. You and me been road dogs ever since Jacktown, Timothy. Make it there, make it anyplace. You'll see."

Waverly glanced over at his partner. B. Epstein, tireless invincible spinner of dreams. Come to me, this dream whispered seductively, come to me and you'll be granted still another chance. One more chance. Waverly knew better. No more pardons for them. No more chances.

He was mistaken.

"You say this tank belong to Brewster?" Bennie asked him.

"I think so."

"Means we gotta ditch it, first thing."

"Expect we do."

"Whyn't you take a peek in the box. See what you can find."

Waverly opened the glove compartment and examined its contents under the faint interior light. Owner's manual, insurance proof, vehicle registration, couple of pill bottles. Otherwise empty.

"What's that there?" Bennie said.

"Where?"

"On the floor there." He jabbed a finger at the tip of an object projecting from beneath Waverly's seat.

Waverly reached down and slid it forward. "It's a briefcase," he said.

"Open 'er up."

Waverly set it on his lap, snapped the latches and lifted the top.

"Jesus Q. Motherbumpin' Christ," Bennie exclaimed joyously, steering with one hand and running the palm of the other over the surface of the stacks and stacks of banded bills. "Lookit all them gorgeous green dead presidents. Where'bouts you think it come from?"

"No idea."

"Think it was Brewster's?"

"Could have been."

"Well, he got no use for it now. Count it up."

Waverly made a quick tally. "Little over a hundred thousand," he said.

"Holy fuckin' Grail! Hundred large. What'd I say, Timothy? Did I say we was gonna make it?"

"Your very words."

"Hog fat city, boy."

"Dead ahead."

Adrift in their private dreams, they drove on, tunneling through the dark. The engine purred. Clouds smeared the face of the moon. A sturdy wind lifted off the desert floor. Waverly listened to it, to all the old promises carried along on the legions of voices riding the wind. He listened. And although he was no longer a man given to prayer, he prayed for the spirit of his sister, whose unmistakable voice came singing down that wind, and for Roger and his father and what his memory could conjure of a son, and for all the numberless spirits, living and dead, guilty and innocent, of all the victims caught in the undertow and swamped in the wreckage of his life. He prayed for them all. Also for himself.